Camellia Stephens

by

Natalie L. Tawes

DORRANCE PUBLISHING CO., INC.
PITTSBURGH, PENNSYLVANIA 15222

This is a work of fiction. Names, characters, places, and incidents are either the product of the author's imagination or are used fictitiously, and any resemblance to actual persons, living or dead, or locales is entirely coincidental.

ISBN # 0-8059-3988-1
Printed in the United States of America

First Printing

For information or to order additional books, please write:
Dorrance Publishing Co., Inc.
643 Smithfield Street
Pittsburgh, Pennsylvania 15222
U.S.A.

Part One

Chapter One

"What if I were to become an opera singer?"

Camellia Stephens's bold question to her parents that spring evening of 1927 couldn't have drawn a more shocked reaction from her father, Thomas Stephens, if she had suddenly added three "name in vain" words and a string of "bad words" thrown in for good measure.

No matter that Camellia's music teacher, Claudie, said she might have the voice for opera. No matter that Camellia was tall and big for her eleven years of age, strappingly healthy, and downright beautiful. No matter that there was musical heritage from both sides of her family. Thomas Stephens was against opera singers nevertheless.

Camellia, Thomas, and Mary were having a late snack in the kitchen of their home which was also their business—the Stephens Tu-Rest Home. Thomas had just started to put a big forkful of bread dripping with molasses into his mouth when his and Mary's only child sprang the question. His grayish-brown eyes bugged out and he stared at Camellia with his mouth wide open and with the fork and the bread dripping with molasses still poised in mid-air. "Singer?" he shouted. "*Opera singer*? LIKE ON THE STAGE? *LIKE 'MISS CLAUDIA' USED TO DO?"*

Each question got progressively louder.

Camellia lounged back in her chair and puffed up her chest with her not-quite-yet-breasts. She had feasted her childhood fantasies early on *Tristan and Isolde* and *The Ring of the Nibelung* instead of on *Little Red Riding Hood* and *The Three Bears*. So SHE KNEW her life's course was going to be no ordinary one! She could already sing along with Claudie's gramaphone recordings of opera scores, featuring greats like Madame Schumann-Heink, the famous contralto, who was Camellia's favorite.

Camellia eyed her father cautiously. She stroked her long black hair, ran her hands sensuously over her tawny skin, and tossed her head half-teasingly, half-haughtily, exactly the way she'd seen

Claudie do. She partially closed her dark eyes and then seductively smiled.

But the fancy posing cut no ice with Thomas Stephens. He put his syrupy fork down on his plate and sputtered, "Opera singer? Why, that's terrible...sinful...disgusting...."

When he was mad—or anytime, for that matter—Thomas was not a handsome man. He was short and pudgy and had a large beefy face. People around Bell's Island, Maryland, referred to him as "Pumpkin" Stephens. But Camellia knew her father was as strong as an ox as well as a lot more tenderhearted on the inside than he looked or sounded. His early-balding head with its little fringe of short black hair around the edges gleamed in the glow of the candlelit kitchen table. The top of his head was as red as his large ears when he turned to his wife and said, "Mary, did I hear our daughter correctly?"

Camellia glanced at her mother. Mary was trying hard not to laugh out loud at her husband's comical pose with that bread and molasses fork. And oh, so pretty Mary was with those crystal blue eyes and ash-blond hair, with that potato chip-thin body. Island people sometimes referred to her as "Mary Beanpole," especially when she and Thomas were walking along together, she being several inches taller than "Pumpkin" Stephens. And she had that certain polished, intellectual bearing, the result of a good upbringing, but on the inside she was down-to-earth-as-an-old-clamshell-friendly as well as a little on the scampish side.

Mary said, "Yes, Thomas, you heard correctly.... And yes, I would agree that many of the themes and characters of many operas are *not nice*, but opera *is* considered very high-class entertainment and it is certainly not a hootchy-kootchy show—not the kind the Bell's Island watermen around here all go to see when they take their loads of seafood up the Chesapeake Bay to Baltimore."

"We-ell," said Thomas slowly, and Camellia thought she saw her father's ears reddening even more.

Mary Stephens quickly said, "But I wasn't referring to you *now*, Thomas, no matter what you may have been enticed to do in the past."

Thomas said, "My brothers still try to get me to.... But back to the question at hand." He pursed his lips and cocked his eyes off at an angle in that all-wise expression he could sometimes get and he said, "Camellia, aren't those opera things sung in a foreign language?"

Camellia stroked her raven hair and looked off in the distance with a bored expression at her father's ignorance. "Most operas are...in French, German, Italian...." She even *sounded* like Claudie, having picked up that *educated* British accent from her teacher almost as soon as she'd learned her first "do re mi's."

Thomas pursued the matter. "Well, suppose you were singing a lot of words and you didn't know what they were, if they were in a foreign language, and there happened to be some bad words in them...?"

Mary chuckled. "Foreign 'bad words' like you hear on the Baltimore docks where you still go sometimes with your brothers when they need extra help in hauling Bell's Island seafood up there?"

Camellia looked disgusted and tried to set them both straight, though she knew her mother could, when she wanted to, be almost as knowledgeable and accomplished in music as Claudie. "If you are singing opera usually you know what the words mean even if they are in a foreign language—at least, you're *supposed* to know."

Mary didn't help the idiotic conversation any by adding, "Well, Thomas, if there *were* foreign 'bad words' in the opera—which I don't think there are, at least not the variety you might have heard on the Baltimore docks—and if Camellia didn't recognize them as such when she was singing them, what difference would it make?"

"But it would make a difference to God!" Thomas roared. *"God* would know what you were singing, Camellia, whether you did or not. So you'd better not consider any career where you'd have to take a chance like that. Look, if you want to sing, Daughter, couldn't you just keep on singing in English and in our Bell's Island Methodist Church, like you've been doing ever since you were yea high to a grasshopper, singing so beautifully at Children's Day and things like that?"

Camellia puffed up her chest with her not-quite-yet breasts again like a toad whose chin has been rubbed, and very slowly in that *educated* British accent learned from Claudie, with an impudent toss of her head, she said, "Some-day,-Papa,-I-hope-to-rise-above-mere-Bell's Island-and-Children's Day-and-*JesusLovesMeThisIKnow*!"

"Well, you can't rise above *Jesus*, that's for sure!" Thomas bellowed.

Camellia felt like she was either going to burst out crying or laughing or both and maybe do a little Bell's Island-type cussing of her own when she saw her mother eye-signalling her to drop the whole subject. And being a good child, she complied.

When Thomas went to the sink with his empty bread and molasses plate, Mary whispered to Camellia, "Don't you know it's no use trying to argue with your waterman-born father when he's always fancied himself a preacher?"

Largely undaunted by her father's outburst, before going up to bed Camellia checked the music room, a special room between the front room and dining room where her piano was—the baby grand her mother's father, Grandfather LeCates, had given her for her tenth birthday. She would be seeing Grandfather LeCates as well as

Grandmother and Claudie in the morning, as was usual for a Saturday. All of them lived at the other end of the island at the lavish Bell's Island Inn which her grandparents owned and operated.

In her mind's eye, Camellia could see the inn now, that plush establishment built right at the water's edge and on the order of a large colonial home with columns up to the second floor, floor-to-ceiling windows in all the rooms, and first-and second-story screened porches. The inn had its own dock, a clean sand beach for sunbathing, and a crystal-clear swimming area, and the dining room served the most luscious seafood anywhere.

Camellia could see Grandfather LeCates greeting the wealthy Baltimore and Western Shore tourists who came down the bay on the steamboat to vacation at the Eastern Shore's best. James LeCates, tall and gracefully erect, always wore his cutaway coat, pinstripe trousers, and a black bow tie, all of which went so well with his dark hair, fair skin, and smart black moustache. And Camellia could mentally see Grandmother LeCates, too, standing there with him in her gown of soft blue which complemented her silvery hair and peaches-and-cream complexion. Though robust and bosomy, Lucille LeCates was elegantly neat and regal in her bearing. Some said there was a touch of arrogance to her, but most Bell's Islanders overlooked it, feeling the LeCates' position in the community gave Lucille the right to be stuck up. Also, her father had been Judge Johnstone of Royal Hall, the county seat some twenty miles inland, and that "helped a heap," too.

As Camellia prepared for bed, she thought about how her mother had taken her as a baby and young child to Grandfather LeCates's inn each morning to stay awhile with Claudie, who being a childless widow herself, had taken an early and permanent fancy to her. She remembered how Claudie used to put her on her lap when she played and sang for the guests at the inn and how, before long, Camellia was singing and playing, too, just like the little tyke who learns to ride a horse early because his daddy put him in the saddle with him before Junior had ever learned to walk.

In her mind's eye, she could see Claudie now: Claudie had a smile as generous as the sunshine and a pair of merrily dancing violet-hued eyes off of which you couldn't keep your eyes. She had mountains of brownish-red hair piled in loops and swirls and gathered with combs on top of her head. She wasn't very tall, but she was plump and curvaceous and had a certain swing to her hips that verged on what was called "daring" in that day and age on Bell's Island. She had a pair of gold-rimmed spectacles that were either dangling by their neck chain, stuck into the swirls of her hair, or, on rare occasions, perched on the end of her nose.

The British-born Claudie, or "Miss Claudia" Hornsby, to be exact, had been a permanent resident at the inn for many years. She had first sung opera in Europe, then came to the United States and taught for awhile at the conservatory in Baltimore. She had first come to Bell's Island while on vacation with her brother and sister-in-law, the retired Reverend and Mrs. Bowman of Baltimore. Then the three of them became so entranced with the island and the inn that they had all just stayed! Claudie had opened a music studio in the inn and Mary LeCates, before her marriage to Thomas Stephens, had been one of her first pupils. Later Claudie and Mary put on musicals for the entertainment of the guests, and little Camellia had made her singing/acting debut in one of them at age three and was rousingly applauded.

As Camellia was trying to drift off to sleep, she thought she could see why her father objected to the prospect of her singing opera one day. For one thing, he didn't like Claudie. He often said he thought "Miss Claudia" must have been "a fast woman" at one time. He seemed to have the notion that if an opera singer had once sung the parts of gypsies and whores, she must have been that way in real life, too.

Maybe her father got that notion, Camellia reasoned, because his maternal grandmother had come from a clan of gypsy tinsmiths who had taken up residence on the island generations before. Izetta had been a cabaret singer and she had been killed in a barroom fight at Corrigan's Moonlight Casino just over on the Wintergreen County mainland from Bell's Island. The Corrigans had descended from bay pirates who'd used Bell's Island for a base, and Thomas's paternal grandmother had been Kitty Corrigan Stephens, also considered "a fast woman." Thomas was very secretive about his shadowy ancestors and tried to keep Camellia from knowing anything about them. But she had picked up things here and there.

Mary also had told her a little of Thomas's background and how he'd striven to rise above it. Thomas's father, Azariah Stephens—who was still living—was known as the crookedest, meanest waterman and seafood dealer that Bell's Island had produced since the days of the bay pirates. Azariah's half-gypsy wife, Mona (Izetta's daughter), had been a fairly decent sort everybody said, but she had died in a flu epidemic and left Azariah to raise—and corrupt—their four young children by himself.

Mary had gotten to know Thomas personally when she was still living at her parents' Bell's Island Inn and Thomas was delivering seafood there. The Reverend Bowman had also taken an early interest in the young man and the two spent many hours discussing the Bible.

The inn, the Reverend Bowman, and the down-to-earth, love-the-whole-wide-world friendliness of pretty Mary LeCates had caused Thomas Stephens to catch sight of a better way to go than the rough waterman's family he'd grown up in. And Mary, though she could easily have gotten a well-to-do—and handsome—city-bread tourist for a husband and moved away from the island, as her sisters had done, saw something admirable surfacing in Thomas Stephens that she couldn't pass up.

Thomas had told Mary and the Reverend Bowman that his middle name was Bell, and that he'd been named—oddly enough, considering his family—after the evangelist Thomas Bell who had cleaned up the island (originally called Hell's Island) of the carousing, thieving gypsies and most of the brawling descendants of the bay pirates who had held control over the island for centuries. The good citizens who had remained were grateful to the evangelist, Thomas Bell, and changed the name of their homeland to Bell's Island in his honor.

Thomas said he'd always wanted to be a preacher like his namesake, Thomas Bell, but he had so many bad family traits to shake off, things such as stealing, fighting, and running women. And what was more, he could barely read or write.

With the help of the Reverend Bowman and Mary LeCates and with the Bible as a textbook, he did passably learn to read and write, though he never made it to the pulpit. Clean of heart and strong of back, Thomas Stephens still was not overly blessed with brains. But his morals, his manners, and his general behavior became exemplary. In fact, his reformation was so thorough that he impressed even the LeCateses, who at first had disapproved of Mary even talking with him, much less marrying him.

When Mary's parents did agree to the union, one of their wedding presents was to set Thomas and Mary up in business, making them proprietors of the new rooming house that James LeCates had built at the upper end of the island near the bridge that went over to the Wintergreen County mainland. It became the Stephens Tu-Rest Home.

It was designed to catch tradesmen coming in via the wooden drawbridge and road from the mainland—salesmen and the like, and sometimes religious people from the county at camp meeting time who were too fastidious to sleep in the tents—anyone who wanted clean, comfortable accommodations at a reasonable price and didn't bother with the frills. The Tu-Rest Home served no meals, but there was a lunch counter at the drugstore/soda fountain further on down the island. And if a traveller wanted sex, bootleg liquor, gambling, or dancing, he could get all of that at Moonlight Corrigan's place over on the Wintergreen County mainland before even coming on Bell's Island.

Camellia felt her home was nice enough as a large, two-story double house with porches running the width of the front, both upstairs and down, with the roomers on one side and the family on the other, and with all the fine things—mahogany furniture, crystal chandeliers with their myriads of gleaming candles, lovely china and silverware—that her parents had bought for the family side.

And they certainly ate well—in spite of Thomas's bread-and-molasses habit left over from his far less affluent days. They often had the same bill of fare as the inn, including delicacies like filet mignon, caviar, capons, lobster, and rare imported teas and coffee brought down on the steamboat from Baltimore caterers. Thomas would wear his cutaway coat to dinner just like he'd seen his father-in-law James LeCates do.

And if James wore a velvet topcoat and high silk hat to church of a Sunday, you could be sure Thomas Stephens would be similarly attired the very next Sunday. And Camellia, being a young clotheshorse herself, revelled in all the finery her parents and grandparents bought for her.

Thomas and Mary didn't *own* the Tu-Rest Home outright, but Grandfather LeCates allowed them to keep all the profits from it in lieu of a salary, and business had been terrific ever since they'd first hung out that Stephens Tu-Rest sign some twelve years before. Island people had at first laughed when "Pumpkin" Stephens and "Mary Beanpole" started the business, but they didn't laugh anymore.

Still, Camellia felt life at home could not begin to compare with life at the Bell's Island Inn of her LeCates grandparents. At the inn there were always well-to-do people from the city for whom she could sing. They made a far more exciting and sophisticated audience than the *JesusLovesMeThisIKnow* hayseeds at the Bell's Island Methodist Church. And when her mother's sisters came with their families on vacation there were several cousins near her age and of her same social class with whom to pal around. They always went swimming together and had picnics on the sand beaches and went on boating cruises with Grandfather LeCates.

Since she was having trouble getting to sleep, Camellia got up and went to the front window or her bedroom and looked out. It was well after midnight and everything seemed still and dark outside, but in the partial light of a clear sky she saw a tall, shadowy figure weaving around in the dark and coming from the direction of the drawbridge. As the figure went on by the Tu-Rest Home and disappeared down the shell road, she thought nothing special of it as sometimes a lone drunk would wander by late at night, having come from Moonlight Corrigan's place over on the edge of the mainland. She turned from the window and went on back to bed.

Tomorrow then—to the inn...and her grandparents...and Claudie....

The warm spring sunshine smiled down on Camellia Stephens as she left the Stephens Tu-Rest Home the next morning. She was heading for the Bell's Island Inn, striding rapidly down the shell roadway with her chin held high and her long black hair flowing out behind her, tossed by the ever-present winds that swept across the island. She was pretty, and she knew it. She was talented, and she knew it. And she was smart, and she knew it. So, maybe, like Grandmother LeCates, she had the right to be "stuck-up."

She hoped she wouldn't run into any Stephens cousins along the way. They were the rough, scruffy children of her father's sister and brothers and they lived over on the other side of the shell roadway. Her father would never let Mary say to Camellia, for example, "your Uncle Charlie thus and so" or "your Aunt Amanda said this or that." It always had to be "your father's brother" or "your father's sister." But Camellia had to pass by those three grubby-looking houses with their broken-down docks at the marshy ends of the backyards where one or more decrepit skiffs were tied up.

In her pre-school days, her father had been successful in keeping her away from those kids. But once she got into the Bell's Island public school, she was running into them anyway, and they lost no time in reminding her that she was from the same *pirate-gypsy* stock from which they were, in spite of the fact that she "lived in a mansion, wore fancy clothes from Baltimore, and talked like she wasn't from around here."

"Hey, Cousin!" they would taunt her. "Doncha know you're our cousin? What makes you think you're better'n us? Bet you think yours doesn't stink, hey?!"

And they all would screech and laugh and sing dirty little ditties, and when she would huff up with an air of superiority, they would shriek in mocking laughter. But they never carried it too far, because she was bigger than all of them, in size as well as in years, and they were a bit afraid of her.

When she had been in a second grade play at school, she had been selected to play the witch. She had gotten such a kick out of the part where she muttered the magic incantation and charged after the other characters in the play, causing them to scatter and run, that she would do this same thing to her Stephens cousins whenever she met them on the shell road outside their homes. And she was so dramatically effective with it that they were always startled and would scream and scatter, just like in the second grade play, much to Camellia's satisfaction.

But there was one of the cousins who would always come back and look at her with curiosity and smile at her. That was Snipsey, the oldest child of Thomas's big, boarish sister, Amanda, and her likewise husband, Simon Cartwright. Little blond-headed Snipsey, with her pigtails bouncing and her mouth forever grinning, eventually won Camellia over. She was just about a year younger, and although she was somewhat of a pest, she was very knowledgeable about "things." Being around all the time as compared with Camellia's LeCates cousins who visited the island only once or twice a year, Snipsey became the closest thing to a sister that Camellia would ever have.

Camellia didn't see Snipsey this morning or any of the other Cartwright-Stephens cousins close enough to the front of the shell roadway to give her any trouble, and she was glad of that as she walked on.

The next house was that of her father's brother, Charlie Stephens. Charlie was considered the handsomest of the lot and also the shrewdest, but he had a nasty disposition. He had more of "that gypsy look" to him than the others, with coal-black kinky hair and olive skin. He was lithe and strongly built and had a razor scar across one side of his face left from a boyhood fight with Thomas. That scar gave Charlie a leer that everyone said excited women but scared them at the same time.

Camellia saw nothing of Charlie or any of the children when she went by the house, but she did see Charlie's wife, Agnes, pop out the front door, then just as quickly pop back inside. Camellia figured Agnes had forgotten something in the house and went back for it, and it reminded her of a tale she'd recently heard her mother telling on Agnes.

Mary had been telling the story to "Aunt Sairy" Middleton, the colored woman who did the heavy cleaning at the Tu-Rest Home, and Mary had been unaware that Camellia, as was her pesky habit, was eavesdropping.

It was as much a tale on Thomas and Mary as on Agnes Stephens. But, Agnes being a large, rawboned, blond-haired *immigrant* from one of those early-settled islands out in the bay where they still talked Cockney-like English instead of the *educated* British kind, made it all the funnier.

Anyhow, seems that some twelve years before at the time of their wedding, Thomas and Mary had intended to spend their honeymoon in Baltimore, but the steamboat had engine trouble and couldn't leave Bell's Island until the next morning.

The LeCateses, who had given them a big wedding and reception at the inn, suggested that Thomas and Mary spend their first night together at the brand-new rooming house (complete except that all its plumbing hadn't been hooked up yet), as it was to be their home anyway, and they could be completely alone there.

Thomas and Mary somewhat reluctantly agreed and Grandmother LeCates had Agnes, who at that time was unmarried and a chambermaid at the inn, take over all sorts of things for "a real old-fashion bridal suite" to the new rooming house. There were plush towels and perfumed sheets, bouquets of fresh flowers, little petit-four cakes and cheese tidbits on a silver tray, and *even a bottle of champagne in a bucket of ice!*

After Agnes had gotten everything in order—or so she thought—Thomas and Mary entered the bridal suite and closed the door. They were half-annoyed because they couldn't leave Bell's Island by steamboat that night, but they were trying to make the best of things. They talked awhile and nibbled on the petit-fours and cheese bits.

They stayed away from the champagne, but after awhile Mary said, "A little of this won't hurt you, Thomas, even if you did give up drinking as a part of your new character."

But Thomas said, "Well, I don't know, Mary...."

Actually, the real problem was both of them were trying to figure out how to go about doing what they knew they were supposed to be doing on this, their wedding night.

Thomas was more embarrassed than Mary, even though Mary had never done this before. Thomas didn't drop his new character as a gentleman just because he'd won Mary and gotten her in the bedroom. Thomas believed that *nice girls* (and Mary indeed was a nice girl) weren't really supposed to *want* to do what it was they were supposed to do, much less start it. Yet he couldn't figure out how to start it himself.

So it was Mary who got into that bottle of champagne, and before long that fire got into her veins and she suddenly became like one of those legendary sirens that hide out in the Anderson Sound waiting to shipwreck some poor seaman.

At first Thomas was surprised, then he was delighted, then embarrassed and bewildered, then delighted all over again. He gathered Mary up in his arms, took her to the bed, and they snuggled down amongst the perfumed sheets and in the half-glow of the candlelight it looked like everything was going to be just perfect.

But Thomas had forgotten to bolt the door of the bridal suite, and Agnes was on her way from the inn again, bringing an item she had forgotten.

The unthinking Agnes popped through the unlocked door, carrying the biggest, roundest, tallest, shiniest enameled chamber pot that Mary had ever seen. Without even looking around, Agnes said, "Miz LeKytes thowt you moight naid thiz...AYO! MOI GAWD!!"

Agnes suddenly realized what was going on and in her haste to get out of the room, she dropped the chamber pot! Crash! Bang! Rattle! Rattle! Rattle! The huge vessel and its runaway lid were dancing and rolling all around the floor in arcs and semi-circles until they finally bumped into the wall and stopped....

But Agnes was still running down the hallway...and screaming, "Ayo! moi Gawd! Ayo! moi Leurd! Miz LeKytes! Thomas! Murry! Jaysus Croyst! *Ever'body*! Playze excowse me! Playze forgive me!" When she reached the front door of the new rooming house she went barrelling outside and ran down the shell roadway like a lion was after her.

Mary, whose sense of humor far outweighed any embarrassment she had—or should have had—got into such a state of uncontrollable giggling at Agnes and the chamber pot that she somehow rolled over on top of Thomas and proceeded to thoroughly drench him.

Sober-minded Thomas, unable to laugh, at either Mary or Agnes, yet trying not to be angry or crude, got to stuttering and stammering, "Agnes brought the—brought the—brought the—the" He couldn't think of a "proper" word for it, so he wound up saying, "But it 'pears to me she brought it *a mite late*!"

This understatement of the century, this unintentional bit of humor on Thomas' part, set Mary off into another round of giggling. Needless to say, both of them were done for, sex-wise, that first time around.

For a wedding night, maybe all of that was excusable, but Camellia felt her mother, in spite of her good upbringing and lady-like appearance, was still too giddy-headed at times and still loved the risque side of things too much for her own good.

Camellia continued along the shell road and eventually came to Amos Stephens's house. Amos was the youngest Stephens and even shorter and wirier than Thomas, and of even duller sense of humor. Island people sometimes called Amos "that blond-haired gypsy" because, though one-quarter gypsy like the rest of Azariah Stephens's children, he was light-haired, fair-skinned, and had blue eyes. "But Amos never done nobody no harm," everybody said.

Camellia saw neither Amos nor his wife, Lois, nor any of their children, but out in the front yard she saw Azariah Stephens, her grandfather with whom her father didn't want her to have anything to do. Azariah lived there with Amos and Lois. Camellia didn't know if she agreed with the consensus that Azariah was the meanest, crookedest waterman Bell's Island ever produced, but he certainly was the most peculiar-looking. There he was this morning, wearing as usual his stiff, bib-type overalls that were three sizes too big for him, and he wasn't very big himself anyhow. He told everybody he liked his overalls big because he could hide from people in them.

More likely people wanted to hide from him, Camellia mused. He had bulging, frog-like eyes, a sharp nose, and a small rat-like face that was often covered way down his forehead with a peaked-crown hat which was also too big for him.

Claudie had once told Camellia that Azariah used "gypsy magic" that he'd learned from his wife's people, and that he could mentally command anybody or anything to do his will, from a baby to a barnacle, without their realizing what was going on. Claudie said she had witnessed something like that happen years ago when Thomas had been courting Mary at the inn and Charlie had been courting Agnes. Thomas and Charlie had come to the inn to pick up the girls. It wasn't a double date by any means. Charlie went to the back door to pick up chambermaid Agnes, but Thomas had front door privileges at the inn.

Charlie had made some sort of nasty remark about this to Thomas, and Thomas had lit into him and then the two were slugging it out right there in front of the inn. Suddenly both young men fell down in the dirt, clutching their stomachs, and Claudie said it looked as though they had both knocked each other out at the same time. But that was not what had happened.

Just about then Azariah Stephens, who wouldn't let his offspring fight each other if he could help it (it was okay to fight anybody else), came strolling along, whistling a little gypsy tune. Charlie and Thomas helped each other get up off the ground and Charlie said, "How *does* he do it? I'd give a year's worth of good pussy to know how Paw does that to us!" And Thomas had said, "Shut up or he'll do it again."

So Azariah had his children and most of Bell's Island scared to death of him. When anybody tried to get the law on him for some theft, that person usually had something even more terrible happen, like falling on a boat's deck and breaking a leg or coming down with some strange and sudden illness.

Azariah glanced at Camellia as she passed by, but he didn't say anything. She didn't feel afraid of him, but she did feel curious about him. She had heard that he played the fiddle—usually gypsy music—and sometimes watermen in the Anderson Sound heard it and swamped their boats, mistaking the sound for the voice of a bewitching siren or the beckonings of the very devil himself.

Azariah had come to live with Amos and Lois, so Claudie had said, through an odd set of circumstances. After his children had all married and left the little hut in the marsh they'd called home, Azariah took the old photo of his dead, half-gypsy wife, Mona, out of its frame and put it under his undershirt next to his heart. Then he took his fiddle and bow down from the wall and put them under his arm. He went outside and pushed the coal oil drum off its platform, opened the bung, and let the coal oil spread all around the bottom of his hut. Then he stepped back, tossed a few lighted matches, and walked away.

In a little while he turned around and saw the fire burning down his home. He started playing some gypsy music on his fiddle, then walked away from the place for good and never looked back.

He came up out of the marsh, went right to Amos's house, and said, "My house just burned down, Amos. All right if I stay here with you for awhile?" Amos and Lois took him in and he'd stayed there ever since.

Camellia continued walking the mile-long shell roadway and soon got past all of the small, unpretentious, white clapboard houses at the east or mainland end of the island. There would be more of the same further on, toward the Anderson Sound end of the elongated island. The island contained about seven hundred fifty people, most of them watermen and their families, most of them poor. The only really well-to-do people and grand-looking places on the island were the Thomas Stephenses with their Tu-Rest Home and the LeCateses with their Bell's Island Inn.

Camellia was getting to the section where, on the left or south side of the roadway, there was an untidy string of wharves, shipyards, warehouses, and seafood firms, including A. Stephens and Sons, where her father's brothers and brother-in-law all worked, and where their father, Azariah, still cracked a mean whip over them. Oystering all winter, crabbing all summer—it was an endless routine that had gone on for most of the island families for centuries.

On the right, opposite the wharves, on the north side of the roadway, there was a mixture of small businesses, including a ship's chandlery, a hardware store, a general merchandise store that also housed the post office and the telegraph office, and a combined drug-store/soda fountain/lunch counter with a barbershop on one side and Doc Feldman's office on the other.

Camellia smiled a bit. Doc Feldman—Bell's Island's favorite (and only) doctor; Bell's Island's favorite (and only) Jew. Doc, a lanky, sandy-haired bachelor with horn rims, looked more like a Scotsman than a Jew and more like a professor than a doctor, and lived upstairs over his office. He regularly attended the Bell's Island Methodist Church because, he said, it was the next closest thing to a synagogue and he liked to go there so he could keep tabs on all the courtships, marriages, and pregnancies because more babies meant more deliveries and more deliveries meant more money and more money meant he could spend more time fishing. He was a self-appointed wiseacre whose comments were taken with a grain of salt, and though he wasn't much of doctor, everybody loved him. He had a genuine way with people and if he couldn't figure out how else to treat them when they were sick, he gave them *needles* and that made them feel better.

Camellia was proud that she was healthy and needed no *needles* from Doc Feldman, but she wasn't so sure about her mother.

Everybody said that Mary, in spite of her perpetually cheerful manner, was so thin and "consumptive-looking" and looking more than ever like her nickname "Mary Beanpole" that she must surely be sick from working too hard. True, she was constantly on the go, flitting like a nervous little bird from one pursuit to the next. She did all the bookkeeping and general managing of the Tu-Rest Home, but this by itself was no great chore as she had been bookkeeper and receptionist, too, at the inn before her marriage. But at the Tu-Rest Home, though Thomas did all the heavy maintenance, she also did most of the inside cleaning and laundry—the chambermaid work, if you will. She insisted on doing this even though there were women on the island quite willing and able to do manual labor, and Thomas would have preferred her to just "sit by and be a lady." Camellia thought her mother had more nervous energy than she knew what to do with.

On Sundays Mary was either organist, pianist, soloist, or choir director at the Bell's Island Methodist Church, and sometimes it seemed like she was all of them at once. Mary also did tons of fancy cooking and gave away most of it, taking a lot to the Stephens families across the shell road, much to Thomas' displeasure. But Mary was more tolerant of his rowdy relatives than Thomas was, even though Mary said she suspected they threw her specialty—Maryland Beat Biscuits—at each other rather than eating them. And considering that those unleavened little dough balls were natural-born missiles, Camellia figured that may well have been the case. Camellia recalled Doc Feldman once saying that if the value of Maryland Beat Biscuits had been recognized by the South in the 1860s, they would have been used as missiles far superior to the Minie ball and grapeshot and the South undoubtedly would have won the Civil War. Doc also said that dentists both loved and hated for people to eat Maryland Beat Biscuits because they had been responsible for more broken teeth and cracked dentures than all the sour balls and prune pits in recorded history! One other value of Maryland Beat Biscuits, according to Doc, was that making them was wonderful therapy for pent-up energy that couldn't otherwise be expressed. The dough required hours of continuous beating with the backside of a hatchet!

Maryland Beat Biscuits notwithstanding, Mary's real pride and joy were the afternoons she spent as librarian at the little Bell's Island

Library that she and Claudie had set up years before in the belief that Bell's Island residents needed a bit of *culture* the same as the inn's guests, who were regularly treated to Claudie and Mary's musical and theatrical presentations. The library was in a little storefront location next to Doc Feldman's office and Doc had donated a lot of medical books to its shelves. Not many people ever went in the little library, but Mary had real all the books and encouraged Camellia to do the same.

Mary had recently pointed out to Camellia certain sections of Doc's books and said, "Study this information while thinking about some of the stories in Claudie's 'opera book' and some of the stories in the Bible (she wrote down a few references) and soon you'll know all about men and women...and love and sex...and babies!"

Camellia had found the physical descriptions and technical illustrations pretty weird, but she got the general drift and it all jibed quite well with the wild things Snipsey had been whispering to her and Claudie had been discreetly implying. *But if love and sex and babies were going to get in the way of her musical career, Camellia wanted no parts of any of them!*

Somewhere in the midst of all this learning, she had begun to wonder again why she had no brothers or sisters, when the other Stephens families had hordes of them. She remembered overhearing her father saying something in the hardware store one day that caused everybody to nearly fall on the floor to keep from laughing at "Pumpkin" Stephens. Thomas had said, "Well, big families are nice. I don't know why Mary and I haven't had more than one child. We've been 'naughty' at least a whole half-dozen times in our marriage!"

In his efforts not to sound vulgar, Thomas more often than not ended up sounding silly. But there was something more out of kilter here, Camellia reasoned, than her father's choice of words. Shortly afterwards, Camellia had heard her mother talking with "Aunt Sairy" Middleton, the cleaning woman, and Aunt Sairy had said, "Why you so jumpy all the time, Miss Mary?"

Aunt Sairy was one of those colored people to whom you could tell things, like you would to a pet dog, without fear of embarrassing them or having them scold you or snitch on you. Mary had answered Aunt Sairy something to the effect that she could "almost count *only on one hand* the times Thomas and I have had sex in the entire twelve years of our marriage."

(Then his arithmetic had been literally true!)

"It's not that he doesn't love me," Mary had continued. "I couldn't ask for a more devoted, more easy-to-get-along-with person than Thomas Stephens. He never demands anything, never complains, and it takes so little to make him happy. I give him just a little pat or touch on the arm and he's beaming all day."

And Camellia could have vouched for the same general pleasantness between her parents in the home. And in public, the two were the perfect example of consideration for each other, almost to the point of being silly.

Thomas was forever adjusting Mary's coat or asking her if this, that, or the other was all right; was she warm enough, cool enough, and comfortable enough; and she was always smiling at him and nodding yes, everything was fine, and addressing him as "Mr. Stephens" as was the custom among the better class of people of that day.

Mary had gone on to say to Aunt Sairy, "And it's not that he can't do it. His problem is not down here; it's up here (and she had pointed to her head). Oh, Aunt Sairy, I wish I'd never taught Thomas to read. You should see the places he's marked in his Bible."

Mary and Aunt Sairy had then moved out of range of Camellia's eavesdropping and she heard no more, but she lost no time in checking out her father's Bible. She found passages marked such as: "...abstain from fleshly lusts which war against the soul." "...Flee also youthful lusts..." "...as ye have yielded your members servants to uncleanness and to iniquity unto iniquity; even so now yield your members servants to righteousness unto holiness...."

Camellia had concluded that her father must have thought all sex was dirty and unholy, no matter with whom it was performed. Maybe he thought he was doing Mary a favor by *not* messing with her because *nice women don't like it.* Or maybe he was just *bucking for Heaven* and not even thinking about Mary's feelings one way or the other.

But Camellia knew her mother did have *feelings* and an incident not too long afterwards had borne this out. Mary had sent Camellia over to Charlie and Agnes Stephens's with a plateful of Maryland Beat Biscuits. The Stephens work boat had just gotten back from a trip to Baltimore delivering seafood, but Thomas, who had gone with the brothers as an extra hand, had not yet returned home. Camellia was surprised at first that Charlie was home already—until she overheard Charlie and Agnes arguing with each other inside the house:

"You stye a-whye from me, you filthy thing! You got a smell on you stroong enough to gag a maggot!"

"Goddamit, woman! A little bit of cock before supper ain't gonna hurt you none! You're already pregnant again anyway."

"Nayo! Not loike you are! Why kent you be loike Thomas? He always tykes a beth before he goes hayom."

So that was why Thomas had not yet gotten home. As Camellia left the biscuits on Charlie's porch and scooted home herself, she remembered her mother saying how Thomas always kept soap and a set of clean clothes at the Stephens crab house so he could "tyke a beth" from the rain water tank and change into clean clothes before returning to the Tu-Rest Home after one of those slimy trips up the bay and back.

But when Camellia had reported to her mother—part of it at least—what she had overheard at Charlie's, being careful to leave out the "bad words," she was not quite expecting what Mary remarked in an aside to Aunt Sairy Middleton.

Mary said, "Which is better—or worse—I wonder: To come home with 'a smell stroong enough to gag a maggot' and be all geared up and ready for action, or to 'tyke a beth' before coming home and then do nothing?"

Camellia had puzzled over the remark for a long time. *Nice women didn't like it*...or did they?

In another incident along about the same time, Amanda Cartwright had brought a pair of beagle pups to the Tu-Rest Home.

Amanda was a regular Amazon of a woman—tall, big-framed, and laden with floppy fat, possessing a booming voice that never stopped talking or laughing. She had rather thin, black hair pulled straight back in a ponytail and a heavy, reddish face. She was aggressive, coarse, and comical, but basically harmless, everybody said.

Camellia had been singing and playing the piano in the music room when she looked toward the living room and saw big, sloppy-fat, and unkempt Amanda standing there, holding something in her apron and talking to Mary.

Suddenly Amanda let go of the apron and two beagle pups tumbled down to the floor. They must have heard Camellia singing for they set up a brand of puppy howling that was not of this world.

Thomas had been reading his Bible and abruptly flung it aside. He said, "Amanda, what in...?" Camellia thought he was going to say, "What in hell?" but he didn't quite, though he surely must have been thinking it.

Amanda was cackling. "There you are, Brother Thomas. Singing rabbit dogs! Ahhahahahaha!"

"But we don't—don't—don't—want...." Thomas was stammering.

Amanda was beaming. "They're a present, Thomas. And they *will breed*, even if you and Mary have forgotten how."

Camellia saw her father's ears reddening.

The beagle pups were chasing each other around and around the room, howling, squealing, and making spectacular puddles on Mary's just-waxed floor.

Thomas was furious. "Take those animals out of here, Amanda. We don't want DOGS. Mary's already got a cat."

Amanda threw her hands in the air and said mockingly, "Oh, Brother Thomas! You certainly want something more than *Mary's pussy*, don't you?"

Before anybody had time to react to *that* remark, Amanda had ducked out of the door, leaving the beagle pups in full charge of the household.

While remembering all this, Camellia walked on past the rest of the stores and shortly came to the Bell's Island Methodist Church. The modest white building with its long, multi-paned windows, green shutters, and simple white cross on the front peak of the roof still had not been completely repaired from the explosion during the winter. How close her father had come to losing his life, Camellia recalled.

Thomas was sexton for the church, a lowly position for someone who always dreamed of becoming a preacher, but he was strong, healthy, and dedicated, and everybody said he did the work with such perfection and reverence.

Early that Sunday of the explosion he had gotten the coal oil stove, which had seen its better days, going, and everything seemed to be all right. So he left the church and went momentarily to the outhouse in back. Before he returned, there was an explosion inside the church, the likes of which had never been heard before on Bell's Island.

It seemed the entire population instantly rushed to the scene to assess the damage. Everybody was saying how wonderful that the service had not been in progress when the coal oil stove blew up, and how lucky Thomas Stephens had been not to have been inside, either.

Mary and Camellia were in tears of gratitude when they found Thomas all right. Mary said, "The Lord surely must have been with you, Thomas."

But Amanda Cartwright viewed the narrow escape from a more earthy perspective: "Well, Brother Thomas! That was one time when a piss saved you!"

Oh, these boorish Stephens kinfolk, Camellia was thinking as she walked along, coming now to the Bell's Island School. There wouldn't be any tests on Monday, she felt sure, so no need to study any books this weekend. She could think about music instead.

Whenever her mother had asked her how she got her usual good marks without seeming to do much studying, Camellia always said, "Oh, I don't know, Mama. Maybe I hear the answers before the questions."

And to Claudie's asking a similar question, she had replied "Well, it's like I've heard beforehand—heard in my head—what the questions will be when I get called on in class, and I study only those things."

Mary and Claudie had both shaken their heads and Claudie had said something about "gypsy forebears and telepathy." Still, nobody could dispute consistently good report cards, Camellia mused, and she puffed up her chest with her not-quite-yet-breasts as she walked along.

The island was so full of music this morning. Every sound was a note or combination of notes. Every part of the landscape had its own rhythm. The trees—pine and deciduous—were coming out of their subdued green and winter bareness, and the sedge and marsh grass that had turned a bronze-tan during the cold winter months would soon burst into a full lush green, while the silver poplars would flash striking patches of brilliance as the wind continuously turned their leaves back and forth and around and around.

From the quietness of the starlight to the clamor of the morning when the sunlight first broke out across the water, all was music.

Yet Camellia was not so immersed in the music of the island as to be unaware of its hazards. She knew that the rising of the wind all too often signalled danger to the men working out in the Anderson Sound and that it struck fear in the hearts of those loved ones who waited on shore. The sky whose stars so often sang with tender music could suddenly become a raging electrical inferno that would pummel down hail and lightning and set off waterspouts and twisters capable of capsizing boats and tearing ashore, taking away trees, roofs, and chimneys.

The restlessness of the tides and the uneven glitter of the sunlight on the water made one remember the uncertainly of what lay beneath those waters; whether there would be a good oyster harvest or not; whether the crabs would be plentiful or scarce; whether one's family would live well or poorly in the months to come.

Camellia was always grateful that her father and her Grandfather LeCates both had a more safe and secure kind of business on which to rely than just the life of a waterman.

She was coming now to the last grouping of white clapboard houses at the west end of the island just before the Bell's Island Inn. Here people's yards were neat and clean and in the summer bright flowers would surround the little dwellings. But the land generally was too salty to grow much in the way of vegetables. And far too wet and soggy most of the year even to decently bury one's dead.

Chapter Two

Camellia didn't see her grandfather outside the inn. This was unusual for he always greeted guests coming off the steamboat. The steamboat had already docked and a few final passengers, preceded by porters carrying their luggage, were coming off the gangplank and heading up the walkway to the inn's front door.

Camellia went on in the lobby and, stepping lightly along the plush red carpet, looked around for Grandfather or even Grandmother LeCates, but didn't see either one.

She peeped around the edge of the crimson portiere at the entrance to the dining room and saw the snowy white tablecloths and the fine silverware all in readiness for the noontime meal. But she still did not see her grandparents.

From somewhere in the lobby Claudie crept up behind her and gave her a big hug, and then the two of them jumped into each other's arms in greeting.

"Claudie, you should have seen the way Papa reacted last night when I asked him what if I were to become an opera singer!" Camellia began with a chuckle.

"He didn't like the idea, I'll bet!" Claudie said with an impish grin.

"No, indeed, He nearly dropped his bread and molasses on the floor." Camellia imitated Thomas' actions and words.

Camellia and Claudie had a huge laugh.

Still looking around the lobby of the inn, Camellia said, "Where's Grandfather?"

Claudie seemed rather concerned as she said, "I don't think he's feeling too well this morning. Your grandmother is upstairs with him."

Camellia thought that was strange as her grandfather was rarely sick. At that moment Lucille LeCates appeared, coming down the red carpeted stairway.

"Is Grandfather ill?" Camellia blurted.

Grandmother LeCates stopped in her tracks, hesitated, then said, "He has a bit of a headache this morning, Camellia. I think he's been overworking lately, but I'm sure he'll be all right shortly."

"Have you sent for Doc Feldman?" Camellia asked.

"I don't think that is necessary," Lucille LeCates said.

"I can stop by Doc's office on the way home and tell him to come down here," Camellia offered.

"I don't think that will be necessary," Lucille repeated a little sharply, then turned, and went back upstairs again.

Camellia thought her grandmother was acting a little funny. To Claudie she said, "Claudie, what's going on?"

Claudie, too, had a genuinely perplexed look as she said, "I'm not sure, Camellia. Maybe it doesn't have anything to do with anything and maybe I shouldn't say this anyhow, but it seems to me your grandfather came in quite late from somewhere or other last night."

A flicker of recognition raced across Camellia's face as she remembered the tall, dark, shadowy figure she had seen staggering along the shell road outside the Tu-Rest Home after midnight the night before. But just as quickly she shook off the suggestion. And she even laughed a little, because the notion that *Grandfather* could have been at Moonlight's place was not only laughable, it was unthinkable.

She did, however, say to Claudie, "If Grandfather's not feeling well, maybe I should go home and get Mama."

"We-ell," said Claudie, "if you want to. Yes, I guess maybe you should."

Camellia rushed home and just as quickly returned to the inn with Mary. Somebody must have summoned Doc Feldman in the meantime, for he was going up the stairway of the inn even as Camellia and Mary were entering the front door.

By sundown, James LeCates was dead.

Late that night after the undertaker from Royal Hall had been notified and had come and removed the body, Camellia, Mary, and Grandmother LeCates were sitting in the living room of the LeCates' suite at the inn, trying to make some sense out of the sudden shock of death.

At the risk of being severely reprimanded for disrespect, Camellia, acting on a hunch, point-blank asked her grandmother, "Did Grandfather ever go to that tavern—Moonlight's place—across the inlet on the Wintergreen County mainland?"

Lucille—and Mary, too—gasped, horrified, and Lucille said, "*Camellia!* How can you insinuate such a thing and your dear grandfather a corpse? And as good as he was to you...He gave you that magnificent piano and so many of your fine clothes. You ought to be ashamed...."

Then a strange and angry look came over Lucille's face and she said under her breath, choking, "They ought to close that place down...." But just as quickly she recovered her composure and said matter-of-factly, "Doc Feldman said it could have been a brain tumor."

Camellia, without thinking, burst out, "Doc Feldman doesn't know shit from sugar!"

"Wha-at?!" Grandmother LeCates gasped and to Mary she said, "Mary, if you don't keep your daughter away from those filthy Stephens kids, she's going to be ruined, if she isn't already."

Mary, however, instead of reprimanding Camellia, seemed to be acting on a hunch also and she re-asked Camellia's question: "Well, Mother, *did* Father ever go there?"

Lucille flushed again and said, "If either of you even as much as *think* that again—what you just said—you will live to regret it. Brain tumor. Brain tumor. Doc Feldman said it could have been a brain tumor."

After they left the inn at nearly dawn, Mary said to Camellia, "Like you, I wonder how Doc could have come to such a conclusion. You don't just suddenly die of a brain tumor, I don't think. I'm going to talk with Doc myself sometime today."

Later that day Mary, Thomas, and Camellia, still numb with shock and grief, sat down in the kitchen of the Tu-Rest Home and tried to eat some lunch.

Thomas said, "You've talked with Doc Feldman again, have you, Mary?"

"Yes," said Mary. "He said Father could have either been struck on the head, or fallen somehow and hit his head, thus causing a concussion and his death. By the time Mother had called Doc, Father was unconscious and couldn't give any information himself. Doc wanted to have the hospital in Gainsbiddle do an autopsy, but Mother was violently opposed to it. She even talked Doc into writing brain tumor on the death certificate. Mother is obviously hiding something.

"When I asked Doc if he knew whether Father ever went to Moonlight's place, he hedged, so I didn't press him."

Camellia, not wanting to get Claudie in trouble, did not mention what Claudie had said about James LeCates coming home late the night he was stricken, nor did Camellia say anything about seeing someone staggering past the Tu-Rest Home late the same night.

The news of James LeCates' death from "a brain tumor" swept across the island. Camellia was hearing the question everywhere—at school, in church, in the Bell's Island drugstore—"Who'll run the Bell's Island Inn now?...Oh, no! Surely not 'Pumpkin' Stephens!"

But Bell's Island need not have worried about "Pumpkin" Stephens. There were far sadder things than that about to happen to the Bell's Island Inn and to the Thomas Stephenses, too.

When James LeCates' estate was opened a slew of hard facts came out for which no easy coverup like "brain tumor" could be invented. After the lawyers had talked with the LeCates heirs—Lucille, Mary, and Mary's two sisters—Mary gathered Thomas and Camellia together at the Tu-Rest Home. To Camellia she said, "It's only right that you should hear this, too, and from us, not the general public.

"Your grandfather died, quite frankly, flat broke, penniless, and so far in debt that even the sale of both the inn and the Tu-Rest Home here may not meet the demands of his creditors.

"The lawyers said he had gone way beyond his means in building this rooming house to start with. He had been trying for years to sell the Bell's Island Inn, but had been unable to find anyone to agree to his price. He should have changed us here at the Tu-Rest Home to just a salary instead of letting us keep all the profits. That way he would have had something to apply to his debts, but he didn't want to admit to us that he was in so much trouble. And he had not wanted to risk having us turned out of the Tu-Rest Home, so he had not put it up for sale, but now it most likely will be. We've always lived pretty 'high off the hog', so we don't have much in savings, but I'm sure we'll find a way to survive."

"*Survive?*" Camellia squealed. "Mama, I have to do more than just *survive*. I have an opera career ahead of me, an education to get."

Thomas started to say something, but Mary cut him off and said, "We know that, Camellia. And the Lord will provide, the Lord will provide. Now you get on to bed and we'll talk about this more in the morning."

What Mary had not said to Camellia about her grandfather, she was shortly to find out anyway. Always hungry and even more so now, it seemed, at the prospect of maybe even *going hungry*, Camellia crept downstairs that night to get a sandwich, thinking her parents had gone to bed. But Thomas and Mary were still up and in the kitchen, talking. Camellia paused out of sight to listen.

Mary was saying, "How can one person have made such a mess for everybody? And to think he would have resorted to gambling to try to get out of debt. He never was any good at cards and Doc Feldman finally admitted Father always got drunk over there at

Moonlight's and forfeited what little skill he did have. He had told Doc only a few days before his death, 'Doc, I don't even own the shoelaces that are in my shoes'. Doc said he couldn't say for sure whether Father was at Moonlight's the night he was stricken and if he had gotten his head injury there or just what. And Mother remains as tight-lipped as ever and keeps insisting 'Brain tumor. Brain tumor'."

Thomas scratched his balding head. "You know, Mary, it's funny. My grandmother Izetta got killed at that Moonlight's place and now, several generations later, your father may have had something happen to him there that caused his death, too."

Mary said, "Yes, and you remember that old rumor that said Mother's father, Judge Johnstone, was there that night Izetta was killed, and *he* went there for women, not gambling. That's why Mother is so sensitive and hates that place so much."

Thomas said, "Well, it is an awful place, Mary, and it should be closed down, but I suppose it never will."

"No," said Mary, "probably not. There are always too many *current* Judge Johnstones who still find its wares attractive. But that is neither here nor there. The point is somebody's got to look out for Mother now and God only knows who's going to look out for us. I think either my sister Ruth or Lizbeth will take Mother to live with them. But as for us...."

Thomas sighed helplessly. "Mary, if I hadn't been so intent on seeing that we all enjoyed the good life—you, the way you'd always had it and me, the way I'd never had it—and instead listened to you and put something more away for emergencies...all good watermen do that, but I guess I no longer thought of myself as a waterman. I thought I'd gotten above that. I thought our prosperity was going to last forever."

Mary said, "Don't scold yourself, Thomas. What's done is done. We can't go back now and do it over a different way. But maybe we can convince whoever bids on the Tu-Rest Home when they have the creditor's auction to let us be the ones to run it for them. We might get a salary and we might not, considering the liens against it that the new owner will have to face, but at least we would still have a home. And maybe you could go back to working on the water with your father and brothers. I'm sure I could take care of things here if you did."

Thomas said, "I don't want to work with them if I can help it, Mary. They're dishonest. But I think there might be something for me down at Gainsbiddle. I know a young man down there, name of Norman Travis, who's looking for somebody—somebody honest and a Christian, he says, and somebody who doesn't drink or smoke—to go on his oyster boat with him as mate."

Camellia never did get her sandwich, but went on back upstairs and wrestled with her troubled thoughts. They were going to auction off everything? Was that what her mother had said? Could anybody possibly take MUSIC away from her?

Somewhere in the background of all her misery she heard music. It was such strange and beautiful music—not like anything she recalled having played or sung or heard before. She wanted immediately to go downstairs and try to capture it on the piano, but she knew her parents would scold her, for it was so late.

But over and over those beautiful strains echoed and re-echoed in her mind and she knew first thing in the morning she'd be down in the music room, playing it and writing it down, capturing it before anyone could come and take away her piano.

When the morning came, however, the strange and beautiful music had gone from her and she couldn't hear, remember, or reproduce a note of it.

More troubled than ever, Camellia wandered out into the backyard of the Tu-Rest Home. She was moping around by the beagle pens when Snipsey Cartwright came hop-skipping into the yard, her pigtails bobbing.

Snipsey eased up to Camellia, put her arm around her, and said, "Sorry your grandfather died. You liked him, didn't you, Camellia?"

Camellia tried to be nonchalant though her heart was breaking and fear for the future was making her head throb and her stomach ache. "Well, yes, I rather liked Grandfather. He gave me my piano."

"Well," Snipsey said, drawing in a big breath. "We could lend you *our* Grandpaw for awhile, if you would like that. He has a *fiddle* he plays on!" Snipsey seemed overcome with awe at the mention of "fiddle." Then she cleared her throat a bit and continued, "Would you like that, Camellia, if we lent you *our* Grandpaw?"

Camellia had not even been half listening to Snipsey and wondered what on earth was she talking about. She didn't remember ever seeing Snipsey's father's father. But then the mention of "Grandpaw" and "fiddle" got together in her mind and she nearly burst out laughing.

"Snipsey, do you mean Azariah Stephens?"

Snipsey nodded "Yes" so vigorously that she set her blond pigtails to bobbing.

Camellia drew herself up with an air of superiority. "Snipsey, you may not have thought of this, but I believe Azariah Stephens just happens to already *be* my grandfather, too."

Snipsey had a rather strange look on her face as she tried to take this in.

Camellia helped her a bit: "You see, Azariah Stephens is my father's father as well as your mother's father. Your mother and my father are brother and sister, and Azariah is the father of both of them and that makes Azariah *grandfather* to both of us. Your understand that, Snipsey?"

Snipsey said, "Yes, I think so. But I never thought of it that way before. Grandpaw never goes to see your father like he comes to see us. Why is that?"

"Oh, I don't know, Snipsey," Camellia said, half-angry at this stupid conversation. But then the word "fiddle" seized her again. She said to Snipsey, "Look, Snipsey, the next time you see Azariah—uh, Grandpaw, that is—tell him to come see us—Mama and Papa and me—and tell him to bring that vio—that fiddle—with him. I'd like for him to teach me how to play it."

Snipsey was jubilant. "Okay! I'll tell Grandpaw!" she said. And she scampered off, pigtails a-bobbing, obviously proud as punch that she had done something to make Camellia feel better.

And Camellia *did* feel better. If the creditors were going to take her piano, she'd still have Grandpaw to give her fiddle—uh, violin—lessons. One thing for certain—she knew NOBODY could take *music* away from her for long.

When the word had gotten around the island that the Stephens Tu-Rest Home would likely be sold at auction, Thomas and Mary had a visit from a pair of good Samaritans, eager to help as Snipsey had been with Camellia.

There was a knock on the door of the Tu-Rest Home one evening, and Camellia went to answer it. Standing on the front porch were two slightly built and shabbily dressed creatures—Thomas's youngest brother Amos and his wife, Lois. Lois had an overall faded look just like her faded blue gingham dress. Amos—"that blond-haired gypsy" —had an expressionless face except for his blue eyes, the whites of which bulged like his father Azariah's. Camellia recoiled somewhat at first, but her mother had tried to teach her to accept people for the potential good in them, no matter what their outward appearance.

Camellia smiled as best she could, but it was a little smirky smile because she was thinking of how everybody said of Amos and Lois that they went everywhere together, even to the outhouse together, because neither of them had sense enough to find their way back home without the other's help. Still, people always added charitably, "But they never done nobody no harm."

For all of Mary's good will toward everyone, Camellia could see her mother was annoyed this time at the appearance of Stephens relatives. Mary was still overwrought from the loss of her father and all that it meant, and she was in no mood to entertain or make small talk with people as socially inept and difficult to converse with as Amos and Lois, and in a home that might not even be home much longer.

But Mary bade them come in and sit down, which they did without either of them having as yet said the first word. Thomas greeted them with a grunt, and he did not even bother to get up or set aside his Bible. True, they were *home folks*, in a sense, but they so rarely came to the Tu-Rest Home that they might as well have been strangers. This was mostly, Camellia knew, because of the social distance that her father had erected over the years between himself, his immediate family, and his *lesser* relatives.

Mary made some strained remarks about the weather, and then asked if she could get Amos and Lois some cake and coffee.

The pair looked at each other with their mouths half open, each waiting for the other to say something. But neither did, nor did they answer Mary's question. They merely looked dumbly around the room, then again at Mary the way a cow will look at a person—full-eyed, unblinking, unafraid, unassuming, and completely stupid. But one must remember, Camellia thought: Amos and Lois—"they never done nobody no harm."

But still it was awkward, and Camellia couldn't decide which was worse—to have this kind of people visit who never said a word or to have Thomas's sister, Amanda Cartwright, come over and constantly jabber things that would embarrass a sailor's parakeet.

After an eternity, it seemed, Amos did say, "Uh, no, thanks. We get fed at home."

Then they both got up abruptly as though to leave.

"Not leaving so soon?" Mary said, and Camellia thought she detected a little too much joy in her mother's voice.

Amos and Lois exchanged blank glances as they moved toward the door and then, as Amos opened the door, he looked toward Thomas and said, "Iffen you 'n' yer fam'ly need a home, y'could come live with Lois 'n' me. We've still got Paw—or Grandpaw, as the kids call him—but we ain't got's many kids as Amanda 'n' Simon or Charlie 'n' Agnes."

Camellia was thinking, *So that's what they came for and didn't know how to say it*!

Thomas didn't reply to them, though he had set his Bible aside now and was looking oddly at Amos.

"*Thomas*!" Mary said sharply, "your brother is talking to you!"

"Yes, I heard," Thomas said. He was getting to his feet now—slowly, deliberately, the way he did most everything—and he walked over to the door and faced Amos and Lois.

"I thank you, Amos," Thomas said quietly. "We still may be able to stay here. And there is the possibility of us going to Gainsbiddle. But I thank you for your offer. We appreciate it, and we'll see how things work out here."

At the mention of "Gainsbiddle," Camellia noticed little smiles flitting ever so briefly across Amos's and Lois's faces. It was about the most evidence she'd seen that evening that they were even alive! Gainsbiddle, the rival port down the river, didn't have a very good name among Bell's Islanders. To say the least, it could rouse a snicker from even Amos and Lois. But Gainsbiddle? Live in Gainsbiddle?!

Amos and Lois had barely gotten off the porch when Camellia started yelping, "Gainsbiddle?! Papa, you said 'move to Gainsbiddle?' Why, that's a terrible place to go to live!"

"Oh, stop, Camellia," Mary said wearily. "Nobody said were moving to Gainsbiddle."

"But Papa just said...."

Thomas warned her, "Daughter, if you don't quit butting in on other people's conversations, the devil is going to get you."

Mary said, "And there *are* some nice places in Gainsbiddle. You've only seen that trashy waterfront, Camellia, and the lower end of town where we get off the boat and go for supplies sometimes. And there *are* some nice people in Gainsbiddle, too. We met a couple the other day while you were in school, when you Papa and I had gone down there on the freight boat. They are Norman and Bessie Travis—young people, not been married long, and Norman may give your Papa a job as mate on his work boat.

"But that doesn't mean," Mary continued, "that we have to go to *live* in Gainsbiddle. If the creditors let us, maybe we can stay here and I can run the Tu-Rest Home while your father works on the water. And nobody's going to get your piano, Camellia. We've got that *in writing* from the lawyers."

At least the piano was safe, Camellia sighed with gratitude. But everything else remained uncertain. She reflected with a bit of wry amusement at how all the poor Stephenses across the shell road were offering to help their once well-to-do brother Thomas and his family who were now perhaps worse off than they were. They were being far nicer to the Thomas Stephenses than Thomas had ever been to them during his affluent years.

Snipsey had offered to loan Grandpaw and his fiddle to Camellia. And Snipsey's mother, Amanda Cartwright, had brought two more beagles, proclaiming—pointedly—"And *they will breed,* Brother Thomas, and you can make some money by selling the pups as hunting dogs."

And Amos and Lois had just now offered to give Thomas, Mary, and Camellia a home if they needed it. Camellia didn't think anything had come yet from the Charlie Stephenses, but it wasn't far off.

Mary continued to make Maryland Beat Biscuits and hand them around, as if nothing had happened. At the Charlie Stephenses, Agnes was usually the one who returned the plate if Mary or Camellia couldn't get over there and get the plate back right away, but on this particular day, it was Charlie who came across the shell road with the plate, and this time it had a batch of sugar candies on it. The candies were obviously a maybe-this-will-help-some gift, because heretofore the plate, though always washed when returned, had always come back empty.

Mary was out on the front porch sweeping when Charlie walked up to the porch of the Tu-Rest Home. Camellia had just started out on the porch, but stopped. She didn't like Charlie and that knife scar smirk on his face made him look more leering than ever this morning. And he was leering at Mary.

Charlie said, "Well, now, Mary, and aren't we looking mighty pert and pretty today! Just like we would like to have a big hug from brother-in-law Charlie and then maybe...."

Charlie started to move up to Mary. She grabbed the plate with its sugar candies from him, stepped back, and hissed, "Go home, Charlie Stephens!!"

"Okay, okay" Charlie said. "Wrong time, wrong place, I guess." He gave a suggestive wink, then turned, and left.

Mary dashed into the house and slammed the door, and nearly fell over Camellia, sending sugar candies flying in all directions. "Camellia! You are as invisible as a dead black cat at midnight and forever spooking people!"

Camellia read guilt all over her mother's face and in her voice, yet it seemed shocking and unbelievable that Mary should be registering this kind of guilt. "Mama, why was Charlie talking to you like that?" Camellia asked reproachfully, and then with a certain say-it-isn't-so pleading in her voice, "Your wouldn't.... You haven't...?"

Mary quickly busied herself with picking up the scattered sugar candies and scolded Camellia harshly—harshly, for her, that is, as it wasn't Mary's nature to be harsh. "Camellia, one thing you should learn in this world and learn quickly is to leave other people's business alone."

Something inside of Camellia refused to accept what she feared about her mother, that which Mary would neither confirm nor deny. *Nice women* just didn't want it to start with, Camellia argued with herself, much less with somebody else's husband, and certainly not with a man as mean and filthy as Charlie Stephens. Or did they?

As so often of late, when doubt and trouble edged in, Camellia, the happy, self-assured, aspiring young singer/actress, turned sad and brooding. Yet into the ache of her soul came a brand of music, comforting and beautiful yet so strange, for it was unformed, unstructured, and mostly uncapturable either on the keyboard or with the voice. But it was as alive and tangible as life itself, bigger even than life itself and certainly far better than life as it was now for Camellia and the Thomas Stephenses on Bell's Island.

As the summer of 1927 wore on and no buyer or lessee was found willing to take on the indebtedness of the Bell's Island Inn, James LeCates' creditors, lawyers, and heirs came to the decision to close the inn as there were no longer any funds to keep it operating.

Lucille LeCates had "taken to her bed" in a state of nervous prostration and total humiliation over the circumstances surrounding her husband's death and bankruptcy. Doc Feldman was giving her *needles* daily. Camellia's aunt, Ruth Montgomery (Mary's "California sister"), was making the preparations to take Grandmother LeCates to live with her.

Reverend and Mrs. Bowman and Claudie, along with several other permanent residents at the inn, also had to find other lodging. Camellia had tried to talk her parents into letting those three lifelong friends come to live at the Stephens Tu-Rest Home, but its fate, too, still hung in the balance. Reverend and Mrs. Bowman still had a home in Baltimore that they had kept rented over the years, and so had decided to return to it as the current tenant was planning to leave anyway. And Claudie had decided to go with them.

When Camellia realized her beloved music teacher, mentor, and friend was soon to leave the island, she was nearly inconsolable. It was far worse than losing Grandfather (or Grandmother) LeCates, perhaps even worse than if she had lost her piano.

Camellia had relied on Claudie for far more than just music instruction. Though of advancing years, Claudie was always young at heart and worldly-wise in a practical way. She had been more of a mother to Camellia than Mary, who was always gyrating back and forth between being coolly intellectual one moment and then impossibly silly the next.

When Mary had been stumped for an answer to Camellia's childhood questions, whether they had to do with music, manners, or morals, and couldn't find an explanation in some book or other at her little Bell's Island Library or pass off the whole thing with either an off-color joke or silly remark, Camellia's question usually went unanswered.

Claudie didn't always have all the answers, either, but she had a reassuring *way* about her that convinced Camellia that everything was going to be all right no matter what.

Even as Claudie was leaving the island, she still conveyed this unassailable optimism to Camellia. "I'll write you every week, Camellia," she said as Thomas, Mary, and Camellia had come to the steamboat dock to see her off. "And when I get my own apartment, you can come visit me, and we'll go to concerts and operas in Baltimore and Washington, and maybe even to The Met in New York City!

"I've taught you as much as I can for the time being. But with your mother's help—and don't forget, she knows her music, too, when she puts her mind to it—and with your own continuous effort, you can hold on until you are ready to try for the conservatory.

"Keep singing, keep playing the piano, and performing everywhere you can get the opportunity—at home, in school, in church. Yes, even in Gainsbiddle, if you can get the chance!" And she gave a glorious laugh and winked a violet-hued eye. Ah yes, that was Claudie—good Bell's Islander that she had been for so many years, making one last punch at Gainsbiddle!

The steamboat taking the Bowmans and Claudie away from the island had barely gotten past the first light in the Anderson Sound when carpenters began boarding up the windows of the Bell's Island Inn.

The pounding of the hammers made Mary jump, then weep. "I can't even look, Thomas. My childhood home and all those happy years; the good times we had there when we were dating; having Reverend Bowman tell you about the Bible and all—all of those days gone forever."

"When troubled, turn to God, Mary," Thomas whispered.

But Camellia knew her mother, for all her choir singing and organ playing at the Bell's Island Methodist Church, was not all that hooked on religion and theology. Her mother's brain got in the way of her soul, Camellia thought glumly. Mary's brain...and maybe some other parts of her anatomy, too....

The Thomas Stephenses returned to the Tu-Rest Home, glad at least that the creditors were allowing them to continue to manage it and call it their home. They would get no salary and only a small percentage of the profits, but Thomas had gotten the job with Norman Travis at Gainsbiddle as mate on Norman's oyster boat. There would be income from this even though it meant Thomas would be away from home for weeks at a time as the oyster fleet worked the bay.

Yet absence does not necessarily make the heart—or anything else—grow fonder. Camellia overheard her mother bemoaning this fact to the cleaning lady, Aunt Sairy Middleton, one afternoon when school had let out early, and Camellia had come in as quietly as that invisible dead black cat at midnight.

"Aunt Sairy," Mary was saying, "it was one of the many nights I couldn't sleep. Thomas had just got back from three weeks on Norman's boat. Thomas was fast asleep, dreaming of neutered angels, no doubt. He had hugged and kissed me good night before we went to bed as he has always done, but that was as far as it went.

"So, when I couldn't get to sleep, my thoughts started wandering again to Charlie Stephens. They were 'improper thoughts', to say the least. But my reverie carried me farther than I intended and I suddenly gave an involuntary lurch and cried out. I woke Thomas up.

"'Mary, what's wrong?' he asked.

"'Nothing, Thomas, Just a charley horse', I said. Damn! I was thinking, what a poor choice of words!

"But Thomas never sees double meanings in anything and he wouldn't have then, even if he had suspected my thoughts were on Charlie. But I doubt if he ever thinks my thoughts are on Charlie, because he still has me on a pedestal as 'a nice woman'. So, you know what Thomas said?"

Aunt Sairy dutifully replied, "No'm. What he say?"

Mary burst out laughing. "He—heheh—He said 'Do you want me to rub it for you, Mary?'"

When Mary and Aunt Sairy both stopped laughing, Mary continued, "I was thinking, *Oh, that you would, Thomas*. At least do something. But I couldn't say things like that. Thomas and I are on different wave lengths. So I just said, 'It's okay now, Thomas. Charley horse is all gone. Go back to sleep. I'm sorry I woke you up'. And he did, he went right back to sleep.

"But the incident worried me and I told myself, You've got to stop this business of thinking about Charlie this way.... It's nothing short of committing adultery with him in your heart. I don't know whether Charlie knows my thoughts or just what—some gypsies do, you know—but he can get awfully familiar at time. Now, we've never even as much as touched each other, Aunt Sairy, but still and all...."

Camellia's sigh of relief was so audible, she added a sudden burst of song to cover up and went on into the kitchen big end foremost lest she be caught red-handed at her eavesdropping. And that singing was anything but fake for now she knew—her mother had *not* done anything wrong with Charlie Stephens! Yet Mary had *thought* about doing it...and seemed to be still thinking about it, so all was not completely well.

It had taken a while for Camellia's message via Snipsey to Grandpaw Azariah Stephens to get results. Then one afternoon the odd-looking little man in overalls three sizes too big for him was heading toward the Stephens Tu-Rest Home.

Camellia was in the backyard seeing to the chickens and goat that Thomas had brought from Gainsbiddle so that they'd always have a few eggs and some milk each day in case times really did get bad. Mary was feeding the beagles and everyone was hoping they would start multiplying as Amanda had assured them they would so that there would be a little income from selling the puppies. Thomas was staking up a huge fish that he'd caught while on Norman Travis' boat.

Thomas glanced up from the fish, looked down the shell road, and said to Mary, "Looks like Paw might be coming here. Can't you send Camellia off somewhere, like to the store or in the house to get supper?"

"Why should I do that, Thomas?" Mary asked him.

"Paw's a dirty old man, Mary. *You* know that."

Camellia mused. Yes, *everybody* knew that. Grandpaw was always hugging and pawing on any woman who'd let him. Camellia had seen him catch hold of a lady one day in the Bell's Island drugstore. And there *were ladies* on Bell's Island; Mary LeCates Stephens wasn't the only *nice woman.*

Anyhow, Grandpaw started rubbing up against this lady in the drugstore—with his hands and everything else. The lady gave him a shove and blurted out, obviously without thinking, "Stop it, Azariah Stephens! You've got nothing but a crooked old rain spout!"

The entire drugstore, including Grandpaw, exploded with laughter and the lady looked so embarrassed.

But as Grandpaw approached the Stephens Tu-Rest Home, it was evident he had something with him in addition to his "crooked old rain spout."

Mary said, "Thomas, he's got that fiddle with him. *That* ought to keep his hands busy."

Thomas said, "I don't think Camellia ought to hear that gypsy music stuff."

"Oh, good heavens, Thomas! Some people get itchy pants when they hear *The Old Rugged Cross.*"

"Ma-ry!" Then to his father, "Oh, h'lo, Paw."

Camellia walked over excitedly to greet Azariah. "Grandpaw! You've brought your fiddle! Did Snipsey tell you? Could you teach me to play the fiddle?"

"Mebbe I could, darling." He was gazing at Camellia with his big frog-like eyes.

Thomas was frowning.

Camellia said, "Well, come on in the house, Grandpaw. You can play some notes on the fiddle and I'll play the same notes on the piano and then you can show me where those positions are on the fiddle and...."

"Errrrah, Camellia...." Thomas was clearing his throat in protest.

But for once Mary talked Thomas down. Mary said, "That's fine, Grandpaw! Camellia's been wanting to know something about the violin for a long time now."

Thomas whispered to Mary, "Go in the house with them, will you, Mary?"

"Oh, Thomas, will you never stop...."

"My family are not very nice people, Mary. You know that."

"Maybe it's because you never give them a chance to be. You're always expecting them to do or say something terrible...and I admit, they often do, but...."

Thomas gave Mary a fierce look and jerked his head in the direction of the house.

Mary followed Camellia and Grandpaw into the house and it was a good thing she did. It was not that any sin was bout to occur, but Grandpaw was, of all things, a left-handed fiddler!

Camellia didn't know whether that would have mattered or not, but it still didn't seem to be any way for him to be teaching her the violin. However, between the three of them, they did get the technicalities straightened out as to which hand did what and before long, Camellia was beginning to play that fiddle—and right-handed, too!

In the days and weeks to come, she would write down all the music for the gypsy airs that Grandpaw played for her, and later she transposed them for piano and worked in her own harmonic chords.

She figured it out all by herself because Grandpaw couldn't read music. He couldn't read, period. But he was great as a teller of gypsy anecdotes, and soon he was teaching Camellia things besides music.

One day after Grandpaw left the Tu-Rest Home, Camellia was in the kitchen, breaking open a whole gang of raw eggs in a large bowl. She had nearly a dozen broken open.

Mary caught her at it and fairly screamed, "Camellia, what *are* you *doing*?"

"Oh, Mama, it's just that I'm looking for two eggs with no yolks, so I can make up one of Grandpaw's gypsy potions. He says if you drink the potion it will give you anything you wish—and you *know* that I wish to someday SING AT THE MET! Grandpaw says all you need for that kind of potion are two eggs with no yolks, one hair from a kitten's paw, one...."

Mary was so exasperated she could barely speak. "Camellia, I ought to make you eat all those eggs right now—raw! There's no such a thing as an egg without a yolk."

"Yes, there is, Mama. I've already found one—look here in this saucer—"

But at that moment Thomas came into the kitchen and barked at Camellia with a fury of which she didn't think he was capable: "Camellia, don't you ever try any of that witchcraft stuff in this house again, for if you do, I'll never allow you to see Grandpaw again, not even for the violin lessons."

Camellia didn't verbally cross swords with her father. But when she tried to find that egg without the yolk to show him, it had disappeared. She couldn't find the saucer or anything. She was wondering if Grandpaw had put a spell on her and made her *think* she'd found a yolk-less egg when she really hadn't or if her father's Christian purity had cancelled out the gypsy magic or just what. But she was still the good daughter and she began cleaning up the mess she had made in the kitchen. She could hear her father and mother talking more quietly now in the next room.

Thomas's anger had faded away and with great pride, he was saying to Mary, "Camellia's getting prettier every day, isn't she? And... and...growing up, too! I mean—growing into *a woman*." He said the last two words with a certain amount of awe.

Mary said, "Yes, she's twelve now and no longer a child. And you know where all that 'pretty' comes from? That thick black hair, that tawny skin, those large, dark and intense eyes...?"

"Well, you're pretty, Mary."

"Me? A watery-blue eyed, ash-blond, who's turning gray early? No. Thomas, it's not from me she gets her beauty. It's that gypsy blood that you are so ashamed of in yourself."

Thomas noted, "Camellia's going to be a beautiful woman, I do believe. How strange that anyone so pretty could come from someone as ugly as me!"

"It's that gypsy influence, Thomas. I've been trying to tell you. Admit it now. It might have skipped your generation, although your sister, Amanda, if she were fixed up and not so sloppy-fat and learned some manners—she would make quite a handsome woman and she's got 'that gypsy look.'"

"Mary?"

"What is it, Thomas?"

"Teach her...teach Camellia to be good." He said it imploringly.

"She's good," Mary said.

"Uh, you know what I mean." He paused as though shaking his head to clear out disturbing thoughts, then he repeated, "You know what I mean...Anyone as lovely as Camellia is going to have to be... *extra good*....You know what I mean, Mary."

After the closing of the Bell's Island Inn, the Stephens Tu-Rest Home began to get more roomers, but since almost all the profits were going to James LeCates's creditors, the Thomas Stephenses didn't see much benefit from the increased business. Still and all, they were making out reasonably well thanks to the beagles that were now producing puppies for sale and to Thomas's job as mate on Norman Travis's work boat.

Camellia was no longer receiving the pretty new clothes that had always been lavished on her by both her Grandfather LeCates and by Thomas and Mary. But she was still fixy and fussy about her appearance, even though she was having to do it now with patched elbows, split seams, and out-grown blouses. Big and mature for her early teen years, she was fast growing into womanhood and nothing was fitting her.

But none of this prevented her from being attractive nor did it protect her from the *dangers* of being attractive.

One afternoon she was in the Bell's Island drugstore—and if anything wild was going to happen, it usually happened there. Suddenly Camellia was surprised out of her wits by someone coming up behind her, clasping an arm about her waist, and tickling her "improperly."

Lightning-fast, she gave a vigorous backhanded punch with her fist and made contact with a face—Doc Feldman's face!

There followed a confused and embarrassed flurry of apologies with the mortified Doc Feldman spluttering, "My, I'm terribly sorry, Camellia. I didn't mean to touch you like that. I mistook you for... for...for somebody else. I'm so sorry....I—I....Please forgive me. So terribly sorry...."

When Camellia saw that her punch was drawing blood from Doc Feldman's already-flushed cheek, she began stammering, "Oh, Doc! Oh, my Lord! I didn't mean to hit *you*...That is, I mean I didn't know it was you that I was hitting, that is, I didn't mean to hit *you* that hard if I had known it was you...or...Anyhow, please forgive me. I'm sorry...I really am...."

Doc Feldman went retreating out of the drugstore, holding a big hanky to his bleeding face, and muttering to himself, "She looks like a Corrigan, but she fights like a Stephens!"

Doc, Camellia later learned, cut a right comical figure trying to take stitches in his own face while the Bell's Island barber held up a mirror in front of him.

But Camellia was not laughing at the time, and when she and Mary, who'd been in the drugstore and witnessed the incident, too, got back to the Tu-Rest Home, Camellia said, "Mama, what do you suppose Doc Feldman meant when he said, 'She looks like a Corrigan, but she fights like a Stephens'? *Isn't Papa my father*?"

Mary replied, "Papa is your father, Camellia. Most certainly your father."

"Then what did Doc mean?"

Mary pondered for a while, then said, "The only thing I can figure is that Doc mistook you for one of those Corrigan girls who live over at the tavern across the inlet. You do resemble one of them."

"One of those gypsies, Mama? One of those gypsy cousins of mine that Papa would never let Grandpaw finish telling me about?"

"Well, yes...." admitted Mary. "The person over there called 'Moonlight' Corrigan who's been running that place has a daughter who's about seventeen, I guess. You probably never saw her in school, because she probably never went to school much, but she's got black hair and a big build and I think they call her 'Moonlight', too."

Camellia responded real slowly, "Oh, I–think–I–know–who–you–mean."

Camellia had sometimes seen an overly dressed and heavily rouged, but basically good-looking and well-built young brunette walking down around the Bell's Island docks, drawing wolf whistles from the men working on their boats. And Snipsey Cartwright had made some pretty plain remarks about *why* the girl was walking around the dock area.

Mary, continuing her explanation, said, "I suspect that's who Doc Feldman thought it was when he accidentally grabbed hold of you instead, Camellia."

"*You mean I look like a whore to Doc*? I know these clothes are pretty shabby, but that's not my fault." Camellia was unmindful of her terminology at this point.

"No, no," Mary said. "It's just that Doc mistook you for somebody else. It happens all the time. Some of us have doubles and they don't have to be related to us."

"But that girl *is* related to me, isn't she, Mama? The Corrigans and the gypsies and the Stephenses—they were all mixed up together, weren't they? That's what Snipsey says. But somehow I'd never thought of *that one* as my...."

"Well, it isn't very close a relation, if at all, Camellia," Mary said, trying to soften it. "But if you are so much concerned, why don't you see how the Corrigans and Stephenses look on paper. See which ones are related to which other ones and to the gypsies."

Camellia watched as her mother rummaged through a desk drawer and brought out some pedigree registration forms like the ones she filled out for customers who bought the beagle puppies. Seeing those papers, Camellia gave a howl of her own. "Oh, Mama we're not *dogs*!"

"Very little difference sometimes," Mary said under her breath.

"What's that you say, Mama?"

"Never mind," said Mary, handing Camellia the pedigrees. "Just look these over if you care to. I put them together just out of curiosity one time with Amanda's help. Only don't let your Papa know I have them."

Camellia looked at the genealogies and asked bout the numerous question marks in the blank spaces marked "Sire" on the Corrigan side of the family that the two Moonlights originated from.

"Nobody knows who the father was where the space is left blank or marked with a question mark," Mary explained. "So most everybody on that side of the family goes by their mother's last name which always seems to be Corrigan."

They both were quiet for awhile, then Mary said, "Let's just shelve this whole thing. Your Papa most certainly would say, 'God is the Father of us all'. And maybe that's the best way to look at it."

"But Papa *is* my father—earthly father, that is?" Camellia persisted.

"Yes, Camellia. How many times do I have to tell you that?"

"Then how come there is only one of me?"

"May the saints preserve us!" Mary exclaimed. "As if *one* of you isn't enough!"

Camellia said, "But I meant...you know what I meant....I meant why don't I have brothers and sisters like Snipsey and all the other Stephenses across the shell road?"

Camellia waited for Mary to answer, but it seemed as though Mary couldn't think of a blessed thing to say.

So Camellia probed further: "Haven't you and Papa been...been... 'living together' since you had me?" Camellia assumed as much from the little things she'd overheard at home and from the snickery little things she'd picked up from time to time around the island about "the way it was with 'Pumpkin' Stephens and 'Mary Beanpole'." But she wanted to hear it from her mother herself.

Mary conceded, "Well, Camellia, I guess you could state it that way. I think it's because your Papa doesn't think it's the right thing to do. Frankly, I don't understand your Papa's notions about the Bible and some of the things it says, but it should not be any concern of yours. It's my problem, not yours."

Mary's problem, however, would always be Camellia's problem.

Sexual activity on the other side of the shell road, especially at the Cartwrights, was a little more promising.

Camellia noticed that if the notion struck Simon and Amanda, they'd just as soon start going for each other in the back yard—or in the front yard, for that matter—as to bother to get in the house first.

Big, gorilla-like Simon would run up behind Amanda and grab her back. With his arms linked around her waist and her big backside punching him in the belly, he'd start dry-humping her dog-style, through their clothes. Then he'd let go of her and allow her to take off running, and she would be squawking with laughter the whole time. He'd chase after her, winding her down in smaller and smaller circles that were bringing them closer and closer to the house, and he would be shouting suggestions lewd enough to curl the hair on a cucumber.

Amanda would be howling with delight as Simon scooped her up in his hairy arms and carried her into the kitchen. And never mind closing the kitchen door. He's shove her up against a table, grab up the front of her long-tailed dress in his paws, drop his own pants, and "get awn with business," proving—at least for them—that **sex can be fun for both**!

But things were not all that hilarious next door at Charlie and Agnes's. Snipsey and Camellia had wandered by the house under their bedroom window one evening and such a commotion they heard up there!

Camellia asked Snipsey, "Why is Agnes crying like that? Why is Charlie cussing so much?"

Snipsey said in an all-wise whisper, "Well, Mama says Aunt Agnes's cunt's made backwards and that's why it hurts her and Uncle Charlie both, when they do it."

For a split moment Camellia took Snipsey's physiological information literally and wondered how such a phenomenon could be! She didn't recall any descriptions or illustrations in Doc Feldman's medical books in the little Bell's Island Library to that effect. Then she realized Snipsey was merely repeating Amanda's crazy talk, so Camellia said, "If it hurts, why do they keep on doing it?"

Again Snipsey got that all-wise tone in her whisper and informed Camellia, "Well Mama says they don't, leastaways, not too much any more. Uncle Charlie goes to Moonlight Corrigan's place a lot. You know, 'cross the inlet over there. Only, Uncle Charlie's got to pay for it over there. At home you don't hafta pay for it. Not like in dollar bills, but you sort of pay for it anyhow by earning a livin' for the fam'ly."

With curiosity, Camellia asked Snipsey, "If Charlie goes over to that place across the inlet, then where does Agnes go?"

"Nowheres. Women ain't s'posed to go nowhere else, if it ain't working right at home. And women ain't s'posed to like it nohow."

Camellia almost laughed in Snipsey's face and said, "Well, *your mother* certainly must like it. She and Simon can barely wait to get in the house."

Snipsey corrected herself and said, "Well, I meant women ain't s'posed to *let on* they like it."

"Oh?" Camellia said.

"Not s'posed to let on *to the world,* that is," Snipsey clarified further. "Its's okay to let on to your husband, though."

"Oh?" Camellia said again. "Well, I'm not going to get married. It sounds too complicated."

"Yeah, but you might like it," Snipsey noted.

"But how would I know?" Camellia said. "That would be a right big sacrifice—getting all married, only to find out that you didn't like it."

Snipsey thought for a moment. "Well, you could try it out ahead of time. Say, haven't you had that Ralph Drummond putting his arms around you a lot lately?"

Camellia admitted that she had.

Snipsey said, "Well, maybe you and him could try it out sometime."

"*Snipsey*!" Camellia said. "You're not supposed to talk and think like that, and I'm not, either."

"Well, how's anybody gonna know anything about anything if they don't try it out? I wish I had a boyfriend like Ralph Drummond."

"Well, you can have him," offered Camellia. "I don't want him. He's been pestering me every since fifth grade. Besides I don't intend to get married, anyhow. I've got other things to do."

"Like sing and act, huh?" said Snipsey, a little awe-struck. "Like in the big city, huh? Like in New York City *at The Met, huh*!"

"Yeah, like sing and act. Like in the big city. Like in New York City at The Met," Camellia mimicked her, then sadly walked away.

Claudie, living in Baltimore with the Bowmans, had kept her promise and written to Camellia every week since leaving the island. But she still had not had the opportunity to invite Camellia and Mary up there for a visit.

Camellia, answering one of Claudie's letters, wrote:

> *Oh, Claudie, if only I could talk with you in person. You remember when I was little used to hear melodies in everything: Moonlit diamonds in the snow. Sun gleaming through the icicles. Pretty flowers. Pretty rainbows. Remember how I would work out melodies on the piano for each beautiful thing I would see?*

I still hear melodies, Claudie, but they are different now. There are wild rhythms all inside me and sad melodies—oh, so sad. I try to capture them on the piano, but they get away from me. Maybe I just don't know enough—counterpoint, composition, that sort of thing. Or maybe it's because I can't concentrate. I worry all the time about money and everything. I try not to show it and Mama puts up a good front, but the only one in the family who seems ***genuinely*** *cheerful is Papa. I overheard Amanda once say it was because Papa 'doesn't have sense enough to know when he's bad off'.*

I don't know from where the money will ever come for me to go to the conservatory. Sometimes I think I would like to just run away and try things on my own. Run away to New York City. I dream of doing that all the time. Dream of going there to The Met and getting an audition—you know, I'm big for my age, they never would guess my real age....

But to run away wouldn't be right, it wouldn't be fair to Mama and Papa. I think that Mama may not be well. She's so nervous and works so hard at everything and she's gotten so thin she looks like one of those flat fish that are only a top and bottom skin with nothing inside but a skeleton. Sometimes I find her sitting in the kitchen alone, with her eyes misted all over, just staring out the window, with account books and budgets spread out on the table in front of her.

I ask her what's wrong and she says, 'Oh, nothing. Just tired, maybe'. Sometimes I suggest we go to the Bell's Island Church and practice on the pipe organ that she's been teaching me and that always seems to cheer her up....

The Thomas Stephenses might have eventually adjusted to their cramped financial situation if there had not come two consecutive devastating winter freeze-ups, the first after Christmas in early 1929, and then again in early 1930. It was a time when no Wintergreen County waterman could work for more than a few weeks at a stretch.

The freeze of 1930 was even worse than the previous winter's and nobody had recovered very well from that one, not even during the only-too-short and too-poor crab season in the summer of 1929.

Because of the ice in the waterways, Norman Travis and Thomas Stephens could not oyster again, so Thomas had come home to Bell's Island.

By February of 1930, Camellia, Thomas, and Mary were having one awful time. They had long since sold their fine silverware and fancy appointments—chandeliers, bric-a-brac, and ornate furniture—

that had once been such a prominent part of the residence side of the Tu-Rest Home.

Their diet was down mostly to whatever wildlife Thomas could shoot in the woods and thickets since seafood ordinarily right at their doorstep was buried under the ice and almost impossible to come by. Rabbit stew, boiled goose, and beans were all right for Camellia, who could digest, as Mary once said, a brick-bat covered with green mold, but that sort of fare was not good for Mary, who had a finicky system to start with.

Then there came one of those snow-threatening, gray-skied days when all the color of the Bell's Island land and seascape seemed to have left forever.

Everybody was saying it was too cold to snow, but if it would only snow, the freeze might be broken.

The island looked so weird, Camellia mused. Everything was locked in ice. All the watermen were idle. All the work boats were frozen in the harbor. The skipjacks, bugeyes, and pungys sat so strangely still at their moorings along all the docks.

Their hulls were imprisoned in frozen salt water and their decks, furled sails, and masts were crusted all over with frozen spray. The masts looked like silver skewers piercing the leaden skies.

At the Tu-Rest Home, the family was both figuratively and literally at the bottom of the barrel. The only thing left was some gritty, wormy, moldy flour and some greasy water left from cooking that last goose that Thomas had been lucky enough to shoot. Mary had been saving that water to use on the beagle food she usually made up each week, but she was out of ground corn and had no rabbit or goose entrails left to mix in, either. Camellia asked if she should throw the water out, but Mary said, "No, better keep it. As a last resort I could mix it with those flour dregs and make a paste or gravy out of it, and we could try to eat that in case your father doesn't get a goose or rabbit today."

Geese and rabbits were getting scarcer and scarcer because everybody on the island was doing the same thing—shooting and eating them. At the Tu-Rest Home there were never any eggs in the afternoon from the few hens they had left, and the goat would milk out only once a day in the morning and not give much even then. Mary didn't want to kill any more chickens for food because they would then lose out on the few eggs they still got each morning. Thomas had mentioned slaughtering the goat, but then they would lose out on the milk.

The Bell's Island grocery store wouldn't give Mary any more credit. Or more correctly, she was too embarrassed to ask them yet another time. She didn't want to ask anything from the Stephenses across the shell road as they were having it as bad as anybody this year and with all those kids to feed. Thomas didn't want to ask Norman Travis for any more advances on his wages because he knew everybody in Gainsbiddle was having a struggle, too.

It was useless to try to get anything from Grandfather LeCates's creditors and lawyers. There hadn't been a roomer at the Tu-Rest Home for months, partly because of the ice in the bay which kept the steamboats from running, and partly because everybody was tightening belts after the financial collapse of the stock market in late 1929. Even Claudie and the Bowmans had been affected by the crash, and Mary had not wanted to call on them for help. The family had spent everything available from the Tu-Rest Home upkeep fund just to have a little heat in the kitchen on the residence side.

The beagles were starving. They were so lean their sides were caved in and their ribs were showing through and they cried so piteously when Camellia went anywhere near them that she almost cried, too.

Camellia knew the only thing left for her mother to do was to swallow her pride and contact her Baltimore sister, Elizabeth St. George, and ask her to loan them some money. But the last time Aunt Lizbeth and Aunt Ruth Montgomery from California had visited, there had been cross words all around. Aunt Ruth and Aunt Lizbeth had erroneously believed Mary had gotten the better end of the deal by being allowed by the creditors to keep the Tu-Rest Home, whereas the other two sisters and even Grandmother LeCates had received practically nothing but the proceeds from a few meager insurance policies. The only communications between Mary and her sisters after that time were Christmas cards with no messages and barely a signature.

As evening came on that snow-threatening day, the cold was getting intense. Camellia and Mary kept looking out the kitchen window for Thomas. He had been out hunting all day. They watched the last bit of weak daylight fade out behind the island's skinny pine trees. The gray sky turned to black and they lit the one little oil lamp in the kitchen.

Finally they heard Thomas penning the two beagles he'd taken out hunting with him, and then he came on in the house. He didn't have anything with him but a sad face as he set the shotgun in the corner of the kitchen. He came and sat down at the table, a table with no food on it.

"Sorry," he said with a sigh. "Only saw one or two squirrels and they got away."

Mary got up to get that greasy water mixed with the last of the flour. She said, "Well, we can have this—er—this gravy. But there's nothing to put it on."

She poured the near-rancid mess into a large pan and mixed the gritty, wormy flour from the bottom of the barrel into it. "It may not taste very good, but it's nourishing...I think."

"It sure doesn't smell very good," Camellia said as the mixture began to heat up.

Nevertheless they ate the greasy gray mess. They ate it in silence.

Thomas finally said, "I'll kill and dress that goat in the morning."

Nobody offered a protest.

It was only around six-thirty in the evening, but they prepared for bed. Camellia had not practiced the piano in weeks. The music room was ice cold, dead cold. She stayed downstairs with Mary a while longer after Thomas had gone up to bed. Mary was trying to write to Aunt Lizbeth, asking for money, but she just couldn't do it and set the letter aside.

For the first part of the night, Camellia slept, then she came awake rather suddenly as she heard her mother going downstairs. She got out of bed and into her coat and followed Mary downstairs.

"What's the matter, Mama? You're all bent over."

"Stomach pains," Mary said, then added nonchalantly, "Just hunger I guess." She bowed together again and gasped, "But I never could eat much grease....I better get to the outhouse. I didn't want to wake your father by trying to use that chamber pot upstairs."

Camellia said, "If we could only have some heat upstairs, we could have the bathroom working again."

"We will," Mary said, "this weather can't last forever."

Camellia followed her mother outside and as they crossed the back yard, the beagles started to whine, but they did not bark. The goat baa'd slightly and Camellia thought, *Poor creature, in a few more hours you will be racked up and your life's blood draining out of you.*

Mary said, "It seems warmer, don't you think? Maybe the weather is going to break, and your father can get back to work."

Camellia didn't think it seemed any warmer and figured her mother must be in a fever.

Mary stayed in the outhouse heaving and straining for God only knows how long, and when she finally staggered out, she gasped and said, "I'll wire Lizbeth in the morning. Can't wait on a letter to get there."

When they returned to the house and started back upstairs, Mary said, "I feel better now, Camellia. Thanks for getting up with me. You go on back to sleep now."

When the dawn came, the sky was pale and overcast and it was still bitterly cold, but there was no snow. The family went down into the slight warmth of the kitchen once again. Camellia glanced anxiously at her mother. Mary looked pale and drawn, but managed a smile as she directed Camellia to go to the chicken yard for the eggs.

Camellia returned with but two eggs. Mary said, "Boil them for you and your Papa. I'll go milk that goat one last time and maybe have some of that."

Camellia said, "I'll give Papa my egg to go along with his egg. Maybe I can get something from Snipsey's lunch box at school today."

"*Not steal*?!" Thomas shouted.

Camellia replied indignantly, "Of course 'not steal!' Snipsey *gives* me things sometimes."

Thomas said, "I hate for my child to have to beg. When a man can't support his family...."

"Hush, Thomas," Mary said and started out the back door to milk the goat. As she went, she stumbled and nearly fell.

"Mama, what's wrong? Come back in and sit down. I'll milk the goat."

"Well, all right, then," Mary said and handed Camellia the pail.

Camellia came back in shortly with the milk and said, "She doesn't give much any more."

Mary looked at Thomas and hesitantly said, "Thomas, maybe you'd better not kill the goat right yet. I believe that milk will be all I can take for awhile. I was terribly sick in the night from that supper....I'm going to wire my sister in Baltimore this morning. We should have some cash today."

"Mary, I hate for you to have to crawl to your sister....When a man can't support his family...When he didn't have sense enough to save anything...."

Camellia thought her father looked absolutely beaten.

"Heat me up a little of that milk on the stove, will you, Camellia?" Mary said. "Yes, I know it's already warm, but heat it a little more, will you?"

Camellia, thinking her mother must now be having chills, said, "All right, Mama, I'll heat it."

"You take some of it, too, Camellia," Mary directed.

"There's not enough for both of us, Mama."

"Yes, there is. Divide it. Do as I say."

"All right, Mama."

"When a man can't support his family," Thomas was saying again, as he picked up the shotgun and once again went out to hunt for a rabbit, squirrel, goose, anything.... Anything except the goat, which was spared.

Mary was getting ready to go to the telegraph office, but Camellia said, "Can't I send the wire to Aunt Lizbeth? You shouldn't be going out in this weather."

"I'll be all right, Camellia. You go on to school now. Do as I say."

Reluctantly Camellia did so, but at the lunch hour she rushed back to the Tu-Rest Home.

She found Mary lying on the couch in the ice-cold living room, unconscious, and barely breathing. When Camellia saw the bloody vomit all over everywhere, she went into a near panic, but managed somehow to rush back down the shell road for Doc Feldman.

Once Doc and Camellia got Mary into the kitchen and into a makeshift bed loaded with blankets, she came to momentarily and said, "One hundred dollars from Lizbeth. Bought some food. It's in the kitchen. Paid some on the back bill and on the wood and coal oil bill. The rest is in my pocketbook. Pay Doc...." then she slipped again into unconsciousness.

Chapter Three

"With a proper diet and less worry, you can learn to live with your ulcer."

Mary thought about Doc Feldman's words to her. Maybe she could do just that. She had much to be thankful for. Doc had pulled her through that pneumonia, though the bleeding stomach ulcer remained.

But now it was spring 1930 on Bell's Island and as the ice melted from the rivers and the bay, Thomas returned to work with Norman Travis in Gainsbiddle and soon they were pulling in oyster catches that would bring joy to the heart of even the most "down-troggled" waterman. And gradually roomers began drifting back to the Stephens Tu-Rest Home.

Most of the roomers were men and Camellia had always been told by her parents to stay away from that side of the house. And she always did. Mary herself maintained a stance that was business-like, though democratically friendly, as was her nature. Most of the men stayed only a night or two, and there were no permanent residents as there had been at the Bell's Island Inn. That sorry-looking place still remained boarded up with no one as yet to buy, lease, or re-open it.

In the fall of 1930, Camellia and Mary got their long-awaited trip to Baltimore to see Claudie, who now had an apartment of her own.

Mary had saved enough money to get Camellia some fairly decent new clothes, but there was not anything to spare for a new wardrobe for herself. Also, considering the two winters that had taken such a terrible physical and emotional toll on her, Mary looked so pale and haggard when they got to Claudie's that Claudie gave an audible gasp.

But Claudie was delighted at how much Camellia had matured, now being almost as tall as her mother and nearly twice her girth. "A real Brunnhilde in the making!" Claudie exclaimed, her violet-hued eyes dancing.

They talked about Camellia's future, what music scholarships were available, what she could expect in the rough, tough world of the performing artist, what would be exacted of her, and whether marriage should or should not be a part of all this.

Claudie gave Camellia some good-natured scolding about how rusty she'd gotten with her singing and playing, and Camellia promised never again to let circumstances prevent her from practicing. "I'll practice that piano and sing every day no matter how cold it might get in the house. I'll practice every day even if I have to play the piano with mittens on!"

They attended a number of concerts and a performance of Donizetti's great tragedy, *Lucia di Lammermoor*, by the Baltimore Civic Opera Company, as well as taking a tour of the conservatory where Claudie had taught upon first coming to the United States from England after she had concluded her own opera career in Europe.

Claudie arranged for an audition for Camellia and she sang and played for some of the top instructors. Even though she was out of form, they all said she did exceptionally well. All agreed that she had the voice, the body build and stamina, and the background basics to eventually start operatic training. Claudie said afterwards, "What you need now is to keep on practicing, keep on learning and performing, and *stay with your convictions*! Don't let anything or anybody turn you aside!"

Then Claudie gave Camellia a gift. Inside the box was the biggest pair of bright red mittens that Camellia had ever seen. She and Mary and Claudie all laughed until their sides ached. Camellia said, "I'll hang these mittens on the piano as soon as we get home, so they'll be right there to remind me to keep practicing no matter what!"

Claudie promised that if Camellia was accepted later on a scholarship to the conservatory she could live with Claudie during her training.

They talked a little about composing, too. Claudie said that composing and performing were at opposite ends of the creative emotional scale, and since they came from two very different parts of consciousness, they might cause a conflict inside Camellia. But even so, Claudie gave Camellia a couple of textbooks on counterpoint and a stack of music paper and said to let the Muses guide her from there on.

By the time their visit with Claudie was over, Camellia was walking on air. The trip to Baltimore had been a shot in the arm for Mary, too. A far better tonic, Camellia felt, than any of Doc Feldman's *needles*. While in the city they had visited with Elizabeth St. George, and Mary had tried to pay back the one hundred dollars Lizbeth had sent her during the previous winter freeze. But Lizbeth said, "No, Mary. Put it in a savings account for Camellia's operatic training instead." Mary agreed and the past hard feelings between the two sisters were over.

On that same trip Mary got a pair of much-needed eyeglasses. Camellia had always thought her mother had a *prim look*, and she looked even more that way when they got back to Bell's Island with Mary wearing those silvery-framed spectacles. Thomas was delighted. He said, "Mary, you look just like an angel!"

Camellia couldn't remember seeing any paintings of angels with spectacles on in the Bell's Island Methodist Church Sunday School Room, but "if Papa thought Mama looked like an angel, then there was no arguing with a Bell's Island waterman who *still* fancied himself a preacher!"

Camellia's school work held up well during her high school years, buttressed, it seemed, by her ability to still *outguess* the teachers, to know—or *see* beforehand—what was going to be on tests or questions in class and to study only those things. This left her more time and energy to devote to her music. With her music, however, she did not depend on guesswork. She put in endless hours of practicing with intense concentration, and she appeared in every public performance onto which she could latch. These performances had remained limited to church and school ever since the closing of the Bell's Island Inn.

Nevertheless there were several competitions for young singers and pianists in Baltimore which Claudie arranged for her to enter. There would have been more opportunities to enter if Bell's Island hadn't been so far away from Baltimore, but Camellia was happy for any exposure to the city she could get. She was not too disturbed even when the juries didn't quite go along with her over-flowery interpretations because Claudie made the near-misses a little more bearable by saying she could easily enough learn to "tone it down a little" later. Those visits with Claudie in Baltimore were high points in her young life.

They never did get their talked-about trip to New York City and The Met as Claudie never seemed quite up to travelling that far. She wasn't sick, she said, but she tired easily and wasn't a spring chicken anymore, but "maybe if the right rooster...!" Then with her marvelous smile and her eyes the color of crushed violets, she managed to make a big joke of it all.

Camellia herself wasn't much interested in chasing after boys, though at first they were chasing after her because she was curvy-round and "easy to look at." Then she quickly got the reputation for being "a cold fish" as she turned aside most of the boys, even the promising ones she occasionally met on the steamboat going up to Baltimore. But there was still Ralph Drummond, the lanky, tow-headed waterman's son, whose quiet way of inner strength she admired, though she was reluctant to admit it, even to herself.

Snipsey Cartwright seemed jealous of her and Ralph and pestered Camellia continuously about him. "Has he asked you to do it yet?" Snipsey asked at least once a week.

"We-ell, not exactly," said Camellia, with a coy little smile, revealing that she was flattered that he had been *hinting* in that direction. She liked the idea of being considered desirable, even if she wasn't quite willing to put out for it yet.

"If he hasn't asked you, why don't you ask him?"

"Snipsey, be decent."

"I bet you think you wouldn't like it, but how do you know, if you've never tried it?"

"Well, have *you* tried it, Snipsey?"

Snipsey whined, "No, but nobody's asked me yet. I'm not pretty like you are. But you could easy get Ralph Drummond to...."

"I don't give a hoot about Ralph Drummond!"

"Well, he's in love with you. Anybody can see that. And he's working on the water now with his father and he'd make you a good living and...."

"I'll never marry a Bell's Island waterman!" Camellia shouted.

Snipsey asked, "Well, who *are* you going to marry? I guess they ain't nobody good enough for you 'round here anymore since you been running up there to Baltimore all the time visiting those fancy-pants people. And you still talk like you ain't even from around here."

When anybody wanted to run Camellia down, it always seemed they struck out at that *educated* British accent. To Snipsey she replied, "I don't intend to marry at all!" And she unconsciously pronounced it "ohl" just as she'd "ohl-ways" done, just as Claudie "ohl-ways" did.

As Camellia was walking away from Snipsey, head in the air, Snipsey hollered after her, "Well, what do you intend to do then? Shack up?"

Camellia stopped, turned around a bit and started to *give Snipsey the finger,* but thought the better of it. After all, if she was aiming for the conservatory in Baltimore and eventually The Met, she couldn't be acting like "poor white trash from Gainsbiddle."

Although Camellia could take Snipsey in small doses, she couldn't tolerate the other Stephens cousins across the shell road, especially en masse.

But one day she saw Grandpaw Azariah, in his overalls three sizes too big for him, with a whole bunch of Stephens kids around him in the Cartwright's yard, and he was doing card tricks. Camellia's curiosity overruled her distaste at being around the Stephens cousins, and she wandered over to the edge of the group and tried to appear disinterested.

When Grandpaw finished his demonstration, Camellia bided her time and then followed after him down the shell road as he was heading back to Amos Stephens's where he still lived.

When she caught up with him, Camellia said, "I know which pocket you have the cards in now, Grandpaw."

"Do you now, darling?"

"The right pocket."

"Lucky guess, chickadee."

"No guess, Grandpaw. I saw them there—in my head."

"You *saw* them there—*in your head*?" He seemed much interested now and had Camellia make a whole lot more "lucky guesses." Almost always she had the right answer.

She asked Grandpaw, "Will you teach me what you know of 'gypsy magic', like you taught me the fiddle?"

"Looks like you know already, chickadee."

But he did teach her. That summer he honed up her natural ability to *see through* the opponent's cards, and she beat him hands down almost every time in each of the numerous card games he taught her. Whenever Amos and Lois Stephens weren't home to snitch on them, Grandpaw also taught Camellia how to drink—and hard liquor, too—how to drink without either getting drunk or getting sick.

But Grandpaw warned her. "Don't ever drink when you're playing cards, chickadee, no matter how well you think you can handle both. Your other Grandfather tried that, and you know what happened to him and to his money, too."

Ah, yes, thought Camellia bitterly. How well they *all* knew.

Toward the end of that summer of 1931 Camellia asked something else of "The Wise Old Fool," as Azariah was sometimes called: "Grandpaw, teach me how to hit people in the back from one hundred feet away, will you?"

But this time Grandpaw balked and said, "I ain't gonna teach you how to hurt people, darling."

"Well, teach me how to keep from getting hurt myself, then."

Grandpaw started off with the old favorite—how to knee a man in the groin if he starts to grab you, but Camellia only laughed at him and said, "Oh, for heaven's sake, Grandpaw! Snipsey taught me how to 'cold cock' a guy two or three years ago. What I want to know is *how to use my mind*."

So once again he became her instructor, and they went through many an exercise on mental concentration and silent suggestion. But Grandpaw added some serious advice: "Little chickadee, don't ever be tempted to do evil with the things I've taught you. You never knew your Grandmother Mona, but she was a good person, far better than her own people—the gypsies—but all of them ended up bad or dead early because of this magic and witchcraft stuff. Some of them deserved what they got; others didn't. But none of them with gypsy blood, 'cepting my Mona and her and my son, Thomas—your Papa—ever lived a very good or honest life. So be careful to whom you look for your heroes. You might do well to pattern your ways after your Papa."

Camellia marveled, for this was the first and only time she'd ever heard any of her father's family say anything good about him.

Thomas's kinfolk were usually only too happy to poke fun at him, for his having had only the one child and for his super-cleanliness that almost verged on fastidiousness.

Thomas expected Mary to keep a clean house, and she was only too happy to do that if for no other reason, Camellia suspected, than that it helped her run off some of her sensual energy that even her previous pneumonia and her continuing stomach ulcer didn't take the edge off.

But Thomas did his part to keep things clean, too. He was still 'tyking a beth' before he came home even as he was working on the water out of Gainsbiddle with Norman Travis. And he kept his clothes hung up, his belongings in order, and he cleaned up and put away his tools after doing any maintenance or repairs to the Tu-Rest Home. He even washed empty soda bottles!

Camellia always knew when her father was taking those sparkling clean bottles back to the store because she could hear Amanda Cartwright booming out all over Bell's Island: "Ooooo, looky! There goes Brother Thomas sashaying along with his soda bottles. Will you lookit how they're shining! Almost like diamonds! He thinks he's going to get the same ones back. Hah! Bet he gets back the ones somebody has pissed in!"

Thomas usually took the bawdy banter from his kinfolk with a grain of salt, but when he found out Camellia had been learning "gypsy magic" from Grandpaw Azariah he was furious....

When Camellia came into the house one day—and she always moved gracefully and walked *on soft feet* in spite of her size—she stopped short when she heard her parents arguing in the kitchen. She paused just outside the door, waiting, listening, silent, and invisible as that dead black cat at midnight.

Thomas was going aboard Mary with all four feet: "Mary, I asked you, I pled with you, to teach Camellia to be good. You've always let her run wild with that Snipsey, and now it's Paw, too, who's corrupting her. God only knows what he's been teaching her. Gambling, for one thing, I'm sure of that. I've seen her playing cards and shooting dice with Snipsey, and you know that's against our church. And Paw may have been teaching her to drink liquor, too. I almost caught them at it one day when I went looking for Amos. Now what do you have to say for yourself, Mary?"

Camellia judged her mother's ulcer was acting up, for Mary snapped right back at Thomas: "You might do a little teaching her yourself, Thomas. You're her father. Why do you expect me to do it all?"

"WELL, YOU'RE HER MOTHER!!" Thomas roared. "Girls are supposed to be taught by their mothers. Now, if there was a son...."

There was an angry silence and then it was as though Mary was biting each word off a sour pickle a foot long: "Thomas Stephens, if you had wanted another child, a son or whatever, there was something *you* were supposed to do, *remember*? Just because my name's Mary that doesn't mean I can do what 'that other Mary' did!"

Another unearthly silence. Camellia waited for her father's response. Her mother had just profaned the Trinity and all Christianity. Was Papa waiting for God's hand to come down through the roof of the house and whack Mama to her knees...?

If so, it didn't happen and Thomas seemed completely disarmed as he said, "Well, I—we, that is, we did 'do something' a whole half dozen times and...."

Mary jumped at his throat again, sneering, "Yes, we've been 'naughty' *a whole half dozen times* in our marriage, as you're forever bragging to everybody down at the hardware store and everywhere else. You've made us the laughingstock of this community."

"But, Mary...."

"Oh, go play with yourself, Thomas Stephens. But I suspect you don't even do that."

"I don't," he replied, and there was amazement in his voice that Mary had even thought he might.

Camellia was thinking maybe *her mother should*, or maybe she did, but maybe it still wasn't enough....

Mary was speaking again. "Don't you ever *feel anything*, Thomas? Feel anything 'down there' working on you?"

"When I do, I think of God," he said, and he said it so quietly, yet so assertively, it was as though he thought *everybody* did—or should do—the same.

Again Mary exploded. "I've been told that men, when they get excited at the wrong time—like in church—they think of baseball scores. My sisters, who are 'nice women', and don't think it's right to act like they enjoy it, even with their husbands, tell me they think of hats. But YOU, Thomas Stephens, you think of GOD! What have I married—a saint, a yogi?!"

Camellia shuddered. Her parents were having the harshest exchange of words she could ever remember. And it didn't end with the usual apologies, with patting each other on the hand and exchanging a platonic kiss or two. There was a strained silence between them for days and days.

Camellia didn't let on to them that she was troubled by all of this, but the music that came to her at bad times like these seemed all the more strange this time when she played it out in her efforts to compose on the piano. It was as though the weird rhythms and tones flowing from the keyboard were the very reflections of Thomas's and Mary's anguish.

A number of weeks later Camellia heard them going at it again in the kitchen just as she started in for breakfast. Again she paused and waited.

Thomas was saying slowly and quietly, as though he'd been practicing it for days: "Mary–do–you–want–a–divorce?"

There was a silence of disbelief.

Thomas went on: "I mean—if you are unhappy with me...."

Again a silence. It was as though Mary couldn't think of a blessed thing to say.

Thomas spoke again. "I always though we had a good marriage, Mary, but if for any reason...."

Camellia was thinking he was giving her all the opportunity in the world to say her piece, but she still wasn't doing it. Maybe her mother "knew her place" as a good wife, one who "is subject unto her husband" as the Bible put it, whether that husband be a Charlie Stephens who comes home with a smell on him "stroong enough to gag a maggot" but is all geared up, ready for action, and demanding it or like a Thomas Stephens who "tykes a beth" before coming home and then won't do a blessed thing!

Camellia's ears pricked up for Mary was speaking again. This time she was speaking softly, with good humor and reassuringly. "We *do* have a good marriage, Thomas. Just forget all the things I've said of late. I always was a little crazy."

"Yes," said Thomas.

Camellia didn't know if her father was agreeing with her mother on just her first two statements or on all three of them!

But somehow Camellia knew the crisis—for the time being—was over.

But another crisis was just around the next bend in the road. During her senior year in the Bell's Island High School, Camellia had entered another voice competition in Baltimore, arranged for her by Claudie, and this time she won the unanimous approval of the jury and received a scholarship to the conservatory. Everyone was delighted. All plans were being made for Camellia to live in Baltimore with Claudie, starting in the fall. It was the happiest time of delicious expectation that Camellia had ever known.

Then the bottom dropped out of everything. Camellia had no foreboding of anything, in spite of her off-and-on gypsy intuition, which must have been off at this time. Quite unsuspecting, she came home from school at the lunch hour on what was one of the most beautiful spring days she'd ever seen. She was singing at the top of her voice. And there was Mama, she noticed, right at the front door of the Tu-Rest Home to greet her. How nice! How wonderful life was!

Mary put her arms around Camellia and said, "Brace yourself, Camellia. Some bad news here." She had a piece of paper in her hand.

Camellia thought a notice had come saying her scholarship to the conservatory had been revoked for some reason.

But Mary said, "Telegram here from Reverend Bowman." And she handed it to Camellia.

Camellia didn't get past the first line: "Our Claudie passed away at 6:30 this morning...."

A horrid chill went all through Camellia. She gave one piercing howl, then came the screams and the sobbing that wouldn't stop. She clung to her mother so violently that Mary had to struggle to keep Camellia from unintentionally hurting her.

Mary wept along with Camellia. Camellia knew another era had ended for her mother, too. Claudie had been Mary's music teacher and mentor as well as Camellia's, and now Claudie had passed forever from both of them.

After they both were cried out. Mary said, "You better get back to school now, Camellia."

Camellia glanced in the mirror. "Can't go back looking like this." Her face was tear-drenched and her eyes all bloodshot.

Mary said, "Well, skip this afternoon. I'll write you a note to take in the morning." Camellia knew her mother was in rare mood of generosity, for she never let her skip school unless they were out of town and since she was never sick, there was no other reason to skip school.

For the next several days, Mary tried to convince Camellia that she still had her scholarship to the conservatory and that she could stay with her Aunt Lizbeth in Baltimore. But Camellia was so broken up over the death of Claudie that nothing her mother said seemed to get through to her.

When Camellia abruptly stopped playing the piano and singing, Mary was at a loss as to what to do. When she questioned Camellia about why she had quit practicing, all Camellia could say was, "Every time I try to practice, I see those big red mittens Claudie gave me, hanging there on the piano, and all I can do is cry."

Mary started to say something, but Camellia interrupted her and said, "I know, Mama. You're going to say I put those mittens there to remind me what Claudie said that time about practicing *no matter what*, but I...I...just can't...anymore...."

Camellia thought for a moment Mary was going to say, "THROW THE DAMN MITTENS AWAY!" And Camellia reasoned that if the mittens were going to prevent her from practicing instead of helping her to practice as they had been intended, then maybe she should throw them away. But she knew that would be cruel to Claudie's memory. So she *tried* to practice. And when her eyes would fill with tears, she would throw aside not the mittens but her music and stomp out of the house.

Camellia knew she couldn't enter the conservatory in the fall, cold, and expect to get anywhere. They would throw her out at the end of the first semester, scholarship or no scholarship. But she still did not pick up with her music. Her high school graduation came in June, but she was still in mourning for Claudie and she wouldn't practice her music. She only half-heartedly sang the solo assigned to her at the graduation ceremony.

All summer long, though, she dated Ralph Drummond. They spent many an hour strolling arm in arm on the lee side of the island over in the area of the old Bell's Island Inn where the sand beaches were.

One evening she was coming downstairs at the Tu-Rest Home all dressed up for a date with Ralph and Mary said, "Camellia, you'd better get with that piano."

Camellia answered back, flippantly, "Haven't got time to, Mama."

Mary said, "It's okay to have a boyfriend, and we like Ralph, too, but you *must* practice your music or you might as well forget about the conservatory. Do you want to end up as just another Bell's Island girl married to just another Bell's Island waterman?"

Camellia detected a bit of concealed bitterness in her mother's voice. She knew Mary was thinking of her own situation—just another Bell's Island girl married to just another Bell's Island waterman, when Mary might have otherwise become that schoolteacher she'd always wanted to be.

But Mary's words cut no ice with Camellia, who merely gave an insolent flip of her hips and walked out of the house to where Ralph was waiting for her on the porch.

Camellia knew her parents, especially her father, would be just as happy if she got married and stayed out of music altogether, except maybe to sing *JesusLovesMeThisIKnow* once a year at Children's Day, or rather to produce Thomas and Mary a litter of grandchildren who would do just that.

As for her father, Thomas need not have worried about Camellia and music. Music was the farthest thing from her mind that summer.

Then something strange happened. One afternoon Camellia and Ralph were walking hand in hand, this time over the grassy dunes on the north side of the island. Every now and then they stopped and watched a sandpiper running along the dunes. And every time they stopped, Ralph slipped his arm around Camellia's waist and pulled her close to him. He kept caressing her and blowing at wisps of her hair, and she could feel his body pressed warm and taut against her thigh. She knew very well this time what he wanted.

Ralph said, "Would you like it if we built our house out here on this part of the island, Camellia? We'd be all alone. Nobody's bought any of this land out here yet. My uncle knows who owns it and maybe he could get the people to sell us a lot out here."

Camellia said, "Mmmmm," without really saying anything. She was thinking, Did she really want to be married to Ralph? Did she really want to be married to anybody? She hadn't said "No" when he'd asked her to marry him a couple of weeks before, and she hadn't said "Yes," either. But he seemed to *think* she had said "Yes."

Ralph turned Camellia around to one side and then he eased the two of them down onto a grassy hummock where he sat very close beside her. He was touching her cheeks, her lips, pulling her into his arms, and easing his hand down along the inside of her thigh. He was saying, "Camellia, would you like to...? Would you like...to... just...try it a little? How about it, huh? We could try it...just a little, huh...?"

Camellia was uneasy. She said, "We shouldn't be doing...this...not yet. We're not married."

Ralph said, "But we're going to be, aren't we?" He rolled up against her and she felt him warm and taut against her body. He was kissing her deeper than he'd ever kissed her before. His hand was placing her hand on him and she touched him and felt how warm and taut he was.

She was thinking it would be so easy to yield to him, to yield completely. Still and all she gave another weak protest. "But we shouldn't...not this...not yet." But she closed her eyes, felt his hand, his body, his manhood seeking her and finding her. And as that little sandpiper scurried just at arm's length, keeping tender watch over them, she let Ralph Drummond have his way.

He felt big moving inside her, but it didn't hurt. In a little bit she felt her back arch and her toes curl and a hot shiver go all up through her. Her first time with a man! And over so quickly. But she felt pleasantly content. Ralph was panting softly alongside her and they both were laying very still, side by side, hand in hand on that grassy hummock while that little sandpiper still kept watch over them.

Camellia wondered—had her fate been sealed in that moment? The fate of just another Bell's Island girl joined to just another Bell's Island boy? Just another Bell's Island girl being primed to marry just another Bell's Island boy who was destined to be just another Bell's Island waterman? Just another Bell's Island girl destined to be just another Bell's Island mother, so that the same cycle could continue on for generations yet to come?

But then something happened. Camellia sat bolt upright and exclaimed, *"I hear music*!"

Ralph gave a start, then he began to laugh, and said, "I don't hear anything, Camellia. You must have been asleep and dreaming." He sat up and tried to put his arms around her. He said, "You liked that first time, didn't you? *Let's try it again*!"

But Camellia wrenched away from him and got to her feet. She put her clothes in quick order. Ralph grabbed for her legs and yelped, "Come back here!"

"No!" she said. "NO!"

That music was getting louder.

She heard herself scream, "I'LL NEVER MARRY A BELL'S ISLAND WATERMAN!!"

She ran off like a frightened deer and left Ralph Drummond still trying to get to his feet.

A dark shadow crossed the ground in front of her. She glanced up at the sky and saw a thunderhead coming over the sun. She heard Ralph calling to her, "Hey, Camellia, look! It was only thunder that you heard! *Camellia*! *Come back*! *Come back*!"

By the time Camellia reached the shell road, her heart was pounding nearly out of her chest. *What WAS that music*? It was like nothing she had ever heard, played, or imagined before. It had not been thunder, that was for sure. She did not hear it as loud now, but the spell remained.

When she got home, she went straight upstairs to her room and ignored her mother's call for supper. She needed time to think.

She could hear Mary and Thomas talking downstairs. Mary was saying, "If Camellia doesn't start eating more, I don't know what's going to become of her. She's lost nearly twenty pounds already this summer."

And Thomas was saying, "Mary, it could be...it could be...*love*!" He finished his sentence in a low, awed whisper.

But Mary was not so entranced. She said, "Oh, Thomas, I don't think she's in love with Ralph. Oh, she likes him, but she hangs around with him mostly for something to do. Something to fill up the emptiness since Claudie has gone out of her life. I don't believe she has any intention of going to the conservatory this fall. I'm worried about her, Thomas. She's lost all interest I music...and food. That's not like her, on either count."

Thomas responded, "Maybe love has cured all of Camellia's crazy music idea stuff."

Then Camellia heard Mary get very angry and say, "Oh, Thomas, you make me sick with all your talk about love." Camellia was thinking her mother *still* was not reconciled to her father's abstinence. But just then there was a heavy roll of definite thunder this time, and she heard no more of their conversation.

She looked out the open window of her bedroom and saw toward the southwest that the sun had dropped behind an ominous ridge of dark, rapidly churning, low-hanging clouds. She heard Thomas downstairs, running to put windows down and saying, with the typical dry humor of the island, "It looks like we might be in for a little blow."

But at that point the weather was the least of the things on Camellia's mind. She shut the window and the door of her bedroom and sat for a long while on the edge of her bed, trying to reconstruct what had just happened to her. The picture came back of her laying there on that grassy hummock as Ralph Drummond had taken her from girlhood into womanhood like no amount of high heels, silk hose, or lipstick had done or could ever do.

But that music? From where had it come? What had it meant? Suddenly she thought of Claudie's most important words to her: *Don't let anything or anybody turn you aside from your music*. Yet she knew she had let that very thing happen after Claudie's death. When she should have been turning from her grief all the more toward music, what had she done? She had turned to a young man's arms.

She still did not know from where that music had come, but she knew now what it meant for her to do.

Rain was splattering on the window panes. Trees outside were bending double from a brief, but violent burst of wind, lightning, and thunder. It was but the prelude for something more terrible to come.

But before the hurricane struck Bell's Island the next day, that evening Camellia got her wits together and asked her mother to contact Aunt Lizbeth in Baltimore and ask if she could stay with her while she attended the conservatory in the fall. Joyfully, Mary said she would.

The brief scuds of thunderstorms, more bark than bite, that had occurred at suppertime did not clear the air but left the skies over Bell's Island looking very nasty and wicked.

In the night the winds freshened from the southeast and by morning, a huge swell was rolling white caps all along the south side of the island. The lower parts of the marshland were already covered with rising tide.

By noon gale force winds of better than fifty knots were coming from the south and whipping straight across the island, breaking off tree limbs, ripping up roof shingles, slamming boats against the docks and against each other, and lifting off sections of crab and oyster house roofs. The tide was rapidly rising inland and toward the north and east parts of the island.

Thomas had gone out at dawn. He had not attempted to go down to Gainsbiddle, but instead had gone to help his father and brothers even though he had not been in the employ of Grandpaw Azariah for a number of years. All of them were trying to secure their oyster and crab houses as well as re-moor their work boats.

By two o'clock in the afternoon, hurricane force winds were all but shattering Bell's Island. The sky above had turned a sickly gray-yellow color, not filled with rain, as this has turned out to be a dry hurricane, but with a salty, stinging sheet of mist wildly blown up out of the harbor and nearby Anderson Sound.

The driving mist was laced with flying dirt and all manner of whirling debris—great masses of whole tree limbs, twisted crab floats, huge strips of corrugated metal from off the seafood houses, as well as millions of shredded leaves and twigs, all being blown hundreds of feet into the air, sucked aloft by violent updrafts of the churning winds and then driven back downward and sideways by the erratic atmosphere.

The sound of the steady pounding roar of the winds and the crashing of the waves that the tide was making and swirling all over everything was such that one person could scarcely be heard talking, shouting even, to the person right next to him.

By four o'clock in the afternoon trees were toppling left and right, falling across the shell roadway and across side lanes, onto horse carts, and onto the few autos and trucks that were on the island, into the sides of people's houses and into store fronts. Entire roofs were off some homes and buildings, chimneys were down, store and house windows smashed, horse carts, autos, and trucks blown against one another, and in some places entire buildings and homes were lifted off their foundations and dumped sideways.

Numerous boats had broken their moorings and had been carried ashore by the tide or hurtled there by the winds and left floating on top of the water in people's yards or blown up against houses and trees. Almost all the seafood houses built on stilts and pilings out over the water had collapsed.

And as if to add one last bitter drop of gall to the cup, the wind and surging flood tides were working for all they were worth on the Bell's Island bridge, the only connecting link to the Wintergreen County mainland. The causeway was rapidly washing away at both ends of the old wooden structure.

A. Stephens and Sons Seafood Company had lost both of its crab and oyster houses and two of its large workboats. The men were struggling to re-moor the third boat and seeing it was a losing battle, Azariah screamed, "Let 'er go, boys! Let 'er go! No use killing ourselves!"

But no one could hear Azariah. Thomas, crouching warily in the bow of the pitching boat, caught a rope thrown to him by one of his nephews. In a lurch to pitch the rope over the nearest piling, Thomas lost his balance and crashed chest down across the starboard edge of the deck. Then, just as suddenly, the boat heaved upwards and threw Thomas backwards, landing him on his back on the port edge of the deck and striking his head against a huge iron mooring eye. In one final fury the boat lurched again and pitched Thomas sideways into a crumpled heap against the boat's wheel.

In a few more seconds the crashing waves would have washed over the boat again and carried Thomas's twisted form overboard, but Amos Stephens and Simon Cartwright leaped into the boat from the dock and managed to catch Thomas and hold him, and somehow they dragged him across the bow of the boat and onto the boardwalk of the dock. Simon got a crushed hand as the boat slammed against his hand and pinned it to the boardwalk, and twice the two men misstepped and fell or were blown off the swaying, wave-and-foam inundated boardwalk. But they were able to scramble and climb back up and keep on going until they had half-dragged, half-carried Thomas's limp body through the swirling water and onto the dock.

Thomas lay on the dock unconscious, his face, hands, arms, legs, and shoulders torn and bleeding. Azariah, Charlie, and two of the nephews came to help Simon and Amos. All looked at Thomas for a shocked moment, and then they turned around and saw the boat, in a final mocking gesture, lose its last line and go over on its side like a stricken whale.

The men fought the hurtling, buffeting winds and the stinging, blinding salt mist at every step as they slogged through the rolling tide that was pouring in great waves over the shell road. They carried Thomas to the Tu-Rest Home and laid him on the floor of the open porch. Simon started hollering for all he was worth for somebody to come unlock the door which Mary had bolted to keep it from flying open in the teeth of the relentless winds.

Shortly before Simon and the rest had come with Thomas's broken body, Camellia and Mary had been sitting huddled together in the kitchen of the Tu-Rest Home all but transfixed as they heard one window pane after another break and shatter in pieces throughout the house. Then an unbelievable roar had made both of them jump. An avalanche of bricks plummeted down onto the kitchen roof and bounced off and down to the ground right past the broken kitchen window right before their eyes. "The chimney!" they both gasped.

In the brief silence that followed the falling of the chimney, they heard Simon and the others yelling and pounding on the front door. They both ran down the hallway and cautiously unbolted the door. It almost immediately flung open, pushed in by the wind.

"Thomas is bad hurt," Grandpaw Azariah said in a voice that was but a hoarse whisper, yet they heard him amazingly well in spite of the roaring of the wind.

The men lifted Thomas through the doorway and placed him on the couch in the front room. Mary was so stunned at the sight that she could neither move nor speak. Thomas lay very still, very pale, and gray. It was hard to tell if he was dead or alive. Suddenly a quake shuddered through him. There was a strangling sound in his throat and a reddish-brown foam oozed through his lips.

"Turn his head there, Charlie! Don't let him choke!" Simon barked.

Then underneath his breath Simon said, "My God, I thought he was gone then for sure."

Simon said to Camellia, "Get some blankets and cover him. He's in shock."

To Amos, Simon said, "Go try to find Doc Feldman."

Simon was in his glory, giving orders to people, Camellia thought wryly.

Mary came up to the side of the couch and looked at Thomas. Her face was as pale as his. Camellia brought some blankets and arranged them as softly as she could around her father. He was very still, very silent. Camellia took Mary's hand and together they stood there, waiting, expecting the worse.

It seemed like an eternity before Amos returned. He practically fell forward into the house as Simon eased open the door for him. "You can't even stand up in that wind!" Amos said.

"WHERE'S DOC?" Simon demanded.

Amos struggled to speak. "That damn Jew! He ain't even on the island today. Neighbor lady said he drove up to a medical meeting in Baltimore yesterday and ain't come back yet. And...and...." Amos hung his head. "And the bridge just went down. I saw it. I saw it go...."

The men, salt-water and sweat-soaked and exhausted, and Mary and Camellia, all stared at Amos in stunned silence. No doctor. No way of getting one.

Thomas moaned from the couch where he lay wrapped up in the blankets. Simon went over to him and studied him closely, while the rest of them stood back in silence. Simon then turned to Mary and said, "He may just make it. He's in deep shock right now. Just keep him warm. Don't give him anything to eat or drink. He's probably got a concussion. Don't move him or let him move. I don't think he can anyway. I'm pretty sure his back is broken."

Again there was silence from all of them, and all they could hear was the slamming of the wind and the storm outside. Simon nodded to the others, and they moved toward the door. Simon said to Mary, "I'm going to send Amanda over here to stay with you tonight. Camellia, get some oil lamps ready. And boil any water you use from your tank or cistern. God only knows how many dead fish have been blowing up out of the water and down out of the sky and onto your roofs and into your gutters today."

The men left, their backs hunched against the wind, their heads low.

After they had left the porch, Camellia pushed shut and re-bolted the door against the seething wind. Mary fell onto Camellia's shoulder, clinging to her, trembling, and sobbing. Mary said, "I have had too many un-Christian thoughts about your Papa over the years, I guess. But I—I—have never realized how much he has meant to me...until now...'til now...when it may be too late...."

"Hush, Mama....Hush now." Camellia's own eyes were stinging with unshed tears. How true, she was thinking, how true that we don't fully appreciate something until something tries to take it away from us.

Amanda arrived on the porch, almost bent in two to keep from being blown down in the wrenching, twisting winds. Mary and Camellia were still standing in the semi-darkness beside the couch where Thomas lay inert and silent, but still breathing.

"Don't you have an oil lamp, for heaven's sake?" boomed Amanda as she pushed headlong through the doorway when Camellia slid back the bolt.

"I'll get it," Camellia said and hurried off for the lamp which she should have already gotten.

When she returned with the lamp, Amanda said, "Get some water and a cloth and let me try to get this blood off his face. And boil the water, Simon says."

"Okay," Camellia said, glancing once more at Mary's ashen face and her father's stricken form. She didn't want to leave the room, but did as she was told. All she could think of was that her father was dying and it hadn't even been his boat or his business he was trying to save, but somebody else's. With all the irony and cruelty in life, where was God and justice in all this...?

Darkness fell on Bell's Island. The Stephens Tu-Rest Home quaked and shuddered throughout the night as the lingering gale now started coming out of the southwest. By morning it was on its way inland, giving other towns northward the final lash of its diminishing fury.

Thomas Stephens had survived the night while Mary, Camellia, and Amanda Cartwright had kept their uneasy vigil.

When the morning came the sky was a strange-looking striated mixture of baby blue, green, and pink. But most of the wind had dropped. Camellia stepped out on the porch of the Tu-Rest Home and saw the other Stephenses and various Bell's Islanders moving around in little groups here and there, climbing over fallen trees and other debris, surveying the devastating losses to their homes, their boats, their businesses.

The tide had washed through the Cartwright's yard so forcefully during the night that it had dislodged most of the back foundation of their house. The roof had blown completely off Charlie and Agnes's house. And Amos's house had caught on fire during the night.

Someone had located an intact shortwave radio and had gotten in touch with the Coast Guard station in Gainsbiddle. They were sending a motor launch to transport Thomas Stephens and several other badly injured persons to the hospital in Gainsbiddle.

But first the launch had to pick up Doc Feldman, stranded over on the flooded causeway on the Wintergreen County mainland. Islanders had seen Doc over there at the first light of dawn, wildly waving his arms and pointing to the still-rolling tide tangling all sorts of flotsam and jetsam in and out around the broken sections of the downed bridge. But there wasn't a single craft on the island that had not been either sunk or ripped apart by the winds or damaged beyond sea-worthiness for even so short a run as to the other side of the inlet. So Doc helplessly waited beside his Model T Ford on the one side of the inlet while Bell's Islanders with their sick and injured waited helplessly on the other side.

When the Coast Guard motor launch finally came, it quickly rescued Doc and put him ashore near the Stephens Tu-Rest Home.

Doc rushed into the house and sent soothing jets of morphine into both Thomas and Mary. While the Coast Guardsmen were getting Thomas onto a stretcher, Doc told Camellia what had happened to him the day and night before.

Doc said he had returned to the county from his medical meeting in Baltimore just as the storm was at its height, and try though he might, he could not get his little Model T Ford coupe to make it to Bell's Island before the bridge collapsed. When he saw the washed-out causeway, he said it never occurred to him to seek shelter at Moonlight Corrigan's tavern, just off to the north in the mainland marshes. He would have been safe and sound there, for the tavern, he found out in the morning, had suffered very little damage from either the tide or the wind.

By contrast, Doc had weathered out the storm and the night hiding underneath his Model T Ford coupe, holding frantically onto the front axle and using all his effort and muscles to hold the little car down. Any number of times it started to rear up in the howling winds and threatened either to roll over on him or blow completely up into the sky with him still hanging onto the axle underneath. Doc said, "It was hard to tell which saved who: the car, me or me, the car!"

Ah, yes, that was Doc, Camellia thought with amusement, always seeing the funny side of things and sharing it with his patients. Maybe that's why Bell's Islanders loved him so much. Or maybe it was because of his *needles*.

As Thomas Stephens began his long fight for recovery in the Gainsbiddle hospital, clean-up operations started all over Bell's Island. The tide had caused numerous graves to open in the Methodist Church cemetery, and bits of skeletons had floated out of their supposedly *final resting place* and were left high and dry all over the island as the flood waters receded. Camellia watched dismally as several of the Stephens cousins across the shell road used an anonymous skull alternately as a basketball and a soccer ball. The boys kept that up all day until Simon Cartwright came home and took to their backsides with his big leather belt. As to what happened to the skull, Camellia didn't know.

The skull's fate was no worse, she thought, than her own once-again shattered plans to enter the conservatory. The hurricane had descended so rapidly Mary had not even gotten the chance to contact Aunt Lizbeth in Baltimore. Then after Thomas's severe injuries, it was no use to do so, as Camellia knew she was needed at home to look out for her mother while her father was in the hospital.

Somewhat softening the setback, however, was the fact that she applied for and was accepted as a day student at Halburg Normal

School, which was inland and only about twenty-five miles away, and she could ride up there and back each day with an island resident who was going up in that area anyway, so she would be home each evening. She would start with the 1933 winter term—certainly her father would be home by then—and if she could complete the two-year teacher's course in the music department, she would be qualified to teach music on an elementary school level.

It seemed a poor start toward her goal to sing at The Met, but Camellia spunkily told everybody, "I'm sure teaching will only be temporary for me, if at all." Camellia felt that her mother was secretly tickled pink that she might be teaching rather than performing. That way Mary, who had always wanted to be a schoolteacher herself, could gain some sort of vicarious pleasure from her daughter's vocation.

Most everybody on Bell's Island had sustained some sort of storm damage or personal injury during the hurricane, and all were waiting for the State Relief Administration to send its representatives to make evaluations and take applications for financial aid.

In the meantime, Thomas slowly began to mend in the Gainsbiddle hospital. Camellia and Mary went down on the freight boat to see him every week. One of the doctors told Mary how amazed the staff was at Thomas's strength and ability to survive a broken back, severe internal injuries, a concussion, and many broken bones and lacerations. The doctor said, "We've been told what a good, clean-living, religious man your husband is, Mrs. Stephens, and undoubtedly that is what has saved him."

Camellia was thinking there were two sides to that coin, but Mary seemed only too happy to have Thomas still alive to be harboring any bitterness toward him for his religious beliefs.

When the *state men* came in September from the Relief Administration, there were two of them and they took a room at the Tu-Rest Home. There was one other roomer there at the time, a hardware salesman. Mary showed the two *state men* the outside of the house, pointed out the fallen chimney, the broken windows, and other damage. She then filled out an application and provided a statement from the Gainsbiddle hospital about the extent of Thomas's injuries, the cost of his treatment, and length of time he was expected to be off from work.

Camellia had taken no particular notice of what any of the roomers looked like, but the morning *IT* happened, she could have sworn she saw all three of those men at the Bell's Island drugstore getting breakfast. She had gone down there to pick up some of Doc's medicine for her mother's ulcer.

As Camellia had left the house, Mary said that she was going to put a pot of stew on to cook and then, as was her usual routine in the morning, go to the roomers' side of the Tu-Rest Home and make the beds up clean, dust, and sweep so everything would be in order when the men returned. All three of them had been gone most of each day as there was much storm damage to assess and the hardware stores were having a hard time keeping in supplies for all the repair work that was going on.

As Camellia was returning from the drugstore with Mary's ulcer medicine, she encountered Snipsey who, still in high school, was playing hooky from school that day, and Snipsey followed Camellia home and into the kitchen.

But they were suddenly surprised and enveloped in billows of dense smoke. Camellia had forgotten about the stew pot, but remembered her mother had said something about going to the roomers' side to clean.

Heedless of the smoke, Camellia, with Snipsey right behind her, pushed on through the kitchen to the hallway with the stairway that led up to the roomers' side.

Shouting at the top of her lungs, "Mama! Mama! *The house is on fire*! THE HOUSE IS ON FIRE!!" Camellia raced up the stairway, with Snipsey still right behind her.

Then Camellia stopped as suddenly as if she had run into the side of an elephant, and Snipsey almost catapulted over top of her.

There, in front of both of them, standing in the upper hallway, was Mary with her housecoat open in front, a stack of clean sheets draped over one arm, and a man, naked from the waist down, skewering her to the door of the linen closet.

Hearing the word "FIRE!" and seeing the smoke already seeping up the stairway, the man broke away from Mary, grabbed up his pants from around his ankles, tumbled down the stairway past Camellia and Snipsey, and headed out the front door onto the shell roadway.

With amazing aplomb, Mary gathered her housecoat together in the front and said, "Camellia, Snipsey, I might as well be honest with you from the start. It was NOT rape."

Camellia squealed, "But he...he was...was...!"

"Yes," said Mary. "But it was not rape."

Suddenly remembering the smoke and the fire, Camellia and Snipsey *both* squealed.

Again Mary said calmly, "That smoke. Yes, I'm sure it's only the stew pot."

Mary dropped the stack of sheets over the newel post and shooed Camellia and Snipsey back down the stairway. They all rushed through the smoky hallway and into the kitchen. Mary grabbed the coal shovel and scooped the smoldering, red-hot stew pot off the stove and pitched it out in the back yard.

Camellia and Snipsey started putting windows up all over the downstairs. Mary got a hold of Snipsey by the shoulder and said in a stern warning, "Nothing happened here today except the stew pot caught on fire and filled the house with smoke. Understand, Snipsey? Nothing else. *Nothing*! Now, you go home."

"Yes'm," Snipsey said, rolling here eyes both dutifully and in fear. She ran down the hallway and out the front door.

But Camellia ran out of the house after her, caught her by the shoulder when she was halfway across the shell road, and said, "And if you tell anybody *anything else*, I'll come and beat the shit out of you!"

Big as she was, Camellia could have easily done it, in spite of all the weight she'd lost the past summer.

With Snipsey gone and the worst of the smoke out of the house, Camellia confronted Mary. In total exasperation, she demanded, "Mama! *Who was that man*? Why was he upstairs with you like that?"

"One of the roomers," Mary said, unemotionally.

"But I swear I saw all three of them at the drugstore just now," Camellia protested.

"I thought they had all gone, too, Camellia," Mary said. "Else I never would have gone upstairs on the roomers' side in the frame of mind I was in."

"What frame of mind, Mama?"

Mary said, "Sit down, Camellia. This is difficult to explain standing up."

"But it wasn't too difficult to DO stranding up, eh, Mama?" Camellia sneered.

"Please have a little mercy, Camellia."

"I don't see where you deserve any," Camellia snapped. "But go ahead, what were you saying about frame of mind?"

Mary said, "I'm sure you've thought more than once that I've wanted Charlie Stephens, and I admit I used to. I used to have all sorts of fantasies about him, but I was afraid he could tell what I was thinking and get me into trouble, so I stopped it.

"*But I had to do something*! So, some time back I started thinking 'that way' about first this one and then that one of the roomers here. It was less personal. None of them are ever here that long. I've always tried never to be upstairs working when any of them are still in their rooms. They are always told to use their Do Not Disturb signs if they are going to be in their rooms past eight in the morning or before three in the afternoon. I sometimes clean over there if it gets real late, but never have I gone into a room with a sign on it or said anything to anyone I might see up there except a brief 'good morning' or 'good afternoon'."

Impatiently Camellia said, "Your are not making much sense, Mama. All chambermaids and rooming house proprietresses follow those rules. What's all that go to do with *what happened just now*?"

Mary drew a deep breath. "It's just this, Camellia: Whether you believe me or not I *thought* all those rooms were empty this morning when I went up there. I *thought* I saw all three of those men leave. So when I went up there to clean, I was starting to act out my favorite little fantasy:

"In my mind's eye, I am seeing the door of the one of the rooms ajar. A half-naked man is in there sitting on the edge of his bed. I come up to the door and with my housecoat open in front I say in a low, teasing voice, 'Room service! And wouldn't you like something a little special this morning...!'"

Camellia's exasperation grew even more. "And this invisible man jumped off the bed and came and fucked the hell out of you while your were standing there with sheets over your arm and you thought it was all your imagination!?"

It was as if Camellia was daring her mother, after what Mary had done, to upbraid Camellia for so minor a thing as indecent *language*. "Oh, *Mama*! This is *ridiculous*! If you *had* to seduce one of those men, why didn't you just claim it was rape when Snipsey and I caught you. *That* would have been easy enough to believe—certainly the way you were both standing there. But this incubus-like imagination excuse.... Sheesh!"

Mary said, "Camellia, believe it nor not, I *did* think it was all my imagination until you and Snipsey came running up there, yelling the house was on fire. *That* broke the spell. Suddenly I realized it was all *for real*. But then it was too late...."

After a long and thoughtful moment, Camellia said, "Mama, I don't know whether to believe you or not. But couldn't you at least have claimed it was rape *to Snipsey*?"

"Camellia," Mary said, slowly and deliberately, "I may be crazy and I may be sexually immoral, but I'm not dishonest. Further, if I had claimed it was rape, that would have caused even more uproar. Snipsey would have instantly hollered it all over the island and gotten everybody to try to catch the man."

"And she may yet," Camellia said dryly. "I wonder where the man got to?"

"I don't even know which one it was," Mary said weakly.

"Little wonder," said Camellia. "I'm sure you weren't looking at his face."

They both were silent for awhile, then Camellia fairly shrieked, "Mama! What if that man got you pregnant just now?"

"I might be too old for that," Mary said. "I'm getting pretty close to the change."

Camellia said, "But you're just in your early forties. Claudie always said she was past fifty when....OH, CLAUDIE! *I'll never get to The Met now....*"

It was near Thanksgiving, cold and blustery, and a thin cloudiness was making the already weak sunlight over Gainsbiddle even paler.

"Mama, I suppose you'll be baking and handing out these confounded Maryland Beat Biscuits even on the Day of Armageddon," Camellia said to Mary as they came off the freight boat at the greasy Gainsbiddle dock. The dock was loaded with leering longshoremen.

Camellia and Mary were carrying a huge basket between them as they started picking their way along the stone street that ran from the dock up through the lower business section of the town. They had to negotiate over, around, and through pot holes and puddles, coal cinders, garbage, dead fish, horse manure, and God only knows what else.

"That Day of Armageddon draws ever nearer," Mary said bitterly. "But I do have Bessie to talk with. I can no longer talk with Aunt Sairy Middleton about 'things'. Aunt Sairy's gotten too pious of late."

"Miss Bessie's pious," Camellia noted.

"Yes, but Bessie's much younger and she's...."

"And she's fifteen miles down river from Bell's Island," Camellia finished the sentence for her mother.

"Correct," said Mary, astutely.

They continued up the stone street, following the railroad tracks parallel to it. They had gone past the shabby-looking warehouses, foundries, and hardware stores that were bunched at the depot end. Further along now, rows of identical working-class dwellings began springing up on either side of the tracks. The houses were all alike and all painted a peeling dull yellow. Each had a small front porch and four small rooms, two up and two down, and an outhouse sitting back on the edge of the marsh. The houses were so close together their eaves were touching at their tops, and at their bottoms there were tiny walkways that never saw the light of day.

At the first intersection, Camellia and Mary bore off to the left and followed another road that was now heading into one of the better residential areas. The first place on the left was a fairly large, fairly decent-looking two-story home, painted white and having a bit of yard and trees. To the rear there was a dock out in the marsh with Norman Travis' work boat tied up to it.

Norman was home and he came out on the porch to greet Camellia and Mary. He took the basket of Maryland Beat Biscuits in for them. Norman was raw-boned and strong-muscled, and though only in his early thirties, he already had a weatherbeaten and old look to him.

The life of a waterman doesn't do much for a man's appearance, Camellia thought idly.

Bessie cut a somewhat better figure as a waterman's wife. She was a plump, dark-haired little creature, always chattering, but also always listening, and always scurrying about doing things, which included chasing after her and Norman's lively little toddler, Wayne.

After Norman left the house to continue working on his boat repairs, Bessie got a pot of fresh coffee brewing for Camellia and Mary to have with some of the biscuits and the homemade grape jam she had made.

Bessie said, "Does Thomas suspect anything yet, Mary? You are sort of getting big already, don't you think?"

Mary spread a biscuit with jam and said, "Not yet he doesn't suspect, I don't think, but I can't wait much longer to tell him. But can you believe it, Bessie? Doc Feldman told me it was 'against the law' for him to do anything for me, when he does it all the time for those whores at Moonlight Corrigan's place."

"Well, he's doing it 'against the law' when he does it for them, too, I guess," Bessie offered realistically.

Camellia put in, "And also, Mama, you said Doc told you that you weren't strong enough for the treatment he'd have to give you."

Mary sniffed. "Just his poor excuse. He obviously thinks I'm strong enough to carry and birth it. Right?"

Bessie nodded with a helpless little smile as Mary went on:

"Thomas may want a divorce. He would be entitled to it, I guess. I plan to tell him the truth, to say it was my fault and not try to make out like it was rape. If he doesn't ask for a divorce, he may let me go live with my sister Lizbeth in Baltimore until after the...until after 'it' would be born and I could put it up for adoption. So, he should know all about this as soon as possible, so I can make my plans."

Bessie asked, "What about you, Camellia? Weren't you planning to start at Halburg Normal School after Christmas?"

Camellia said hopelessly, "I guess I won't go. I wasn't going to board there. And Mama doesn't think I should be left at the Tu-Rest Home alone at night. Which is silly, considering...."

Mary seemed annoyed at Camellia's oblique jab, but she shrugged it off, and said to Camellia, "Maybe you could come with me to

Baltimore and have that scholarship to the conservatory reinstated. Only I don't know if that could be done or not. Or if I'll even go to Baltimore. The very thought of having to tell my sister....Also, I don't know who would run the Tu-Rest Home if I weren't there and if Thomas is still in the hospital. I just don't know, Bessie. I just don't know anything anymore."

And Mary started a soft little crying.

Bessie asked, "Don't you think Thomas will be out of the hospital soon? Norman's been going to see him every day or so, and Thomas is talking like he might be going back to work on Norman's boat any day now."

"Thomas is always the optimist," Mary said. "But it all depends on what they find when they take that cast off his back. Everything else has healed up. Thomas is such a good, strong man; why do all these terrible things have to happen to him? And now when I tell him what I've gone and done...."

Mary was sobbing for all she was worth now, and Bessie went over and put her arm around her and tried to comfort her. "Mary, considering all that you've told me of Thomas and his lack of, lack of...well, not *lack* really, but lack of 'attention' to *you*, don't you think what you did is just a tiny bit *his fault*, too?"

"No! It's not Thomas' fault!" Mary shouted.

Camellia smiled at how her mother was always quick to defend Thomas if *anybody else* criticized him.

Mary went on: "Not too long ago we had that big fight over this...this 'lack of attention', as you call it, and he offered to give me a divorce. But I didn't want a divorce. And he didn't, either. Thomas and I *love each other*, Bessie....Why do these things have to happen? Why did God make me the way I am—no different physically than my beagle bitches—and then punish me, and Thomas too, for doing what I couldn't help doing because of the way God made Me?"

"I don't know, Mary," Bessie said slowly and wonderingly. And Camellia was wondering why, just as much as the other two.

When Mary could no longer hide the truth of her pregnancy from Thomas, she and Camellia again took the freight boat down to Gainsbiddle to talk with him in the hospital. Camellia was dreading this trip. She felt that her mother's encounter with the roomer had been an unforgivable character weakness, and she feared her father would feel the same way.

Camellia had done essentially the same thing a few months previously with Ralph Drummond but this did not seem to bother her. The big difference was that her mother had gotten pregnant and Camellia had not!

But Camellia still resented having to go to the Gainsbiddle hospital with Mary on this mission.

Oddly, since the water was "slick ca'm" that day and Camellia had never in her life before been affected by a boat's motion in any kind of weather, this time she was seasick the whole trip. She guessed her own scrambled-up feelings about everything had caused it.

She barely made it to the toilet in Thomas's semi-private room when they got to the hospital. While she was in there, Mary started telling Thomas what she had to tell him. His bed was near the toilet, and there were no other patients in the room at the moment, so Camellia could hear the conversation through a crack in the door:

"Mary, aren't you hot with that coat on?"

"Not really, Thomas."

"Well, seems awful hot today to me. They say it's the hottest December on record."

"Thomas, there's something I have to tell you."

"What is it, Mary?"

"Thomas, there's...uh...we're...uh, that is, I'm....Uh, there's-going-to-be-a-baby, Thomas. That's why I'm keeping my coat on."

There was a long, long silence while Camellia waited in the toilet, listening....

"But Mary, how can there be any baby? We haven't been 'naughty' for years."

Mary replied slowly, sadly, "*We* haven't, Thomas. But...but...but... but I have."

"Mary, I don't understand."

"It was a one-time-only thing, Thomas. I lost my head with someone. But it meant nothing whatsoever. It was momentary lust and nothing more. And it was entirely my fault. But sometimes, Thomas, even *nice women* need it once in a while...and if their husbands don't...."

There was another long silence. Thomas broke it. "Was it someone I know? But no, you don't have to answer that, Mary."

Again silence. But Thomas's curiosity must have gotten the better of him and he asked, "One of my brothers?"

"No."

"Simon Cartwright?"

"No."

"Not Grandpaw?!"

At the mention of Grandpaw, Camellia nearly choked there in the toilet on an unholy combination of horselaugh, hiccup, and heave!

Thomas was speaking again, slowly and very strangely. "Mary, you once said that just because your name was 'Mary' that didn't mean you could do...what 'that other Mary' did....But-could-it-mean-that-now...?"

Mary completely lost her composure. "Oh, for heaven's *sake*, Thomas! No! *It wasn't God*. It was one of the roomers."

Thomas was quiet for awhile, then he said slowly and softly, "Yes, I was afraid that might happen some day....But it's still hard to believe it of you, Mary."

Mary was crying now, sobbing.

"Stop that, Mary." Thomas said it firmly, but not unkindly.

Mary spoke through her tears. "Thomas, if you want to be rid of me, I'm sure I could be taken care of. I haven't told my sister in Baltimore yet, but I'm sure she'd let me stay with her temporarily or even permanently. Doc Feldman won't do anything about taking the baby. He could get in trouble with the law, he says. And he says I'm not strong enough for an abortion, anyhow. So, I'll have to keep on carrying it and have it, I guess, but there are adoption agencies in Baltimore and...."

Thomas interrupted her. "Mary, there's something I have to tell you, too."

"What is it, Thomas?"

"They took the cast off my back yesterday, examined me, then put a new cast right back on. I didn't heal right. They're sending me home in a day or two. They can't do any more for me. They say I'll never be able to walk straight or work on the water ever again. Mary, I need you now, no matter what you've done, and whether you realize it nor not, you need me, too. *Don't go to Baltimore*."

Again there was a long silence.

"How far are you along, Mary?"

"About three months."

"And I've been here in the hospital longer than that. But people on Bell's Island never could count, so to 'the eyes of the world', Mary, the child will be mine."

"Thomas, you are too kind." Mary was crying softly.

"I guess it's the least I can do now, Mary. I guess I could have been a different kind of husband to you, but I never thought you really wanted that. You always seemed so much *a nice woman*. And the Bible says we're supposed to be putting off our carnal natures, anyway. I take the Bible seriously. And somehow I'd always thought you'd like to go on that upward path with me. But I guess I just didn't understand you, Mary."

"Nor I you, Thomas."

But there was the sound of relief in Mary's voice. And Camellia was relieved, too, that her father had not sent her mother away from the home. But it had not fully hit Camellia yet what Thomas had said about not being able to work on the water ever again.

After the ordeal of confronting Thomas was over, Mary and Camellia returned to the freight boat. They didn't even take time to go see Bessie Travis. Camellia was feeling back to her old self again, and by now she was hungry as a wolf. She saw a plateful of baked yams, still hot and in their skins, in the boat's wheelhouse. She guessed they were for the captain, but asked him if she could have some for herself and Mary. Before the captain could answer, Camellia had grabbed two of them and peeled one and started to eat it.

The captain said, "How in hell ken yer eat a yam pertater on yer raw stummick?" He had been only too aware of Camellia's condition earlier in the day, as the boat came down the sound.

She answered him by saying, "Well, you see these still have the skins on them," which made no sense at all because she'd peeled the one she was eating. But she was so happy now, she didn't even know what she was saying. Thomas had not turned Mary out of their home in spite of her awful mistake, and Camellia's heart was singing.

She said to the captain, "I'm going to take this other yam to Mama." She went out of the wheelhouse fairly dancing even though the freight boat was lurching around in the now very choppy waters of the Anderson Sound.

Camellia found Mary sitting off to herself in the passengers' section with "the puke pail" not too far away. Without thinking about what her mother's condition might be, Camellia stepped up beside her and said, "Want a nice yam, Mama?"

Mary took one look at that huge, steamy, stinky, green-orange thing and turned just about the same color. "Jesus save us, Camellia! Get that goddam potato out from under my nose!"

It was not an ordinary thing to hear Mary swear like that. But his was no ordinary day.

"Okay Mama," Camellia said. And she ate the second yam herself!

As soon as they got back to Bell's Island and the Tu-Rest Home, Mary sent Camellia out back to kill a chicken to cook for their supper. Camellia was still trying to hold onto some refrains that had come to her mind on the boat—happy music for a change this time—and she wanted to write it all down. She was trying to keep it separated in her head from the usual Bell's Island cacophony of whirring boat propellers, gasoline engines firing up, dockmen yelling to each other, the gangs of shrieking sea gulls over head, and Mary's ever-squawking chickens and yapping beagles.

Camellia went to the chicken yard and grabbed the first chicken she got her hands on, forgetting all about the one being purified off to one side in its own little coop.

She was about to come down on the chicken's neck with the hatchet when somebody yelled out, "Camellia, DON'T! You've got the wrong chicken!"

"Grandpaw!" Camellia dropped the hatchet and let go of the chicken. It ran off from her, heading for the thicket. Grandpaw made a dive and almost slid completely out of his overalls three sizes too big for him, but he caught the chicken and put it back in the chicken yard.

"All chickens look alike to me, Grandpaw. Oh, I know, I should have gotten that one." Camellia pointed to a lone chicken clucking happily away in its own private death row cell.

Grandpaw said, "They make better meat when they ain't been eatin' the rest of 'em's shit a few days before you kill them."

"*I* know that," Camellia fumed. "I just overlooked it, that's all." She went to the coop where the one being purified was, but it didn't seem very pure in there to her. She was sliding her hand around in that slippery mess, trying to catch hold of the chicken as she yelled to Grandpaw, "I guess it doesn't matter if they've been eating their own, huh?"

"That's the way life is, darling," said the Wise Old Fool. "Our own shit never bothers us, it's only other people's."

How true, Camellia was thinking. Her own *sin* with Ralph Drummond didn't bother her, but her mother's *sin* with that roomer certainly was bothering her. Why should she compose even the happy music?" The full ramifications of that visit to the hospital were just now beginning to get through to her. She'd never get to college now, not even to stinky little Halburg Normal School to learn to be a music *teacher*, much less to the conservatory or to The Met. With her mother's baby coming and her father's back not healed right, who was going to support the family?

Camellia grabbed hold of that purified chicken by the neck, almost as though it were Mary, but before she could get the pleasure of decapitating it herself, Grandpaw had taken it from her and with a flash of his hunting knife, head and body parted company.

"My knife gives a cleaner cut," Grandpaw explained as they watched the headless chicken flop all over the back yard in bloody spurts. Grandpaw tossed the severed head with its dead and staring eyes into the beagles' pen and nearly caused a fight in there as to which dog was going to get it and eat it.

"Life," Camellia muttered. With a sigh, she walked to the end of the yard and picked up the dead lump of a chicken, bringing it back to a small wash tub where she poured a kettle of steaming water over it.

Grandpaw grinned and said, "Been to Gainsbiddle today, ain't you?"

"Uh huh."

"How's your Papa?"

"About the same." Camellia didn't want to have to talk about her father's back and certainly not about what Mary had told him, but Grandpaw persisted.

"Your Mama told him yet?"

"Told him what?"

"Darling, everybody on Bell's Island knows your Mama is goin' to have a baby. Why else is she goin' around all the time wearin' a coat when this is the warmest December on record? But the big news is that the baby ain't even Thomas'!"

"Damn people," Camellia exclaimed out loud. And she was thinking *Damn Snipsey, too*—wait until she got a hold of her!

Grandpaw said, "You oughtn't cuss like that, darling. You're goin' to be a schoolteacher, ain't you? We island people like our teachers to be a cut above ourselves in character as well as brains."

"Well, you can't expect everything, not from me, you can't." Camellia fished the headless chicken out of the bloody water. "But once I learn to teach, I won't teach for very long. I've other things to do." She was still handing everybody The Line. But the thing she wanted most to do right now—after her mother—was to kill Snipsey. She chopped the dead chicken's feet off with the hatchet and gave the body a furious, but not a very thorough, de-feathering.

Grandpaw said, almost mockingly, "Still want to go to New York to sing?"

Camellia picked up the sorry-looking chicken and headed for the house, calling back over her shoulder to Grandpaw, "*Of course*, I still want to go to New York to sing."

"Think you're gonna make it?" Grandpaw called back. He spat tobacco juice on the ground at the same time as if to say, *We all doubt it*. And then he headed back across the shell road.

Damn him, too, Camellia was thinking.

When she went in with the chicken, she found Mary sitting in the kitchen, half asleep. That music was still persisting in Camellia's mind, but it was now mixed with sadder undertones. Yet she was still fascinated by it and wanted to write it down. But the chicken came first.

Then, since her mind was divided, she forgot to cut the chicken up and instead put it in the kettle whole. When the water started to boil, Mary gave a jump and came wide awake, crying out, "What's wrong with that chicken? *It smells*!"

"All chickens smell like that when they first start to boil," Camellia said, aping the Wise Old Fool's omniscient tone of voice. "You've just got a sensitive stomach today, Mama."

"It's not just my stomach, Camellia," Mary said. "Did-you-take-the-insides-out-of-that-chicken?"

"Of course I did....Well, I *think* I did....But maybe I didn't....And I don't believe I cut the chicken up, either."

"Oh, *Camellia*!"

"Mama, don't cry! I'll fix it. *I'll fix it*!" She scooped the chicken out of the kettle and started the eviscerating job, promptly getting burned by the scalding flesh. But this time instead of merely saying damn either aloud or to herself, another form a craziness took over. "Mama," she said, "did you ever try to write your name with chicken guts?" She was hauling the pale white stringy intestines out of the chicken and onto a piece of newspaper, trying to loop them around and around into Old English Script.

"Camellia!" Mary whimpered.

But Camellia went on jabbering and playing with the chicken entrails. "Writing your name in chicken guts is just about as tricky as Amanda's boys trying to piss their names in the snow, don't you think so, Mama?"

Mary gathered up what little energy she had left at this point and came and stood in front of Camellia with a threatening look. "You'd better watch your language, young lady. You want people at Halburg Normal School to think you're *POOR WHITE TRASH FROM GAINSBIDDLE*?!"

Camellia threw a knife and the chicken guts down on the table. "There's not going to *be* any Halburg Normal School."

Mary shot Camellia an awful glance. "What do you mean, there's not going to be any Halburg Normal School? You've been accepted there for the winter term. I won't be leaving home myself now and your Papa will be coming home, too. So why, why do you say no Halburg Normal School? Don't tell me you're pregnant, too? You haven't started seeing that Ralph Drummond again, have you?"

"Oh, Mama, no! NO! None of that. But I overheard what Papa said in the hospital today. His back didn't heal right. He can't work anymore. What's going to happen to us? Where is the money coming from for us AND a baby?"

Mary hung her head.

Camellia went on. "Grandfather LeCates's creditors are still getting almost all the profits from the Tu-Rest Home here. And better that we'd never been allowed to live here and run it in the first place, considering the trouble it has got you into."

Mary was crying for all she was worth now. Camellia was wishing she wasn't feeling so mean and could be forgiving like her father. But for all her resentment, she still wanted to help and she said, "Mama, I'm going to forget about college and go to work in Gainsbiddle to see if I can help out here with expenses."

Mary's tears turned to helpless laughter. "Camellia, there's no work in Gainsbiddle for a young girl. There's hardly any work for a man. Don't you read the newspapers? Aren't you aware of the terrible times in our nation?"

"Yes," said Camellia. "But remember that time recently we were at Bessie Travis's and what she said about some girl who was going to quit her job at the drugstore soon. Maybe I could get that job. Somebody from Bell's Island goes to Gainsbiddle every morning by boat and I could go with them, and somebody is always coming back every evening and I could come back with them and be home every night with you and Papa and could cook your next day's meals and all...."

"Camellia, don't go to Gainsbiddle. It's an awful place."

"Well, I agree. It *is* awful. But you've always said I should see the good in everybody, in everything, in every place—even Gainsbiddle. After all, Gainsbiddlers are only just poor—like Bell's Islanders."

Camellia had the chicken all cut up now and Mary was speaking again. "Gainsbiddlers are poor and, with but a few exceptions like Norman and Bessie, they are also wicked. But then, come to think of it, I guess I am, too—poor *and* wicked."

Camellia was trying to decide whether to agree with her mother's last statement or not when suddenly Mary squawked, "*Camellia*! Don't-put-that-chicken-back-in-*THE SAME FILTHY WATER FROM WHICH YOU JUST TOOK IT OUT*!"

But it was too late. Camellia's attention being everywhere but where it should have been, she had dropped the cut up chicken back into the same dirty water.

"*Lord*! *Will I ever get through this day*?!" Mary and Camellia cried out the exact same words at the same time.

Once again Camellia fished the chicken out of the dirty water, washed the pieces off, emptied the kettle, refilled it with fresh water, and everything was started anew.

With the chicken at last straightened out, Camellia went and sat down in an exhausted heap at the kitchen table with Mary.

Mary said, "Why don't you go practice your music? That always makes you feel better. The chicken will take care of itself now."

Practice her music? What was Camellia to say? She said nothing.

Mary sighed and said, "I know what you mean. You think it's no use. But, Camellia, don't go to Gainsbiddle looking for work. Go on to Halburg Normal School as you had planned. Stick with your music and your highest hopes for it. There'll be a break for you sooner or later."

Then it was as though Mary were turning things over in her mind, for she stopped talking abruptly. Camellia waited. Finally Mary said, "I'm not much of a believer in religion, Camellia, even though I've gone to the Bell's Island Methodist Church ever since I was a child and I've given it my best service in the choir, as soloist, and with the organ and piano.

"And I've tried to follow the church's moral teachings. I had never let a man even as much as touch me 'that way' until your Papa came along and not even him until we were duly married. What happened between me and that roomer was spawned by desperation, whether you want to believe it or not. I know I don't deserve much in the way of mercy, but nothing can make me believe that either you or your Papa should be punished, too, for what I have done. So, whether I believe in God or not, I do believe that a way will be provided for you, Camellia, a way for you and your music...."

Camellia looked at Mary for a long time, then said, "Sometimes I think you mean what you say, Mama, and then sometimes I'm no so sure. But I will go and practice the piano, now, if that will make you happy. I promise I will not give up my music entirely, but *I am going to Gainsbiddle to work*. I've made up my mind to that."

Camellia left the kitchen and went to the music room and diddled a while with the piano. She wrote down some of what had come to her on the boat, but she couldn't concentrate. She couldn't get her mind off the things Grandpaw had said. She had a score to settle with Snipsey....

When Camellia found Snipsey in the Cartwright's backyard, she jumped alongside her and whispered, "Remember, I told you I'd beat the shit out of you if you told? Well...I'm here to do just that."

Snipsey looked terrified, but she didn't run. She said, "Camellia, please listen before you start beatin' on me. My daddy did enough of that the day of your fire over there at the Tu-Rest Home."

"Simon beat you. Why?"

"He asked be what had happened over there that day an' I said, 'Mary's stew pot caught on fire'. That was what she told me to say, remember? or something like that. But I got to gigglin' when I said it because you could take it another way....And rememberin' the way your mother looked, standin' there with that roomer....Hehehehe! But Daddy thought I was being snotty an' laughin' at him an' he started slappin' me across the mouth an' said, 'Don't you be smart with me, girl! You were over there messin' 'round with one of them roomers'.

"An' I said, 'No, Daddy. Honest, I wasn't.' Then he hit me again an' he said, 'Your mother said she saw you come runnin' outten that Tu-Rest Home like you was crazy an' Camellia was runnin' right after you, a-hollerin' at you. An' before that, one of them roomers come runnin' outten there half-naked an' tryin' to get his pants buttoned up. Now, which one of you was it with that man? You or Camellia?'

"An' I said, 'No! Neither one of us!' And Daddy hit me again an' said, 'You tell me the truth'. Camellia, I was tastin' that blood all inside my mouth an' I was scared he'd keep on hittin' me, so I said, 'Don't hit me no more, Daddy. I'll tell you the truth: It was *Mary* with that man'. An' then I had to tell Daddy what we done seen that day, you an' me....I couldn't help it, Camellia, honest, I couldn't...."

Camellia let Snipsey go. Snipsey had been chastised enough. They all had. But it was only the beginning....

Chapter Four

Thomas Stephens had little reason to feel *Joy to the World.*

This Christmas of 1932 meant a broken back that had healed wrong, a wife who had cuckolded him and gotten herself pregnant, and now a daughter who was about to go into the big, wide, wicked world of Gainsbiddle to look for work to support the family.

Thomas was out of the hospital and back home on Bell's Island. He could walk fairly well with the new cast on and with assistance, but most of his time he spent sleeping. On Christmas Eve he wouldn't even go to the Bell's Island Methodist Church to hear Camellia sing her choir part in *The Messiah.*

But Thomas need not have worried about Camellia and Gainsbiddle. She was not exactly going forth as an unprepared novice. Just a month short of seventeen years old, she had already known both high affluence and deep poverty. She had learned how to drink, gamble, and cast "gypsy spells." If the occasion warranted it, she could cuss as good as any Bell's Islander, even if she did still do it with the *educated* British accent. She knew what death and grief and fear were. She had witnessed her mother in an illicit sexual union with a stranger. And she knew what it was like herself to lay in the arms of a lover.

She was built "like a brick shithouse" and at the same time had the graceful bearing of a fashion model. She had magnificent long black hair, tawny skin, and compelling black eyes that could look your soul inside out. And she had a mezzo-soprano voice that, whether singing or speaking, could charm a rattlesnake. Physically, she had the strength of a draft horse and mentally, the courage of a lion.

The aptitude for "gypsy magic" with which she'd been born and which had been further honed under the tutelage of Grandpaw Azariah helped a heap, too.

On her first day alone in Gainsbiddle, before she'd even completed the short walk from the dock to Middleton's drugstore, she'd already seen a half dozen white boys chasing a bevy of Negro girls up and down the marsh; three pairs of mating dogs strung together in the middle of the road, blocking traffic; two drunks thrown out of a saloon followed by a rattle of gunshot; a fight between a peddler with a wooden leg and a woman who claimed he had shortchanged her; and a monstrous fire deliberately set in a trash wagon by a bunch of children with matches and coal oil.

It was just a typical Gainsbiddle morning, and Camellia had determined ahead of time she was not going to let anything rattle her, so she was not at all surprised when she landed that drugstore clerk job even though there were six other girls trying for it.

Mary seemed pleased enough when Camellia got home to the island that evening, but she did say, "You didn't use 'gypsy magic' on that druggist to get your job, did you?"

Camellia said, "All Grandpaw ever told me was 'Don't ever do evil with what I've taught you'. Getting a job to help my family and my music isn't evil, is it?"

Mary had to admit that no, perhaps it wasn't evil. But Camellia could see her father silently shaking his head. And it wasn't too long before she was indeed using that "gypsy magic" in a more questionable venture.

Camellia could tell that the drugstore cowboys that hung around Middleton's soda fountain were out for "only-one-thing" when they joshed around with her and the other girl clerks. So Camellia turned her usual cold fish treatment on them.

Then one day she heard one of them—Wylie Hovey—bragging about his gambling and lottery winnings. It occurred to Camellia that here might be an opportunity for her to make extra money. Though the numbers games were probably rigged, she still had the feeling she would be able to mentally *see* which numbers would win each week.

She waited for an opportunity, then got Wylie Hovey off to himself. She maneuvered him around, trying to get him to ask her for a date. Then, when he did, she stalled him off, playing him like a fish on a line. But she did act as though she would like for him to walk her to Bessie Travis's that Saturday after she got off work. No boat was going back to Bell's Island that late or car going by way of the county road, so she always stayed Saturday nights at the Travises.

That Saturday night Camellia had her pay envelope with her and, acting like it was all a big joke, she asked Wylie if he would take a dollar and place it on her number in the Gainsbiddle lottery the next week. Since no woman could do that alone for herself in a place like Gainsbiddle, she needed a *bookie*.

Wylie agreed, and as they chatted on, Camellia discerned that this greasy-haired, semi-illiterate Gainsbiddle wharf rat fancied himself somewhat of a comedian. So she made out to him like she thought he was just about the most comical person she'd ever known and that he could make her laugh when none of the other fellows hanging around the drugstore could.

Camellia could tell Wylie was beginning to think she was something great, so she turned on her best mixture of refinement AND sensuality and talked to him "real educated, real citified" and laughed herself silly at his jokes. Before too many weeks went by, there wasn't a thing he wouldn't do for her.

When she won on her first attempt at the lottery, she made a big show of laughing and joking to him about it, saying how much fun it had been and would he place a bet for her again, if she paid him a certain percentage in case she won again? In short order they had quite a little business going.

As the spring of 1933 came on, Camellia was earning twice as much from the lottery and various other gambling opportunities for which Wylie served as her *bookie,* as she was from roasting peanuts and making double banana splits in Middleton's drugstore. And she was sending modest, but regular deposits to that nest egg saving account in Baltimore that Mary and Aunt Lizbeth had opened for her a couple of years before.

But gambling was no get-rich-quick deal. Camellia did not want to arouse Wylie's or anybody's suspicions, so she had to hold herself in check. There was a great temptation at times to bet on a large jackpot when she *knew* intuitively that her number was *the one.* Instead she would sometimes mentally suggest that number to Wylie for him to play. Then, if he would voice it back to her and try to get her to play it, she didn't agree and instead let him win. He would laugh afterwards and say, "Well, I told you which number, but you wouldn't listen to me." Then Camellia would say, "Oh, dear! You are always right, and I'm so foolish, but I do it only for fun, you know, and to be with you."

Nevertheless, she let herself win often enough that Wylie could get his cuts, too, and make the whole thing worth his trouble.

Only too soon the time came that Wylie was expecting more from Camellia than just percentages on her winnings. His attention to her had gone from just holding hands as they walked to Bessie Travis's on a Saturday night, to arms about her waist, to his lips pressed hard against hers, to his hands slipping around and up and down into places on her that they had no business being.

Again, when danger seemed too near, Camellia resorted to "gypsy magic." And Wylie, no doubt, experienced a sudden lowering of spirits as well as other items of his anatomy.

Bessie Travis eventually called Camellia on the carpet over Wylie Hovey. Bessie said, "Camellia, it's none of my business, I guess, but I don't think your Mama would think too much of it if she knew you were hanging around with a man like Wylie Hovey."

"Well, *at least I know his name,*" Camellia said viciously. "And I'm not doing what Mama did anyhow."

Bessie looked at her and said, "You've still got it in for your mother, haven't you?"

Camellia didn't comment on that, but she did say, "I only let Wylie walk me home to keep the others away. I can handle him, if I have to." She wondered, though, just how much longer it would be before "gypsy magic" might have to step aside in favor of the old *knee in the groin.*

Bessie surveyed Camellia's current strength and voluptuousness and said, "Yes, I believe you could. And I bet you would make some man a good wife some day and some kids a good mother. That is, if you would want that sort of thing."

"I've got other things on my mind, Miss Bessie."

"Yes, I know you have, Camellia. And one day I know you're going to make it."

But before Camellia was going to "make it" anywhere, she became a sister—or more correctly, a *half*-sister. In mid-June 1933, as she had done before in so many of her mother's crises, she stood dutifully beside Mary in the Gainsbiddle hospital in Thomas's absence. Thomas, still ailing, remained at home on Bell's Island. Doc Feldman, fearing complications, had not tried to deliver Mary's baby himself, but had sent her to a surgeon colleague at the Gainsbiddle hospital.

After a night of terribly harsh labor, the surgeon finally had to do a high forceps job on Mary and dragged out of her what was surely the ugliest, screamingest, stinkingest piece of ill-conceived humanity that had ever gotten into the womb of woman. And the thing had *red hair*!

When the nurse brought the baby boy to Mary and she saw he was redheaded, she tried to cry. Camellia knew that crying was a little trick her mother had always been very good at when both reason and humor failed her. But this time Mary was so exhausted she could only gasp.

"Camellia, (gasp!)...nobody...on either side of (gasp)...your Papa's family...or (gasp!) mine had ever had...(gasp!) red hair. What—will—people—THINK!?"

"BUGGER WHAT PEOPLE THINK, MAMA!" Camellia yelled, trying to be heard above the squawking of the baby. She was feeling both cross and coarse. "Tell everybody he's a throwback. That's what you tell out-of-town tourists when you try to sell them an inferior beagle that looks like a Chihuahua. Tell everybody your baby is a throwback to some great Celtic sailor-warrior in Papa's pirate ancestry...like Eric the Red, maybe."

"Camellia," Mary said weakly. "Eric the Red was a Norseman. Didn't you learn *anything* in school?"

Thomas had indicated no preference of a name for "his" child-to-be, so several weeks before going to the hospital, Mary had Camellia haul out the huge dictionary and open it to the section on masculine and feminine first names. Mary chose a page at random in each group, flipped a toothpick down on the page, and the name the sharp end pointed nearest to she wrote down on a piece of paper.

And so it was that Mary's baby—sired anonymously, named by the flip of a toothpick, destined for trouble, and according to many on Bell's island, the very incarnation of the devil himself—became officially Roger LeCates Stephens.

Thomas was true to his promise to Mary to accept the child as his own ("in the eyes of the world," at least). He even passed out cigars and was telling everybody he'd finally gotten a son to carry on the Stephens name. (As if he didn't have enough Stephens nephews to do that!) Thomas was winking his eye mischievously and saying to everybody, "I caught Mary 'on the change'!"

Well, Mary wasn't even "on the change." Thomas was silly as usual when it came to sex, and he overdid his act but Camellia noticed that people just smiled and humored him. She guessed that they thought Thomas had taken enough lickings in the past year or so, what with his hurricane-incurred injuries and his broken back that hadn't healed right, so they were not about to *rub his nose in it*—this new thing, too, this "indiscretion" of Mary's, as Thomas himself had now taken to calling her encounter with the roomer and its results.

In the meantime, Camellia, after becoming a *half*-sister, had her own dilemma with Wylie Hovey still waiting for her: How to keep him from doing what he wanted to do with her and still retain him as her *bookie*.

Toward the end of summer of 1933, fate solved the problem for her. She had gone home to Bell's island as usual one Friday night. And that was the night of The Great Gainsbiddle Fire.

The old waterfront town—about half of it—including many of the docks and seafood places, and almost all of the businesses and homes in the lower end of town, including Middleton's drugstore, went up in flames. It was one of those "Mrs. O'Leary's cow" things: Somebody had stumbled in the semi-dark, knocked over a lighted candle onto some flimsy window curtains, and it was "kitty bar the door" for the next three days.

Fire companies from all the nearby counties and towns came and did what they could but their efforts were largely ineffective. The wind changed three times that first night and the wooden construction of the densely packed together old businesses and tenements caused them to go up like paper, flinging sparks into other residential areas of town, and taking away people's homes right and left. Norman and Bessie Travis's home, though right near the thick of it, was somehow miraculously spared.

The fire light was so intense it was seen low in the southeastern sky as far away as Baltimore and caused Mary's sister, Elizabeth St. George, to wire and ask: "Are you folk all right? What is happening down there on the shore?"

And Mary had wired back, "Oh, nothing much. Just Gainsbiddle burning."

Nothing much? Just Gainsbiddle burning? Gainsbiddlers didn't exactly think of it as *nothing much*. And neither did Camellia when she realized Middleton's drugstore, her job, and her last pay envelope with its cash had all gone up in smoke.

So Camellia was out of work and she could no longer get that *extra income*, either. But she had avoided the showdown with Wylie Hovey. She never saw him again after that.

However once again the Thomas Stephens family was without a source of income. What was coming in from the Tu-Rest Home was practically nothing, and considering what it now symbolized to them, Mary was all for closing it up. Nevertheless it was still their home and they had been paying a little to the LeCates creditors every now and then toward eventually owning it.

Mary had long since given up her special delight—her little Bell's Island Library—for lack of funds to pay the rent. The community had never had any interest in it anyway. Mary stored the books at the Tu-Rest Home and the little library was boarded up. It looked as forlorn as the old Bell's Island Inn, which also had never been sold, rented, or re-opened. It was just a bad time all around for everybody during those Depression years.

Camellia even had to draw out most of the money from her nest egg Baltimore savings account to help pay expenses at home. That it had so much in it amazed Mary, but Camellia managed not to have to admit where most of it had come from by suggesting that maybe Aunt Lizbeth had been adding to it from time to time.

Much of the family expenses were doctor's bills for the baby, Roger. Doc Feldman told Camellia and Mary there was nothing seriously wrong with him. Still and all, the redheaded terror was awake and trying to fight at everything within his grasp more than he ever seemed to be asleep. He was sick and screaming almost all the time.

Doc was constantly changing his formula, and still he couldn't digest anything. Mary herself had no milk. She hardly had any blood, except what ponded up in her stomach ulcer all too often.

So Camellia ended up with the main burden of Roger. It was Camellia who rolled him out in the baby buggy. It was Camellia who washed and hung out his diapers. It was Camellia who bought milk for him at the store and prepared his formula. It was Camellia who took him to Doc Feldman's office.

Some folks on the island, seeing Camellia instead of Mary with Roger all the time, started whispering that Camellia was Roger's real mother and the family was passing him off as the new baby brother. "After all," so went the gossip, "Camellia had been in Gainsbiddle working, hadn't she? And girls who go to *Gainsbiddle* to work always wind up pregnant!" The fact that Camellia hadn't gone to work in Gainsbiddle until nearly January 1933 and Roger was born in June of the same year—a six-months baby, yet!—didn't seem to disturb these people's conclusions one little bit.

As if she wasn't stone deaf anyhow from Roger's yellings, Camellia turned a deaf ear to all the loose talk, most of it relayed to her by Snipsey. Snipsey often helped Camellia with Roger, but on those trips to Doc Feldman's office, Camellia was on her own.

Going to Doc's office was enough of an annoyance in itself. On the wall of his examining room there was an ornately engraved plaque which read:

The Definition of a Woman
A woman is an animal
that
urinates once a day
defecates once a week
menstruates once a month
parturiates once a year
and
FORNICATES ALL THE TIME

Camellia had a choice. She could look at that plaque and get mad. Or she could look at Roger and get mad. On one occasion she looked at Roger and asked Doc Feldman, "What is the matter with this baby, anyway? He never stops crying and fighting at everything. He won't sleep and he keeps boiling over out of both ends faster'n I can clean him up. I know you are going to say he's only nervous, but isn't there something you can do for him, Doc? Is he going to turn out, like everybody says, to be one of those 'crazy kids' that women have when they 'get caught on the change'?"

Doc said, "Your mother *didn't* get 'caught on the change'. How did that notion get around?"

"Oh, from Papa's silly talk, I guess."

Doc smiled. "Your Papa overdoes his playacting, Camellia. He was unintentionally real comical when I told him that your Mama shouldn't have any more children because this one tore her up inside for good. Your Papa got this real serious look on his face and said, 'Mary and I promise that we won't "be naughty" anymore'. Your Papa is quite a card, isn't he, Camellia?"

Camellia made no comment.

Doc babbled on. "Your Papa thinks he has to maintain his pretense even in front of me, his doctor. I started to offer him some sample condoms to go along with my warning about 'no more children', but I figured that would be an insult to his religious beliefs about self-control."

Camellia grimly ignored Doc Feldman's jabber. He wasn't telling her anything she hadn't already known or surmised from things Mary had said all along, but she still didn't like Doc rubbing it in about her father.

Doc was giving Roger an overall exam in spite of all the squirming, squalling, kicking, sputtering, and bubbling he was doing. Camellia said, "Honestly, Doc, what's wrong with him? He doesn't seem right to me. You sure he hasn't swallowed a pin or something? And he smells so bad all the time. I don't care how much Snipsey and I scrub and clean him up, he still smells. What's wrong the him, Doc? Something must be."

Doc only laughed and said, "I've yet to see a sweet baby; I don't care what your poets and songwriters say. But this Roger here—I think the trouble is that your mama doesn't love him....She hates him, in fact. And he's reacting to that. Hate breeds hate, you know. Roger is playing a part; that is, he is what the old gypsy folks used to call 'the incarnation of the devil'."

"My! That's a terrible label—even for this child," Camellia said in protest.

Again Doc smiled and said, "Did you ever hear your Grandpaw Azariah speak of the Legend of Boro?"

Camellia thought for awhile, then said, "Wasn't Boro the gypsy boy that my great-grandmother Kitty Corrigan lived with and had lots of children by before she walked out on him at the old tavern and came back on the island and legally married George Stephens who was Grandpaw's father?"

"That's right," said Doc. "And remember that part of the legend that says Boro vowed to kill Kitty for leaving him, vowed to kill Kitty and George Stephens and all their children?"

"Yes, I remember. But Boro never got around to killing anybody."

"Right!" said Doc. "Even Eastern Shore *gypsies* are lazy."

Camellia sniffed. She was thinking, *Yes, this is Doc, the ex-Balto moron, talking.* So she shook on a few more grains of salt. To Doc she said, "But what's this gypsy stuff got to do with the baby here? He's no gypsy. He's not even a Stephens."

"It's like this, Camellia," Doc said. "Boro's curse on Kitty Corrigan and her progeny still holds. Boro can come back in a new life whenever he wants to and do what he didn't get around to doing when he was alive before. He can terrorize any of those Kitty and George Stephens descendants still left."

"Roger is Boro?!" Camellia exclaimed. "A redheaded gypsy? And he's come to kill Grandpaw Azariah and Papa and me, not to mention Mama, whom he's almost killed a'ready, anyhow?"

"No, no, Roger isn't Boro exactly. I don't believe the *bodily* incarnation mentioned in the legend. But Roger could be the incarnation of the *influence* of Boro's original evil intention. In this sense Roger may indeed have 'come to kill you', as the expression goes. When an evil vow or curse is made and not either carried out or annulled, the thought of it remains and it will eventually come out somewhere in the family descendants wherever the mental atmosphere is right for it to germinate.

"It could have happened in Amos's family, right where Azariah is still living, or in Charlie's family or in Amanda's. But apparently their mental atmosphere has been somewhat different than in your family, Camellia. All the other Stephenses, mean as they are, may be something like the publicans and harlots that Jesus talked about when he said those would get into heaven before the priests and elders did. The priests and elders being the so-called 'better' people of the world who do everything according to the book...like your Papa does."

Camellia looked at Doc angrily and said, "Well, nobody has tried harder to live a decent life than Papa. And even though I still find it hard to forgive or excuse Mama, I believe she did her damnedest to keep from having something happen like what did happen to her, so how can you imply that our family's 'mental atmosphere', as you call it, is somehow inferior to the other Stephens's?"

Doc Feldman said, "I am only suggesting answers to your original question 'What is wrong with Roger?'. If someone in your family is racked with guilt over something—in this case, your mother because of what she did with that roomer—then that is a very ripe mental atmosphere in which the devil can set himself down."

"But why must the innocent suffer?" Camellia demanded. "Papa doesn't deserve this. Nor do I. Why is Mama's sin backing up on us? I think she's got it in her mind to dump most of the responsibility of this baby on me—to both raise and support him. I have planned three times to go either to teacher's college or the conservatory and something has happened in the family each time to prevent me. *Why must the innocent suffer, Doc?"*

Doc would only give a "Who knows?" shrug.

Camellia thought for a moment, then said, "You said something about if the curse is not annulled....Can anything be done to annul it *now*?"

Doc smiled mischievously and said, "I've been told there is only one thing that can completely annul evil and that is love. You see this baby here? Love him. LOVE HIM!"

Just then Roger gave an ear-splitting scream that would curl the hair on a cucumber and he let go both ends, inundating the examining table and filling Doc's office with an aroma "strooong enough to gag a maggot."

Camellia screamed at Doc. "Love him? Love *that*? Doc, you're crazy! I don't believe what you say about love and gypsy's curses and influences and Boro and all the stuff you've been talking about. I believe this child is really sick and you just don't know what to do for him. I believe you make up all these crazy stories because you are so bored with your life on Bell's Island that you have to do something to entertain yourself. You're nothing but a bum ex-Baltimore doctor that we islanders have to put up with because we're too poor to afford a decent one. And you're nothing but a no-good Jew who sits Sunday after Sunday in our Christian Methodist Church, silently mocking everybody and everything you see and hear. If anybody on Bell's Island is the incarnation of the devil, I believe it's YOU, Doc Feldman!"

Doc roared with laughter. Camellia saw nothing to laugh at and figured that by her disrespectful outburst she had merely given Doc Feldman one more reason to believe all Bell's Islanders were crazy.

When Roger was about four months old, Thomas heard that an evangelist, a "healer," was in the Gainsbiddle area, holding revivals at the Holy Roller Church near where Bessie and Norman Travis lived.

As Camellia and her parents were sitting around at the Tu-Rest Home one evening, Thomas said, "I want to go to those services in Gainsbiddle where that healer is preaching. I think he can heal my back. Will you go with me, Mary?"

Mary answered downright disgustedly, "Oh, *Thom-as*! You never go to our own church any more. Do you realize about which church it is in Gainsbiddle that you are talking?"

Thomas said, "I don't know exactly. It's one of them."

Camellia marveled at how even-keeled her father could be at times once he'd made his mind up about something.

Mary said, "It's that Holy Roller church."

"So?"

"Thomas, do you realize what kind of people go to that church?"

"I don't know. Sick people, I guess, if a healer is there."

Mary said, "Sick-in-the-head people. The church is not too far from Bessie and Norman's house—it's in an old auto repair garage. Bessie says she can hear them in there screaming half the night. They holler and faint and roll all around on the floor and sometimes mess on themselves and foam at the mouth and God only know what all."

Thomas didn't say anything to that. Then after a bit of silence, he said, quiet-like but with authority, "Mary, I want to go to those services. You will go with me?" It was more of a command than a question. Mary didn't answer. Camellia remembered that Ephesians 5:22 had been one of the places Thomas had marked in his Bible along with all his favorite anti-sex passages. It read, "Wives, submit yourselves unto your husbands, as unto the Lord."

It was doctrine that was still taught and obeyed on Bell's Island, and Camellia was not surprised when her mother said, "Yes, Thomas, I will go with you."

Camellia decided to go with them the first evening or so because Mary seemed so apprehensive about going into a place like that. They left Roger in the care of Snipsey who came over to the Tu-Rest Home to be there along with Aunt Sairy Middleton who was taking care of the house in their absence.

They put up at the Travises and that evening after the big supper that Bessie had for them, they started out toward the Holy Roller Church.

Mary had hold of Thomas's arm as she had always done in public during their married life, and as usual she leaned forward a bit and sideways to accommodate her taller height to him. Camellia found it hard to decide who was leaning on whom. Thomas could walk, but he moved with a stiff gait because of the cast on his back, and he looked so awkward. Camellia thought her father was in pain a good bit of the time, too, but he never complained.

So, there they were—Mary "Beanpole" and "Pumpkin" Stephens—sojourners in the rough, tough community of Gainsbiddle, which had still not cleaned itself up after The Great Fire and was stinking to high heaven amid the tide-soaked rubble. Two pilgrims, arm in arm, lurching and limping along a dirt road that was full of cinders and coal dust from the nearby railroad tracks, pressing on toward a ramshackle, unpainted hulk of a building on the edge of the marsh.

Camellia was saddened at this caricature of the once hale and hearty young couple of nearly twenty years before who had set out similarly on a Sunday evening for their first date, attending a service together at the Bell's Island Methodist Church.

Camellia knew her mother was feeling poorly, but she was thinking if Mary had even a smidgen of the faith that Thomas had, she might have been less uncomfortable and apprehensive. Also if Mary had more of Thomas's faith all along and if Thomas had more of Mary's sense of humor, they might have made a better-matched couple. But custom-made couples didn't seem to be in God's plan. Camellia toyed with the picture of God dropping a whole bunch of jigsaw pieces from separate boxes onto the earth, scrambling them all together, and then making couples out of random pickings.

But her little reverie was cut short as they entered the Holy Roller Church. It was steaming AND stinking in that terribly overheated dark barn of a place. And the people....Ugh! The women all wore drab, shapeless, more or less unclean dresses with wide skirts that went down to their shoe tops. Their sleeves were baggy, went clear down to their wrists, and were held in place with tight elastic. Their necklines were tight up under their chins. They had hairdos pulled back in buns and almost hidden by hats that looked like upside down pans.

The men wore heavy baggy trousers with dirty white shirts collared tight up under their chins and sleeved down to their wrists, with badly fitting suit-type jackets over their shirts.

With that sort of clothing it was little wonder either men or women wanted to take it all off and put it all back on very often in order to bathe and get rid of their smell.

Music, such as Camellia and Mary knew it, was no part of this congregation. Instead there was a sort of buzz-like moaning going on continually and this became almost deafening as the service started. The moaning was accompanied by a constant jingling of tambourines which every other person seemed to have.

Up on a platform in front of the rows of wooden benches was as pulpit of sorts with two people sitting up there that faintly resembled a man and a woman. They were both dressed in dirty whitish clothing and for a moment there Camellia thought she was seeing two ghosts.

There was a film of coal oil fumes coming from several big stoves in the huge room and the fumes were mixing with a conglomerate body odor so thick you could cut it.

Camellia suddenly recognized the woman up front on the platform as the one who had once been pointed out to her while at Middleton's drugstore as the leader of the Holy Roller Church in Gainsbiddle. She was called "Glory Anna God's Hosanna." She was an odd-looking critter with a grayish-pink face. It was said she was baldheaded and that was why she always wore her pan-like hat so far down on the back of her neck. She even had that hat on in the pulpit!

The man sitting beside "Glory Anna God's Hosanna" was the healer-evangelist and he was a fat, beefy-looking character. He kept clearing his throat and looking with shifty eyes at all the people jammed into that room.

The first part of the service was announced as "The Love Feast." Several helpers got up and moved to the platform. "Glory Anna God's Hosanna" started handing out long wads or loaves of what appeared to be half-baked dough or bread.

Camellia noticed a shudder go through Mary. Thomas looked at her in a bit of alarm and took her hand in his, held it tight, and smiled at her. Mary smiled back at him as if to say *I know it's right for me to be here with you, even if it kills me.*

The sight of the bread being handed out had excited the people, and the moaning-buzzing noise grew louder along with a low sobbing noise. Every now and then there was a shriek as somebody jumped up—leaped up straight into the air, it seemed—then fell back down and rolled to the floor writhing like a doubled-up sack of potatoes. And all the while there was that constant cricket-like jingling of the tambourines.

"Glory Anna God's Hosanna" had come down off the platform, and she and her helpers were handing out the loaves of bread. They would give a loaf to the first person at the beginning of each bench, and that person would grab it with sticky, filthy, sweaty hands, jam one end of it in the mouth, and viciously chew off a bite, then hand it to the next person who would do the same thing. As the loaf of bread moved along from person to person, it got shorter and shorter, but also sweatier, filthier, smellier, and slobberier.

Even Camellia was feeling sick, and she knew her mother surely must be. When "Glory Anna God's Hosanna" came to the bench where Thomas, Mary, and Camellia were sitting and opened her mouth in a dark toothless grin, then started a loaf of bread down the line, Camellia saw Mary suddenly clench hold of Thomas's knee. Mary croaked, "Thomas, I think I'm going to...!"

But she didn't! In fact, after a long moment of staring at the floor, with her hand clapped over her mouth, she suddenly looked up, smiled, and winked at Thomas. Camellia was congratulating herself on the quick use in her mother's behalf of one of the more positive aspects of "gypsy magic"—the mental healing touch. Only that was *not* what had brought Mary about, as Camellia was to learn a bit later when they got back to Bessie and Norman's.

In the meantime, the saliva-slippery loaf of bread had gone on by Thomas, Mary, and Camellia as they had each quickly shunted it on down the line without even as much as making a pretense of trying to partake of it.

The second part of the service featured the evangelist and his healings. Even though Thomas was not one of the ones who were healed that time around, neither he nor Mary seemed discouraged as they walked back to Bessie and Norman's several hours later.

Camellia listened with a certain amount of wonderment as Mary told Bessie what had—or had not quite—happened to her in that horrid old building.

Mary said, "It was so sickening in that place I was just about as close as you can get to depositing on that greasy concrete floor a used version of that wonderful supper you had for us, when something under the bench in front of me caught my eye. Bessie, you won't believe this, but down under that bench there was a huge mouse—not a rat, but a mouse, a huge one—and it was bucktoothed, bright eyed, and smiling at me. Suddenly it was sitting up on its haunches just like a dog begging for a bone and while it was sitting up like that, it started washing its face just like a cat and it even winked its eye at me! I was so completely amused and fascinated by it that I didn't feel in the least bit sick any more, not even for the whole rest of the service!"

Well, Camellia had seen no mouse and she didn't think her father had, either. But if her mother saw a cartoon-like mouse, if that was the way God came to her, if that was the way even "gypsy magic" sometimes worked, then who was she to question? She only wished her father could get healed as readily.

However Camellia did feel that Mary was in good enough command of herself, now that she'd had "the vision of the mouse," to continue going to those Holy Roller services without Camellia having to be there with her. So the next day Camellia returned to Bell's Island on the freight boat.

Thomas and Mary remained in Gainsbiddle with the Travises nearly two weeks while the healer-evangelist services continued at the Gainsbiddle Holy Roller Church. Then one morning a message from Mary came to Camellia on Bell's Island via the captain on the freight boat. Mary and Thomas were coming home the next day and "with good news!"

The word spread quickly and the next morning nearly the entire population of Bell's Island was gathered at the docks, waiting.

Camellia and everyone saw the boat coming and Thomas and Mary were standing in the bow. When the boat was about one hundred yards from shore, they could see Thomas holding something up for everybody to see. It was that old plaster of Paris cast that had been on his back!

As if that wasn't enough proof of "good news," Thomas suddenly took off his coat and shirt, and picking up the cast again in one hand, he leaped into the water and swam the rest of the way to the dock, holding that cast victoriously aloft for everybody to see.

The crowd on the docks gave such a chorus of cheers that for once the Bell's Island sea gulls were out-voiced.

Many a tale has been told of cripples coming out of churches, throwing their crutches in the air, and leaping and praising God, but Thomas Stephens had come home to Bell's Island, swimming the last one hundred yards and holding his cast in the air.

As the boat caught up with Thomas and eased into the dock, Mary shouted to everybody above their cheers, *"Thomas is a new man today and Gainsbiddle and those Holy Rollers did it!"*

Thomas's healing was all anybody could talk about for weeks and weeks. And for once, nobody was making nasty cracks about Gainsbiddle!

Grandpaw Azariah and the brothers offered Thomas a job at the Stephens Marine Railway, a venture they had started after the hurricane when there had been such a demand for both new and re-built boats. Thomas accepted with misgivings at being a part of what he feared was just another crooked gypsy Stephens outfit, but he didn't have his job as mate on Norman Travis's work boat any more. Norman had been obliged to get someone else in Thomas's long and indefinite absence. But the friendship between the Travises and the Thomas Stephenses continued without interruption.

With her father well and working once again, Camellia wasted no time in re-enrolling as a day student at Halburg Normal School for the winter 1934 semester. A whole year had been lost and she would have preferred to have tried for a new scholarship at the conservatory in Baltimore, but Mary's postpartum crazies were still acting up. Camellia felt she had to stay as close by Bell's Island as possible.

Mary's attitude toward Roger didn't improve much. She tolerated him and took care of him after a fashion, but more often than not she left him unattended diaper-wise during the day for Camellia to have to struggle with when she came home late in the afternoon from Halburg.

"Why *don't* you clean him up?" Camellia often roared at her mother.

And Mary would say, "But he'd only just get that way again."

If Camellia fussed too much, Mary would start crying.

Thomas, who, like Doc Feldman, had been reminded of the Legend of Boro in all of this, *tried* to love Roger. In his own silly way he would cuddle the boy, play with him, talk to him. Usually all

Thomas got for his efforts as Roger began to grow, crawl, and talk was a good sound kick on the shins or a poke in the eye or a cuss word.

Mary often said, "Roger's only a baby; how can he have gotten such a rotten vocabulary *this soon*?"

Camellia offered, "Maybe from Snipsey when she used to help me take care of him."

But Thomas said, "The incarnation of the devil comes already equipped with a built-in supply of 'naughty words'. So Mary and I will just have to 'love the hell' out of him, that's all."

Camellia conceded that Mary outwardly tried to love Roger, but so often he recoiled from her as if she were a poisonous snake. Sometimes he couldn't even stand for her to even touch him and would scream and turn a bluish-red if she even approached him. Mary often said, "I do believe Roger is allergic to me."

There was one comical aspect to her parents' situation that Camellia learned about when Bessie Travis came to see her and Mary at the Tu-Rest Home one day.

Mary was saying, "Bessie, if I ever needed to be cured of lust, this baby has done it. I'm only too glad now for Thomas's religious beliefs or his beliefs about *nice women* not wanting it or whatever it is he's always been hung up on. For I no more want sex now, much less another baby, than I want a hole in the head."

"Your change of attitude must be pleasing to Thomas, eh?" said Bessie.

Mary paused a moment, then said, "Well, maybe yes; then again, maybe no. The darnedest thing happened the other night. I had gotten up half asleep and went to the bathroom in the dark. Without looking or even thinking, I automatically flipped up the tail of my nightgown and sat down—*on Thomas*!

"I thought he was in the bed! But he'd gone in there and fallen asleep on the toilet. '*Mary*!' he yelped. '*For God's sake*! *Get up*!'

"I nearly jumped halfway out of my skin. I said, '*Thomas!* What on earth are you doing in here?!'

"Bessie, if Thomas had half the sense God gave green apples, he could have thought of at least a dozen good excuses to a ridiculous-to-start-with question. Instead he made a clumsy attempt to tell me the truth....

"He said, 'Well, Mary, I...I....It's funny, I guess, seeings I've never been bothered much by...by...carnal lusts...or that is, whenever I have been...I've always been able to turn to God, but—but—ever...ever since that Gainsbiddle healing....'

"By now I was fully awake and it hit me of a sudden-like what Thomas was trying to say....Bessie, supposed I'd gone in that bathroom and sat down on Thomas *before* he'd finished handling his 'carnal lusts'?"

By now Bessie Travis was in stitches. "Well, Mary, I've always heard that when you get a Gainsbiddle Holy Roller healing, you get healed *all over*! Remember how you told everyone Thomas was a *new man*!"

Camellia waited to hear what her mother would say to that. Mary thought for awhile, then her momentary lighthearted mood got a touch of bitterness in it. She said, "You know, Bessie, it's a shame Thomas didn't get that broken back years ago...."

Camellia was hoping her parents would start being husband and wife again and chuck out Thomas's religion or whatever it was, but there was no real indication that this happened.

Camellia went through the two-year music teaching course at Halburg Normal School in only one and half years, getting her certificate in 1935. Once again Mary accused her of using "gypsy magic" on the instructors.

Camellia hadn't found it necessary to do that as she learned easily and quickly, could concentrate intensely in spite of the worries and distractions at home, and she was miles ahead of most of her instructors to start with.

But there was one instructor whom she learned was dabbling in horse race betting. In short order, Camellia made a new "Wylie Hovey" of him, and once again extra money was coming into her hands. When she slipped Mary a ten or twenty to help with the household or decked herself out in a new Sunday ensemble, she implied the money came from giving piano lessons to kids in the Royal Hall area, which she in fact did, but not to that great an extent. Mary, however, did not question Camellia. Mary had enough on her mind trying to resign herself to the fact of Roger, who remained an ever-present reminder of her past sin, her "indiscretion" as Thomas still maddeningly referred to it.

Had things been better at the Tu-Rest Home and had there not been a new position opening up in the Wintergreen County school system—that of itinerant music teacher for the elementary grades—Camellia might well have hied herself to Baltimore in search of a teaching job, as well as a voice teacher for herself which she so desperately needed. There she could more readily enter vocal competitions and auditions and maybe even get into the chorus of the Baltimore Civic Opera Company, with tries for The Met, even, not that far away.

She wavered back and forth so long about what to do she was just about to use her mother's method of making a decision—toss a toothpick!

Camellia decided to at least *apply* for the new county position, mentally reserving the right to refuse to take it if wisdom so dictated in the meantime.

When she was notified that she had been accepted for the position, once again she wavered and then once again went forward with it, but with essentially the same reservations, telling herself, "I can always quit it the very moment things get better at home and then go to where the grass is greener—on the other side of the bay or up to New York even." In her moments of fantasy she could see herself already floating up into the air over the island and going way up above the Wintergreen County marshes and on and on northward, ever northward.

The position as itinerant music teacher required that Camellia travel from elementary school to elementary school throughout the county, catching each one every week and giving each grade one to two hours of "music instruction," which mostly boiled down to leading the children in group singing to the accompaniment of the invariably out-of-tune school piano. She taught them the words and music to old standards like the state song, *Maryland, My Maryland* and numerous selections from Stephen Foster.

To get to all these schools, Camellia had bought herself a little Austin car, which Norman Travis said was some sort of engineering miracle in that it could comfortably seat someone as tall and well-built as Camellia. Which was Norman's nice way of saying, "She's built like a brick shithouse!"

On her "Gainsbiddle Day," Camellia would go to the Travis's for her lunch. Bessie always had a big sandwich and a piece of fresh home-made pie for her. It was a treat for Camellia as she couldn't stand the filthy Gainsbiddle school cafeteria and, what with having to fool with Roger so much of the morning, she never had time to fix herself a box lunch at the Tu-Rest Home before getting out on the road.

Those noon hours at Bessie's were the high spot in Camellia's work week. She always took the time to play ball with little Wayne, Bessie and Norman's son, who was now about five years old, a big chap, and a mite too heavy to bounce on her lap like she'd done when she'd stayed a part of each weekend with the Travises during her days of working at the drugstore in Gainsbiddle.

Camellia was also finding Bessie as much of a confidante as Mary always had. "Miss Bessie," Camellia said one day, "Roger is about to drive me insane. He's all the time hugging on me, pulling at me, making funny mouth noises at me, and looking at me like I am some sort of mother-god to him."

Bessie laughed. "Maybe it's because you *look* more motherly to him than thin, prim Mary with her silvery angel eyes—isn't that what Thomas calls those eyeglasses she wears?"

Camellia said, "Well, none of us seems to be doing much with Roger. Mama acts like she's afraid of him and he acts like he's afraid of her, even when he's just looking at her. Papa won't discipline him and I think it's because deep down he feels he has no right to, because Roger isn't his child. Mama thinks I should discipline him simply because I took a required course in child psychology for my teaching certificate. I went to Halburg to get qualified to teach music, not to be a child psychologist.

"And I'm sure no psychologist would have approved of the way I handled Roger the other day. I'd bent over to pick up a coat hanger—one of those thin wire kind—and I didn't even know Roger was anywhere around, but he came up behind me and goosed me! *Where does he learn these antics*! I nearly jumped over the piano!

"I was so mad I took that coat hanger and started thrashing him across the seat of his pants. And he was yelling and screaming and hollering, 'Sister! Sister! You son'f-bitch! You son'f-bitch!' I felt like saying, 'Look who's talking!' And he kept on yelling and crying at the same time, 'you son'f-bitch! I love you! Love you! Love you!' Calling me a 'son'f-bitch' and saying he loved me all in the same breath!

"It was a good thing for him that Mama heard all the ruckus. For once she took the initiative and came and broke up the battle."

Camellia often mused that you might survive being involved with the Gainsbiddle Elementary School during the 1930s and the Depression if you were a native Gainsbiddler to start with or a seasoned health nurse or just plumb crazy.

Since she was neither of the first two, she concluded she must be the third.

The Gainsbiddle school was full of mean and ignorant, ragged and dirty, smelly and sickly, undernourished wharf rats whose heads were loaded with lice and whose intestines were filled with worms.

In the course of a normal teaching day in the old wooden building, you were likely to get stung by an army of mason wasps tumbling off the ceiling and down into your collar; scalded by steam from an improperly working radiator; bopped on the head by falling plaster and blinded by the shower of lime; kicked, buffeted, bullied, and spit on by any number of roughneck boys—and sometimes girls; wet or messed on by some kid who'd waited too long to ask to leave the room; or thrown up on by some deathly sick kid whose parents had sent him to school anyway.

Those Gainsbiddlers, Camellia thought, needed and appreciated singing lessons about as much as a hole in the head. The dirty ditties that they sing-songed at recess and lunch time they did quite well by instinct alone and they didn't need a piano, a metronome, and a charming lady music teacher to instruct them further.

Yet Camellia was there, always poised as an actress, always immaculately groomed. Always with her *educated* British accent and her voice as smooth and golden-rich as honey poured from a jar. Her black hair was bobbed short now and marcelled in the style of the 1930s. Her lips were colored a cherry red and she wore gold earrings that sparkled and dazzled as she turned her head in the sunlight. High heels and brilliant, multi-colored sheath-type dresses completed her ensemble.

Next to the other teachers of drabber attire and aspirations, who looked like last year's dried-out cattails, Camellia stood forth like a tall and colorful wildflower of the hibiscus variety often seen in marshy farmland areas. Like just one graceful wildflower? Why she knew she look like a *whole field of beautiful wildflowers*!

And if there was just a little touch of haughtiness in her bearing, she felt she needed it as a buffer. If she came across to the children as someone they hoped would one day slip on a banana peel, she knew she had the aplomb for any contretemps.

Such as the day she was right in the middle of "Thou shalt nawt cower in the dust/ Mary-lahnd, my Mary-lahnd." She had sung that line a cappella in the full resonance of her mezzo-soprano voice and with great pomp and ceremony. So far, so good. Then to illustrate the music further—music adapted form the German *O Tannenbaum*—she sat down on the piano bench, raised her hands...and suddenly.... *Praise Jesus*! She had sat down on a mason wasp! And it was letting her know exactly how it felt about the indignity. Its sting delivered a far worse jolt than being goosed by Roger. Her hands crashed involuntarily onto the keyboard in a rattle-rumble of discordant notes.

Yet not a child in the room dared laugh. Camellia arose calmly from the piano bench, picked up by one leg the flattened and now quite defused mason wasp, and dropped it very dramatically into the wastebasket. Then back to the piano, *O Tannenbaum,* and "Thou shalt nawt cower in the dust/ Mary-lahnd, my Mary-lahnd!"

Like "Mary-lahnd, my Mary-lahnd," Camellia Stephens was "nawt" about to cower in the dust...in the dirt of Gainsbiddle or anywhere else.

Roger continued to be the bane of the Thomas Stephens's existence, but as he began to grow up a bit, and especially by the time he was old enough to start school, the screaming, yelling, crying, and sickliness of his earliest years tapered off. Or else, Camellia reasoned, the family had gotten so used to it that it didn't even register with them any more.

But Camellia did note that Roger seemed to be doing more listening now than mouthing off. He wasn't, however, listening to his family's weak attempts to raise him right. He was listening to a different world of sound....

Mary and Camellia let him play outside the house by himself a lot since he was not one to run off or get himself hurt. He didn't have much to do with the other Stephens kids, most of whom were older, but he did become pals with all the animals, birds, and insects. He would crawl around on his hands and knees in the grass and thickets, stalking them, but never hurting any of them, and he was learning to imitate their sounds.

Camellia noted that he wasn't too good at it at first, but he soon got so proficient that often neither she nor her mother could tell whether it was a real cricket in the house of just Roger *sounding* like a cricket. Eventually he could do the sounds of frogs, sea gulls, ducks, geese, beagles, locust bugs, chickens, horses, bumblebees, and mosquitoes. After Thomas had taught him to swim at the harbor, he learned to imitate things like gasoline engines, waves hitting against the docks, and shipyard sounds like winches, saws, and hammers. And he was great at wind, rain, and thunder.

Camellia appreciated his unusual ear for sound and his ability to reproduce what he heard, but she never knew quite what to make of it. Roger would never do any of these imitations if he were asked to. He didn't revel in an audience the way Camellia did.

But that didn't mean he wasn't trying to get people's attention. The thing that set everybody on their ear was when he started grinding out his *farts repertoire*—his thousand and one variations on the one basic theme. And at least 50 percent of them were for real—no imitation—and he'd learned to time them at the most pertinent moment—like when somebody had just told an obvious lie. He had also learned some crude ventriloquism (though not from Grandpaw Azariah, who despised Roger) and could usually make it seem like the farts were coming from somebody else.

He just about wrecked a church social one Sunday afternoon with his *talent* and got Camellia so mad at him she was about to box his ears off. Amanda Cartwright boomed at her, "Why don't you dress up that monkey-ass brother of yours in a red suit and little round hat, give him a tin cup, put a leash on him, and see if you can't make a million dollars!"

By the time he was in first grade he was periodically disrupting every class with this nonsense. But he won himself a pal in Jim

Stephens, Amos's youngest son, and Roger and Jim became the best of buddies. In addition to vying with each other on fart sounds (Roger always won), the pair started their earliest sexual investigations regarding girls together.

When the notes from the teacher would come home pinned to Roger's shirt, Mary always shunted off onto Camellia the responsibility to "straighten Roger out" and "Go see his teacher for me, will you, dear?"

Upon one such visit to Roger's teacher, Camellia was informed that when the teacher caught Roger and Jim trying to see how many little first-grade girls they could get to pull their panties down for them, Roger spoke up real innocent-like and said, "We just wanted to look at her a little bit, ma'm. We didn't aim to *do* nothing with her."

The teacher looked half-amused, half-infuriated at Camellia and said, "At age six, what did they *expect* to do with her?"

Camellia felt like saying, *Well, when you are the incarnation of the devil, anything is possible, I suppose.*

And it wasn't just an occasional boys-will-be-boys prank with which Roger was involved, either with or without Jim's help. Finally Roger's teacher and the principal of the Bell's Island Elementary School both went to see Mary. They rattled off a half-dozen or so adjectives to describe Roger's behavior ALL THE TIME: bullying, quarrelsome, inattentive, overactive, disrespectful, and unteachable.

The principal said to Mary, "What has happened to you, anyway? Your raised a wonderful child in Camellia here, but this boy Roger—I'm telling you, Mary, if you don't do something about him, and quickly, he's going to be in reform school before he's in the third grade."

When the principal and Roger's teacher left, Mary tearfully turned to Camellia and said, "Roger is bad, yes, but he can't be all that bad. Reform school? We'd be the disgrace of the island. Camellia, maybe you can talk with the school board about Roger. After all, you are in the school system. They would listen to you better than to me. And with my stomach condition...."

Exasperated, Camellia said, "Mama, it's a funny thing. Your stomach condition never seems so bad you can't play that damn organ in church on Sunday mornings. Yet if it's a matter of going to PTA meetings or to see somebody about Roger, no, you can't do that. *I'm* the one who has to go and have the sermon preached to me about Roger."

Mary whined, "But it's my duty to my church to be there on Sunday morning."

That made Camellia all the madder. "Mama, it's your confounded guilt that's making you go. You feel you have to do all this service to atone for your violation of church teachings when you got with that roomer. But for the life of me I can't see why you are bothered by the *teachings* when you once said to me that you didn't believe in God to start with."

Mary sniffled and said, "I just keep hearing it inside me all the time, something whispering 'Sinner! Sinner! Sinner!'"

Camellia thought for a bit, then said, "But there are other parts to Christianity than just condemnation. Can't you take any comfort in the fact that even Jesus didn't condemn forever the out-and-out prostitute, Mary Magdalene? He forgave her and told her to 'Go, and sin no more'. Why can't you see yourself forgiven in the same way?"

When Mary couldn't or didn't answer, Camellia threw her hands in the air and said, "Frankly, Mama, I think you've put a self-woven crown of thorns on your head—or in your stomach, maybe—and are not about to let anyone remove it. I believe you get some sort of perverse pleasure out of wearing it."

In spite of all the tension and contention at the Stephens Tu-Rest Home over Roger, Camellia managed to go to summer school at Halburg Normal during the 1938 and 1939 sessions. The school had now expanded into a four-year system and was called Halburg State College. Camellia was picking up credits right and left toward a bachelor's degree in music and drama. During the winter months, too, after her boring-as-hell school day was over, traveling around the county teaching Stephen Foster tunes and "Mary-lahnd, my Mary-lahnd" to the elementary grades, she would drive on to Halburg for evening classes.

It was usually so late by the time she got back to Bell's Island that Mary and the rest of the family had gone to bed, and thus any arguments over Roger were happily avoided.

With Camellia's somewhat begrudging influence on both Roger *and* the school board, Roger had stayed out of reform school and by 1940 he was in the second grade at the Bell's Island Elementary School. That was the year Mary's California sister, Ruth Anderton, and Grandmother LeCates (who was still living), sent word that they were coming to visit Bell's Island. This was the first direct communication Mary had had from them in over ten years.

James LeCates's debts had finally been squared when the old Bell's Island Inn was sold. The remainder owed on the Tu-Rest Home had been paid for out of Camellia's school (AND still-secret horse race earnings) and the business was deeded to Thomas and Mary. There was even a little pittance left in the estate for the other heirs. No more than it was, checks could easily have been sent to Ruth Anderton and Lucille LeCates as was done with Elizabeth St. George in Baltimore. But Camellia's Aunt Ruth had decided that she and Grandmother

LeCates would "come east" and receive their checks directly from the lawyers, then go on down to Bell's Island from Royal Hall to see Mary and Camellia.

Both Camellia and Mary were dreading this visit. Camellia was home for the weekend from her teaching chores, and she had Roger trailing along with her from a grocery story errand just as Aunt Ruth and Grandmother LeCates came over the Bell's Island bridge in a cab. Camellia knew they were coming sometime during that day, but she didn't recognize them at first. The window of the cab rolled down and someone said, "Is this Tu-Rest Home still run by Mary Stephens?"

"Well, yes, Mama runs it," Camellia said.

Suddenly the lady speaking exclaimed, "It's Camellia!"

"Aunt Ruth!" Camellia exclaimed right back.

There was a lot of hugging and kissing, and then they helped Grandmother LeCates out of the cab. All the while Camellia could see Aunt Ruth eyeing the redheaded Roger who was hovering at Camellia's side.

"Oh, Camellia! We didn't realize you were married!" said Aunt Ruth, and she was glancing all around as if to see some red-haired waterman husband of Camellia's approaching in hip boots with a string of fish on a wire. No such husband appeared, of course.

Camellia said, "I'm not married, Aunt Ruth. This is my...my...uh, my brother Roger."

"Oh," said Aunt Ruth. She studied Camellia for a moment, then said "Oh" again and added, as though talking to herself, "I didn't realize Mary...uh...I mean, Thomas always was a little funny...I mean, uh...uh....Well, Camellia, I trust your mother got my letter about us coming...and...."

"Yes, we got your letter." Camellia was wondering, didn't Aunt Ruth *know* about Roger? Hadn't Aunt Lizbeth told her? Aunt Lizbeth had kept in touch through the years, but maybe Mary had passed Roger off to her, too, as Thomas' kid.

Camellia shook off uneasy thoughts the best she could as they all went in the house. Roger followed along with them. He was quiet, but Camellia was quaking with fear as to whether he might try his *farts repertoire* on these fancy relatives of his mother's.

And all the while Camellia was thinking how much older and frailer Aunt Ruth looked than when she'd last seen her, and she wondered if Aunt Ruth was thinking the same about Mary. As for Grandmother LeCates, she must have been close to seventy now, but Camellia couldn't see where she had changed much at all. She was still big, well-dressed, silver-haired, and elegant-looking, just as she had always been. She was smiling and pleasant, but she really hadn't said much of anything.

Mary greeted them with her usual *in public* friendliness that hadn't suffered too much in spite of all the rough years. She launched into her reserve of polite *nothing talk*, used for occasions such as this when she didn't know quite what else to say or do.

As they were all sitting around, sipping the coffee and nibbling on the cake Mary and Camellia had served them in the front room, it was hard for Camellia to tell just when she realized Grandmother LeCates was "not quite right." Of course, she hadn't been exactly "right" before leaving Bell's Island, after the shock of Grandfather LeCates's death and the humiliation of his bankrupt estate. But what with Camellia's own family's struggles in the intervening years, she had lost sight of her grandmother's nervous breakdown at that time.

Suddenly Grandmother LeCates said directly to Aunt Ruth—not to Mary—"Mary, isn't it time to tell Agnes to change the blankets from summer to winter weight?"

Camellia noticed her mother give a start at hearing her name when it was obvious that Grandmother LeCates was speaking to Aunt Ruth.

Aunt Ruth said to Mary sotto voce, "Uh, she thinks I'm you, Mary. Thinks we still live at the inn...long time back."

Grandmother LeCates was speaking again as though to "the middle distance." "When James get home from Royal Hall this evening, I must remind him to go over those accounts again with Mary. I think there may be a mistake...and...." Then her voice trailed off.

Camellia felt weird and uncomfortable at all of this. Her mother, too, had a puzzled, then an embarrassed look when she recognized Grandmother LeCates' "condition." The last thing any of them wanted was insanity in the family. That was even worse than adultery. But it looked like they had them both.

Aunt Ruth was speaking now: "Mother's no trouble really, Mary. She's not unhappy. She'll do anything I tell her...that is, most of the time. She's perfectly healthy except for...except for....Well, anyway, I thought a little trip would do us good and so that's why we're here." Aunt Ruth forced a little laugh.

Aunt Ruth was putting up a good front, Camellia thought. It was called "keeping up appearances." Mary, too, had been doing a lot of that in the last seven or eight years. It was hard for Camellia to tell which had come off the worse for wear—Aunt Ruth or Mary. Aunt Ruth looked like she'd had it plenty rough, and she'd had no financial problems like Mary. Camellia noticed her mother perked up considerably when she seemed to see how bad Aunt Ruth looked. There's nothing in this wide world that makes you feel better any quicker when you're down than to find out somebody else is hurting, too. But Mary still had some explaining of her own to do....

Roger was still hanging around inside the house, but so far he hadn't done anything out of the way. No cuss words or vulgar mouth—or anal—sounds. In fact, he hadn't said anything and had merely nodded when Mary had introduced him to his grandmother and aunt. Mary had simply said, "This is my boy, Roger." But there was a little more to Roger than just Mary....

About then the kitchen door opened and Thomas came into the house. He was tweeting on his beagle whistle. He bumped around in the kitchen for a minute or so, then came into the front room where they all were. He didn't see Roger at first, but nodded politely to his mother-in-law and sister-in-law. Then he looked all around and got a big smile on his face. "Where's my boy?" he said. "Where's Roger? We got beagles to train this afternoon!" He tweeted the whistle again.

Camellia knew her father never took Roger beagle training. Roger still wasn't all that fond of Thomas and he still would fling him a cuss word every now and then. But this time Roger didn't seem about to cause any trouble.

Aunt Ruth looked oddly at Thomas, then at Mary, then at Roger, then at Camellia, as though she were trying to put all of them together—including Roger's red hair—and make some sort of sense. Thomas gave Aunt Ruth some help:

"Lot of difference in their ages—Camellia and Roger, eh? But I...well..."[he lowered his voice to a whisper] "...I caught-Mary-on-the-change!" Then he gave that silly little laugh of his.

Camellia was thinking her father was not the best actor in the world, nor was this a very elegant way to explain Roger—to say nothing of his red hair—but it was the line he'd been handing everybody over the last seven years or so. And he must have convinced Aunt Ruth, for she dropped the censuring look she'd had on her face ever since she'd arrived.

Roger now, without a word, whimper, or vulgarity of any sort, followed Thomas out into the kitchen and on out of the house to go beagle training, and Camellia and Mary breathed near-audible sighs of relief. Camellia didn't know if her father had used "gypsy magic" or not. She doubted if he even knew how to. But with him maybe it was that love that he always said they needed to have for Roger in order to get the devil—or Boro's incarnation—or whatever it was out of him.

Mary suddenly jumped up and said she was going to get some more coffee for everyone and hastened to the kitchen. Camellia quickly followed her, not knowing if her mother's ulcer was about to explode, as it periodically did, or just what. But Mary was only fighting off some tears...as usual.

"What's the matter, Mama?" Camellia said, "Roger didn't do a thing."

Mary said, "I know that. And you must have been 'working on him' mentally."

"No, I wasn't," Camellia said, honestly.

Mary sniffed. "And I think *I've* had it tough....Your Aunt Ruth looks a hundred years old....But did you see how your Papa covered for me? 'Caught Mary on the change!' he said. Tired old story, but bless him for it. And it seemed to work with Aunt Ruth, did you notice? He even got Roger out of the house on a pretense of beagle training and Roger didn't say a word. Oh, Camellia, your Papa is such a good person, such a kind person; he deserves something better than this old bitch—uh, this old sinner he's got for a wife...."

Mary gave a big sob, leaned on Camellia, and was all set for an out-and-out cry. But Camellia pushed her aside and said, "Mama, if you don't stop this self-chastising crap, it's going to kill you!"

"Hush, they'll hear you!" Mary said in alarm. Then she pulled herself together and said loud enough so that they *would* hear: "Open that new can of coffee, Camellia. I don't think this is any too fresh."

And so with the fresh pot of coffee, Mary and Camellia went right on "keeping up appearances."

By the end of 1940, for five years Camellia had been giving Wintergreen County elementary school kids "those inane singing lessons."

She was getting mighty restless. She was already twenty-four years old and felt that *life* had completely passed her by. She had her bachelor's degree in music and drama as well as many credits toward her master's, but to what avail? She felt she was fast becoming an educated fool.

She was doing a lot of singing here and there—on Bell's Island, at Royal Hall and other towns up and down the shore, at church events, public gatherings, Masonic banquets, and patriotic affairs. But none of this was like the city would be.

Yet every time she was set to go to Baltimore, either for an audition or vocal competition or to enroll at the conservatory, Mary would come down real sick or Roger would do something terrible and again be threatened with reform school.

The closest Camellia was getting to The Met was to listen to its radio broadcasts on Saturday afternoons. For a couple hours she would be deliriously lost in those fantasies of music and drama.

One other opportunity for her musical fantasies to run freely were those precious moments she had alone while driving throughout the county to the elementary schools. Caught between the discordant situation at home and the boring and grubby working conditions of the county school system, she treasured those moments when her own sad and angry feelings could find their unique expression.

The entire Wintergreen County landscape seemed pulsing with music, so much of it strange music—from the weird gypsy-like sounds in the miles and miles of desolate marshland between Bell's Island and Royal Hall, to the sad, bitter-sweet strains of black spirituals like Aunt Sairy Middleton hummed, rising up from the worn-out Depression-racked farmland and the remains of old Civil War mansions still standing in the southern section of the county.

At times the music seemed like an eclectic blend of all that Camellia had ever heard or played or sung or studied, from Beethoven's *Ninth Symphony* to *Ave Maria*. Yet at other times it seemed like *nothing* she'd ever heard before, like nothing that had ever been written, played, or sung before by anybody, like it was the very soul of *music* itself speaking to her.

"I must write all of this down," she kept saying to herself. And sometimes she did manage to scribble some of it on some of the music paper Claudie had given her so many years before. But it seemed that when her little Austin car stopped at whatever school was on her schedule for the day, that strange music stopped with it. It might return on her way back to Bell's Island in the evenings, only to flee again the moment she stepped inside the Tu-Rest Home to be greeted either by Roger's cussing and farting or Mary's crying.

There was always that nagging little belief that as a woman she wasn't supposed to write music even if the Muses were hollering their heads off at her to do so. She could acknowledge that Nadia Boulanger, Fanny Mendelssohn, Amy Beach, and a few other women had indeed written and had music published, but even they had never gained much recognition. The general belief was that women didn't have the intelligence to compose. A woman's *place* was to perform, or at most, to interpret while performing what some man had already created.

The music world might say it was all right for a woman to compose little "nothing pieces" of chamber music for a piano or violin or "I'm a Little Teapot"-type songs for children to sing, but anything complicated, like a symphony or opera...? Oh no! Yet it was just that sort of as yet unformed, as yet unharnessed, metaphysical music that so often came to Camellia during those times when driving the back county roads.

Camellia had long since parted company with the Halburg instructor who had placed bets for her on the horses. She missed that extra income, but there was still one thing she wouldn't do and that was go to bed with a man in order to get or to keep getting favors from him. She was clever enough to make men *think* she was about to do just that, but eventually there came the time when she reneged on her promises just too many times and their interest in her ended.

Then one day she had dropped into the board of education office in Royal Hall to complain about the bad working conditions in the county schools, notably in Gainsbiddle. Nobody was paying her any mind except the principal of the Royal Hall High School, who happened to be in the office at the same time and overheard her.

Afterwards they both were walking out of the building and Hugh Forrester remarked that he for one agreed with Camellia. The county could do something to insure better school standards, at least in sanitation, if it really wanted to. They got to talking and Forrester asked Camellia for a date that evening. He was a regular mountain of a man, a former football player, and not bad looking, either.

Camellia knew he was married, but also that he was having trouble with his wife, so she decided to go out with him. She did not go home to Bell's Island even though she was dying to get into some dressier clothes, but instead, as it was getting late, she followed Forrester to the Royal Hall High School, left her little Austin car there, and joined Forrester in his car. They drove to a restaurant and night club up the shore where there was drinking and dancing.

Forrester offered Camellia a cigarette. Smoking had been on Grandpaw Azariah's curriculum when tutoring Camellia earlier in life but she had declined that course because she knew smoking was no good for an aspiring opera singer. She had later, however, at least tried cigarettes with Snipsey, so she was not unprepared. She looked at the pack of Luckies that Forrester was holding out to her and thought, *Why not*? If all she was ever going to sing was *I Love You Truly* at weddings and *Old Black Joe* in the county elementary schools, she might as well smoke.

She had also never before accepted a drink with a fellow on a date—the scattering of fellows she had gone out with at Halburg and in the shore choral society to which she belonged—and there *had* been dates that were *real dates* and not just occasions to euchre something out of a fellow, as with Wylie Hovey and the horse racing enthusiast who had been her instructor at Halburg Normal. Yet when Forrester suggested they have a cocktail before dinner, Camellia did not hesitate. ANYTHING, she reasoned, to keep her mind off Bell's Island and the county school system for awhile.

The cocktails of that evening were so effective in doing just that (doing it just short of making her drunk, that is, for she had not forgotten Grandpaw's coaching) that she was all for another date with Forrester when he asked her again the following week...and the next and the next....Before she realized what was happening, she was hooked on a married man because of the liquor he could provide her.

Liquor didn't bring in any extra income for her like gambling had, but the inevitable price to pay to keep on getting that liquor was the same. Camellia used every bit of her acting ability AND her "gypsy magic" to keep Forrester where she wanted him—on the front seat of his auto and on the driver's side. But he was a tough one and she didn't know how long she could hold out against him. Yet that liquor—the cocktails they had when on dates and the little flasks he gave her as gifts—was the buffer she increasingly needed to have between herself and an impossible world.

And as long as Roger was around, that world would remain impossible as illustrated in the episode of The Gainsbiddle "Crees".

Camellia had been teaching at the Gainsbiddle school that day and had brought home to Bell's Island "a mess of 'crees'," a gift from Bessie Travis to the Thomas Stephenses.

"Crees" was that peculiar kind of Wintergreen County watercress that popped up in the cornfields after winter. They were flat, star-shaped clusters of leaves and looked somewhat like huge green snowflakes. Quite pretty, in fact, Camellia thought.

When it was cooked right and used right, crees was very tasty and considered "good for you." Used wrongly—that is, if too much of it was eaten at one time—or cooked wrongly—that is, if cooked with too much, too old fatback, crees could act as a powerful cathartic, emetic, and diuretic, and sometimes all three at the same time!

Anyway, Camellia came home to Bell's Island with her little Austin car loaded with a dozen or more large grocery bags filled with crees that Bessie had freshly picked from cornfields just outside of Gainsbiddle. The car was so full of crees that Mary told Camellia she could hardly see her in the driver's seat as she rolled up to the Tu-Rest Home.

Camellia didn't wait for Mary to cook the crees because she was in a hurry to get along to her foreign language courses that evening at Halburg State College. She had to settle for a sandwich and cup of coffee and was somewhat disappointed because Mary "cooked good crees."

When Camellia got back to Bell's Island late that evening, she found everybody had gone to bed, the crees was all gone, and the kitchen was filled with Maryland Beat Biscuits. *Uh-oh,* Camellia was thinking, *Mama must have sex on the mind again*!

The next morning, however, Camellia learned that the Maryland Beat Biscuits were merely a thank you present to take to Bessie Travis in appreciation for the crees. Mary then went along with Thomas to Gainsbiddle on one of the Stephens's boats to deliver the biscuits.

This was Camellia's Bell's Island day for the elementary school singing classes. Roger, now in the second grade, had left for school ahead of Camellia and she hadn't paid too much attention to him.

When she started walking toward the school herself, she noticed a lot of commotion at the Cartwright house across the shell road. There were a lot of kids running back and forth to the outhouse, but she didn't pay them much mind.

Snipsey, now married and with a couple of little ones, still stayed at the Cartwright's along with her husband, and suddenly *she* darted out of the house and ran next door to Agnes and Charlie Stephens's.

When Camellia came along in front of Agnes's, she heard Agnes laying the law down to Snipsey:

"You say you used up all your newspypers to sop up the floor? Well, Oi ain't givin' no newspypers to a bunch of idiots! Serves you people roight bein' such hogs an' eatin' all that crees at one toime. What? You say it warse *Gynesbiddle* crees. Jaysus Croyst! That's the worse koinde. You better call the undertyker!"

Camellia saw Snipsey thumb her nose at Agnes and run further on down the shell road to Amos and Lois Stephens's. Snipsey ran in there for a moment, then ran right back out, and went pell-mell toward their outhouse on the edge of the marsh.

When Camellia got down to Amos and Lois's, she met Grandpaw Azariah, in his overalls three sizes too big for him, with an armful of newspapers, strolling along and taking his own good time.

"Mornin', chickadee!"

"Morning, Grandpaw. Where are you going with the newspapers?"

"To Amanda's. They've all got the shits there this mornin'. Crees sickness, you know. It's that time of year."

Camellia smiled a bit but it didn't quite sink in, the connection between what had happened at the Cartwrights (Amanda was a terrible cook) and the fact that the culprit was *Gynesbiddle* crees, as Agnes put it, the Gynesbiddle crees that Camellia had brought from Bessie Travis's.

Camellia's first singing class—the first grade—went by without incident, then came the second grade. She had barely got them going on "Mary-lahnd, my Mary-lahnd" when instinct made her glance at Roger.

His hand was jammed into his crotch and his face was as red as his hair. Still not making any connection, Camellia merely walked up to him and whispered, "If you have to go to the toilet, GO!"

Roger went—and fast!

But when he didn't come back for so long, Camellia sent Jim Stephens, his buddy, to look for him. Jim came back quickly enough but without Roger. Jim blurted, "He h-h-he d-d-done it all over hisself—EVER'THING! BOTH ENDS!"

"Jesus!" gasped Camellia and out loud, too. Quickly, she got the regular teacher back in the room and went to see to Roger herself.

As she approached the boys' toilet, she could hear Roger cussing even louder than he was gagging: "GOD*DAMN*!—Aaaagh—GOD-DAMN *CREES*!—Aaaagghh—GODDAMN *AMANDA*!—Aaagghhh—GODDAMN *GAINSBIDDLE*—Aaaghhaawrrr—*GODDAMN GAINSBIDDLE CREES*!!—Aaaahhhhh."

NOW Camellia made the connection and only too well. Her mother had given the Cartwrights some—some? much!—of the "Gainsbiddle crees" and Roger had eaten supper with the Cartwrights as he did every chance he could get because he liked to hear Amanda and all of them blackguarding.

As Camellia was trying to figure out what to do with the wet, shitty, and pukey Roger, she turned and saw little Doris Thornton peeping in the doorway of the boys' toilet.

"Miz Camellia! Miz Camellia!" the little brown-haired, hazel-eyed eight-year-old was whispering as loud as she dared. "Miz Camellia!"

"What is it, Doris? You're not supposed to be *here*!"

"Miz Camellia, if there ain't nobody to Roger's house to take care of him, he could go to *my house*! Me an' Mama could take care of him for you. We know all about crees sickness. We get it, too, sometimes."

Camellia didn't know how Doris knew there was nobody at the Tu-Rest Home to see to Roger, unless Roger had earlier told her himself or maybe Doris had seen Thomas and Mary leaving on the boat. She said to Doris, "For heaven's sake, Doris, you can't take him home with you. He's in a terrible mess. Your mother wouldn't want him in her house. I'll take him on home and stay with him till my folks get home. Would you go and tell Mrs. Morgan for me, please."

But little Doris kept persisting. "Miz Camellia, Mama and I know all about crees sickness. Even *Gainsbiddle* crees sickness. We know how to *cure it*!"

Camellia had always heard that *Gainsbiddle* crees sickness was *in*curable.

By now Mrs. Morgan, the second grade teacher, had come looking for Roger, too. And she was shaking her head and saying, "*Gainsbiddle* crees sickness? Oh, my. Oh, my. Oh, my."

Camellia said, "Doris here says she can take Roger to her house, but I don't know...." Camellia was thinking that Doris's mother was an all right person, but she couldn't say much for Doris's father, "Hambone" Thornton, who was vaguely related to some of Grandfather LeCates's *lesser* cousins on Bell's Island. "Hambone" had once referred to Roger as "Mary LeCates's bastard young'un" and Camellia had overheard it, and though it was the truth, certainly, she still despised "Hambone" for having said it.

Mrs. Morgan studied Camellia a bit, then said, "Let Doris take him, if she wants, so you can get back with your classes. 'Hambone' is on his boat today, if that's what you're worried about."

So Camellia turned Roger over to the little eight-year-old Florence Nightingale and good Samaritan all rolled into one. Camellia watched, marveling, as Doris took Roger by the hand, heedless of his smell and mess, and led him out the side door of the school and on down the shell road toward the Thornton home. Roger didn't resist Doris's tenderness but seemed grateful for it. He was as quiet now and as humble as Camellia could ever recall seeing him.

At the end of the school day, Camellia went to pick up Roger from the Thorntons. Mamie Thornton, Doris's mother, reported that she had cleaned Roger up, put some fresh clothes belonging to one of her own kid's on him, and put him to bed. While Mamie had washed out, dried, and ironed Roger's clothes, Doris sat by his bedside, holding his hand, and soothing his brow with cold cloths. Every now and then she would read to him out of one of her storybooks or just sit there quietly with him while he dozed.

Roger was still asleep when Camellia went to get him, but Mamie Thornton woke him enough that she could re-dress him in his own clothes so he could walk home. When Camellia got him back to the Tu-Rest Home, she put him to bed and let him finish sleeping off his crees hangover.

When Thomas and Mary got back from Gainsbiddle later in the afternoon, the first thing Mary said to Camellia was, "Where's Roger?" He was forever a thorn in Mary's flesh, but Camellia guessed her mother still didn't want to misplace him.

"Upstairs taking a nap," Camellia said.

"At this time of day? Is he sick?"

"Not now, he isn't. I trust you had a good day in Gainsbiddle? Miss Bessie like her biscuits?"

"Yes, we had a good day. And Bessie liked her biscuits. But you sound a bit sarcastic, Camellia. Is something wrong?"

Camellia tossed her head and shrugged wearily. "Well, let's put it this way, Mama....I hope your biscuits don't do to Miss Bessie and half of Gainsbiddle what her crees did to Roger and half of Bell's Island."

As soon as Roger recovered from his crees sickness, he was back outside again almost all the time, crawling around in the muck and mud, looking for shore birds, frogs, and insects to imitate their sounds.

He got so wet and stinky that Thomas often stripped him down in the back yard and turned the cold water hose on him before letting him go in the house, no matter how much chill there was in the air. Roger didn't seem to mind this, but Mary kept saying to Thomas, "I wish you wouldn't wet him down and make him shiver like that. You'll fill him full of cold. He stays full of cold enough as it is."

But Thomas said, "He's soaking wet anyhow from crawling around in the marsh. How's a little more water going to hurt him?"

Camellia knew one thing about her father—that though he had his silly ways and notions about some things, he was as tough as any when it came to *not* coddling children. Thomas had been a hardy outdoorsman all his life. He'd fallen into the icy Bell's Island harbor more than once during winters and always came away none the worse for wear. He still took those cold water baths all year long at the crab house or the shipyard before coming home in the evening from work, and he saw no reason why everybody shouldn't be as tough as he was. He reminded Mary that Camellia had never had a cold in her life and yet she got soaked to the skin many a time walking to and from school in the rain and sleet during those bad years when they barely had money for food, much less rainwear.

But Camellia was thinking her father failed to recognize that Roger was not as strong as she had been when she was growing up. Roger was *not a Stephens*, no matter how many times Thomas continued to tell the whole wide world, "I caught Mary on the change." Roger was Mary's son, though, and there was a history of tuberculosis in the LeCates family. Camellia often wondered how her mother had escaped it, thin as she was. Maybe her ulcer had scared it away!

Toward the end of the summer of 1941 Roger and his sidekick, Jim Stephens, were going on nine years old. They both could swim and were able to handle a skiff with considerable expertise, so Thomas and the men at the Stephens Marine Railway started letting them fool around by themselves with one of their old skiffs.

They took to going around the edges of the harbor and marshes, looking for shore birds to watch and listen to, so that Roger could imitate their calls. Sometimes they poled the skiff across the inlet to the old Corrigan tavern. One of the men at the shipyard told Camellia that the boys sometimes would go and talk with the Moonlight who was running the place now. She was the same Moonlight for whom Doc Feldman had mistaken Camellia a number of years before in the drugstore and Camellia had socked Doc in the eye for it.

This current Moonlight was close to thirty now, Camellia judged, about five years older than she was, but they still looked a lot alike—black gypsy hair and all. Even Roger had once commented on the resemblance and made everybody ill at ease at the Tu-Rest Home. Moonlight came onto the island for groceries and supplies, but she kept out of the way of "good people" and no one paid her much mind. Everybody knew what she was, and they let it go at that.

Camellia didn't like the idea of Roger going over there to that tavern, but she seemed to have no more control or influence over him than did Mary or Thomas. And another problem was about to surface, something they all had been dreading.

Roger and Jim Stephens were wrassling and tussling one evening out in the yard of the Tu-Rest Home when Camellia heard Jim call Roger a 'bastid." It might have been just in fun, Camellia figured, for she didn't hear any more of the conversation.

But a day or so later Roger asked Camellia, "Sister, what's a 'bastid'? Jim called me a 'bastid' and said it meant I didn't have no father. I told Jim he was crazier'n shit because Pop's my father."

Camellia guessed she must have given a little start. She had known this question was going to come up sooner or later, but she still was not prepared for it. Roger misinterpreted her reaction and said in utter boredom, "Oh, I know....Pop ain't much, but he is my Pop....So what's a 'bastid', Sister?"

Camellia was amazed that Roger had never heard—or at least never questioned—the word before or maybe it was just because of the way Jim had pronounced it that he was questioning it now. But Camellia was in no mood for questions. Roger had already been dogging her all day, following her around and whining and asking unanswerable riddles, such as "When can I quit school? I don't like school. When is Mom going to die? She don't like me. Why don't Pop grow whiskers so's I can pull 'em all out with the pliers?"

And now, "Sister, what's a 'bastid'?"

When Camellia continued to hesitate, Roger whined and said, "Don't you know the answer, Sister? I though you was a teacher. Teachers s'pose to know all the answers, ain't they?"

As she was stalling for time, Camellia was reciting to herself the old adage about teachers and adding her own ending: Those who can, do. Those who can't, teach. Those who can't teach, teach...half-brothers—'bastid' half-brothers, that is.

She felt compelled to say something, though, so she started with the only thing she could think of at the moment:

"Roger, you remember last summer when the beagle that was in heat got out of her pen and Mama had everybody on the island chasing after her?"

Roger got all excited and said, "Yeah! And before anybody could catch the bitch, she ran right up to Charlie's old bulldog, turned her ass around to him, and he jumped on her and fucked the hell out of her!"

Well! Camellia was not quite expecting Roger to give *that much* of a blow by blow recount of the incident, but he rattled on:

"Nobody could get 'em pulled apart. We threw water on 'em and kicked 'em and threw rocks on 'em, but nothing did no good. Mom kept screaming, 'He's got my best bitch! *He's got my best bitch*! Lady was intended for Samson, but now she's ruined! She's RUINED!' And Mom was crying and begging Pop to get his rifle and kill Lady and Charlie's bulldog, too. But Pop wouldn't do it."

Camellia said, "And a couple months later Lady had some puppies, right?"

Roger nodded.

"Were they beagles?" Camellia asked.

"Naw, they wasn't much of nothing," Roger said, disgustedly. "Couldn't sell 'em. Couldn't even give 'em away. They wasn't no beagles."

"They were 'bastids', Roger," said Camellia.

She paused a moment, then plunged on: "A 'bastid' or 'bastard' doesn't mean there wasn't a father. It means the father was not the one it should have been. Papa was in the Gainsbiddle hospital with his broken back and the other injuries he sustained in that hurricane, but it was right at that time that Mama got pregnant with you, so Papa couldn't have been your father."

Camellia waited to see if this would sink in. Finally Roger nodded and Camellia felt that he understood. He might be incorrigible, she mused, but he was not stupid. Yet for some reason he didn't right then ask the next inevitable question: Then *who was* my father?

Camellia reasoned that Roger may have begun to think that Charlie Stephens was his father. Charlie did take a lot of interest in Roger, more than any of the other Stephenses, more even than Thomas. Charlie played baseball with Roger and Roger tagged along with Charlie everywhere he went. A number of people on the island had always thought that Charlie was Roger's father. Charlie was forever making overtures to Mary. When Charlie and Roger were together, Camellia often heard comments from people such as, "Hey, looky there? There they go, off to play baseball. Make a right good father and son team, doncha think?" "Yeah, one's jes' 'bout as nasty as t'other!"

Something else happened late that summer of 1941 that may have made Roger think that Charlie might be his father. The men were working late at the shipyard that evening and Mary had sent Camellia to the docks with a basket of supper for Thomas.

Camellia was coming back alongside the warehouses just as it was starting to get dark, woolgathering as usual. Her mind was jittering between strains of unwritten music begging to be captured and wearisome thoughts of the too slowly moving days and the too swiftly moving years. (She was twenty-five now and still no closer to The Met.) And she was worrying as to just how much longer she could hold out against Forrester's expectations of her.

Suddenly she was startled out of her troubled reverie by someone whispering in the dusk: "Camellia. Camellia! Come in here a minute." She recognized Charlie Stephens' voice, and unthinkingly she stepped inside the corrugated tin warehouse where his voice was coming from.

Immediately when she was inside, Charlie shut the door. He was all geared up and ready for action, and he grabbed her in the half-dark of that old warehouse. When she resisted for all she was worth, he said, "Oh, come on, Camellia. Don't say you don't do this. What of Forrester up there in Royal Hall? The whole damn county knows what you and he are up to."

Well, Camellia knew she hadn't done *anything* with Forrester, but she was thinking she might as well go ahead and do something because people were saying she was anyhow.

Charlie kept tugging on her, and she knew it was no use trying to resist him by physical means. He was strong as an ox as were all the Stephenses, and though she was a Stephens, too, she knew as a woman she was no match for Charlie. So, she had to try something else. It was becoming darker by the moment in that warehouse but she was still able to see Charlie's face, and she managed to make direct eye contact with him. Grandpaw Azariah had said years before never hurt anybody with what he'd taught her, but this was an emergency!

She felt Charlie's grasp on her give way and he grabbed his head with both hands and started moaning. Quickly Camellia said to him, "And if you ever again try to do to me what you just now tried to do to me, Charlie Stephens, or if you try it on any of your other nieces and I find out about it, I'll tell everybody on this island what sort of person you are. Your name will be shit and your own children and grandchildren won't be able to hold their heads up any higher than a frog's asshole." She pronounced it "ahhs-hole," which was nothing unusual as she still used that *educated* British accent, but it seemed to drill right through Charlie's head just as her eyes had done.

Charlie started whining. "Aw, Camellia, lay off, will you?" He was holding onto his head and rubbing his eyes. He said, "I've never been able to get anywheres with your mother, so I thought maybe you'd do, instead."

That made Camellia even madder. She didn't know what Charlie could see in Mary to start with as her mother still looked and acted as she always had—like *a nice woman,* but then you can't tell a book by its cover.

Camellia said, "You'd take me as *second choice* to Mama, huh? What's the matter with you, Charlie Stephens? Why can't you either stay with your own wife or else be satisfied with Moonlight and her girls and leave respectable women alone?"

Charlie gave an insinuating, mocking laugh. "You and your mother—*respectable* women?! Hah!"

They heard a clattering in the dark toward the back of the warehouse and both of them jumped. Charlie said, "That damned brother of yours had got in here, I'll bet....Go on, Camellia, get out of here."

Camellia scurried across the shell road, went directly home, and sat down on the front porch of the Tu-Rest Home alone in the dark. It seemed like hours before she could stop shaking. Part of it was retroactive fear of Charlie and part of it was that she needed a drink and had none left from the last little flask Forrester had given her. But she also knew more than ever now that she was going to have to kick that habit and be rid of Forrester forever. Or at least be rid of Forrester. Maybe she could buy her own liquor on the sly from Karl Jurgensen, "that Mennonite bootlegger" in the eastern part of the county, about whom Forrester had once told her. But no, she knew she wouldn't do that.

As she sat there, trying to size up what had just happened, she heard Roger creeping along the edge of the porch in the dark. He was whispering, "Sister. Sister! Will you talk to me, huh? Talk just a little, huh?"

"Come on up on the porch, then."

Roger sat down in the swing beside her and said, "Sister, Charlie had a-holt of you there in that warehouse and he had his pants open and...and...his-his....Was he aiming to f—?"

"Don't you say that word!" Camellia cut in. Roger was quiet.

Then in a little bit he said, "Is Charlie my father?...Are you my mother, Sister?"

Oh, *God*! Camellia thought. To Roger, she said, "Charlie is *not* your father, Roger. But why should you think I'm your mother?"

"Well, you were fussing to Charlie there in the warehouse about bein' second choice to Mom, weren't you?...Has Charlie been f—" [he muffled down the middle of the word] "—ing *both* of you!?"

"No, Roger. NO!"

But Camellia knew even less now how to talk to Roger than she had when he'd first confronted her weeks before about his questionable origins. To tell him he was the result of the chance coupling between his mother and one of the Tu-Rest Home roomers, a man Mary hadn't even been able to identify by name, seemed as unbelievable and ridiculous as telling him the stork—or the sea gull—had brought him.

When the new school year started in the fall of 1941, Camellia was in the lowest spirits she could ever remember.

Mary, however, seemed delighted that Camellia was just a music *teacher*. It was considered a woman's *right place* in the world.

Thomas also seemed pleased that Camellia had not broken away to become that opera singer he feared she might. He often remarked about "so many temptations out there in the world." Camellia had to smile inwardly at that. Had not enough temptations and yieldings happened right at the Stephens' doorstep or thereabouts? Camellia suspected her father would always remain one of those blessed people who have the ability to *not see* what they don't want to see and to forget what they wished had never happened.

Both Thomas and Mary stewed over the fact that Camellia had not yet found a husband. Thomas often said, "It's always safer for a woman to be married." The absurdity of what he was saying, in the light of Mary's "indiscretion," never seemed to dawn on Thomas.

Neither Thomas nor Mary was very keen on Camellia's friendship with Forrester even though the Royal Hall High School principal was now legally divorced from his first wife. Mary acted as though she suspected Camellia was giving sex in exchange for the liquor that Camellia finally admitted to her mother (after Mary found one of the empty flasks in the garbage) that Forrester was providing. But Mary didn't moralize. Camellia sensed her mother knew enough not to, considering her own shortcomings in the past.

In the fall of 1941 Roger really turned on. It seemed as though he was doing his best to live up to all the dirty names people called him: "Mary Stephens' bastard son." "A turd that come out twisted." "The incarnation of the devil."

Roger was in the third grade now and getting terrible marks. The teachers were complaining to Mary and Camellia that he was continually fighting with the boys, cussing at the teachers, and making "those crazy fartsounds" in the classroom...and somehow making it seem like the teacher was doing it! He was also fooling with the girls all the time, running his hands up their dresses, and trying to feel them up. But he didn't do that with Doris Thornton and it wasn't because she socked him or ran from him or ignored him. Doris and Roger were even better pals than Jim and Roger. Even the teachers noticed the deep admiration and respect that Roger and Doris seemed to have for each other.

But aside from that one positive element, Roger remained a holy terror. When reform school was again threatened for him, Mary and Thomas talked about putting Roger in military school. Camellia hit the roof and said, "Not if I'm going to have to finance it, you're not!

Let him go to reform school where he belongs and the state will pay for it."

Camellia often said to Mary, "Papa ought to take a belt to him once in awhile."

But Mary always replied, "Well, you know your Papa is not going to do that. Now, if Roger were his own son....Your Papa once said Roger would be his son 'in the eyes of the world', but I guess he never meant it to go much further than that."

Camellia tried to appeal to the one thing Roger could do well—that of imitating sounds. Considering his ability at ventriloquism, too, she tried to get him interested in putting on some vaudeville-type shows with her for Bell's Island or anywhere they could get an audience.

Camellia met with a dead end. Roger said, "Shit! Music an' actin' is for girls." Camellia started, as usual, to correct his grammar and shush his obscenity, but then she thought, *T'hell with it; he came from the devil; let him* go *to the devil*!

And Roger almost did! He'd come home from school one afternoon in early November, reeking of marsh mud, dead fish, duck manure, and God only knows what else. He'd been out stalking shore birds again. Thomas turned the cold water hose on him to clean him up some before letting him go in the house. Roger took a bad cold right after that, and it went into pneumonia.

Doc Feldman's medicine didn't seem to help one bit and they all were awaiting for Roger to die. Mary wept and wrung her hands while Thomas prayed and asked God to forgive him for causing Roger's pneumonia. He asked God to heal Roger.

The whole business got on Camellia's nerves so bad she couldn't practice her music or do anything. At one point she, too, almost came to tears. It was a Saturday night and Roger was in a high fever and deep delirium, and Mary was bending over his scrawny body with the tears running down her face. She was whispering to him, "Please don't die, Roger. I don't want you to die. I have hated you at times, yes. I have ignored you so much, I have even wished you were dead. But give me the chance to be a better mother to you. Don't die, my son...."

Camellia could not fathom just what happened—whether Roger responded to Mary's plea or to Thomas's prayers of finally to Doc Feldman's medicine....Or to something else....

The next day was Sunday....Sunday, 7 December 1941. It was the day President Roosevelt said would "live in infamy."

For the Thomas Stephenses it had started off as normally as a Sunday could with someone as sick and near death as Roger was. Camellia played the organ at church that morning in Mary's place as

Mary wanted to be with Roger all the time now. Thomas was at church, too, praying for all he was worth.

When Thomas and Camellia returned home, Thomas sat down with his Bible alongside Roger's bed. Mary was bathing Roger's forehead and hands in cool water. Emotionally exhausted, Camellia sank in a chair beside the radio, turned it on low, and sat back half-dozing, half-listening to some classical music. Suddenly the music stopped....

"We interrupt this program to bring you a bulletin...."

The Japanese had attacked Pearl Harbor!

Roger—and he'd been nearly dead for days—sat bolt upright in bed. He looked around like he didn't know where he was. Then he raised both hands and arms together like he was aiming some sort of weapon and he started squawking: "Airplanes! *Goddamn Jap airplanes*! Att-att-att-att-att! Eeee-errr-ooommmm! Splaaatoosh! Got 'in! Fuckin' Jap airplanes! Att-att-att-att-att! Eeeee-errrr-oooommm! Splaaatooosh! Got 'im, too!"

Thomas, Mary, and Camellia all stared at Roger in amazement. Camellia remembered Doc Feldman once saying that a dying person will sometimes have a strange and sudden rally, and then in the next minute fall back down on the pillow...dead.

But Roger did not fall back dead. Camellia guessed the devil or Boro the gypsy or something or other still had some unfinished business with the Thomas Stephenses.

But for the moment, they were all so startled—and happy—at Roger's sudden turn for the better that the war bulletin had not sunk in.

In fact, Camellia had gone outside for something or other and saw all the neighbors running around on the shell road, and when one of them asked her, "Did you hear the radio just now?" Camellia beamed with her magnificent smile and said, "Oh, *yes*, and isn't it *wonderful* what has happened!"

The woman gave Camellia the weirdest look and went off muttering, "Well, what do you expect? Those Stephenses probably got *Jap* blood in 'em, too, along with the gypsy!"

Part Two

Chapter Five

"This war is doing so much good, it's a shame we didn't have it sooner."

Amanda Cartwright's statement was considered by most people on Bell's Island as atrocious at the time and even worse in retrospect when she and Simon lost two sons in that war.

But the statement had more truth in it than most people cared to admit. The war broke the back of the Depression finally for the Stephens clan and prosperity came to many others on the island as well.

Thanks to Charlie Stephens' shrewd, sharp, go-get-'em maneuvering amongst all the right politicians, the Stephens Marine Railway landed one fat navy contract after another to build landing craft for the Normandy and other invasions.

The Stephenses formed a legal corporation of the Marine Railway and elected Thomas president. Camellia could tell her father hadn't felt so big since the early prosperity days of the Stephens Tu-Rest Home when Grandfather LeCates was still living, and they all dined on lamb chops and caviar, and Thomas wore his cutaway coat to meals.

The wages were high at the shipyard, and all the members of each Stephens family were on the payroll, including all the grandchildren—even babies—and yes! even Mary's beagles came in for their cut, being listed in government reports as "security dogs." A good deal of this was little more than high-tone gypsy thieving, but it didn't seem to upset Thomas too much, seeing that he was *president* of the firm.

The Pearl Harbor bulletin on the radio may or may not have been the thing that roused Roger out of his coma and the pneumonia, but he did get well, he didn't get sent to reform school after all, and Mary did a 180 degree turn in her attitude toward him. She couldn't give Roger enough attention now and she was praising him for every little good thing she detected in him. She went to bat for him in his school difficulties and in his neighborhood brawls and no longer pushed these problems off on Camellia.

Camellia calculated that it had taken her mother nine years to get over her postpartum crazies, but thanks to the war, which had diverted everybody's attention, Mary was back to her lighthearted, giddy-headed old self again. She even reopened her little Bell's Island Library. She said she was sure some servicemen on leave from Camp Conover near Royal Hall would find their way down to Bell's Island's "center of culture and knowledge."

Camellia, too, experienced a remarkable surge of good fortune and new-found happiness. In a few short months, she marshalled her courage and gave up smoking, drinking, AND Forrester.

She had long since quit playing the horses, but now with a clearer head to hear her gypsy intuitions she invested in the legitimate stock market and once again began building her music nest egg.

In the summer of 1942, after her teaching year in the county was over, she lost no time in getting to Baltimore for a quick stint at the conservatory, staying at her Aunt Lizbeth's home for those months. She was still working on her master's in music and drama and was even considering going for her doctorate.

All this music education wasn't getting her any closer to The Met, but it did go a long way in landing her the position of music director for the Royal Hall High School. She felt it was a plum too good to pass up.

By this time Forrester had been appointed superintendent of the county schools, so there was a new principal at Royal Hall High and Camellia didn't have to answer directly to Forrester. But he was still trying to lure Camellia back into his nest. Only this time she was not as vulnerable as when she had been on liquor and only a lowly traveling singing teacher for the elementary grades.

When Camellia came back from her courses at the conservatory in Baltimore, she rented a sumptuous apartment in a sumptuous colonial mansion in the heart of "historic Royal Hall," then she stole Aunt Sairy Middleton away from the Stephens Tu-Rest Home and brought her to Royal Hall to be her maid!

Camellia was totally delighted with Royal Hall. It was truly a gentle, genteel town. It had its roots in the Church of England wealthy class who had settled in the area in the 1600s and built large plantations along the Mocoteague River.

There was a distinctive well-bred aura to Royal Hall as Wintergreen County's seat of government. The town's arrow-straight avenues with their carefully right-angled cross streets and the exquisite architecture and landscaping of the homes and buildings all spoke of well-to-do colonial times. There were large Georgian, Federal, and Victorian dwellings bordered with neatly trimmed hedges and boxwood. The brick sidewalks and cobblestone streets were dotted here and there with ladies in blue-rinsed hairstyles, walking arm in arm toward the banks and stores.

Camellia suspected that Royal Hall ladies always walked in pairs, for who knew when there might be some "bad people" from Gainsbiddle coming through town? The ladies might see and hear things they shouldn't, and the shock at such a time might be too great for their genteel sensibilities if they were walking alone.

Royal Hall had its "poor people," but they "knew their place." The roughly dressed, weather-beaten workingmen, farmers, and Negroes walked the streets of Royal Hall along with the ladies with the blue-rinsed hairdo's, but they were quiet and respectful with no spitting on the sidewalk, no rough language or lewd horseplay like one was likely to see on the streets of Gainsbiddle.

Royal Hall was where the courts, the government, and authority were. Through the business-like, almost stern atmosphere, Camellia perceived something very pretty about it all, especially the scene at the main intersection of Wintergreen Avenue and Prince Edward Street, looking west up along Prince Edward Street in the general direction of the courthouse. The courthouse, with its sandy red brick facade, sat back a bit from the north-south running Wintergreen Avenue and overlooked a well-trimmed green.

Beyond the courthouse and all along Prince Edward Street were very judicious-looking county government buildings, followed by large white colonial residences, all nestled under huge green umbrella trees arching over the cobblestone street from either side and forming an emerald tunnel. At the end of Prince Edward Street was the Royal Hall High School. And not too far from the school was the old colonial mansion where Camellia had her apartment. Back down at the beginning of Prince Edward Street where it intersected with Wintergreen Avenue was the old ivy-covered Episcopal Church.

To add icing to her Royal Hall cake, late in the summer of 1942 Camellia became the soloist in that grand old Episcopal Church. She was really putting distance between herself and Bell's Island now!

Her first Sunday morning as soloist came on Labor Day weekend. And it was hot! One of those "wringing-wet sweatin' hot" mornings as they said on Bell's Island. But Camellia didn't feel it one bit.

When she looked out her bedroom window, she saw a hazy reddish cast to everything—the sky, the cobblestones, the white houses all along Prince Edward Street. Leaves hung motionless, no birds were singing, and even the cicadas were silent. The weather was grossly uncomfortable, but there still was an unspeakable beauty to everything.

There was music in Camellia's soul. She could hear it, feel it. It went far deeper than just the notes on her sheet music for the morning solo.

Before leaving her colonial apartment, she opened both the front and back doors and all the broad windows. The most delicious scent of rose blossoms from the surrounding yard drifted into the house.

It was one of those moments when she wanted to live forever.

As she prepared to leave the house, she looked great...and she knew it! What a headiness to know that you are good-looking, talented, educated, tasteful in manner and dress, and have the money once again to keep all this up!

She appeared taller and unusually lithe this morning for all her tendency to be heavyset. Her black hair curled softly around her face under one of those huge, wide-brim hats of the 1940s.

She went down the steps of the mansion and out onto the brick sidewalk, her high heel white pumps clicky-clacking to the spritely rhythm in her soul. She felt like a gossamer gliding on the air in her filmy, powder-blue dress. Her little purse and her sheet music folder were clutched to her bosom.

As she walked along beneath the emerald boughs of the umbrella trees along Prince Edward Street, she was aware every now and then of little patches of red sunlight glinting down through the leaves onto her head and shoulders. The heat? She didn't feel it at all. She was in another world!

After performing her successful solo at the Episcopal Church and basking in all the compliments and greetings from the parishioners, Camellia returned to her mansion apartment where Aunt Sairy Middleton had lunch all ready for her. They had hoped to have Mrs. Elderkin for lunch, too. Mrs. Elderkin—one of the typical blue-rinsed ladies of Royal Hall—owned the mansion and had her residence in one of the wings. But she was off on one of her Sunday jaunts, traveling and visiting as usual, in spite of gasoline rationing and all the inconveniences of a nation at war.

As Camellia sat relaxing on the porch of the mansion that afternoon, the heat had not let up one bit all day, but she still felt cool and fresh and elated. All around everywhere there was such a aura of peacefulness. No roughneck Stephens cousins running about. No blackguarding kinfolk shouting back and forth at each other. No vulgar kid brother snooping around, fighting, fussing, and making obscene noises. No unpredictable mother, at one moment cheerful and wisecracking, at the next, ailing and weeping. No well-meaning, but slightly cracked father, all primed for the Kingdom of Heaven, while driving everybody around him straight to Hell.

No longer would she have to brace against the wildness and clamor of Bell's Island's wind, rain, and ice storms or instinctively recoil at the sickening smell of its marshes and waterfront. No longer would she have to shuck those jagged-shelled oysters for the family meals and scar up her piano hands when Mary didn't feel like shucking them and Thomas was at work. No longer would she have to travel the rough county roads to the elementary schools, especially to that stinking, filthy Gainsbiddle one, to give those stupid singing classes.

Here in Royal Hall was quietness, gentility, and beauty, a colonial sense of orderliness, respectability, and stability. The long drawn-out Depression of the 1930s had not seemed to affect Royal Hall as it had the other towns and the rural areas. There was no lack of elegance and pleasant living here. And the war didn't seem to be affecting Royal Hall adversely either.

In spite of the oppressive heat, Camellia remained immersed in a deep sense of well-being such as she'd rarely experienced before. It was the beginning of a glorious era for her. A time when all the frayed ends of her psyche could mend themselves. It was a time of rejuvenation from all the roughness and frustration of the past decade and a half that had wrung some of the natural exuberance out of her. And though she may have been roughened and toughened on the inside, she had lost none of her high classiness on the outside. What she had learned in her earliest associations with the Bell's Island Inn, with her LeCates' grandparents and with Claudie, still remained. And she quickly became the talk and toast of Royal Hall society.

Mrs. Elderkin took Camellia under her wing as the weeks and months progressed. The rich old dowager introduced Camellia to "all the right people." Mrs. Elderkin threw tea parties, dinner parties, bridge luncheons, and "just little get-togethers" at the mansion, and Camellia was the guest of honor and shown off like a pedigreed poodle. And she won blue ribbons in every category—for her looks, her poise, her musical talents, and "that charming British accent."

Aunt Sairy Middleton served at all these affairs, as well as at many of the community do's such as church suppers and Masonic banquets where Camellia was either the special soloist or the guest of Mrs. Elderkin.

Aunt Sairy watched, well pleased, as Camellia won the favor of all the Royal Hall ladies' cliques. There was one clique made up of church ladies and they passed God's judgement on everything from how long a woman's skirt should be to what angle a woman should or should not let a man look at her bosom. There was another clique composed of middle-aged garden and bridge club ladies: they were the ones who had lived long enough to solve all their own life's problems (or else successfully hide them), and now they were qualified to solve everybody else's. And there was the lodge sisters' clique—the Eastern Star, the Historical Society, and the Daughters of the American Revolution—all those which touted honor and loyalty, patriotism and civic-mindedness and, perish the thought! Maryland Beat Biscuits!

There were men in the picture for Camellia, too, at this time. She had many opportunities to attract dates as she was well-liked and into everything: her job as music director at Royal Hall High with its many public song services; her special engagements to play the piano or sing at weddings, banquets, and patriotic affairs; her regular soloist spot at the Episcopal Church; and her recently being chosen head of the Shore Choral and Dramatic Society.

To everyone she appeared to be enjoying her big fish in a little pond success and her social whirl with a variety of escorts—some young, some older, some grandsons and nephews of Royal Hall rich ladies like Mrs. Elderkin, sometimes a lawyer or politician, and she could have picked up again with Forrester, if she had wanted to.

Yet often Camellia would notice Aunt Sairy Middleton slowly shaking her head and mumbling, "Umm, umm, umm" when she accepted yet another date or agreed to sing for perhaps the ten billionth time, *I Love You Truly*.

For only too quickly it was 1945 and Camellia was twenty-nine years old. She was still lovely to look at, still full of talent and still in demand locally, still taking courses toward her master's degree....But she had neither married nor had she tried any further to break into opera. She was not even composing music or rather she was no longer *hearing* any *to* compose.

For so many years things had been too adverse for her to get away to New York City or even Baltimore. Now, she wondered, could it be that things were *too good*? And too good even for her to hear that strange and beautiful unwritten music that had sustained her when all else had fallen through?

As for men...? Aunt Sairy said to her one day, "Mis' Camellia, yo' mind is like a house full o' rooms. Yo' got a middlin' size room with yo' music in it; yo' got another room—an' it's a BIG one!—with all yo' fancy livin' in it; then yo' got a li'l tiny room with yo' Bell's Island folks in it an' yo' hardly even look in dat room no mo'....An' Ah sees....Yas'm, Ah sees *one mo' room*—but it's empty. Mis' Camellia, it's empty—an' it's locked—an' dat's de-room-dat-belongs-to-have-a-man-in-it!"

Camellia was thinking, *A man in it? What for?* She wasn't out to attract men to exploit any more as she was rolling in the dough from her wise investments on Wall Street. And she still believed men would exploit her once their acquaintance got beyond mere superficialities, so sooner than having to resort to "gypsy magic" to hold someone at bay, she usually dropped a fellow after one or two dates.

It was a cold, dreary winter afternoon in February 1945 when Camellia went to the USO canteen in Royal Hall to check out some details on the upcoming show her Shore Choral and Dramatic Society was going to put on at Camp Conover just a few miles southeast of Royal Hall.

She was dressed to the nines as usual and she talked at length with the officer in charge. Out of the corner of her eye she kept noticing a stocky young sergeant with rusty-colored hair looking admiringly at her. Well, this was nothing new, she had been looked at before, so she continued to go over the arrangements with the officer and tried to ignore the sergeant.

Yet every time she turned her head slightly, she'd see the sergeant still looking at her. There was lust in those mild blue eyes, yet it was an innocent kind of yearning, like what is often seen on a child's face when he's looking in a candy store window.

Camellia suddenly caught herself returning the sergeant's gaze with an intense curiosity, as though she were seeing some rare breed of male animal that she'd never run across before. The sergeant smiled giddily at her, as though he were seeing some sort of magical nymph that the gods had materialized just for him out of some ancient mythology.

Camellia could feel the color rising in her face and a certain biting desire race through her like she had not felt since she'd lain on that grassy hummock in the Bell's Island sands dunes nearly a decade and a half before.

It was not often in her life that Camellia ever lost command of herself or wavered in that ever-so-slightly arrogant pose that made people defer to her. But something was happening. The lock on a certain empty room in her mind was being jiggled loose.

She looked again into the wistful eyes of the sergeant. She was surely not the first woman he'd ever looked on to lust after, she reasoned. And he certainly was not the first man who had ever looked on her to lust after her. But suddenly she knew what it was—*He* was the first man *she* had ever looked on to truly lust after!

The sergeant was still gazing at Camellia when she turned to leave the USO. As she walked by him, she smiled playfully, touched his barrel chest, and said, "Sergeant, you remind me of a teddy bear!"

He beamed at her. "You want to hug me?"

She slipped her arm around his waist and said, "I believe I do."

His arm went quickly around her waist, and they walked together out onto the Royal Hall street.

"It's cold standing out here," Camellia said, "Would you like to come to my apartment for some hot coffee, maybe? I live right over there, just a ways from the courthouse."

The sergeant looked toward the imposing white mansions down Prince Edward Street and smiled eagerly. "I think that would be fine!" he said.

He was clean-cut and polite, yet had a worldly wise bearing, Camellia noted. Obviously from a good home but had been around a bit, too.

They went the few short blocks to her mansion apartment. Mrs. Elderkin (bless her!) wasn't home. Aunt Sairy was there. *But never mind Aunt Sairy,* Camellia was thinking. And she didn't intend to play with her "teddy bear" just yet anyhow.

Over hot mugs of coffee brought to them by Aunt Sairy, the sergeant told Camellia he was from South Dakota; that he had no family—no close family, that is. That he had been raised by an aunt and uncle in Chicago after his parents had both become too ill to take care of him.

"Then you are a long way from home," Camellia noted.

The sergeant had just taken a sip of his coffee, and he seemed to have difficulty in swallowing it.

"Coffee too strong? Too hot?" asked Camellia.

"No, no. It's just fine," said the sergeant, clearing his throat. Then he smiled broadly at Camellia and picked up with the original conversation. "Yes, this is an entirely new part of the United States to me."

Camellia reflected for a moment. He had said his name was Jurgensen. Should she mention—even in a joke—"the Mennonite bootlegger," Karl Jurgensen? Maybe not. It would hardly be polite. He couldn't possibly now the bootlegger, so any reference would be lost on him.

The sergeant had said his first name was Anselm, which was German since his mother had been born in Germany. "Yes," said Camellia, "I thought I detected a slight German accent."

The sergeant asked, "Are you originally from England?"

For a moment Camellia couldn't figure out what he meant. She had never connected her *educated* British accent with *England,* only with Claudie.

"Why no! I just sound like that," she answered him.

"Well, you sound mighty good to me!"

Camellia was trying to keep her wits about her. The sergeant—Anselm—was stirring up fires in her she didn't possibly even know existed. But she knew one thing—she couldn't possibly let him find out she was from Bell's Island.

He was speaking again. "Miss Stephens, if you need an extra accompanist for your Choral and Dramatic Society program at Camp Conover, you could call on me. I'm pretty good on the piano."

He noticed Camellia's baby grand, walked over to it and said, "May I?"

"Sure," said Camellia. "And call me 'Camellia,' okay?"

"Yes. Camellia," he said. Then in an aside, "The accent is British, but the idiom is...well...American."

Camellia said quickly, "I'm from Royal Hall. It was settled by the British."

"Yes, I know," said Anselm, absently. He had started playing Beethoven's *Emperor Concerto* from Camellia's sheet music. But after a few bars he abruptly stopped and with a nervous laugh said, "Uh, that is, somebody at the USO told me it was."

Camellia looked at him blankly. "That it was what? That what was what?" She was totally confused and only because she wasn't listening to Anselm as much as she was reacting to him.

"That it was settled by the British," he said.

"Oh, yes, the British!" said Camellia with a glorious smile that turned into a helpless laugh. Her hand came down on his arm with the gentlest touch. "You know, Anselm, I don't think either of us knows what we're saying."

She sat down beside him on the piano bench. "You play beautifully, Anselm. Shall we try a duet?"

"On the piano? Or...?" Anselm asked her, rolling his blue eyes in mock innocence.

"The piano. The piano," said Camellia soberly. Wisdom bade her not rush things.

A day or so later, after Camellia and Anselm had concluded their first meeting at her mansion apartment and promised to have more of the same, Camellia drove down to Bell's Island in response to her mother's phone call. Mary, who had never learned to drive a car, was out of her ulcer medicine and the Bell Island pharmacy was out of it, too, so could Camellia come get the prescription and have it filled in Royal Hall?

Glumly, Camellia agreed to do so. She drove along for about twelve miles, thinking of Anselm, trying to figure out how old he might be, finally deciding on twenty-five and hoping that wasn't enough difference between her twenty-nine to make people talk.

She was coming to that vast stretch of weird and lonesome marshland that started where the little black village of Satin (Aunt Sairy's home base) left off and continued on for several miles until the Bell's Island bridge was reached.

The pines and deciduous trees further back had stopped abruptly, and on either side of the narrow, winding roadway there were now acres and acres of dead trees, the salt marshes having crept in at their bases over the years and gradually taken their life away from them. Their bleached-out, bark-less trunks rose up without any branches left and looked like thin tombstones to a bygone era. On some of these silent sentinels were perched black buzzards, their wings outstretched, giving a totem pole effect. Deep ditches were on either side of the roadway and there was nothing but a thin strip of winter-browned and withered grass between the concrete and the gooey muck of the marsh-bottomed trenches.

On past the dead trees and stretching to the horizons all round to the west, south, and north, there were vast expanses of low, brown marshlands with numerous guts and gullies of salt water snaking in and out, and strange-looking shore birds dotted here and there. Suddenly a great blue heron rose up almost in front of Camellia's car and flapped its way awkwardly to the other side of the road.

As always, this was a wild, forsaken, and mysterious area through which to drive, yet Camellia felt strangely exhilarated. Drifting across the marsh there seemed to be...strains of music? Music? Could she possibly be hearing music again—those eerie unformed sounds she hadn't heard in so long? And if so, why? Why now?

She shifted uncomfortably in the car. Something hearkened her back many years before to the first time she'd heard strange music and had taken it as a warning, leaving poor Ralph Drummond alone in the sand. Her throat tightened. Ralph Drummond had been one of the first Bell's Islanders killed in the war. Though she hadn't thought of him in years, suddenly she deeply missed the first and only man to whom she'd ever given her body.

She listened intently. What was this music *now* trying to tell her? It seemed so ethereal, so beautiful, in spite of its mysteriousness. It couldn't possibly be another warning, could it?

Before she could answer her own questions, she realized she was rolling over the Bell's Island bridge and her reverie ceased. Off to her left she could see the Stephens Marine Railways and the trim white skipjack the men had recently completed. With the war nearly over, they were already converting to peacetime operations. Her eye was suddenly drawn to the stern of the big boat: *Camellia Stephens, Bell's Island, Maryland.*

Camellia couldn't believe what she was seeing and she was furious. She braked her car to a noisy halt in front of the Stephens Tu-Rest Home and was barely inside the house before she was blaring at her mother:

"What's the big idea of painting *my name* across the ahhs-end of a Bell's Island oyster boat?"

Mary shrugged. "Why not? You paid for it."

Camellia had never begrudged the large sums of money for which Mary had asked.

Mary knew she did well with her wise investments on Wall Street, so Camellia felt she couldn't very well withhold capital that was going into the business to shore them up for when the government war contracts would cease. But putting *her name* on that damned boat....

Camellia said, "And I guess you are going to remind me how beautiful and graceful skipjacks are. Well, *I don't care*. They still say 'waterman's family' to me."

Mary looked appropriately hurt and said, "Well, the stern of an oyster boat is not quite the marquee of The Met, I admit. But why is it, Camellia, that you are so ashamed of the name 'Stephens' and your hometown of Bell's Island? We are all living honorable lives now and we're not exactly poverty-stricken any more, either."

Camellia snorted and started to say, *Honorable lives? When you have your beagles on the government payroll as security dogs*? But she decided not to argue with Mary as she could see her mother wasn't feeling well.

While Camellia was at the Tu-Rest Home, she helped Mary straighten up Roger's chaotic bedroom. Camellia began wondering what was happening to her sense of time. It seemed Roger had gone from baby smell to boy smell to man smell so fast it was unbelievable. He wasn't even a teenager yet, but his clothes reeked of beer and cigarettes which she supposed Charlie Stephens was sneaking to him. And the sheets on his bed....?

She showed them to Mary and said, "Do you realize Roger is 'at that age'?"

Mary shook her head and said, "At what age?"

Camellia said, "Oh, for heaven's sake, Mama! How naive can you be? You better re-read some of Doc Feldman's medical books in your little Bell's Island Library—the chapters on male adolescence."

Mary said, "Oh," and woke up a little bit. Then she added, "But he's barely twelve years old."

Camellia felt like saying, *So was Jesus*, but thought the better of it. She did say, "Well, just watch him. I don't supposed there is anything you—or Papa (perish the thought!)—can tell him that he doesn't already know about his body, about sex, and about girls, so long as he hangs around with Charlie Stephens and sneaks off to Moonlight's place all the time. But talk to him anyhow, please, Mama, and warn him to leave girls alone...unless you don't mind becoming an unplanned grandmother...."

"But he's barely twelve years old," Mary kept insisting.

"But he won't *stay* barely twelve years old'," Camellia reminded her.

The next time Camellia saw Sergeant Anselm Jurgensen it was on a Saturday and at the USO again. She had gone in there to check once more about her Choral and Dramatic Society's performance at Camp Conover. Anselm didn't see her come in this time, because he was absorbed in banging away on the piano and belting out an extra potent version of *Barnacle Bill the Sailor* to a roomful of lonely young recruits obviously away form home for the first time and happy to hear anything that would make them laugh, the more vulgar the better.

Camellia watched and listened, trying to decide whether to be amused or perturbed. Anselm was really hamming it up—putting on a silly wig with yellow curls and singing falsetto for the part of "the fair young maiden," then changing to a sailor's cap and corncob pipe and singing bass for the part of "Barnacle Bill."

Who's that knocking at my door? Who's that knocking at my door?
Who's that knocking at my door? Cried the fair young maiden."
"It's only me, I'm home from the sea. Cried Barnacle Bill the Sailor."
"What's that thing between your legs? What's that thing between your legs?
What's that thing between your legs? Cried the fair young maiden."
"It's only a pole to put in your..."

Anselm stopped and his normally ruddy face went a shade deeper as he caught Camellia's eye.

A bit of a scowl had come over her countenance, but Anselm was one of those people she couldn't say angry at for long.

She walked up to the piano. He whispered, "Are you mad at me?"

"Not really," she said. "Has anyone ever called you a Danish ham?"

Anselm looked at her in mock amazement. "To you, I am a 'teddy bear' AND a Danish ham?"

"To me, you are...."She couldn't finish the sentence because she honestly didn't know what he was to her.

"You going to be in your apartment later this afternoon?" he asked.

She nodded.

"Okay if I come over for awhile?"

Again she nodded.

He came as promised. He talked a little about his aunt and uncle in Chicago. "Aunt Wilma always said I had musical talent and she saw to it that I had lessons. She thought I should be a concert pianist, but she had some funny ideas. She didn't want me to eat meat. She said she was afraid it would make me virile."

He said it with such an air of innocence that Camellia's funny bone was set to throbbing. After she caught her breath from laughing, she turned serious, and let her eyes roam admiringly over him. At length she said, "But obviously you *did* eat meat."

He smiled, acknowledging the compliment.

It wasn't that he was handsome or especially sexy, even, not in the way the movies portrayed a sexy man, but to *her*, he was...both handsome AND sexy!

He had such a low-key playful streak in him—like he was laughing both at the world and at himself. Camellia had been amazed when he'd said he was only twenty years old because he *seemed* so much older. At times when he would turn reflective, he had sort of a world-weary look, like the kind of look one gets when they've "seen it all and done most of it." Yet there was something open and uncomplicated about him, too, like there was still a kid in him, wanting to see and experience even more.

At one point he asked her, "Your folks? They still living?"

And she said simply, "Yes, they live away from here."

She hadn't said where. But he did not probe. He was full of curiosity about everything, but mannerly with it.

Later they both waxed philosophical.

Anselm said, "There's something deep in me that rebels against fighting. Yes, I'm in the army, because like any good red-blooded American male, I'm supposed to be. But I've always been in the supply department where I'm less likely to have to kill anyone. I welcomed the service in a way because I could get to see the world and get some education. I've always read a lot. I've always wanted to know things. To know why everything is the way it is. Camellia, do you ever wonder why everything is the way it is?"

Camellia thought for a bit, then ventured, "I have found music to be the panacea for whatever I can't understand and perhaps couldn't do anything about even if I did understand. For all my life I have wanted to study and sing opera. So far that wish has eluded me."

He became thoughtful and said, "And I always wanted to be an inventor. I was always examining my old man's still—I mean, my *uncle's* Stillson wrench...to see how it worked....Hahaha...used to call Uncle Johann 'the old man' sometimes...hahaha..."

In Camellia's concern to keep her own family a secret, she was barely noticing how nervous Anselm was when he mentioned things about *his* family.

As though to change the subject, he said offhand, "I thought I might go to Bell's Island sometime. I'd always heard of it, but like the New Yorker who's never been to the top of the Empire State Building or the Philadelphian who's never seen the Liberty Bell, I am a

Wintergr—uh, I mean, uh, a Camp Conover soldier who's never been to Bell's Island. Isn't that something?"

His awkwardness still didn't arouse Camellia's suspicion. Instead, thinking of the shipyard and the skipjack, she nervously said, "Oh, you don't want to go to Bell's Island."

"Why not?"

"It's nothing but fish and crabs and smell and things like that."

"Have you been there? I guess you have, living here in Royal Hall, so close....But the farm wasn't that far away, either."

"What farm?" Camellia was beginning to think Anselm wasn't making much sense.

"Oh, Camp Canover has a farm, didn't you know? Fresh eggs for the soldiers every morning and...and...."

"No, I didn't know that," Camellia said flatly. *Why did Anselm seem so uneasy*? she began to think. *Did he have something to hide, too*?

Next thing Camellia knew, he was suggesting, "Let's go get a sandwich at the drugstore, huh?"

Camellia was game. Food, she was thinking, was always a good way to change the subject.

They started in the Royal Hall drugstore. There was a tall ugly-faced man hulking around in there. He was dressed in a ragged suit jacket, overalls, and a battered old hat. He exuded the smell of dirt, stale sweat, plug tobacco, and whiskey. Camellia gave a little jump. She had once before had Karl Jurgensen walk across her path and she remembered him. He was not somebody you'd easily forget.

Anselm stopped abruptly, halfway in the door, and then backed out, almost trampling on Camellia's feet. He said, "Oh, let's go to the movies instead. They've got popcorn and soft drinks, if you're hungry."

Camellia laughed and said "okay." Then she added, teasingly, "What's the matter? You don't owe that 'Mennonite bootlegger' any money, do you?"

Anselm was visibly sweating. "Wh-what 'Mennonite bootlegger'?"

"Oh, just one of our Wintergreen County 'characters'. Didn't you see that man in there? And, oddly enough, he happens to have the same last name as yours."

"Jurgensen?"

"Yes," said Camellia. "But there are a lot of *Stephenses* around, too. Doesn't necessarily mean anything." Camellia was happy to get that little disclaimer in.

They went on to the movies, but it was obvious to both of them that neither of them was paying much attention to what was on the screen.

Camellia's Choral and Dramatic Society put on their program at Camp Conover, as planned. She saw Anselm there but didn't get to speak with him. She was also busy with her regular work as music director at Royal Hall High, so it was several weeks before she could accept a date again with Anselm. In the meantime, she had missed him, she had literally ached for him.

The next time they did get together it was at her mansion apartment again. After a flurry of hugs and kisses, Anselm said, "You mentioned the last time I was here that there were a lot of Stephenses around, but that didn't necessarily mean anything. But tell me, is there more than one *Camellia* Stephens in this county?"

"You've been to Bell's Island?" she said tensely.

"Yes."

"And you saw that skipjack?"

"Yes."

"So, okay. Some outfit named a boat after me. Big deal." Camellia was getting a little angry.

"But it's a beautiful boat. And so are you....But did some people name a tourist house and a shipyard and a seafood place after you, *too*? The name Stephens is all over that island!" he said incredulously.

"All right, Anselm. You might as well know. You'll find it out anyhow. I'm *from* Bell's Island. Those Stephenses are my people."

"What's so terrible about that?"

"For one thing, Bell's Islanders are so crude. My father and mother aren't, but the rest of the Stephenses are. And the Stephenses have never had a very good reputation. In short, they are crooks—except, and once again, for my father."

Anselm studied her for awhile, then said, "Okay. So, you might as well know something about me, too, as you're likely to figure it out anyway, if you haven't already. Remember that 'Mennonite bootlegger' you saw in the drugstore the other evening?"

"Yes."

"That was my old man. I'm from Wintergreen County, Camellia."

Camellia was completely taken back. At length she found her voice and said, "Then all that talk about South Dakota and Chicago and your Aunt Wilma and Uncle Johann...Not true, huh?"

"Partially true," Anselm said. "There is a Wilma and a Johann Jurgensen, but they are the old man's cousins—and they are much better people than he, let me assure you. They live in Wilmington, Delaware. I stayed with them for a year or so after I ran away from this county when I was sixteen. Wilma and Johann were the ones who got me at least helf-way civilized."

Anselm paused a moment, then said, "Do you want to hear any more or do you want me to leave?"

Camellia thought in spite of herself. "No, I don't want you to leave. Continue with what you were saying."

Anselm went on. "In this county, early in this century, the old man was known as 'that bit of Danish-Norwegian crap that filtered out from the Delaware Swedes'. He came to Maryland in 1905. He had with him his German-born woman, Maude Vogel. He'd found her selling sex on the streets of New York and 'saved her from a life of sin', he always bragged to everybody. But they were never married, I don't think—and eventually there were ten children. I was the last one. 'The corn on the outside row', the old man always called me. He always hated me, but no more than I hated him.

"He and my big, fleshy German mother had their first two children while still in Wilmington when he was working as a laborer in a railroad yard. Then they came down here and became squatters on a Mennonite farm in east Wintergreen County. They had come originally as caretakers of the farm while the owner was away, but the owner never did come back. But the old man and his family stayed. After awhile he let the property fall apart except to plant it in corn for his whiskey still. He never paid taxes on the property, always claiming it belonged to somebody else. The county once tried to auction the property off for back taxes, but the old man bribed the county commissioners with his moonshine whiskey, and they dropped the matter and never bothered the property again. And there have been about four generations now of Jurgensen blood living there, scot-free."

Anselm glanced anxiously at Camellia. "Shall I go on?"

Camellia nodded and smiled at him reassuringly.

Anselm continued. "The Jurgensens weren't Mennonites—parasites says it better—but the old man always tried to make out like his family were Mennonites. That's why he is known as 'that Mennonite bootlegger'. There were Mennonite farms all around him and his was like a sore thumb in the midst of their orderly and clean community. But they tolerated him because they liked to buy his whiskey which he sold them cut-rate.

"All my older brothers and sisters, except Margarethe who married a Mennonite, married into the bohunk clan off a bit to the north of the farm. They were the descendants of the Slav and Pole immigrant laborers who were shanghai'd on the Baltimore wharves and brought to the shore to work in the tomato canneries. The cannery owners never paid them half the time and they were forced to subsist off the rotting tomato skins piled up in mountains alongside the canneries."

Camellia was trying to assimilate all this. She said, "Then *you* spent your first sixteen years of your life right over there in the ethnic section of this Wintergreen County?"

"Yes."

"And it never rubbed off on you?!"

"Did Bell's Island rub off on *you*?"

"I should certainly hope not!" Camellia said in a big huff.

They nearly rolled onto the floor laughing. There was an instant camaraderie now as they recognized they had something very basic in common—both had backgrounds they wanted to hide and from which to hide.

When they caught their breath a bit, Anselm said, "Shall the waterman's daughter and the moonshiner/bootlegger's son go get that sandwich at the drugstore from which they got scared away the other night?"

"Fine with me," said Camellia. "Unless you'd rather go to Bell's Island, eat clams and turnips with my Grandpaw Azariah, and hear all about thieving gypsy Stephenses?"

"We'll do that tomorrow night," said Anselm, helping her into her coat.

Camellia was in no hurry to take her "teddy bear/Danish ham" to Bell's Island. She no more wanted her parents to suspect who Anselm really was than he had wanted her to know. And there was Roger. She didn't know how he would react to the sergeant. Roger was so scrappy.

During the next several dates Camellia and Anselm, now with their pretences off (though they'd not yet gotten their clothes off), became even more intrigued with each other. They became instant confidantes. They told each other everything—skeleton-in-the-closet tales on themselves and their families. Nothing was too personal or too shameful to divulge. Neither was shocked or embarrassed by anything the other said.

Anselm told her, "As I grew up, almost my entire energy and wits were taken up with trying to stay clear of the fighting, beatings, and commotion between my old man and my mother, between their children and the bohunk children and all the grandchildren who came and made the old farmhouse a hotbed of ethnic carousing and confusion.

"The old house by then had no paint on it. It was dirty inside and out. The windows were never washed. The furniture was smelly and rat-infested. The ceilings were cracked and the floors warped. Everything in there shook and swayed and rattled when they all got in there doing that yelling and stomping that passed for old world singing and folk dancing. There was constant boozing and plenty of fornication—and yes, incest, too—to keep things lively.

"There was an old piano in the house, also some fiddles and an accordion that the bohunks always brought, and I taught myself how to play all of them and was good enough at it that they often let me be their accompanist for their singing and dancing. I liked that because that way I was less likely to get stomped on or pummelled.

"The old man was always bragging to the Mennonites who came there to buy whiskey, bragging about what a good father he was. He said stuff like, 'I make sure my kids and grandkids work hard. Beat 'em when necessary, too. But I can't do nothing with the youngest one, Olaf'. The family all called me 'Olaf', which is my middle name. The old man went on, 'Olaf's fat and lazy but he can wriggle or roll away from me most every time I have to cane him. You know what the saying is, Brother Holbein, about "never plant corn on the outside row"...because it never amounts to nothing.

"'That's what Olaf is—"the corn on the outside row." The last seed I planted. Total waste. He won't work, he runs off every chance he gets, he's always got his nose in some book or other he gets from those cousins of mine up in Wilmington where we go visiting sometimes'."

Anselm continued, "Early on in my life something inside me said of my family, 'I do not like these people; I will not *be* like these people'. It was always such a relief—those trips to Wilmington. The old man would take us up there for a week or two at a time to sponge off his cousins, Johann and Wilma. They owned a wholesale grocery and we had some decent food for a change. The old man bought the sugar for his whiskey-making operation from Johann.

"Johann and Wilma had an attic full of books—all kinds of textbooks, science books, classics, histories, literature—and I would fill a suitcase full each time to bring back. The old man hated me for it, and the rest of the family teased me. The old man was nothing but an ignorant laborer who could barely write his name, and my mother could barely speak English, much less read or write it. The old man finagled the Mennonites into letting his kids go to their grade school, but he pulled them all out by the third grade to work on his farm. All but me. He let me go the full seven grades. He said I was no good to him anyhow on the farm."

Naturally they got around to stories of their adventures—mostly misadventures—with the opposite sex. Camellia told Anselm about Charlie Stephens nearly raping her and Anselm told about his niece, Peachie, trying to do somewhat the same thing to him:

"Peachie was my oldest brother Harald's oldest daughter. She and I were about the same age—fifteen—when she and her bohunk girl pal hid a rope in the grass between the barn and a shed. When I came along the path that evening, the two girls—and they were hidden in the bushes, one on one side and one on the other side of the path—they raised up the rope and down I went. Both girls jumped on me and held me to the ground. Peachie got one hand down inside my pants and Christ-a-mighty! She wouldn't quit! I wrenched loose after a while and started chasing after Peachie to bop her for the indignity, not to rape her, though by all rights I should have. Peachie and her bohunk girl pal went bawling and screaming up to the old farmhouse, claiming *'Olaf tried to do something nasty to us!'* I to them, yet! 'And he's my *Uncle,'* Peachie wailed. And they were making all kinds of gestures to indicate what the 'something nasty' was.

"The old man was in the yard talking with one of the Mennonite elders and he took the opportunity to show off to the Mennonites that he was a father who would not allow his children and grandchildren to make such breaches in the moral law. Never mind that the old man himself had sex with some of my sisters and with his granddaughters, too, after he'd worn my mother out. Anyhow, he picked up a horse whip and started after me, but I got away from him.

"At one other time, though, I didn't get away from him. That time a Mennonite elder was there at the farm to buy whiskey and the old man had taken him back to where the still was. Just beforehand, the old man had told me to move the nanny goat from one spot to another so she could clear off more of the weeds. I was absent mindedly leaning over her back end, pushing her along, when an impulse from my newly sprung adolescence seized me. I'd often heard some of my older brothers joking about what they had done—when they were boys in a similar situation. I thought, "Why not?'

"But before I could do much more than get my pants open, the old man and the Mennonite elder appeared from out of nowhere, it seemed, and the old man saw another opportunity to show the Mennonites how well he dealt with any moral irregularities in his sons.

"He picked up a barrel stave and came down across my back, yelling *'An abomination to the Lord*!' The goat hadn't seem to mind, so I didn't know what business it was of the Lord's. But I think it was in that moment that I gave up forever God, religion, and fathers. I'd not had much use for fathers to start with and it wasn't too hard from then on to chuck 'Father God' out the window, too."

Camellia asked Anselm, "But if you didn't want to do it with your niece Peachie and if you didn't quite get to the goat, either, then when did you have your first woman?"

Anselm said, "I ran away—stowed away on a freight train going past the farm—just at the start of World War II and went to live with Johann and Wilma. They got me enrolled in high school. Even though I was behind those my age because of the Mennonite school here having only seven grades and I'd been finished that for several years and had not gone to high school in this county at all, I quickly caught up and was doing tenth grade work by the end of that first year when I quit and enlisted in the army.

"But it was in that one year of high school in Wilmington that I started dating a girl, and I think she was trying to find somebody to pin what she thought was her pregnancy on. So she initiated me, you might say, and then a few months later claimed I had gotten her pregnant. She was going with three or four others at the same time and it turned out that she wasn't even pregnant to start with. Her double dealing gave me one more reason not to trust women."

Camellia told him about her equally low opinion of men and how they could so easily be conned. She mentioned Wylie Hovey, Forrester, and the horse race enthusiast at Halburg College. She even confessed to him her first time with Ralph Drummond. "But," she said, "that was merely youth on both our parts. Neither was trying to harm the other."

"Is this Ralph still around?" Anselm asked with some concern.

Camellia said wistfully, "Ralph was one of the first Bell's Islanders killed in the war."

After a brief silence, Camellia set aside her nostalgia and told Anselm about her mother's "indiscretion" and how her father claimed "for the eyes of the world" that Roger was his own son. She told him of Thomas's religious cuckooism that had led to her mother's desperation in the first place and how that had led eventually to Roger.

"For my own part," Camellia admitted, "sex—I can take it or leave it, and church has mainly been just another place where I can sing before an audience."

Anselm mentioned that he had sometimes attended the Lutheran Church that his father's cousins, Johann and Wilma Jurgensen, belonged to, but that his mind was more on the girls in the congregation than on God, whom he invariable saw as made in the image and likeness of Karl Jurgensen.

He told Camellia how puffed-up and self-satisfied the tall, silver-haired Johann was as a successful wholesale grocer. "Johann paid for my music lessons, but he also made me work in his grocery business, and he lectured me continuously on the value of 'the great American work ethic.' Johann's talking did as much to make me *not* want to work very hard at anything as the old man did in trying to physically beat industriousness into me."

Camellia was beginning to recognize that Anselm was not somebody *she* would ever be able to push around, either, with "gypsy magic" or any other way, and she respected him for it.

Anselm told her that Wilma was a short little woman with bright blond hair the color of brass and was a sight kinder than most of the women in his own family. His mother had virtually ignored him, turning him over as a baby to be raised by his oldest sister, Gerta, who was just about as mean and whiskey-soaked as was his mother. And another sister, Raghnild, always used him as a camouflage, putting him on top the watermelon she stole each day from the Mennonite fields, taking him and it home in a little wagon.

"It wasn't until I got to know Wilma," Anselm said, "that I found a woman any ways at all decent. It was Wilma who taught me manners and how to dress. But for all her goodness, she nearly drove me crazy with her mother hen mentality. She'd inquire each day as to the state of my bowels and she'd hand me a towel every night with specific instructions as to what to do with it in case of a wet dream or other indulgence."

Camellia told Anselm about Claudie, Doc Feldman, the gypsies, "gypsy magic," Moonlight Corrigan, the LeCates's bankruptcy, the Thomas Stephens' years of poverty and disgrace, and on and on.

Sometimes they laughed so hard at the comedy that was interspersed with all the tragedy and cruelty in their lives that they were too weak to talk any more. Then they would just play the piano together and listen to the Muses.

At one point he told her, "You are the first woman I feel I can trust enough to want to share my soul with. Yet how odd, since you admit you've made a habit of conning men to your own advantage. Am I being a fool?"

Camellia said, "No, Anselm, because you are the first man, *the one man*, I have no desire to con." She meant that honestly and not because of her realization that he probably couldn't be conned anyhow.

There's nothing more powerful than an idea whose time has come. Camellia couldn't remember where she'd heard that aphorism, but she knew there was plenty of truth in it....

Anselm had suggested that they have dinner one Sunday at her mansion apartment rather than going down to Bell's Island and meeting her folks as they had halfway planned. This was fine with Camellia as she dreaded any meeting with the Stephenses anyhow. She was not in the habit of taking her boyfriends there to start with. She was not proud of Bell's Island or her family, and with the exception of Forrester she had never dated anyone long enough to even bother taking them to Bell's Island.

Camellia said, "I'd be glad for you to come here for dinner, Anselm. The only problem is I can't cook. Nor can my cook, cook."

Anselm rolled his blue eyes innocently. "Who says we have to eat anything?"

Come that Sunday morning, shortly after 9 A.M. Camellia heard a knocking at her front door. She was still in her undies prior to getting dressed for the Episcopal Church service and her solo spot. She hastily threw on a housecoat and went to the door.

She was greeted with song:

"Who's that knocking at my door?

"Who's that knocking at my door?"

At least he didn't have the yellow wig on.

"Anselm! I thought you were coming for dinner, not breakfast!"

"And I thought you wouldn't mind seeing this lonesome soldier a bit early. I thought I might go to church with you."

"Come on in, then. But I'll be in the choir, remember?"

"I know that. I thought I'd like to hear you sing." As Anselm crossed the threshold into the house, he walked in front of her, brushed her brow with a kiss, and touched her lightly about the waist.

Camellia said, "You've heard me sing plenty of times already with the Choral and Dramatic Society." She grasped both of his hands as though to keep him at bay. This was not the right time to be starting something they'd never done yet, even though they both knew Aunt Sairy had the day off, and Mrs. Elderkin was out of town and would not be jingling the phone or tapping on the side door as she would do sometimes when Camellia was entertaining a date and she sensed hanky-panky might be going on.

Anselm said to Camellia, "But I haven't heard you sing in church."

"No," she admitted.

He said, "You sing a lot at weddings. Ever thought of singing at your own wedding?"

Camellia studied him....That rusty hair and ruddy face. Those twinkly, clear blue eyes. That "teddy bear" physique. That "Danish ham" humor. His air both of innocence and worldly wiseness. Damn! *She wanted him*! But she knew she didn't want marriage—there was still The Met to get to—and she feared an affair would damage her local reputation. After all, Royal Hall was not Paris or Greenwich Village. But still SHE WANTED HIM!

Anselm studied her now and said, "You know something, Camellia, you are a storehouse of sublimated sensuality, just waiting for the right catalyst to come along."

Then he surprised her momentarily by loosing his hands from hers and walking to her piano. He struck a few notes and said, "How much does your music mean to you, Camellia?"

"Mostly everything."

"*Mostly* everything," he echoes. "But not *every* everything?"

"We-ell," she said.

He asked, "Don't *I* mean anything to you? I mean beyond being just a father confessor?"

She couldn't answer. She was fighting a profound stirring inside herself.

But she wouldn't give in to it. Instead she tried to change the subject and said, "Anselm, you want some fried eggs and bacon? Maybe I could cook them halfway decently."

"Damn the bacon and eggs," he said huskily. He left the piano and came toward her. He said, *"Can't you tell?* I want *you*! And you want me! I would prefer to have you legally, as my wife, but if you won't hear that because of your music, then...then...."

"Then what?" she said.

"Then this...!" He reached for her, grasping her waist and pressing himself against her body with an intensity that knew only one resolution.

Neither of them were virgins, but neither were exactly old pros, either. They came near to blowing it right at the start.

There was a long moment of mutual hesitation after that first hefty embrace. Camellia was struck with a stage fright like she'd never felt before. She was used to fending off men's advances, but she barely knew what to do when it came to accepting them. Anselm seemed to have a flush of sudden modesty come over his face.

As they remained paralyzed, Camellia remembered a D.H. Lawrence book she had stuffed into the bottom of the piano bench. She wondered if what they needed was a little pornographic reading to get them going. She said brightly, "Anselm, have you ever read that dirty book—*Lady Chitterling's Lawyer*?"

Well! Talk about wild malapropisms! They both recognized it at the same time and got into such spasms of laughter that they were falling all over each other.

Yes! Hahahaha! They had both read *Lady Chatterley's Lover*! But, no! Hahahahahahehehehe! They didn't know that "chitterlings" (which are fried hog guts, often pronounced "chitlins," and which they had both eaten at one time or other) ever...hahahahehehaha... *needed* a lawyer, not even *lady* "chitterlings!" Hahahehehehaha!

All fear and awkwardness had now fled, but as Anselm was about to get out of his pants and Camellia out of her housecoat, the zipper on that housecoat somehow caught a button on the fly of his pants and held it fast. They were trapped! Struggle though they might, they could neither get apart from each other nor get any closer to each other.

"Scissors!" Camellia exclaimed. "I have some!"

"Please don't make a Jew or a steer out of me!" Anselm cried out in mock alarm.

"I wasn't about to," Camellia reassured him. "I meant I'd cut the housecoat. It's an old one anyway."

They were still howling with laughter and still hooked together, front to front, as they went inching along, sideways, crab-fashion, down the hallway to Camellia's bedroom. Once there, she tried to reach around in back of her for the pair of scissors on her dresser when suddenly Anselm's feet slipped from under him on a little scatter rug and they both went sprawling across the bed. The mean little housecoat zipper had relented on its own and they were quickly freed for a more fleshy encounter.

They rolled around on her bed like a pair of happy puppies and neither of them could remember afterwards whether they'd ended up missionary style, doggy-style, side by side, "sixty-nine" or just what; or whether Anselm had remembered to put on any protection; or when, how, or even if, either of them had come. But they knew they'd had fun and they knew they were going to try it again...and again... and again until they got it just right!

The hall clock was chiming and Camellia said, "We'd better get ready for church...."

Anselm said, "I feel like we've been to church already and to a vaudeville show, too. *Lady Chitterling's Lawyer*! Goooood Lord! Do you pull malapropisms like that often? Or should I call them 'Camellia-risms.'"

"When I get excited or am woolgathering, I'm likely to say anything, Anselm. You might as well get used to that."

They were both feeling lighthearted and lightheaded as they left the mansion together. Camellia was a little too lightheaded, for her solo didn't come off as good as usual. She realized it, but she didn't care. She didn't fall into any malapropisms, but even as she was singing the exalted *Archangels Gathering on High*, she kept looking down at Anselm with an amusement coupled with a steady longing for him, and he was looking up at her with similar emotions written all over his face.

After the service Anselm went to get a Sunday newspaper from the Royal Hall drugstore while Camellia went on back to her apartment to start fixing dinner for the two of them.

When Anselm came in about ten minutes later with the paper he said, "Camellia, you realize you were off you form, singing, this morning?"

She said, "I know that, and little wonder."

"Well," he said, "when I went to get this newspaper, I was walking behind two ladies and I guess they didn't know I was that close to them. Do you have a 'Thelma' and a 'Winifred' in your church?"

Camellia laughed. "Oh, yes! They, along with Mrs. Elderkin, are the guardians of our church music and community morals."

"Well," Anselm said, "your 'Thelma' and 'Winifred' were walking along arm in arm, like this...."

And he began pantomiming.

"They were all silly and dainty-like in their blue-rinsed hairdos and their lacy collars and cuffs and hankies. And Winifred, I guess it was, said...."

And he began mimicking their voices....

"'You know, Thelma, we pay Camellia Stephens to be our soloist, so you'd think she'd do the job right.'

"'Yes, Winifred, *she should* do the job right.'

"'But she fluffed every other note of her solo this morning, Thelma. Did you notice that?'

"'Yes, Winifred, I did notice that.'

"'And, Thelma, did you notice how she kept looking down and giving that sweety-sweet smile of hers to that soldier in the congregation—the one we've been seeing going to her apartment a lot lately?'

"'Yes, Winifred, I did notice that, too. And that soldier was just a-looking back up at her, all moon-eyed. And, at one point, they both looked like they were going to burst out giggling, like they had some sort of private joke.'

"'I saw that, too, Thelma. And you know, I do believe Camellia has...'

"Baarrroooooommmmmmm!" Anselm imitated the sound of the motorcycle that had just gone by and momentarily drowned out Thelma.

"'...on the mind!'

"Winifred's hand flew to her mouth. *She* had heard Thelma even if I hadn't and she gasped,

"'Thelma! What you said!'

"'I'm sorry, Winifred. Truly I am. It just slipped out. And maybe you wouldn't say it quite like that of a woman, anyhow. You'd say that of a man, wouldn't you, if he...if he had...well, you know what I mean. But how would you say that of a woman?'

"'Well, Thelma, I don't quite know. Could it be she has....'

"Skreeeee! Bang!" Anselm imitated the truck braking to a halt at the red light and then backfiring which had prevented him again from hearing the vital part of a sentence.

"'...on the mind?'

"'Uh...hehehehe....No, not that! Oh, it couldn't be *that*, I don't think, Winifred. You would hardly say that. But maybe it could be....'

"Thelma whispered real low into Winifred's ear just as another car zizzed by and I never got the end of that tantalizing bit of after-church commentary on you, Camellia. Both Thelma and Winifred crossed the street at that point and they were out of hearing range. All there was left were the little birdies chirping in the trees all up and down Wintergreen Avenue. So *you* tell me, Camellia, what *was* it you had 'on the mind' in church this morning?"

Camellia was laughing to the point of nearly choking. "Anselm, the way you tell it, anybody would think you were exaggerating, but I know that pair—Thelma and Winifred—and they have both long since forgotten—if they ever new to start with—what it was like to have *anything* on *their* minds!"

Camellia and Anselm decided that he should continue with his South Dakota identity whenever they got around to approaching her family and hope for the best that they would not connect him with the Wintergreen County Jurgensens. After all, Anselm was such a cut above his local kinfolk and almost all of Wintergreen County, too, that one would hardly take him "from around here." His year with the Wilmington Jurgensens and his time in the city high school, plus his tour of duty with the army, and his own continuing self-education, all together, had put considerable polish and sophistication on him. At times Camellia thought he was almost as *citified* as she was!

To get Anselm gradually introduced to the Thomas Stephenses, Camellia suggested they go first to Mary's Little Bell's Island Library. Anselm had seen it when he'd been to the island earlier, but it had been closed that day.

"You'll like Mama," Camellia said. "She's the brain in the family. She's actually *read* all those books in that library. She always wanted to be a high school teacher, but like with me so far, her dreams didn't work out for her. But, like you, Anselm, she's cheerful and instantly likeable, in spite of all that's happened to her over the years. I've told her a little about you—keeping it in the Sough Dakota context just like you had told me originally. I told her we may be dropping in at the library some day."

And when they did, later on that week, Mary and Anselm greeted each other like old-time buddies. They chatted away for hours, it seemed, about books and music and Anselm's "South Dakota" home from which he was "so far away."

Mary said enthusiastically, "Well, our home will be your home now."

Camellia at first was pleased that her mother liked Anselm, but soon she became a little annoyed as Mary seemed to be taking her "teddy bear" right out of her hands.

When they finally did get ready to leave, Mary gave Anselm a standing invitation to come have a meal at the Tu-Rest Home whenever he was on leave from Camp Conover, whether Camellia was free to come along with him or not.

As they rolled over the Bell's Island bridge in Camellia's car, Anselm said, "You may not like Bell's Island, Camellia, but is seems like a philosopher's paradise to me—serene, isolated, a little mysterious. I could easily make it my Walden."

Camellia felt a little alarm. Anselm wasn't falling *in love* with Bell's Island, was he? She said, "You liked Mama, didn't you? But wait till you meet Roger. You may then get a totally different feeling about Bell's Island."

"I don't think so," said Anselm. "Camellia, if you could ever bring yourself to having me for a husband, maybe after the war we could have a home down on that appendage called Little Bell's Island. I understand some county land in there is for sale. Yeah, I know part of it is a tide-washed garbage dump, but there's an old hunters' cabin in there that could be restored and made real 'rustic like.' You could still teach at Royal Hall High, and I could fish and crab at Little Bell's and maybe work on some inventions in my spare time. Watermen seem to be pretty much their own boss when it comes to what they do and when they do it.

Camellia heard herself screaming at him: "*Anselm, you want to do something better than just fish and crab*! You've got too much intelligence and too much musical talent for that."

Anselm laughed. "I don't even have a high school diploma."

"Well, get one!" Camellia ordered. And from out of the past she heard an echo, *I'll never marry a Bell's Island waterman*! She gave a little shiver. That warning again!

To Anselm she said, "And by the way, *I've* got something better to do, too, than teach music at Royal Hall High all my life."

"The Met, huh?" said Anselm.

Camellia didn't answer.

They were coming along now by that long, eerie stretch of marshland on the Wintergreen County mainland. Music—strange music—filled the car.

"Anselm, turn that radio off," Camellia said, a little peevishly.

"Radio's not on," he said.

Camellia shifted around uncomfortably. "Funny, I always seem to hear strange music along this section of the road to Royal Hall."

Anselm strained as though to hear it, too. But he said, "I don't seem to hear anything."

Disappointed, Camellia was thinking, Oh, if only he had heard it, too....

The long-awaited meeting with the rest of the family at the Tu-Rest Home came on a Sunday. Mary and Anselm had already met several weeks before at the Bell's Island Library. Camellia was pleased now to see that Thomas and Anselm took an immediate liking to each other, too.

There *was* that likeable quality to Anselm, Camellia was thinking. He was respectful, but he didn't kowtow to anybody. He was reserved and quiet when it was appropriate to be, but he was not shy. He was curious about everything, but not prying. He knew how to make a racy remark, but he was wise enough to know who to say what to and when.

While they were in the kitchen of the Tu-Rest Home having some coffee before dinner , Anselm cocked an ear at something outside and said, "Is that a duck?" He and Thomas had just been talking about Bell's Island wildlife.

"No," Camellia said, and with no little consternation. "That's my kid brother."

"Your brother is a duck?!" Anselm said and burst out laughing. His bit of absurdity struck Mary funny, if not Camellia. Camellia was thinking, *My brother is the devil, and I fear that we're all about to have its proof demonstrated.*

Roger came in the house, walking lanky and looking untidy. He was growing like a weed and had his first few reddish-yellow whiskers, of which he was unbearably proud. His voice had started to deepen, and as he came in the house, he was grumbling, cussing, and quacking all at the same time.

He was also eating a box of Crackerjack, and half-spilling, half-spitting it all over everything. He didn't notice Anselm at first. He tossed the Crackerjack box on the kitchen table and went to the refrigerator, looking for Lord only knows what, but not finding it. Then he turned around and made some sort of half-burping, half-surprised noise when he saw Anselm.

Mary said to him, "Roger, here is a soldier for you to talk with—Sergeant Anselm Jurgensen."

Roger looked at Anselm closely and growled, "He ain't no airplane pilot."

"Anselm's a supply sergeant, Roger," Camellia said. "He's stationed at Camp Conover. He's also a good musician."

Roger grunted and sat down. He eyed Anselm suspiciously. Anselm looked back at him with mild curiosity, but he made no comment.

Then Mary put another two cent's worth in and said, "Roger's hoping the war will last long enough for him to be of age to enlist in the air force."

"Either that or drive a tank," Roger confirmed. Then Roger punched Camellia on the arm and whispered—loudly—"What did Mom say his name was—'Asshole'?"

Camellia was thinking, *Damn*! Anselm had an unwieldy enough first name without Roger re-doing it. Camellia said, "It's An-selm, Roger. An-selm Jurgensen. It's German, the Anselm part, isn't it, Anselm?"

Now Camellia would have done just as well to have left that German part unsaid.

Before Anselm could say anything, Roger was jumping up, banging on the table and hollering, "*German*! A goddam kraut! What's *he* doing in the American army? A spy, maybe? And in this kitchen?"

"Sit down and shut up, Roger!" Mary barked at him.

Camellia noted that her mother, since getting some of her health back, had more control over Roger, or maybe it was just that she kicked up more racket than she used to in *trying* to control him.

Mary said, "Anselm's all-American, Roger. He just happens to have German in his background, along with a Scandinavian mixture. A lot of folks in the Midwest part of the United States have that."

Thomas picked up at this point and said, "Roger, how about taking those crates of sodas on the back porch over to the shipyard so they'll be there for the men in the morning?"

Poor ole Papa! Camellia was thinking. He usually could get Roger out of the way, if necessary, but he still couldn't do much about making it necessary for him to be gotten out of the way in the first place.

Roger obeyed.

"Sorry about him," Camellia apologized to Anselm as the screen door slammed and Roger yelled back, "See ya later, Asshole!"

Mary looked thoroughly embarrassed.

But Anselm seemed amused. He said, "Back in South Dakota the family called me "Olaf', which is my middle name, but I never liked it, so I started using Anselm when I got in the army, but maybe I should have stuck with 'Olaf', huh?"

Anselm had a nice way of putting everybody at ease.

When Roger came back after delivering the sodas to the shipyard, he was the model of perfect behavior all during the time they were having their meal. But Camellia had a feeling he had something up his sleeve. And he did!

While they were still lingering at the table, talking, the black fuzzy cat they kept in the house strolled into the dining room from the kitchen, and Roger scooped it up in one hand, put it in his lap, and said, "Aaaah! Just what I've always wanted—Sister's hairy pussy!"

And it wasn't even Camellia's cat! At best, it was the family cat. And if there was anything Camellia hated more than her mother's beagles, it was that cat.

Mary, quick as a wink, suggested they all go into the front room for coffee, and as they all got up, with the horribly embarrassed Thomas clearing his throat about a dozen times, Camellia took the opportunity to reach over and bop Roger on the top of his head and hiss at him, "You dahmn Jahk-ahss!"

When Camellia glanced around at Anselm, he was all but "busting a gusset" to keep from laughing out loud.

Anselm might be laughing, but Camellia knew there was more than just an intentionally lewd double entendre in what Roger had said: It was the wicked truth!

Later, when Camellia and Anselm were driving back to Royal Hall and she could talk freely to him again, she said, "Anselm, did you ever look 'wrongly' on any of your sisters? I mean—sexually?"

Anselm gave a hoot of derision. "None of them were worth looking wrongly *or* rightly on. Except maybe Ilse—she was closer to my age and kind of cute. But we never messed with each other, if that's what you mean."

Camellia went on. "Roger keeps looking at me and pawing on me—wrongly—whenever he gets the chance. Not too long ago he said, 'What's so bad about it, Sister; We're only *half*-brother and sister, ain't we?'"

Anselm chuckled. "Roger is just an animal growing up. Kinship means nothing to him biologically. He'll get over it. But remember, you *are* 'easy to look at'."

But Camellia remained troubled. Roger was only a little over twelve years old, but Camellia had been informed by Snipsey that he'd already been to Moonlight's place and had his first real sex, and he'd bragged about it all over Bell's Island. Amanda Cartwright had observed at the time, "Roger's not going to live very long. He's ripening too fast."

But Moonlight's girls weren't enough for Roger. He still wanted Camellia. One afternoon when she was at the Tu-Rest Home again, Roger again got after her. When she pushed him away, judo-fashion, he looked real mean and said, "Well, keep your old cunt for 'Asshole', then. There's somebody I know who looks like you and is probably twice as hot."

Camellia told Anselm about the incident and about the current Moonlight strongly resembling her. Camellia said, "Roger's jealous of you, Anselm. I believe one of these days you'll have to fight him."

"He's just a kid, Camellia, just a kid. He's just trying to prove himself," Anselm said, trying to reassure her.

Toward the end of that summer of 1945, when Camellia and Anselm were again having dinner with Thomas and Mary, Roger had another crack at trying to get Anselm angry enough to fight.

Roger said everything he could to provoke Anselm and made a lot of references to Moonlight's place, which catered to Camp Conover soldiers. At first Roger was implying that he'd seen Anselm there (which he hadn't because Anselm had never been there), and when that didn't cause Anselm to react, Roger implied there must be something wrong with Anselm or he *would* be there.

Anselm still wouldn't react. Camellia was expecting Roger at any moment to start yelling "Pansy!" at him. But Roger chose a more colorful insult.

After they'd finished their meal, Roger saw Camellia going onto the back porch with a tin tray full of empty crab shells from their dinner. He grabbed her by the arm and whispered loud enough for everybody back in the dining room—Mary, Thomas, and Anselm—to hear him: "What's wrong with 'Asshole', Sister? Why won't he fight me like a man?"

Camellia said nothing. She just stood there, biting her lip, glowering at Roger, and holding the tin try full of crab shells. Then Roger got all sarcastically sweet and whispered—loud again—"Tell me, Sister, tell me honest now—DOES HE SQUAT TO PEE!?"

Camellia crashed the tin tray down on the porcelain table top and picked up a butcher knife that was lying there. She waved the knife around about waist high—or a little lower—at Roger and yelled, "NO! But when I get through with you, you dahmned shithead, *YOU'RE GOING TO HAVE TO*!" British accent—Bell's Island vocabulary!

Roger scrambled off the back porch and headed straight for the thicket. Everybody in the house—even the straight-laced Thomas—was in stitches.

When Anselm had the chance to speak to Camellia alone, he gave her his most approving grin and said, "With the right provocation, you can come up with more damn wit and more damn temper than anyone would think possible of you."

"Well," she sighed. "With someone like Roger around, it brings out all sorts of hidden talents."

On their return trip to Royal Hall, Camellia casually said, "Anselm, I feel there's soon going to be a band at Royal Hall High, and that means a bandmaster will be needed. If you get your high school diploma and a few credits at Halburg State in their music department, I believe you could qualify for it. You already have the musical aptitude and most of the basic training."

Anselm immediately said, "Oh, I wouldn't want to be cooped up in some classroom or auditorium. I want to work outside where there's sky and water and...like at Bell's Island, for instance."

Again casually Camellia said, "Anselm, that bandmaster job will be out under the skies. Think of all the parades and football games....A high school marching band is always the center, you know."

"Naw," said Anselm, "I'm not cut out to be a *professional* musician."

Camellia said no more, but she was tempted to use her "gypsy magic." Anything to keep her "teddy bear" from becoming a Bell's Island waterman. Yet at the same time she respected him deeply because he did have a mind of his own and she loved him too much to want to control him. But *to marry* a Bell's Island waterman...?" She wasn't even too sure she would continue to date Anselm if he became a Bell's Island waterman, for that image surely wasn't compatible with the image she had of herself as a part of Royal Hall society.

V-J Day came in August of 1945 with the Japanese surrender, and that officially ended World War II. Camellia knew Anselm would now have to do something. He didn't even have a home to which he wanted to go once he was out of the service. Or so Camellia thought.

How surprised she was, then, when he came to her mansion apartment one evening and said excitedly, "I've got a job, I've got a home, and I'm going back to school!"

He had done some rapid footwork, he said, since she'd seen him last and even without a high school diploma, he'd passed an extensive exam at Halburg College and got himself into their music department program under the condition that he attend high school classes, too, until he could pass a high school equivalency exam and get his diploma, which he had agreed to do.

Camellia was overjoyed. Then came the "other part" of his good news:

"I'm going to be working part-time on your family's skipjack, the *Camellia Stephens*, AND I've rented a room at your parent's Tu-Rest Home."

What could Camellia say? She said the only thing she could rightfully say: "Anselm, that's *wonderful*!" (If you couldn't get a whole loaf, you took a half, as they always said on Bell's Island!)

When the hot sultry fall of 1945 rolled around, World War II had been over for a couple of months, Anselm was out of the service and into his new work/study routine, and Camellia was beginning the new school year at Royal Hall High.

When Anselm stopped by Camellia's mansion apartment early one evening on his way back to Bell's Island, she told him she'd been feeling a little sickish of late and had even missed a period....

"Great!" said Anselm. "We can get married right away!"

Camellia said, "But I don't *want* any kids. We've talked about this already."

Anselm squirmed and said, "But we could at least get married. A lot of people do when something like this happens."

Camellia made no reply. Anselm took her hands in his, looked into her eyes, and said, "What have you got against marriage? Or maybe you just don't want to marry me because I'm nine years younger than you. But you've often said I actually look older than you. Do you resent it that I'm working on that skipjack that's named after you? That I'm working as a waterman? But I am also gearing up for that bandmaster position, remember?"

But all Camellia could say was, "Anselm, you talk too much. You confuse me."

It was the start of a bad evening. They began arguing, and then there came a series of fierce thunderstorms—one right after the other—that plagued the whole county all night. Each time Anselm started to leave for Bell's Island and his room at the Tu-Rest Home, a new outburst of thunder, lightning, and torrential rain occurred.

Camellia and Anselm sat back down and huddled together, first arguing and them embracing, first in the dark, and then back in the light as the electrical power alternately went off and on. Even though they knew Mrs. Elderkin didn't happen to be home or even in town, they still stopped short of actually going to bed for neither of them especially wanted to risk being electrocuted while making love. Some of their couplings were electrifying enough without additional fireworks!

Each time the storm abated, they began arguing all over again. Anselm said, "Well, dammit, Camellia, we'll build two houses—one for me on Bell's Island and one for you in Royal Hall, and we'll visit each other."

Camellia said, "We're as good as living that way now."

Anselm countered with, "Yeah, but we're not married, and if you are pregnant, what about your job as Royal Hall High's music director and your reputation?"

Camellia exploded, "The hell with *that* job and my reputation! What about my *real* music career? One of these days, believe it or not, I *still* intend to leave here and go sing at The Met. But now, it looks like that dream has gone again to the four winds."

Camellia sneaked a quick glance at Anselm. He looked like he felt like the proverbial five cent's worth in a ten cent bag.

He said, "So you've never really considered marrying me anyhow, then? Just wanted to keep me around, so I could make love to you, eh? Well, if you won't marry me and if you are pregnant, would you at least consider going to a doctor—not Doc Feldman, for heaven's sake—but to a city doctor and having something done? With your 'wise investments' that you keep telling me about, you've certainly got the money to have it done and have it done right. And I know you don't have any more religious scruples about abortion than I do."

Camellia didn't say anything.

So Anselm said, "Camellia, have you forgotten about your mother's experience and what her failure to 'do something about it' resulted in?"

"Mama's experience was entirely different," Camellia snapped.

"True, but the result—"Anselm began, but again Camellia waved him to shut up.

Clearly frustrated, Anselm reached for his second pack of cigarettes in almost as many hours, and Camellia poured each of them another glass of wine. Before they knew it, they had argued nearly the whole night through. It was coming on dawn already. The thunderstorms had quit finally. Camellia took Anselm's ashtray and their two empty wine glasses into the kitchen, and he prepared to leave.

"Anselm, you want any breakfast?" Camellia wearily asked.

"No, I don't think so. I better get down to the island, so I can shave, bathe, and change clothes before coming back up to today's classes. I guess your mother will wonder what has happened to me."

Camellia said, "Well, the thunderstorms are a good enough excuse. It's going to be my excuse if anybody in Royal Hall says anything about your car being here all night."

As Anselm turned to go, he said, "I'll check by here when I come back to Royal Hall."

But Camellia said, "I probably won't be here—teachers' meeting today in Gainsbiddle. I have to leave early."

Anselm said, "That's right. You did mention that. Gainsbiddle, huh? Why do they have any meetings in *that* God-awful place? The board of education is here in Royal Hall."

Camellia said, "We alternate for some crazy reason. I don't know just why. Anyhow, it's Gainsbiddle High's turn to host. Now, you'd better get going out of here, Anselm, or you're going to bump right into Aunt Sairy."

Anselm got away quickly.

When Aunt Sairy came in the apartment, Camellia was alone trying to eat some breakfast, but she was having a hard time getting it down. She could barely speak to Aunt Sairy.

Aunt Sairy began bumping around in the kitchen and in the other rooms, and Camellia knew she was finding incriminating evidence because she could hear her mumbling to herself: "Ummmm,

ummmm, ummmmm....*Two* wine glasses in de sink, *still cold....* Ummm, ummmmm, ummmm....Ashtray full of cigarette butts, *still warm*—An' yo' doan smoke, Mis' Camellia....Ummmm, ummmm, ummmm....Toilet seat up in de bathroom....Ummm, ummmm, ummmmm...."

Aunt Sairy glanced in the bedroom, too, but Camellia knew she didn't find anything there. The bed hadn't even been slept in, much less *played in.*

Suddenly her stomach gave a lurch, and Camellia jumped up from the breakfast table and nearly knocked Aunt Sairy over in her haste to get to the bathroom....

When she came back out giddily, Aunt Sairy said, "Dint think yo' ever drink enough to have a hangover, Mis' Camellia."

Camellia gasped, "I—don't—think—it's—a—hangover."

"De heat, maybe....? Or sumpin' goin' 'round?"

Camellia smiled wanly. Aunt Sairy was giving her plenty of good enough excuses.

But Camellia said, "I doubt it."

Then Aunt Sairy said, "Well, den de on'y thing ah knows it could be is...." And she started shaking her head and saying, "Oh, my, my, my....Ummm, ummmm, ummm."

Camellia wiped the sweat from her face, rustled around in her handbag, and pulled out a twenty dollar bill. She placed it gently in Aunt Sairy's hand and said, "Aunt Sairy, you've neither seen nor heard anything unusual here today. Understand?"

And Aunt Sairy said, "Yas'm, Mis' Camellia. Ah understands." And she gave Camellia a little wink and a little chuckle.

"How come yo' gittin' ready so early dis mornin', Mis' Camellia?" Aunt Sairy asked her after a few moments of thoughtful silence.

"Teachers' meeting in Gainsbiddle."

Aunt Sairy said, "Oh, my...oh, my...oh, my....*Gainsbiddle*! Lawd, Mis' Camellia, dat's a TURRIBLE PLACE to have to go when yo' feelin' sick to start with!"

It was enough to tickle Camellia's funny bone, for Aunt Sairy was as good a Bell's Islander when it came to making cracks about Gainsbiddle as if she had been born and raised right on the island instead of in the little nearby black settlement of Satin on the mainland.

After a good hearty laugh, Camellia said, "Aunt Sairy, you are a prize! I feel better already."

For a moment there, Camellia thought Aunt Sairy was about to say, *Another twenty dollars, please.* But Camellia knew Aunt Sairy "knew her place" and had never been "a smart-ass nigger." So, she was not about to take advantage of Camellia, not even in jest.

Anselm's day had also begun on a wild note, he reported to Camellia that evening:

"When I got back to my room, I fell asleep across the bed and had a nightmare that quick. I woke up screaming, 'Camellia, don't! Don't do it! DON'T!' I saw you walking alone somewhere in the dark—it was in the marsh, maybe. And then it was as if you were heading out toward deep water and you were saying, 'The child and I will go together.'

"I was screaming so loud, 'Camellia, DON'T!' that your parents heard me and came running up to my room.

"I was sitting there on the edge of the bed, half-yelping, half-weeping.

"Your mother said to me, 'What are you talking about, Anselm?'

"I said, 'Nothing, Miss Mary. Only a dream. Just a bad dream'. I fell back on the bed, exhausted.

"Your father said, 'Is Camellia all right? We tried to phone her last night but our line was out. That storm....'

"I said, 'Camellia's all right, Mr. Stephens. I had to stay there last night because the storm was so bad in Royal Hall. But she's okay.'

"I couldn't tell them of my dream and what you'd said last night about maybe being pregnant which, I guess, set off that dream....God! That dream scared me!"

Gratefully, Camellia was able to report to Anselm that during the day—and at Gainsbiddle, yet—she had *come about.* Ah, yes, Gainsbiddle—that place would either kill you or cure you.

Both of them were vastly relieved. Camellia wanted no children for a dozen good reasons, not the least of which was that she tended to believe all children were like Roger. And Anselm had often said he was no more cut out to be a parent than Camellia was.

They were relieved, too, that a potential scandal had been averted, for people all over Royal Hall and Bell's Island were talking enough anyhow about their having an affair.

The two of them didn't do anything to alleviate that talk, either, on the Sunday Camellia agreed to substitute as soloist at the Bell's Island Methodist Church.

She had been asked to substitute for them any number of times and had always refused, even though she'd cut her musical teeth in that very church as a child. But this particular Sunday, and on very short notice, she agreed. She was on vacation from her soloist duties at the Episcopal Church in Royal Hall, but she still could have told Bell's Island she was going to the beach or give some other excuse as she had always done before. But this time she agreed to sing for them.

Although she could sing most anything on sight, she had not even had time to pick out a solo beforehand, much less to practice with the organist. Just before the service was to begin, and even as the organist was playing the prelude, she appeared briefly in the empty choir loft, just long enough to consult with the organist about her solo.

Out of the corner of her eye she could see people down in the congregation whispering, and she could easily imagine what they might be saying:

"Oooooh, look who's going to sing for us today! Can it be she's finally condescended to favor us?"

"Yes, but you know why, don't you?"

"No, why?"

"Well, look over there—sitting with Thomas and Mary....There's her fellow. She calls him her 'teddy bear' And—hehehehe!—he does look like a 'teddy bear', doesn't he? Has that stocky build and that ruddy, wholesome look, those baby blue eyes and rusty hair and that innocent little smile."

"Yeah, she's really got a case on him like she's never had for any of the others who've been after her. She told somebody she'd never had a *teddy bear* when she was a child but NOW she has one. And somebody else said—I think it was Forrester, one of her old beaus—'Camellia, have you taken your "teddy bear" to bed yet?', and they say she turned as red as one of our Bell's Island sunsets!"

"So, you think Camellia came here to sing today just because of her 'teddy bear?'"

"Well, what do *you* think?"

Camellia tried to get her mind back on her job. The organist suggested "just a hymn from the regular hymn book," so Camellia flipped hers open at random and scanned the first page she came to, paying more attention to the music than the words. She showed the page to the organist and the organist nodded. Camellia clutched the hymn book to her bosom and slipped back into the wing of the choir loft. And then a moment later, there she was again, filing in with the rest of the choir. And was she ever "in character!"

She was dressed to the nines, as usual, wearing a shimmery summer frock (as it was still sultry hot), long white gloves up to her elbows, and one of those huge wide-brim hats for which she was famous. She radiated her tall, but bosomy, majestic presence to its fullest and she had her black hair done in a large chignon with a big multi colored flower in it. With her brilliant makeup and her high-flown opera diva manner, she was a mite over doing it for a *Bell's Island* church, but "they'd asked for it," she felt like saying.

She maintained that pose all through the first part of the service—the initial hymn by the choir and congregation, the responsive readings, the prayer by the minister, the second hymn by the choir and congregation, the announcements, and then....HER SOLO...!

The hymn she had picked at random was one of those old Methodist "doozies" that can really "work on you," but as Camellia arose, puffed up her bosom, and nodded her magnificent smile to the organist, she still wasn't fully aware of THOSE WORDS. One line, however, was all that was needed...!

Who at my door is standing?
Patiently drawing near
Entrance within demanding.
Whose is the voice I hear?

Sweetly the tones are falling:
Open the door for me!
If thou wilt heed my calling,
I will abide with thee.

All through the dark hours weary,
Knocking again is He.
Saviour, art Thou not weary,
Waiting so long for me?

Sweetly the tones are falling:
Open the door for me!
If thou wilt heed my calling,
I will abide with thee.

Lonely without He's staying,
Lonely within am I;
While I am still delaying,
Will He not pass me by?

Sweetly the tones are falling:
Open the door for me!
If thou wilt heed my calling,
I will abide with thee.

Door of my heart, I hasten!
Thee will I open wide;
Though He rebuke and chasten,
He shall with me abide.

Camellia went through that entire hymn with a flawless technical perfection. She was rolling out those words—THOSE WORDS—in her *educated* British accent and with tones as powerful, beautiful, and soul-tugging as those of any dramatic mezzo-soprano of the Metropolitan Opera.

No matter that "in mind's ear" all through her solo she was hearing a bawdy echo sounding unmistakably like:

Who's that knocking at my door?
Who's that knocking at my door?
Who's that knocking at my door?
Cried the fair young maiden.

It's only me, I'm home from the sea,
Said Barnacle Bill the Sailor.

What's that thing between your legs?
What's that thing between your legs?
What's that thing between your legs?
Cried the fair young maiden.

It's only a pole to put in your hole!
Cried Barnacle Bill the Sailor.

No matter that when she looked down at the congregation and at Anselm, she saw that his face had turned as red as any Bell's Island sunset. He had his fist jammed against his mouth to keep from laughing out loud, he was chewing on his knuckles like a beaver, and his shoulders and back were quaking like he was operating an air hammer.

No matter that Mary was looking at him as though she were desperately trying to think of some way to keep him from flying completely to pieces. No matter that at one point she even cracked him sharply on the knee with her hymn book. And 'twas some sort of miracle that Anselm hadn't yelped out loud.

No matter that other people in the congregation, too, must have been noticing double and triple meanings in THOSE WORDS of her solo. No matter that by the end, finally, of that solo there was an electrified atmosphere in that church, which, if it could have been harnessed and stored, it would have run all the dynamos, machines, and lights on Bell's Island for the next forty years.

Consummate performer that she was, Camellia *did* get through that solo without a missed beat, broken note, or flubbed word. By the time she sat down, however, she was "in a way." She started hankying beads of perspiration and tears of embarrassment out of her eyes. Every two minutes or so she fell into an uncontrollable half-coughing, half-sobbing murmur that kept up for a good twenty minutes, off and on, into the preacher's sermon.

For all anybody in the congregation knew, she might have been having some sort of religious re-conversion. After all she had been a dropout from the very church she was now singing in. And if there was anyone a good Methodist believed was hell bound and in need of urgent redemption, it was an Episcopalian. Were not some of those good Methodists in the congregation expecting at any moment to see white-winged doves come floating down from the ceiling and Jesus and all the angels come winging out from behind the choir loft to take Camellia to their bosoms like the Good Shepherd finding His lost sheep and whisk her away to heaven in one grand chorus of "Amens" and Hallelujahs!"

But that didn't happen. And somehow Camellia and her "teddy bear" down there in the congregation and all the rest of the church managed to endure through the remainder of the service without having to get up and dive for the nearest exit. There were no fainting spells, heart attacks, upturned stomachs, or suddenly damp undies.

By the end of the service Camellia had recovered her composure completely and had stopped that little whimper-murmuring and the daubing at her face with her hanky. Anselm, too, was sitting more relaxed. His flushed face had turned back to normal, and the quaking in his body had ceased. And, as everybody was leaving the church and "how-dee-doing" to each other, and to Thomas and Mary, and to Camellia and Anselm, nothing was said openly of the incident.

But the four of them had barely gotten back to the Tu-Rest Home when Amanda Cartwright rushed in to report:

"Such a chitter-chatter you have never heard before, once you all go out of earshot," Amanda chortled. "People were stumbling all over each other and asking: 'What in the world do you suppose was wrong with Camellia?'

"And some said, 'That solo, that solo, didn't you hear those words? Didn't you see that fellow of hers, how he reacted?'

"And somebody else said, 'What do you supposed has gotten into Camellia? But, on second thought, DON'T ANSWER THAT!'

"And some fights even broke out as to just which different meanings you could put on those words depending on where your mind was at the moment. And you know what the organist is going to do this afternoon? Run off mimeographed copies of that hymn. Uh, huh, because everybody wants his own copy to study. And she'd going to sell them for five dollars a piece and donate the receipts to the church building fund!"

Finally Thomas had enough, and he bellowed at his booming, bawdy sister, "Amanda, GO HOME!"

When Camellia and Anselm got their first private moment together, they glared furiously at each other, pointing fingers, and each exploding at the same time: "DON'T YOU EVER PULL A STUNT LIKE THAT AGAIN?—ME?!—IT WAS *YOU*!"

Mary overheard them and said softly: "It was *both* of you. Now hush your fussing with one another, and help me get dinner on the table."

Ah, yes, thought Camellia....Mary...*she* knew which way the tide was running!

Camellia sensed that her mother, instead of being embarrassed by Camellia and Anselm's affair, took a vicarious pleasure in it.

Camellia was glad that Mary wasn't any younger, or she might have gone for Anselm herself. He was cuddly-cute, decent, and the kind of man over which a woman liked to fuss like a mother hen, then give herself to. But age was toning Mary down now, doing what Methodist morality had failed to do earlier—at least in one instance.

About all Mary could do now was regard Anselm as an adopted son. And she made much to-do about this, telling everybody of the many hours Anselm spent in her little Bell's Island library, talking with her and telling her how much his Bell's Island *family* meant to him. Little wonder, then, as Roger got wind of all this, that he was furiously jealous.

By the time Roger was in high school, he had turned into "a bullying old stud dog," chasing everything in skirts from Bell's Island to Gainsbiddle to Royal Hall and back again, including all the *girls* at Moonlight's place.

Camellia felt her mother took some sort of twisted pleasure in Roger's disreputable behavior. Roger was defying all the rules, regulations, traditions, and mores that Mary herself perhaps had always wanted to defy—and wanted Thomas to defy, too, so that he could have been a little more of a man to her.

But "in the eyes of the world," Mary played out her traditional role as wife, mother, homemaker, and church worker. Even in her one "indiscretion"—which resulted in Roger and which everybody more or less knew about and which Mary *knew* everybody knew about—she did not openly heap ashes on her head and wear sackcloth, but she carried on outwardly as though nothing wrong had happened. She "held her head up," as they said on Bell's Island.

But Camellia knew the wide gap between Mary on the outside and Mary on the inside—that inward truth of things which Mary could never forgive herself for letting happen—was forever working on her health like termites in old lumber.

After his discharge from the service, Anselm started cramming studies right and left at both Royal Hall High School to get his diploma and at Halburg State to get enough music courses and credits to give him a shot at that bandmaster position.

Camellia, at the same time, was on leave of absence from Royal Hall High so she could complete her doctorate in music theory at the conservatory in Baltimore. She stayed at her Aunt Lizbeth's and was back in Royal Hall on weekends.

It was a frenzied two years for both Camellia and Anselm. During the times she was back on the shore on weekends and in the summer, she coached Anselm diligently in conducting and in how to hold a group's attention and respect without actually going so far as to divulge her own "gypsy magic" techniques in such endeavors.

Finally she pulled every string available in the school system short of going to bed with Superintendent Forrester, and by the opening of the school year in September 1947, all of their efforts paid off. Anselm was chosen over six other applicants as Royal Hall High's first bandmaster. And Camellia was back as music director.

The kids in the newly formed band quickly called Anselm the "Big-Bellied Dutchman" because of his stocky beer-belly physique and because of that slight German accent, which he told everybody he got from his German-born mother "out in the Midwest." And, as on Bell's Island, nobody in Royal Hall seemed to have connected him with the Wintergreen County Jurgensens. Camellia said she could never remember a child in either elementary or high school with that surname. Anselm said the Jurgensens of east Wintergreen County had either not gone to school at all, or had gone to the Mennonite school—possibly even to a school in the next county as the clan was so close to the county line—or else there had been so much intermarriage with the "bohunks" that the surname Jurgensen was disappearing altogether.

So, the "Big-Bellied Dutchman" and "Miss" Camellia at Royal Hall High were not so much scrutinized as to their background as to their current love affair. And one day they came close to making complete asses of themselves.

There was to be a meeting of some of the faculty members and students at one o'clock that afternoon in the library regarding the school's music program.

During the lunch hour that preceded the meeting, Camellia and Anselm were out on the sidewalk in front of the school looking at a huge empty box that had held the band's new sousaphone. Several of the boys and girls who were to be in the music meeting were lounging near by.

The huge box was slated for the trash collector, but Camellia said she would like to have it for housecleaning—for Aunt Sairy to store blankets in. Anselm was examining the box to determine which was the best way to get it to Camellia's mansion apartment just a short distance away on Prince Edward Street. Anselm decided to pick up the box, but with his stocky and somewhat clumsy physique, he was having a real struggle to get the right purchase on it.

Camellia heard one of the boys standing nearby whisper, "Pssst! Look! Look at the "Big-Bellied Dutchman"—*in front*!"

"'The "Big-Bellied Dutchman" in fron—'?" whispered one of the girls. "Oh! Ho! Ho Ho *Ho*!"

Then everybody, including Camellia, was looking.

Royal Hall High's "Big-Bellied Dutchman" had more than just a big belly at the moment. Anselm was poked way out in the front of his pants just like he'd been watching a whole bevy of naked dancing girls gyrating towards him. Camellia had heard some of the men at the shipyard once say that straining to lift a heavy object would do that to a man sometimes, but *that empty sousaphone box wasn't heavy*—a bit awkward, maybe, but not heavy. Sooooo....

Just then Anselm got his arms around the box, lifted it way up in front of his face, and started right down the middle of Prince Edward Street with Camellia first beside him, then in back of him, then in front of him, checking for traffic and giving him directions.

They got the box safely to the mansion and up onto the big open front porch, only to find that it would not go through the doorway into Camellia's apartment. *But Camellia and Anselm did*! They eased around the big box and slid into the house, closed the door, and left the box all alone on the front porch.

There was no time for complete undressing and Anselm didn't even take off his pants or jacket. After they were done, Anselm was ready to leave the house first. Camellia couldn't find her undies and was starting to look for another pair. She told Anselm to wait a minute, and she would be right there to help him get the box back to the school in time for the trash collector, as it was no use keeping it if they couldn't get it in the house.

Anselm waited out on the porch while Camellia was putting on fresh makeup at the vestibule mirror. She noticed his reflection in the mirror and saw him looking at the box, taking something from his coat pocket, and dropping it inside the box. Camellia couldn't see what it was, but figured it was probably a piece of scrap paper. Then she saw him pick up the box, take it off the porch by himself, and start down the middle of Prince Edward Street with it.

Without Camellia to direct him AND traffic, Anselm and the box were soon bringing down a barrage of blowing horns and screeching brakes. Camellia dashed out onto the sidewalk, calling to him and trying to catch up with him. But he was soon back at the school—safely—and had left the box on the curb and gone on inside the school to the library where the music meeting was to be held.

When Camellia got up to the school, she paused a moment and looked at the box, but she didn't look inside it.

She went on to the library whose windows faced the street. She wondered why everybody in the room was tittering. When she looked at Anselm, she got a general idea. On the knees of his blue pants and forearms of his jacket were little white bedspread tufts! *That blasted shedding bedspread*! She'd intended to throw it away a dozen times already and never had. She knew none of the tufts had gotten on her for she had made a quick survey all around before leaving the apartment and had not even been thinking about bedspread tufts anyhow or what they might have done to Anselm.

She started to say something to him, but right at that moment *he* discovered the tufts and started frantically picking them off his clothes and stuffing them into his pockets. The tittering, of course, grew louder. Camellia sat down beside him and tried to act *poised*.

Then Anselm got a look of double consternation on his face as he began digging in all his pockets as though searching for something. Suddenly he sprang out of his chair and went flying out of the library, out the front door of the school, and onto the street.

One of the boys said, and not in a whisper this time, "Do you suppose he's got another 'hard-on?'"

Everybody was looking out the window of the library as Anselm was waving his arms in a "No! No!" fashion to the trash collector who had just rolled up and was about to heist the sousaphone box into the truck. Anselm ran up to the box, and standing on his tiptoes, looked inside it, then almost *fell* inside it as he reached down and grabbed something off the bottom.

Surreptitiously he lifted out a pair of black lacy bikini panties, and before he could stash them in his pocket, he DROPPED them! A bit of a breeze caught the bikinis, lifted them gracefully into the air, and carried them down the sidewalk twenty or thirty feet before Anselm, running awkwardly after them, could catch them. When he did catch them, he stuffed them into his pocket, breathed an obvious sigh of relief, and came red-faced back into the building and into the library.

A sudden round of applause greeted him as he came through the doorway with his hand clamped tight in his pocket, making sure his purloined prize did not get away from him again. Everybody was bent double laughing except Camellia who could feel across her face every sort of emotion from surprise to outrage, from exasperation to embarrassment, from anger to a wild sort of amusement usually reserved only for idiots, hyenas, and Cheshire cats!

While Camellia and Anselm were holding forth at Royal Hall, another romance was brewing down on Bell's Island. For all of Roger's wildness with girls, there was one and one only who was special. And little Doris Thornton *still* had a case on Roger.

Camellia remembered how good Mamie Thornton, Doris's mother, had been to Roger that time back in elementary school when he had been so sick, and Doris had taken him to her home for Mamie to care for while Camellia was trying to finish her singing classes for that day. But when Roger and Doris started growing up and coming of courting age, Mamie joined with her husband, "Hambone" Thornton, in forbidding Doris to have anything further to do with Roger. But sometimes that's all it took for a girl to be all the more determined to have her fellow.

Doris and Roger got together every chance they could and sometimes it was at Bell's Island High basketball games. Roger had tried for the basketball team, but had not made it, although the team made him an honorary member anyway because of his ability to spook all visiting teams with his ventriloquist ability and his farts repertoire. At each home game they would plant him near the visiting team's cheering section with disastrous results to the opposition.

Camellia and Anselm went to one of those Bell's Island-Gainsbiddle basketball games one cold winter night in 1948. Roger was there, and Camellia and Anselm got so fascinated with *Roger's* performance, they barely noticed the basketball game.

Roger—tall, stringy, dirty-looking, and sporting his scattering of reddish-yellow whiskers—came into the gymnasium of the Bell's Island High School, eating a bag of popcorn and spilling and spitting half of it onto everybody's head as he climbed into the bleachers right behind the Gainsbiddle High cheering section near where Camellia and Anselm were sitting.

Roger was muttering obscenities as to what should be done to the Gainsbiddle team, and he smelled of a combination of stale cigarette smoke, three-day-old sweat, used beer, and crab scrap.

When the Gainsbiddle girls in the cheering section realized—they didn't even have to turn around to see—who was there, they looked at each other in dismay and cried, "Oh, my God! There's that horrible Roger Stephens! And you know what he does!"

Well, anybody who didn't know was soon to find out. At first even Camellia and Anselm thought Roger was merely throwing stink bombs under the seats of the Gainsbiddle cheering section. Some of the girls thought this, too, but the wiser ones said Roger was doing those farts himself, smell and all, and somehow ventriloquizing them! Some were gigantic and atrocious, some sneaky and drawn out, some even downright comical, and he was making them all seem like they were coming from the girls in the Gainsbiddle cheering section.

He kept pointing his finger at first this girl and that, laughing, holding his nose, and waving his hand around as though trying to chase away the smells. He was so clever with it all that it was hard not to wonder if some of the girls were not the real culprits after all. The girls got to arguing among themselves: *Was* it Roger doing it or was it really one of them? *How* was Roger doing it? By mouth imitations or the real thing? And all the while they seemed to forget *why* Roger was doing it. But his mission succeeded very well, and Anselm said it was the raggedest cheering he'd ever heard any squad ever put on. By half-time the Gainsbiddle team was trailing far behind Bell's Island in the scoring.

Twice a policemen—there always had to be policemen at those Gainsbiddle-Bell's Island basketball games because of the beastly rivalry and hatred between the two towns, both as seafood ports and as high school sports competitors—came and said something to Roger, then the third time the policeman came to him and called him down, Roger jumped up, and in no uncertain terms told the policeman where to go and what to do with himself when he got there.

The policeman got Roger by the scruff of the neck, removed him forcibly from behind the Gainsbiddle cheering section, and dragged him out of the bleachers and down across the back of the gymnasium with Roger cussing and hollering the whole time. When the policeman got Roger to the exit and tried to toss him outside, Roger set up a mighty scuffle, and that's when little Doris Thornton appeared from somewhere and went to Roger's rescue.

Doris was "no bigger than a minute," goes the saying, and she was not about to wrestle physically with that policeman. But Camellia and Anselm could see her doing quite a piece of quiet talking. They didn't know what she was saying, but it must have been mighty persuasive.

The policeman let go of Roger and turned him over to Doris, and the two of them came and sat quietly in the Bell's Island section of the bleachers, away from the Gainsbiddle cheering section for the rest of the game.

Camellia was wondering how Doris could even sit next to Roger for that long, the way he was smelling, but if love was blind, maybe it also was deodorized. Camellia and Anselm were pleased, as no doubt were Roger and Doris also, that Bell's Island won that basketball game. Gainsbiddle never overcame the lead Bell's Island had at the half, and if Roger's farts had helped them in getting that lead, then for once Camellia could say *Bravo, Brother Roger*!

Camellia's contacts with Gainsbiddle had been few and far between since she was no longer teaching "those inane singing classes" in the county elementary schools. Thomas and Mary still visited their old friends, Bessie and Norman Travis in Gainsbiddle, but Camellia, in her high-flown residency in Royal Hall, had all but lost touch with the Travis family. That is, until Wayne Travis, Bessie and Norman's now-grown son, became a night cop in Royal Hall.

Anselm had run afoul of Wayne right at the start. They seemed to invariably meet in the Royal Hall barbershop at a time when Wayne was off duty and out of uniform. In fact, Anselm didn't even realize Wayne was a cop. But Wayne was a big, strapping fellow with wiry, curly brown hair and a tendency to keep a chip on his shoulder.

Wayne and Anselm took an immediate dislike to each other, partly because Wayne was a Gainsbiddler and scrappy, and Anselm, a Bell's Islander by adoption, was a pacifist of sorts who had still not fought Roger. And if there was anything a Gainsbiddler couldn't stand more than a Bell's Islander, it was a Bell's Islander who wouldn't fight.

Wayne somehow knew that Anselm and Camellia were lovers. (And who didn't?) Wayne also no doubt remembered the time when he'd been a little kid and Camellia, then just a teenager herself, had set him on her lap and played with him those weekends she had stayed with the Travises when she'd worked in Middleton's drugstore in Gainsbiddle.

Wayne, undoubtedly to annoy Anselm in a nasty Gainsbiddle way, switched time and circumstances around and bragged that he had held Camellia on his lap and she had played with him—and he implied it was recently!

Wham! The non-aggressive Anselm leaped out from under the barber's scissors and landed a punch right square on Wayne's eye as Wayne sat waiting his turn for a haircut. They would have had a dingbuster of a fight, Anselm later told Camellia, had not another cop—who was on duty and in uniform—walked in, and Wayne did not return Anselm's punch.

But Wayne Travis was a Gainsbiddler and not one to forgive and forget. After the cop left, he made the vow right there in the barbershop that he was going to get even with Anselm, if not one way then another....

Eventually there came a Saturday night in the summer of 1948 when Mrs. Elderkin *was* at home at her mansion, so Anselm and Camellia decided to take a little walk as part of their date that evening. They wandered over to a little off-the-beaten-path lover's nook in the tree-lined border right next to the Episcopal Church cemetery....

Well, they certainly weren't bothering anybody, both Camellia and Anselm agreed. They were out of public sight and as for any "disrespect to the dead," those dry bones in their graves were probably getting their best thrills in centuries.

Camellia and Anselm were in for a little surprise, however. Patrolman Wayne Travis, walking his beat through the town, stumbled—literally—over them. When he saw who they were, he actually arrested them—on a charge of fornication. He ordered them to accompany him to the Royal Hall police station where he started to write out the formal charge.

Then suddenly Patrolman Wayne Travis looked and acted as though he were going to faint. He clutched his head, stopped writing, blinked bleary-eyed, and said, "You-you two c-c-can leave now. I'll-I'll be con-contacting you...later."

Wayne never did "contact them later."

A couple of weeks later Camellia was at the Tu-Rest Home, and Mary and Thomas had just returned from Gainsbiddle. Mary was saying, "Bessie told us that Wayne's finally got back to work. He was taken with a horrible spell of some kind while on duty in Royal Hall two Saturday nights ago. Bessie said Wayne felt there was something very mysterious about it, but Bessie said she thought it was just his wife's cooking. Wayne's not been married too long, you know, and Bessie says his wife has a lot to learn about what combination of foods she cooks together."

Camellia smiled innocently and said, "Yeah, I'll bet." She was thinking, Sorry, Wayne, that I had to do that to you, and Thank you, Grandpaw Azariah, for your "gypsy magic" lessons long time back.

Anselm later said of the incident, "Camellia, couldn't you just have told Patrolman Travis that we were merely looking at tombstones, trying to find that 'missing link' to the colonial ancestor on your mother's Judge Johnstone side of the family so you can get in the Daughters of the American Revolution?"

Camellia exploded in laughter and said, "I hardly think *that* would have convinced Wayne Travis....Or anybody else, considering what we *were* doing."

Camellia's pursuit of the elusive ancestor from Grandmother LeCates's side of the family had been going on ever since Camellia started serving as hostess at Mrs. Elderkin's mansion during Olde Royal Hall Days. Each fall she dressed all up in colonial costume and greeted guests, smiling and curtsying just like a plantation mistress of old time. It was about as close to a Metropolitan Opera costume as Camellia was getting, as absorbed as she was in her own Royal Hall *Daze*.

Anselm wasn't much more tolerant of Camellia's whim than Mary, who once said the Daughters of the American Revolution was nothing but a room full of silly ladies trying to be super-patriotic and out-snoot all the other ladies in the community who didn't have a blood ancestor who had fought in the American Revolution—and no matter if that ancestor in civilian life had been an illiterate drunk who stole horses.

Anselm said his "old man"—Karl Jurgensen—always bragged to the Mennonites that he had an authentic Indian princess in his ancestry. Anselm said, "I don't know how that could have been possible. According to what Johann in Wilmington always said, a boatload of Swedes had set out for Delaware, and one Hjalmar Jurgensen of Copenhagen and his Norwegian wife, Astrid Ingarsdatter, had stowed away on it. That Hjalmar and Astrid were the old man's father and mother, and Hjalmar was also a brother to Johann's father who didn't come to America until later. Johann had a bit of a Scandinavian accent, but the old man didn't. I guess he learned his American pronunciation from the Indians....Camellia, don't you think this whole business is a mite silly?"

But for quite a few years now Camellia had been carefully building her *Royal Hall image* and Daughters of the American Revolution membership seemed a *must.* She also thought Anselm's image needed a little shoring up, too. It was fine that he was of Danish-Norwegian-German ancestry "from the Midwest" and she could even take it that he was Royal Hall High's "Big-Bellied Dutchman" bandmaster, but she didn't want him to ever be classified as a "Bell's Island waterman." She didn't like the grubby work he was doing for the Stephenses on weekends on the crab and oyster boats and in the shipyard. She thought it would be much nicer if she could say to the Royal Hall gentry, "Oh, yes. My friend Anselm *is* working part-time for the Stephenses family firm. He's working *in the office.*"

Camellia knew she was taking considerable chances with her *image* just by having Anselm at her mansion apartment so much. Yet she felt the presence of Aunt Sairy as her maid and her official chaperone was sufficient to hold off much of the gossip. But Aunt Sairy wasn't there *all* the time anymore than Mrs. Elderkin was home all the time. And it was in those *unprotected* times that Camellia and Anselm had many of their rendezvous.

Anselm was there, tucked away asleep in Camellia's bedroom, one spring afternoon in 1949 when Mary came to ask Camellia for money. A Johnny Come Lately to Bell's Island, one Barney Sedge, who must have thought the Stephenses had money, had been to Thomas and Mary, claiming that Roger had knocked up his daughter. Sedge had suggested the Stephenses could "settle friendly-like" (that is, with money) or else Sedge would be obliged to pursue other measures.

Camellia started wailing, "Mama, for how many years now have you drained me either of time, money, energy, or opportunity because of that half-animal, half-demon son you whelped? And now you want money *again*. NO! I'll not pay to raise a bastard's bastard. Or to have it terminated. Whichever way that Sedge man is trying to con you."

Mary started up a wailing of her own: "Camellia, you don't love us any more. How can you just stand aside and let us suffer when you could so easily help us. It's not that you can't afford it....And...and while we are on the subject, the firm is in other trouble again, too.... Notes are coming due on the shipyard and...."

Camellia cut in and said, "Mama, what *is it* with the Stephens family? And I don't mean just you and Papa, but the whole gang from Grandpaw Azariah on down. You all are totally incapable of doing your business unless somebody is holding your hand. And I'm tired of being *that somebody*!"

But Mary looked at Camellia so "down-troggled" that Camellia relented and said, "Well, all right, then." She went and got her checkbook.

Camellia heard Anselm chuckle out loud from back in the bedroom, and Mary, realizing he was there, quickly took the check and immediately left the apartment. She rejoined Thomas who was waiting for her out in the car.

Anselm came into the living room rubbing the sleep out of his eyes.

Camellia said, "I guess you heard?"

Anselm nodded.

Camellia reflected. "I've never had any trouble as a teacher controlling a classroom of kids, not even those rotten Gainsbiddlers back in the 1930s. I've never had any trouble controlling Royal Hall High's glee club or the Shore Choral and Dramatic Society. I never had any trouble controlling my questionable men friends of the past. But when it comes to the Stephens family I have been totally powerless to keep myself from *being controlled by them*!"

Anselm said, "Instead of pouring your money into a bottomless pit by giving them donations all the time, why don't you put your brain or your 'gypsy magic' to work in the business. Your 'special powers' along with your mother's intelligence ought to be enough to keep that firm out of debt."

Camellia said, "That might seem to make sense, Anselm, but that bunch of Stephens men, Papa included, wouldn't listen to me any more than they'd listen to Mama, who's always kept quiet when it came to what was best for the company—just like she always kept quiet when it came to what was best for herself—and all because, as a woman, she 'knows her place'. And furthermore, I don't want to be involved in the running of that business anyway."

Anselm thought for a moment, then said, "Then I guess you aren't aware that Charlie Stephens has talked your parents into putting double insurance on that skipjack—your namesake—*The Camellia Stephens*. You have any idea why?"

"They probably intend to burn it," Camellia said unemotionally.

"But why would they burn it?" said Anselm. "We've been working on her ever since January, sprucing her up like she was going to be on display in some special mid-Atlantic work boat show. Hahahaha! Your father keeps saying to me at the end of each week, 'Next week, Anselm, I want you to work again on *Camellia's* bottom'. Hahahaha! Your father never realizes how some of the things he says sound. But Charlie once whispered loud enough for everybody on the island to hear, 'You do that just about every night, doncha, pal!?' Well, now! I don't mind working on that boat's bottom—or yours, either! But you haven't answered me—why would they burn the boat after it's been repainted and all?"

Camellia said, "Less suspicion that way. They've pulled tricks like that before. The Stephenses have 'the thieving gypsy genes' in their blood. It's the only way they can 'do their business' successfully. Papa tries to hold the others down, but when the firm is hard put, they don't listen to Papa, but go ahead and fight dirty like they've done for generations. I've told you all of that, and yet you still wonder why I don't like to be associated with them OR Bell's Island. And I wish you weren't, either."

Not too many weeks later, Camellia was wakened one night by the Royal Hall fire siren and a large red glow in the sky toward Bell's Island. Fearing it might be the Tu-Rest Home, she rushed to the phone and called her mother.

Mary was in tears. "It's *The Camellia Stephens,*" she reported dolefully.

"Oh, that dahmned thing," Camellia yawned, hung up the phone, and went immediately back to sleep.

So, "that dahmned thing" with her name across its "ahhs-end" passed forever from the mortal scene, and Camellia couldn't have cared less. After all, she had only that morning located "that missing link" in her ancestry—one illiterate buck private—Jeremiah Johnstone (who'd also been a horse thief)—and with him her niche in the Daughters of the American Revolution was finally secured. So, Bell's Island and everything about it could go hang.

However everybody didn't feel the same indifference about *The*

Camellia Stephens." Anselm said to her the next evening, "The firelight woke me. I never did hear any Bell's Island siren. Along with your father, I rushed out to the docks.

"There wasn't a spot on *The Camellia Stephens* that wasn't aflame all at one time, from the top of her mizzenmast to the tip of her bowsprit. The whole sky was red, and the flames were reflecting in all the windows of the houses. It was a ghastly sight.

"The Royal Hall fire truck was there, but about all the men could do was spread foam around everywhere to keep the whole wharf, with all its gasoline and other fuel storage tanks, from exploding.

"All around me I could hear people grumbling:

"'It was a setup job. It *had* to be. The Bell's Island fire alarm didn't even go off....'

"'Yeah, I know. Probably the wire was disconnected. Somebody at the station just now said the fire truck had been drained of gas and the battery removed. And you know, some of Azariah's grandsons are in the fire department....'

"'Will you lookit the way she's burning! All at one time! Don't tell me she wasn't set. Can't you smell that coal oil...?'

"'Those damn Stephenses. They fix her all up with new paint and everything, then toss the match. And she was loaded with cargo, too. She was supposed to go to Baltimore in the morning.'

"'Bet they collect big on this one....'

"'Yeah. Ever so often they'll pull something like this. Was born into 'em. Bunch of crooks, pirates, and gypsies....Goes way back, you know....'

"'But *Thomas* Stephens is not like that....'

"'No, Thomas is okay. A little silly, but okay....'"

Camellia looked rather pleased that her prophecy had been born out. She said, "I told you they were going to burn it."

Anselm said, "It was such a beautiful craft, so wonderfully built—just like you are."

Camellia chuckled.

Anselm went on. "Doc Feldman was standing near me in that red firelight and I guess he saw the anguish on my face, Doc said, 'Don't take it so hard there, Jurgensen. One would think you were in love with the boat instead of the woman!'"

"Sometimes I think you *are* in love with Bell's Island instead of me," Camellia remarked a little peevishly.

Camellia never did know what became of the Sedge man's paternity claims against Roger. In the meantime Doris Thornton and Roger had continued their courtship, and they were married in September of 1949. They were little more than sixteen years old, and neither returned for their senior year in high school. Roger continued to work for the Stephens firm, so they did have some income on which to start a household.

Camellia thought Roger looked rather handsome, for once, on his wedding day. He was all cleaned up, shaved, and dressed in a nice suit, and for once he wasn't cussing. He had a happy look on his face and in his blue eyes. As he was tall and skinny, there was something unmistakable about him that reminded Camellia of Mary; maybe it was his little upward tilt of the chin, sort of as if he were telling the world to go fuck itself!

Camellia thought Doris, too, seemed happy even though none of her people attended the wedding ceremony at the Bell's Island Methodist Church parsonage, and rumor had it that the Thorntons had completely disowned Doris for marrying Roger.

The pair had a short honeymoon in Atlantic City, and while they were gone, Simon Cartwright hastily threw together a one-story, box-like dwelling for them on a tiny narrow lot next door to Charlie and Agnes Stephens. Simon even built a little white picket fence around the house.

Even though Roger was married now, Camellia felt he was still lusting after her and still trying to provoke a showdown fight with Anselm.

Marriage did not seem to cure him of his whoring around, and he would go to Moonlight's place, have his women, and get beered up, then go home to Doris and raise hell. Agnes told Camellia that Doris often spent the night with her when Roger got on his rampages, raring and cussing and throwing dishes and furniture all over the house and scaring Doris half to death.

According to Agnes, Doris always said Roger never hit her or hurt her; he only tore up the house. Agnes told Camellia, "Roger is so hoigh-strung. Doris thinks he has pynes in his stermock all the toime. She thinks mye-bee he's got 'dee-fishy metal-bolly-ism.' It's sumpin' what Doc Feldman tol' her—loike when you diges' your food too fast or not at all."

Camellia tried not to laugh. Doc had originally attributed Roger's condition to the Curse of Boro. Now it was 'dee-fishy metal-bolly-ism." Medical science was advancing all the time. Camellia said, "Did Doris mean deficiency metabolism, maybe?"

Agnes said, "Yes, I think that's what she said. You know Doris alwyes talks loike she knows what she's sying, whether she does or not."

Also according to Agnes, Roger's farting (which Doris told her might have been due to his "dee-fishy metal-bolly-ism") was nearly the undoing of him in the shipyard one day.

Said Agnes to Camellia, "Charlie tol' Roger if he farted one more toime in his fyce, he warse goin' to fix him. Roger dint pay no 'tention to Charlie an' kept roight on fartin' an' when he come out with one of them long, drawn-out, stinky-smelly ones, Charlie whipped out his cigarette loighter an' flicked it at Roger's behint an' Jaysus Croyst! thar warse a sheet of flyme whippin' crost Roger's arse. His pants warse on farr an' he warse hollerin' and jumpin' 'round for all get out. Iffen it hadn't been Amos Stephens shoved Roger overboard, he woulda burned up roight thar on the dock!"

Ah, yes, thought Camellia, Amos Stephens—he "never done nobody no harm."

When the new year of 1950 came in, Anselm was finally working "in the office." Camellia had managed to talk to her mother into letting Anselm be the one to take the deposits to the bank instead of Mary all the time.

"Office?" That loosely formed federation of fools now calling itself The Stephens Enterprises didn't even have an office except for the big front room on the residence side of the Tu-Rest Home where Mary did the firm's bookkeeping.

And one day *too many Stephenses* got in there all at the same time. They had some matters Thomas, who was still president, wanted them to vote on, and they were also waiting for Roger and Charlie to get back from selling a truckload of seafood in Baltimore.

It was one of the hottest April days Camellia could ever remember. Even though the temperature was 90 degrees or more outside, everyone was scared to put on lighter clothing or turn off the stoves lest a blizzard blow in by mid-afternoon. So everybody just sweated and swore all day and wondered why anybody had to be this uncomfortable.

Camellia and Anselm, Thomas and Mary, and Simon Cartwright were already there in the "office" for the meeting. Yet to arrive were Amanda, Amos, and Grandpaw Azariah, as well as Charlie and Roger. Camellia was astounded to learn that Charlie and Roger for sometime had been trusted to bring home *cash* from these Baltimore transactions when it was well known they often used these trips to do a little drinking, gambling, and whoring as well as seafood trading.

So, the tension of waiting for them was building, and they were so wrought up they all nearly jumped through the ceiling when they heard the truck come barrelling over the Bell's Island bridge, tailgate and chains a-slamming. The truck screeched to a halt in front of the Tu-Rest Home. Two doors opened and slammed shut.

Roger came loping up on the porch with Charlie scrambling along behind him. Roger was reeking of liquor, cigarettes, sweat, filth, and

God only knows what all else, and the whole house seemed to fill instantly with his smell. Before he even got the front screen door open, he started bragging. "We done every girlie show and every whorehouse from Pratt Street to York, Pennsylvania!" And he proceeded nonstop with the vulgarest of obscenities to describe just what all they had seen and done on their trip, while Charlie stood there beside Roger, leering through a drunken haze and obviously enjoying the recounting of it.

Camellia and Anselm were sitting at a large table along with Thomas and Mary. Thomas and Mary were braced as usual for these unpleasant tirades of Roger's. Their eyes were on the table, their fists jammed against their chins, and they winced every now and then at Roger's foul talk the way one still winces in a violent thunderstorm at each crack and flash even after living through such storms time and time again.

Camellia had heard all this sort of thing from Roger so many times over the years that it had all but lost its effect on her, and Anselm was no stranger to Roger's vileness, either. But since Anselm was "in the office" now, Camellia felt obliged to offer some sort of counter-comment lest he think she was overlooking or condoning Roger's behavior. So, she nudged Anselm and whispered half-heartedly, "I think I'm going to vomit."

"Please don't," Anselm said wearily.

"Roger always makes me feel that way," Camellia said peevishly.

"Roger makes *everybody* feel that way," Simon Cartwright observed. Simon was standing by the doorway to the front porch, trying to get a breath of fresh air, which was hard enough to come by in that day's heat, much less with Roger in the room.

Mary got up from the table and got Roger by the arm and shook him a bit. She asked, "Roger—the money?"

"Ah, yes, indeed," Roger said. He started swaggering all around as he pulled a bulging wallet from his pocket, dumped a huge pile of large denomination bills on the table in front of Anselm, and said, "Count up that load, Asshole, and the rest of you will see if me and Charlie ain't the big businessmen in this firm."

Thomas stared bug-eyed as Anselm counted out the money. Thomas said, "Why, that's four times the amount that load of seafood was even worth. Roger, did you and Charlie *gamble* to get this—?"

"It isn't hard when you have the right cards," Roger said with an insolent shrug. "Take your own deck, you know. Har-har-har-har!" Then he added, "Just remember who's the most valuable employee to you when you decide on a new 'junior partner'."

Camellia saw Anselm squirm a little. Thomas had said any number of times he'd take Anselm into the firm as a partner provided he and Camellia were *legally* married....

As Roger continued to boast and blackguard, Camellia looked through the front window and saw Doris Thornton—Doris *Stephens*, she was now—coming toward the Tu-Rest Home. Doris was already showing her pregnancy and acting like she was scared to approach the family inside the house.

To Simon, who had gone out on the front porch to meet her, Doris said cautiously, "Please, can I talk with Roger? I've been waiting for him to come back. The pipes in the house are all fouled up."

Everybody said when Simon built Roger and Doris's house, he must have been three sheets to the wind because nothing had worked right in it from the beginning.

Thomas got up from the table, went on the porch, and said to Doris, "Roger is on one of his rampages right now and he's saying things you—uh—best not hear."

"'Mister' Thomas," said Doris, "I'm sure he's not saying anything I've not heard him say already. *Please* let me talk with him."

Thomas tried to put Doris off. Simon came back in from the porch and pushed in from of Charlie, who was leaning against the wall, half-asleep. Charlie roused, swore, swung a fist a Simon, and missed. Simon grabbed Roger by the arm and commanded, "Go to the door. Your wife wants to talk to you."

Roger went sulkily onto the porch and bawled at Doris: "Woman, what in hell are you doing here when us Stephenses are doing our business?"

Everybody chuckled in spite of everything and there was even a flicker of amusement on Mary's tired, thin face.

Doris begged Roger, "Please come home just a minute and at least shut that main water valve off under the house. I can't reach under there any more. The house is flooded inside. You are the only one in the neighborhood skinny enough to get under there."

Camellia didn't think Doris meant any wisecrack at Roger's physique, but he thrust out his arm as if to hit her. Simon Cartwright, ever the self-appointed guardian of the weak and helpless, came from out of nowhere and flew between them, snarling at Roger, "Don't you hit her! In her 'condition.'"

Roger obeyed. He hit Simon instead!

"You damned bastard!" Simon croaked. He was clutching his stomach, and then a flurry of fists flew between him and Roger.

Then they both stopped punching at the same time and looked up to see Grandpaw Azariah ambling across the shell road in his overalls three sized too large for him and with the fly buttoned up cross-hoppled.

"See how fast Grandpaw's presence, even, stopped that fight?" Camellia whispered to Anselm.

Anselm said, "Grandpaw can't get his pants buttoned up right, but he can keep his kinsmen from killing each other, right?"

Camellia said, "Amos's wife, Lois, makes those overalls for Grandpaw. He says he likes them big like that. Claims he can hide from people in them. Amos and Lois bought him some with zippers when zippers first replaced buttons on the fly. But the very first day Grandpaw had them on he got himself hung up in the zipper, and he swore he'd never wear anything like *that* again! Lois went back to making them with buttons for him."

"Goooood Lord!" exclaimed Anselm. Camellia knew he'd heard that same story a dozen times from the men at the shipyard, but she went through it again anyhow. It helped ease the tension.

Camellia also remembered the tales from the shipyard and from Grandpaw Azariah himself about how he could hypnotize anything or anybody from a baby to a barnacle with his "gypsy magic" and without them knowing what was happening to them. Anselm said he'd seen it happen once himself. When the Conservation Commission had started their surveillance of oyster boats, the police boat caught up with *The Camellia Stephens* one day, and Anselm happened to be on board.

Anselm had told Camellia, "The inspector came aboard and started looking for undersize oysters. The oysters were okay as to size, but the inspector was suspicious of the way we were transferring oysters to the buy boat. He took a shovel and hit the side of one of the buckets, and all the oysters fell in to only half-full. Charlie had been shoveling the oysters into the buckets in such a way that they stood up on their ends instead of laying flat. And of course we were dumping those half-buckets as full buckets onto the buy boat. And they did *look* like full buckets. Your father wasn't on the skipjack that day and so the rest of them were taking the opportunity to slip back into their old crooked ways.

"But the inspector was on to them and was about to tip off the buy boat. Charlie grabbed a rifle and was going to drill the inspector in the back. But Grandpaw Azariah signalled 'No!' to Charlie. Then, without a shot being fired or a hand being laid on that inspector, he suddenly stiffened, clutched his head, and fell backwards overboard. (Something like you did to Wayne Travis, by the way.)

"Grandpaw signalled to Amos at the wheel to move out quick. *The Camellia Stephens* got away, and that inspector all but drowned right there in the Anderson Sound. We'd unloaded and sold most of our catch that day before the inspector got on board...and at double what they were worth because our buckets were only half-full."

Remembering Anselm's account, Camellia was thinking of Grandpaw and that less-than-admirable phase of "gypsy magic"—concentrate intensely on your adversary/ see him as terribly sick or gravely injured/ *see him as dead*/ see total evil for him/ and that way you can get him out of your way. Yes, Grandpaw could do all of that with "gypsy magic" and still couldn't get his pants buttoned up straight!

Camellia mused on that for awhile then forcibly snapped her attention back to the scene on the porch. Roger had ignored Doris's plea to fix her pipes, and he had come back into the house.

Doris was still standing outside and almost weeping. Grandpaw eased up to her, touched her on the shoulder, and said, "What is it, darling? Is it those pipes again? I'll fix 'em for you, honey."

"Well, I wish someone would," Doris said. And she and Grandpaw went off together across the shell road.

Simon stepped back in the house, then jumped right back out on the porch again, bellowing to Grandpaw: "Hey, Grandpaw! Wouldja tell Amanda and Agnes to come over here right away so the two of them can get Charlie out of here before he messes up hell and creation?"

Charlie was reeling around in the front room, burping dangerously, and trying to locate the downstairs bathroom.

"Charlie's getting old," Roger observed. "Can't take the whoring and boozing like he used to."

Camellia jumped up and gave Roger a swat. "Why *don't* you shut up!" she rasped at him.

"Aw, now, Sister," Roger said in mock concern. "What's the matter with you these days? You are so crabby, people would think you weren't getting it any more from ole Asshole here." Roger reached out and grabbed Camellia.

"Let me *go*, Roger!" Camellia seethed. She shook off his sensually pawing hands. Camellia saw Anselm tense and thought he was about to jump on Roger and really give him the works, but Amanda Cartwright came bursting in on the scene, big end foremost, brushing aside Simon, who was still standing by the door.

Amanda, in her booming voice, let everybody know that "Agnes says she won't come over here and help me get Charlie out. Says it's not her place, as only a sister-*in-law* to be in on family business proceedings."

"Oh, goddamn her soul," Camellia muttered. Her nerves were taking away her usual politeness.

"Where is that sodden fool," demanded Amanda, looking for her brother Charlie, who had staggered out of the bathroom, wiping the slobber off his chin, then just as quickly ducked back in there again.

Thomas nodded in Charlie's direction and said quietly, "Take him out the *back* door, Amanda, please. Mary just scrubbed the front porch this morning."

As Amanda was dragging the retching and wretched Charlie out the back door of the house, Camellia saw Doris coming up on the front porch again.

Roger roared, "What in hell—? Why doesn't she stay home like a decent pregnant woman is supposed to?"

Simon met Doris at the door and asked, "For God's sake, Doris, what's wrong now?"

Doris seemed near the breaking point. She snapped at Simon, "Don't you ever do anything but act as a doorman for people, Simon Cartwright? If you'd built that house right to start with—but I don't know what Grandpaw has done. He's got the cold water coming out of the hot water faucets, the hot water coming out of the cold water ones, and he's somehow got the *gas line* tied into the water line. There's water spurting out of all the gas burners on the stove, and gas is coming out from under the toilet seat. All I asked him to do was shut off the main water valve. *Please let me talk with Roger.*"

"Where's Grandpaw now?" Simon asked, virtually ignoring everything Doris had said.

"I don't know," Doris wailed.

Anselm was laughing so hard he nearly turned the table over. Camellia glanced at her parents. Thomas and Mary were glumly hanging on, as though they were wondering how much longer anybody could take all of this.

By now Amos and Lois had walked up to the house. Lois was only a sister-in-law, too, but she had no qualms about coming in onto "family business." She still followed Amos around, because Amos still didn't know how to get home from anywhere without her. But "neither of them never done nobody no harm," everybody on the island still agreed.

"'Mister' Amos," Doris began. She turned toward the goofy-looking "blond-headed gypsy" (as everybody still called him) and pleaded, "Would you do something for me?"

Amos looked Doris up and down as she stood there in her new maternity dress. He looked her up and down two or three times, and then without cracking a smile, he said, "Looks like something's already been done."

Again Anselm nearly turned the table over trying to hold down his laughing. *He* was enjoying all this idiocy, if nobody else was, Camellia thought irritably.

Doris continued pleading, "Would you come to my house, 'Mister' Amos, and shut the main water line and the gas line off? Roger won't help me, and Grandpaw's got everything mixed up."

"I'll do what I can, Doris," Amos said. "Come on, Lois, let's see what we can do."

Thomas hollered out the door to Amos, "Amos, I need you here! We're about to start the meeting."

"Only be a minute, Brother Thomas," Amos answered.

"Oh, go on, then," Thomas growled.

Amanda was back now, having deposited Charlie at the doorstep of his house for Agnes to do with him as she saw fit. Amanda looked at the retreating Amos, Lois, and Doris and boomed, "Where are *they* all going?"

"To fix Doris's pipes," said Simon.

"Oh, my good Lord!" Amanda boomed. "That pair wouldn't know how to pour piss out of a boot with the directions written right on the heel."

Amanda came into the front room and turned to Roger, who was leaning against the doorway into the hall, picking at his fingernails, and grunting like some sort of uncomfortable pig. Amanda said to him, "What's the matter with you, you scrawny shithead? Why don't *you* fix her pipes? You're her husband."

Roger made an obscene gesture toward Amanda's back as she walked past him, which she apparently didn't see or else she would have pummeled the hell out of him. But Camellia noticed the gesture and it made her wince.

Thomas walked up to Amanda and said, "Would you go and try to find Grandpaw? We've got to vote on some stuff here and with Charlie, Amos, and Grandpaw gone, we won't have enough for a quarrel."

A 'quorum'," said Mary wearily.

"Yes, that's what I said," replied Thomas, "...a quarrel....Or is it a quarium? No, that's what you put fish in. Anyway, we won't have one if Grandpaw doesn't get back."

Camellia pressed her face against Anselm's shoulder. She was hovering between laughter and tears.

"Don't cry, honey," Anselm begged her. "There ain't ho hell."

Camellia gave a short laugh and said, "No, I know there isn't. It's all here on Bell's Island!"

Amanda, trying to get out the door, suddenly boomed at Simon, "Don't you ever do anything but act as a doorman, Simon Cartwright?"

Simon scratched his head. "That's funny. Doris asked me the same thing."

Thomas called out the door to Amanda, "Make sure Amos gets back here, too."

While they all waited—and it seemed to be getting hotter and stuffier by the minute—Roger started amusing himself by singing some dirty little tongue twister about the "rich bitch's ditch in which the rich bitch's britches dipped" or "dripped" or something like that.

Camellia could take it no longer. She got up and grabbed Roger by the front of his sweaty shirt. "What's with this 'ditch bitch' business? Where do you pick up all this filth?"

Roger scoffed at her. "Aw, come on, Sister. With all your musical education and degrees and things, don't tell me you ain't never heard the song about the 'ditch wich bick...the which bit...the dict witch the bit...AW SHIT!"

Camellia burst into such a frenzy of laughing at Roger that he became all the more infuriated. But he didn't turn on "Sister." He shoved Camellia aside, and without any provocation from Mary, he glared into his mother's eyes and screamed, "There's only ONE BITCH in this family!"

Camellia watched her mother reel back from Roger's outburst. Then suddenly something totally unexpected happened. Something not one of them would have dreamed possible in a million years. Thomas's patience slid off him like raindrops running off an oilskin slicker, and he caught hold of Roger by the head, dragged him out into the hallway, threw him face down across a table, and with his leather belt began unmercifully thrashing him across his butt.

Roger let out a bloodcurdling yell and writhed like a snake, trying to free himself, but Thomas held him fast. Camellia shuddered. One should never underestimate the strength and fury of a Bell's Island waterman, even if he was someone "bucking for Heaven" like Thomas Stephens.

Thomas held Roger in a vise-like grip and kept on beating him with that leather belt until a red dampness began to show through the seat of Roger's pants.

Mary made no attempt to go to the rescue of her son. She just stared tensely at the brutal scene out there in the hallway.

Camellia sensed that Anselm's basic humanity made him *want* to go to Roger's rescue even though she knew he despised him, but even Anselm failed to budge.

It was not until Thomas realized the blood was running out of Roger's behind that he let up on him. He pulled Roger to his feet and shoved him down the hallway toward the front door. "Now—leave—this—house!" he ordered.

Roger uttered not a word, whimper, oath, or tear. He looked at no one, but limped out of the house, holding the seat of his pants with his hands as the blood seeped through the cloth.

Simon stepped aside as Roger went out the door. Doris was again standing there on the front porch. Nobody bothered to find out why she was there this time. Camellia thought maybe she had sensed some awful thing had happened, and she had come intuitively to her young husband's aid. Simon said to Doris, "Thomas just now beat Roger. Beat him bad. Take him home, Doris. Take care of him."

Roger reached out and grasped for Doris's outstretched hand. Together, silently, heads down, hand in hand, they walked away from the Tu-Rest Home. There was something poignantly touching about the scene. Camellia turned to Anselm and whispered, "Ah, yes, that Doris....Some people are unutterably kind."

Amanda, coming across the shell road again, this time with Grandpaw in tow, stared at Doris and Roger retreating toward their house. The blood was still oozing through Roger's pants. "What happened?" Amanda asked Simon.

Simon cleared his throat. "Never mind. I'll tell you later. Meeting's postponed until further notice." He and Amanda walked away from the Tu-Rest Home.

Grandpaw apparently didn't hear Simon and walked up onto the porch and into the house. He soon caught the drift of what had happened. Grandpaw looked overjoyed as he said, "You should have whipped the shit out of him years ago, Thomas. What took you so long?"

Thomas made no reply. He just stood there in the hallway, motionless, looking very strange, Camellia thought, and not like her father at all.

Mary had disappeared upstairs in a state of choking tears, and Camellia ran up there after her.

Mary said, "It's all right. I deserved it."

Camellia replied, "But Mama, you didn't do a thing."

"Long time back," Mary said, sniffling. "Roger's been wanting to say that to me for years, and I deserved it."

Exasperated, Camellia said, "You, you! That's all you think about is you, Mama. I think you enjoy suffering. But what about Roger? Papa nearly killed him!"

"Maybe your Papa's been wanting to do that for years, too," said Mary. "After all, he was only trying to defend my honor."

"Your *honor*?!" said Camellia, shaking her head, perplexed, but she wouldn't be so cruel now as to ask *What honor*?

Mary said, "Go on downstairs, Camellia. I'll be all right."

Camellia went on back downstairs. She found Anselm still staring in disbelief at Thomas.

Thomas asked Camellia, "Is your Mama all right?" Some of his old self seemed to be coming back in him now.

"She'll be all right," Camellia assured him. To the still-shocked Anselm she said, "Come on, Anselm, let's you and I walk Grandpaw home. Would you like that, Grandpaw?"

Grandpaw shrugged but didn't offer any objection.

Camellia whispered to Anselm, "Best to leave Mama and Papa alone to say whatever they have to say to each other in privacy."

Anselm nodded in agreement.

After they'd chucked Grandpaw off at Amos and Lois's, they walked down by the sound side of the island, trying to find a cool spot on which to reflect what had just happened.

Anselm said, "I could not believe what I was seeing. I could not believe your father could do anything so violent."

"In a way I'm glad he did it," Camellia said. "And so was Mama. Roger's had that coming to him for years and years. Everybody has his boiling point—saints and sinners alike—and Papa finally reached his today."

"But did your father have to beat Roger until the blood ran out of him? I thought there was one person on this earth—your father—who wasn't tainted like the rest of humanity. He's always been a hero to me because he dared to be different from his horrible family. Now I'm not so sure any more."

Camellia said, "If Papa flew into Roger for what Roger said—implying Mama was a bitch—it was only that Papa was not about to let any man—son, stepson, or whatever—insult Mama and get away with it, no matter what Mama may have done in the past to deserve being insulted. Papa has always idolized Mama, you know."

"Well, maybe so," said Anselm, reluctantly.

Camellia went on. "I think Roger has always hated Mama for bringing him into existence in the first place, especially in later years since he learned the *way* she did it. I think that's why he's always been so mean and probably why he said what he said to her today. And Mama has always hated Roger, because she has hated herself for the way she conceived him. In recent years she's tried to be more loving to him, but it doesn't seem to have done much good."

They both fell silent for awhile and just stared out across the languidly rolling waters of the Anderson Sound.

Finally Anselm said, "I thought I'd found a family here I could love and believe in. But now I don't know anymore. Your father has really let me down."

Camellia didn't reply.

Anselm said, "Camellia—" then he stopped.

"What is it, Anselm?"

"I think I might leave Wintergreen County."

Camellia stared at him open-mouthed. "And quit your job as bandmaster at Royal Hall High?"

"Oh, that position means nothing to me. I've only done it to please you."

"I sort of figured as much," Camellia said. "But you.... *Leave Bell's Island*? And after you've bought that property on Little Bell's? I thought you were in love with this part of the world. Or is it that you've only been staying here to indulge your need for a pair of surrogate parents whose daughter has been willing to strip for you?"

When Anselm didn't reply, Camellia stormed at him, "Well, leave, then, dammit! Leave!" And after a long silence, "...But take me with you," she begged plaintively.

Anselm looked at her incredulously. "Take you away from all your luxury living in Royal Hall? Your position at the school as music director—the highest paid teacher this county has ever had? Your post in the church, in the choral cociety? Your love affair with the Daughters of the American Revolution?"

Camellia huffed. "All of that 'big fish in a little pond' stuff—I'm sick of it, Anselm. You're the only thing holding me here now. Let's both get away. Greenwich Village, maybe. I wouldn't have to worry about my small town image and small town morality there. We wouldn't even have to be married. You could be anything you wanted—inventor, philosopher—whatever. My 'wise investments' would carry us through. I could find a good music teacher and get groomed for my bid to The Met. I could write symphonies...!"

Anselm laughed. "You are an incurable optimist. But you talk about singing opera and writing symphonies in the same breath. Didn't you say your old music teacher, Claudie, warned you about thinking like that? Performing and creating come from opposite ends of the emotional spectrum. If you have both on the mind, you'll end up doing neither, like it seems you already have, except for your 'big fish in a little pond' capers around here."

Camellia said, "There have always been two beasts in me—one wants to perform, the other wants to create. Yet they are *not* mutually exclusive. And with your knowledge and ability at music, you could help me with both...and 'in the big time.'"

Anselm whooped. "A soprano need lots of sex, they say, and I could supply that. But, otherwise, the Bible says woman was made for man, not the other way around."

"Mama tried to follow that Bible belief, and you see what it's done for her," Camellia observed. "I once said I would never marry. Many times I have said I would never marry a Bell's Island waterman."

When neither could find anything else to say, they left their conversation in the air and returned to the Tu-Rest Home. The shell road was empty—all Stephenses having crawled away to nurse their wounds, physical and mental, and to sweat out the remainder of the uncomfortably hot April day. Anselm went on up to his room on the roomers' side of the Tu-Rest Home. Camellia returned to Royal Hall.

The day after Roger's beating, Camellia drove back to Bell's Island and first went to his little house. Doris met her in the yard and said Roger was still sleeping. Doris told Camellia that Amos and Lois had their plumbing fixed by the time they'd gotten home the day before, and she was able to clean Roger up right away and put a big poultice on his raw backside. Then she cooked him a big plate of bacon and eggs, filled him full of aspirin, and put him to bed. She stayed up all night with him, watching over him.

Camellia, in telling this later to Anselm at her apartment in Royal Hall, said, "I wish I could remember Doris's exact words of how she examined and treated Roger because it was as priceless combination of medical terms, nautical—and 'naughty'—terms and good ole Bell's Island vulgarisms all rolled together in Doris's own special style!

"She described how she'd checked out all of Roger's lower systems and parts, both fore and aft, both internal and external, and found him in remarkably good shape, considering. And she said the cuts and bruises will eventually heal.

"She was so 'down-to-earthy', yet at the same time so enthusiastic about everything from bowels to bladders and loins to groins that I felt like I had walked in on a County Home Extension Agent's Ten-Star Seminar on hem stitching, furniture re-doing, and how to make salad dressing!

"Doris also said that she didn't think Roger had any resentment toward Papa for the beating. So when I went to the Tu-Rest Home and reported, there was a great feeling of relief from both Mama and Papa....But what about you, Anselm—?"

"Well, what about me?"

Camellia said, "You acted so shocked at Papa's actions that I thought you didn't want to stay around here any more."

Anselm said, "It would be hard for me to leave Bell's Island. After all, I've got that piece of property on Little Bell's. It's got an old hunting lodge on it that could be done over into a home...."

"Oh, Anselm," Camellia wailed, "you wouldn't want to live in a garbage dump!"

"The cabin is way off from the dump."

"But you have to go through the dump to get to that cabin," Camellia reminded him.

Then, seeing the senselessness of this line of conversation, she began playing the piano softly like she often did before they got together. Anselm came up behind her and rested his chin on the swirls of her hair.

But she kept wandering off every now and then from the soft music to something strange-sounding in a minor key.

Eventually Anselm became annoyed. "If you'd rather play endlessly with the keyboard than play with me tonight, maybe I'd better let you alone. I can just head on back to Bell's Island and maybe stop in and see Moonlight before crossing the bridge."

Camellia shot him a glance that was not of this world.

He laughed at her and said, "I was just kidding!"

Camellia noted, "The world's oldest profession got started because men couldn't get what they wanted at home."

"Well, I get what I want," said Anselm. "But what for God's sake are you trying to find there on the keyboard? I've heard of *The Lost Chord,* but this...! Jeez!"

Camellia stopped playing and gave Anselm a fierce look. She slammed the keyboard shut and got up from the bench. She gave an impertinent little twist of her torso, suggestive of bawdy house antics and said, "Here, then, take what you want if 'it' is the only thing you can get your mind on this evening."

"Camellia, listen," Anselm said, "forget sex for a minute and listen to me. We're both following that 'different drummer'. We've got more in common than you realize. The only trouble is maybe you take yourself too seriously, and I don't take myself seriously enough. The 'old man' always called me 'the corn on the outside row'—you know that part of the field that never amounts to much. I must have taken the message to heart for I've never applied myself to much of anything—not even things that I've liked to do.

"The men at the shipyard accuse me of 'having pussy on the mind' when I am daydreaming and do something stupid like drop a mooring line directly in the water instead of over the piling. But there is so much more to life than just earning a living. There is so much to see and marvel at. You ask me what do I see in Bell's Island. I don't know. Maybe it's the isolation of the place. You can talk with your soul there."

Camellia thought for a moment, then concluded, "So you *don't* intend to leave Bell's Island...?"

Anselm shook his head no.

She had hoped they could get away together, but it was not what he wanted. And she was not about to force him. Still, there was no coupling that night.

Their rift didn't last very long. The following week Camellia and Anselm were locked together in one of their wild preliminary embraces in her Royal Hall apartment. Camellia ran her hand down below the waistband of his shorts and exclaimed, "What in the deuce is this?"

Anselm chuckled. "If you don't know by now, you'd better go look at some of Doc Feldman's old medical books in your mother's Bell's Island Library!"

"No, not *that*. This—it's a bandage!"

"Cut myself while shaving," Anselm muttered.

"Where were you shaving?" Camellia exclaimed and explored further.

"I had a scuffle with Roger the other night on the Bell's Island docks. He jumped at me with a straightedge razor. He was throwing obscenities at me and flashing that razor and laughing.

"I was trying to get into position to grab him karate-fashion, which was about the only tactic I wanted to use on him, but when I made my move I missed him and caught the edge of his razor right below my belt.

"He was about to make another swipe with that razor—this time at my throat—when suddenly the boardwalk gave way under me. Roger disappeared from my view as I got baptized in that cold slimy Bell's Island harbor....

"What had happened was that Amos Stephens had seen us and was afraid he'd make it worse if he jumped between us, so he'd gotten down under the wharf and pulled down some loose boards which he thought were under Roger, but they were under me. But the commotion caused Roger to run off. And maybe even saved my life."

Camellia laughed, "Yes. Amos. He 'never done nobody no harm', they like saying. But Anselm, you got cut. You got dunked. Why should you always get the shit end of the stick when it comes to Roger? Why don't you fight him for real?"

Anselm exploded. "God's sake, woman! I was *trying* to fight him—fight him my way. I didn't want to hurt him."

Camellia "tch'd-tch'd." "Too bad you grew up 'mongst the Mennonites. But if you don't fight him—and lick him—I'm afraid he'll never let up on you."

"That's the chance I'll have to take, I guess," Anselm said, unconcerned.

The Royal Hall High band under the baton of their "Big-Bellied Dutchman" had won first place with Sousa's *High School Cadets* march at the 1950 Fourth of July parade in Ocean City. Camellia was still bursting with pride over her "teddy bear's" accomplishment, but Anselm took no particular joy in the honor. He was rather in high glee now that it was summer once again, and he was working full time for Stephens Enterprises. And that didn't necessarily mean "in the office," either.

Thomas sent Anselm to Centerbridge in the company fish truck one morning to pick up a boat engine. Camellia's car had quit on her the night before while on Bell's Island, and she had to spend the night with Thomas and Mary. When her car still wouldn't start in the morning, Anselm said he would take her to Royal Hall in the fish truck as he was going through there anyway.

Camellia wasn't looking forward to any ride in that ugly, odoriferous heap of junk metal called "The Bell's Island Express," but she had to get to Royal Hall. Regular school was out for the summer, but there was a board of education meeting for department heads that morning. Superintendent Forrester would be mad if she wasn't there. He was mad anyhow because Anselm had cut him out from pursuing her.

Anselm wanted to avoid some of the heat and humidity of the day, so he and Camellia left Bell's Island before dawn. He was in his work clothes, and Camellia was still in what she had on the evening before, but she knew there would be time to bathe and re-dress before going to the meeting, assuming the fish truck didn't foul her beyond repair.

They crossed over the Bell's Island bridge shortly before sunrise. The first wisps of bright-rimmed clouds were stretching across the eastern horizon in front of them.

They weren't saying much to each other. They both were still half-asleep, but Camellia felt a restlessness inside that usually meant just on thing. She was aware that Anselm sensed it in her, too, and she said, "I have no business feeling like this in a fish truck with you at this hour in the morning, still this close to Bell's Island."

Anselm giggled. "Sex on the sly with me in staid old Royal Hall for the past five years has never seemed to bother you, but so close to Bell's Island, you hesitate, huh?"

"Un huh," said Camellia. But there was plenty of time to kill before she had to be in Royal Hall, so she didn't protest too much when Anselm turned off the main Bell's Island road and headed down a long narrow dead-end stretch of part macadam, part dirt that went to an isolated, unused wharf area on the Wintergreen County mainland.

When they came to the road's end and stopped, Camellia exclaimed, "Will you look at that sunrise!"

They both stared in awe at the flaming burst of crimson and gold. Suddenly Camellia heard music accompanying it. But it was not the warning kind of music that she had heard too much of in the past. It was a stay-here-and-enjoy-yourself kind of music. Ordinarily, if there was *anything* she would bypass sex with Anselm for, it was music. But this time the music and the sex seemed all of one package....

A bit later when Camellia and Anselm got unwound from each other, she said, "I don't know how you do it, Anselm, but more and more and more you set the Muses on fire in me!"

Well, Muses or no Muses, fire or no fire, they both knew she was supposed to be at the board of education meeting at Royal Hall. Anselm started up the motor of the fish truck, but quickly Camellia said, "No, wait." And her eyes were asking for it again.

So they did it again! And then again!

"Really, Anselm, I'm not interested in sex," Camellia said.

Anselm looked over at her in amazement. "May the saints preserve us! And Heaven help the man who has you when you *do* get interested in it!"

"It's not the sex, exactly, it's that music, Anselm. Maybe you don't hear it, but it's you that's causing me to hear it. And it's happened before, too. But it's so elusive. I never can hang onto it for long....So maybe...? Just once more...to fasten it in my memory?

By mid-morning they were still sporting around in the fish truck. Each time Anselm said they should leave, Camellia said, "But I can't go back there to Royal Hall in the middle of the day looking like this. Love in a fish truck is not exactly the cleanest way...."

Anselm whooped. "That's the bummest excuse I've ever heard. You're the one wanting to stay here. I am supposed to pick up that engine at Centerbridge, remember? And you are supposed to be at that meeting. And you are supposed to give a report, too, aren't you?"

Camellia was unimpressed by what either of them was "supposed" to do. By noon they were still in the fish truck, and Camellia had already missed her meeting, but still she wanted to stay right where they were. She kept insisting she heard music every time they got together. But she claimed she couldn't capture it because she didn't have her piano!

Anselm was sweating, thirsty, and exhausted, but Camellia still felt cool as a cucumber. Anselm said, "If we'd known all this earlier, we could have put your piano here in the fish truck along with a basket of sandwiches and two kegs of beer. *Aren't you hungry*? I can't imagine you not wanting to eat something every two or three hours."

"No, I'm not hungry," Camellia said. "Don't you ever get serious about anything?"

"Of course I do," Anselm said. "I've got a bunch of unpatented inventions and processes in my head the same as you have a bunch of unpublished, largely unwritten, musical compositions in your head. I don't talk a lot about them, lest I sound silly."

Camellia said, "Maybe we're both silly. I can't catch the music I hear so vividly. You think your inventions are too unbelievable. Maybe it's the 'beyond the beyond' that we are both reaching for."

She looked at Anselm, and again her eyes were asking for it.

Anselm gestured toward his billfold lying on top of his folded-up pants and said, "You might as well know there are no more of 'those' left, and I don't mean 'greenbacks', either."

"Well, Columbus took a chance," said Camellia.

So, by mid-afternoon, when they were still "at it," Anselm said, "You remember what your mother once said about a pair of beagles she'd left too long in the breeding pen? It all but killed her best stud dog. She said his sides were all caved in and he looked terrible, but the bitch seemed none the worse for wear. I don't know about you, but I'm beginning to feel like that stud dog."

Later on in the afternoon, Anselm quipped, "If a baby comes of all this, you can always print the announcements to read, '8 pounds 10 ounces; conceived in a Bell's Island fish truck; born of a frustrated music teacher who always wanted to sing at The Met and/or write symphonies; sired by an incurable dreamer who has a chicken feed formula he believes will produce all white meat and drumsticks; delivered by a Bell's Island doctor, half-Jew and half-Methodist...."

Camellia turned on Anselm her most worried look of the day.

He laughed at her and said, "Don't look like that! I'd marry you in an instant. I *want* to marry you. Why do you think I bought the license three years ago and have carried it around in my pocket ever since.?"

Camellia said, "I fear if we married and all I could do was hear unstructurable music and still dream of The Met, and all you did was sit on the Bell's Island wharf and think up impossible inventions, we wouldn't make very good parents for any baby."

"Granted," Anselm said, "but I don't think we have to worry about babies. I'm sure my sperm count went down to zero before I ran out of 'those things', considering that workout you gave me this morning. And we have more immediate things to worry about anyhow."

"Yes," agreed Camellia. "I can't go back to Royal Hall in the day-time covered all over with fish scales, semen, and seaweed. And you cant go back to Bell's Island with me still in the truck and *without* that engine. What are you going to tell Papa anyhow?"

Without hesitation Anselm said, "I'll tell him the fish truck broke down, and I didn't get to Centerbridge until after the shipyard closed."

"Papa will never believe that," Camellia said. "Oh, maybe *he* would, but Charlie and the rest certainly won't."

"Well," Anselm said, "what are *you* going to tell your old boy-friend, Superintendent Forrester, about not being at that meeting or even as much as phoning in? I think he's been itching to get something on us."

"I'll think of something by tomorrow," Camellia said, unconcerned.

"Once more as the sun goes down?" Anselm asked her with a chuckle.

"Maybe let's just *watch* the sunset," Camellia suggested.

Anselm agreed.

So they sat on the tailgate of the fish truck, slightly apart from each other so as not to stir things up again. And they watched the sunset.

When Anselm returned to Bell's Island, sans the boat engine, as he later reported to Camellia he got his expected questioning looks from Thomas Stephens and much ribbing from the other brothers.

But the consequences to Anselm for their folly in the fish truck were not as great as to Camellia.

The music Camellia had heard so easily and persistently there with Anselm, so near to Bell's Island, had turned to glue in her head once she got back to Royal Hall that night. How frustrating, she fumed, to have gone through all that previous conservatory work, studying under Nadia Boulanger, the famous French teacher of musical composition when she was in the United States; getting a doctorate in theory and composition; composing stacks of student concertos, cantatas, fugues, and even symphonies; and STILL not be able to capture on paper the kind of music she was hearing. She tried practically the whole night to reproduce on both the piano and the violin exactly what she had heard during the day but came nowhere near it. Toward dawn she finally gave up and went to bed.

She slept as though drugged for about an hour, but when she did get up, she was so tired and haggard-looking that she didn't seem like herself at all. She hadn't even thought of an excuse to give to Forrester. So she didn't give him any. She just walked into the board of education room where the second day of meetings was about to begin, ignored everybody, and sat down.

After the morning session, Forrester called her into his office. Through a blur of fatigue, Camellia turned on him her best "gypsy magic/get-lost-buster" look, but he didn't seem in the least bit fazed. He had a little amused grin on his face when he reminded her that she had neither come to the meeting the day before nor phoned in nor had she asked anyone to give her departmental report for her.

"The truck broke down," Camellia said to him. She was grabbing for a straw now and used the only thing she could think of—Anselm's excuse.

Forrester said, "I beg pardon?"

Camellia repeated. "The truck broke down. I couldn't get here. No telephone on the road." She said it loudly and firmly. At this point she'd forgotten about her own car still out of commission back on Bell's Island, which would have made a more plausible excuse.

Forrester wavered for a moment, and Camellia thought she had him. Her take command voice and a positive mental set had more than once over the years saved her from censure, embarrassment, and exploitation, and not just from Forrester, but in all kinds of circumstances. But Forrester was not about to be cowed this time.

He got a look of mock amazement on his face and he said, "*Miss* Camellia! You need a *truck* now to get from your residence just across Prince Edward Street over on the other side there to the board of education office over here on this side!?"

Camellia didn't answer him. She was simply too tired, and she wanted nothing better than the chance to just go to sleep, so she didn't try to defend herself further. She just kept quiet and frankly didn't care too much any more what else Forrester might say. She didn't think he knew exactly where she'd been the day before, but there was no doubt in her mind that he knew she had been *somewhere with Anselm.*

Forrester got up from his desk, which meant their little talk was over. As Camellia got to her feet, Forrester said very quietly and very sweetly, in that sugary kind of way guaranteed "to gag a maggot," "Miss Camellia, there *is* a time-honored, widely accepted solution to a problem such as yours. And it is a solution heartily recommended by our Wintergreen County education system with regard to our teachers and their conduct. I don't know if you've ever considered it specifically applicable to yourself in your current situation....But it is called...*legal* marriage."

Although Camellia had squeaked by the possibility of an unwanted pregnancy as the result of her frolicking in the fish truck with Anselm in that summer of 1950, there remained other pressures on her to "marry or get off the bed." The formidable Wintergreen County public opinion was still putting the heat on her. There had been that ultimatum in so many words from School Board Superintendent Forrester and, then, in rapid succession Camellia lost a number of her private music students and received censuring phone calls from the parents of most of the rest. No one out and out accused her of wrongdoing, but they always dropped into their conversations that incriminating little aphorism "Where there's smoke, there's fire."

So, seeing no other alternative, Camellia and Anselm set their date for Christmas of that year, 1950. They agreed to live officially at Camellia's apartment in Mrs. Elderkin's Royal Hall mansion and have

Anselm's cabin on Little Bell's as a second home or summer cottage, either expression sounding rather nice.

Almost immediately after Camellia told Anselm she would marry him, she started to regret the decision. People had not seemed to regard her "teddy bear" socially unacceptable so long as he was just her *lover*, but Camellia didn't know how it would be for her image to have him as a husband. She feared he would never come up to the Royal Hall standard for a husband for someone of her position in the community. and if she was going to remain in Wintergreen County, she felt she had to "keep up appearances."

In an effort to get herself together and stop worrying, she started doing something she hadn't done since being the traveling music teacher for the elementary grades back in the 1930s—driving around a lot by herself on the back roads of the county. She was hearing a great concoction of music ringing in her head on these rides, yet when she came back to her apartment in Royal Hall and tried to tickle any of that music out of her piano, she found most of it had gone off into the sky. Oh, she wrote music—reams of it—but when she would play it back to herself it was never what she had heard.

She knew she was upsetting Aunt Sairy, who kept mumbling all the time, "Mis' Camellia, if you doan stop fillin' up de wastebasket with dese scraps o' music yo' keeps writin' down and den tearin' up, "I'se beginnin' to thinks yo' goin' crazy."

Camellia was woolgathering a lot at school, too. She sensed the teachers and students were aware of it. But she also noticed everybody was good-natured about it and seemed willing to pass her odd behavior off with a laugh and a behind-the-hand whisper: "Miss Camellia's just in love, that's all. She'll settle down once she and the 'Big-Bellied Dutchman' are married."

But Wayne Travis didn't act very good-natured the evening Camellia backed her car out of her driveway on Prince Edward Street directly into the side of Wayne's car as he was coming into town to work the night police shift. Wayne bellowed at her in his best Gainsbiddlerese: "Wyin hell doncha watch whutcher doin'?"

Camellia was all full of apologies and said her insurance company would take care of it. But then Anselm appeared from somewhere and yapped at Wayne nastily, "Why don't you go back and be a cop *in your own damn town*, you blasted Gainsbiddler?"

Anselm had the reputation for standing politely aside in most controversies, but he was all snarls and snorts when it came to Wayne and Gainsbiddle. Anselm had not forgotten Wayne's attempt to book Camellia and him on that fornication charge that time. And Wayne had not forgotten nor completely avenged himself for that black eye Anselm had given him in the barbershop that time.

Wayne again threatened to take both Anselm and Camellia to court. But cooler heads prevailed...and without "gypsy magic" this time. Thomas and Mary were still bosom buddies with Norman and Bessie Travis in Gainsbiddle. The word got to them from Camellia, and Bessie managed to talk her son Wayne out of any lawsuit over his damaged car. Camellia's insurance company paid for the repairs, and the ruffled Gainsbiddle and Royal Hall feathers gradually smoothed out.

Anselm began rebuilding his cabin on Little Bell's in early fall 1950. Camellia often spent whole night down there with him. If teased or questioned by anyone, she would say she had gotten stranded there because of the tide coming over the causeway between Bell's and Little Bell's. She said it, but she knew nobody believed her. Nobody would believe that a waterman's daughter, a native of Bell's Island herself, wouldn't know enough about tides to avoid getting caught in a place like Little Bell's. And if she didn't know, her "teddy bear" surely would have—or should have.

Camellia felt that Roger was till trying to drive a wedge between her and Anselm.

"Sister, you know why Asshole is fixing that cabin up, don't you?"

"Roger, I don't see where it's any concern of yours," Camellia coolly reminded him.

"He's got another girl besides you—or didn't you know?" Roger said.

Camellia wavered.

Roger continued, "Some kids paddling around in their skiff have seen Moonlight going there to Asshole's cabin."

Camellia burst out laughing. "For God's sake, Roger, Moonlight and I *look* somewhat alike. The kids have just seen me there at the cabin, that's all. But Moonlight and I do look somewhat alike. You've said so yourself. We are fifth cousins, and we have been mistaken for each other in the past."

Roger shrugged. "Maybe so. But if you really want to know for sure, come down to the island some night, and don't tell Asshole you're coming. I'll take you out there in a special hiding spot, and you can see for yourself."

Again Camellia wavered and she let Roger talk her into doing just that.

That particular evening, they had not been stationed there in the bushes too long before someone in a skiff paddled up to Anselm's wharf and called out, "Anselm. Honey?" Camellia stiffened. It was Moonlight Corrigan in that skiff. Camellia saw Anselm come out of his cabin, and she saw Moonlight scramble up on his wharf. And it appeared as though the two of them were rubbing all up against each other and laughing "fit to kill."

Camellia wanted to stay there and check it out further, but Roger was beckoning that they should get out of there lest they be discovered. Not a little shaken, Camellia returned with Roger to the main pathway out of the pine woods, back through the garbage dump, and onto Bell's Island proper again.

Several nights later when Anselm came to her mansion apartment in Royal Hall, Camellia confronted him in anger at what she and Roger had witnessed from their hiding place in the bushes outside his cabin.

Anselm said, "Camellia, believe me, it *was* odd what happened because I've never had any dealings with Moonlight. Moonlight *said* she wanted me to help her fix her canoe."

"Canoe, hell!" spat Camellia. "*Cunt* says it better."

Anselm yelled, "You don't believe all that pawing on me was for real, do you? If your rat brother took you down there to see that bumly staged act, then can't you see it was he who set it up? He *wants* to break us up. You've always said that, haven't you?"

"Yes, Anselm, but how could he get Moonlight to 'stage an act', as you say?"

Anselm said, "Roger is always over there at that tavern, taking Moonlight free seafood and stuff he's caught himself for her, and she'd do anything for him. The men at the shipyard say she's like a real mother to him. She never had any kids of her own that lived, and she took a liking to Roger when he and Jim Stephens used to go over there in a skiff when they were just kids. Moonlight was fascinated by Roger's duck calls and they always played 'Pull my finger'. Roger would say "Pull my finger' and just as Moonlight did, he'd let one of his magnificent farts and she's laugh like crazy with him. I guess he thought that attention was more positive than what he was getting at home."

Camellia didn't say anything.

Anselm, obviously exasperated at her hesitation to accept his explanation, said, "Well, do you believe me or not?"

"Oh, I don't know, Anselm. I don't believe Moonlight's visit there was for real, no. But...."

"But what?"

Camellia didn't answer.

Anselm got her by the arms, looked her square in the eyes, and said, "Maybe YOU set it up? Hm? Hm? Hm? You've been acting so weird lately, maybe you're just looking for an excuse yourself to break us up. Hmmmm? Hmmm?"

They argued back and forth, but got nowhere. There was no coupling that night.

After Anselm left Camellia's mansion apartment, she lingered out on the porch for a few minutes. There was a mugginess in the October night air like summer was trying to give one last snarl before capitulating to the upcoming winter. Thunderstorms had been predicted but the skies were hazy clear, and everything pointed to another humid and uncomfortable day in the morning...

The next day, after the usual school routine, Camellia went down to Bell's Island and along with Anselm had supper at the Tu-Rest Home. Afterwards they walked down by the sound side of the island, trying to get a breath of cool air. They did not go to Anselm's cabin on Little Bell's. Camellia said nothing further about having seen Moonlight Corrigan there trying to fool around with Anselm. Nor did Anselm. Neither of them had seen or talked with Roger since that incident.

It was coming on dusk, and Camellia said she'd better get back to Royal Hall. As they turned to walk toward the Stephens Tu-Rest Home they saw a dark cloud in the east, just across the inlet, hanging over Wintergreen County mainland.

Camellia said, "I'd better hurry and go on. Left my windows up in Royal Hall."

Anselm waited outside while she went in the house to get her purse. Mary asked her if she would get her ulcer prescription re-filled at the Royal Hall pharmacy where it was a bit cheaper than at Bell's Island. Mary gave Camellia a twenty dollar bill which Camellia absent-mindedly slipped in the pocket of her dress rather than in her purse.

When Camellia came back outside to get in her car, Anselm was looking at the threatening sky toward the east and said, "You better stay here a bit longer. You're going to run right into that. They're bad when they come up from the east like that."

Camellia gave a little sniff of unconcern and said, "Oh, I've been through storms before."

"Okay, then," said Anselm. "See you at school in the morning."

"Okay. See you tomorrow," Camellia said. They exchanged a brief kiss and embrace that was no different from hundreds of such brief—and some not so brief—kisses and embraces and 'see you tomorrows' that they had exchanged over the last five years.

As Camellia rolled away over the Bell's Island bridge, in her rear mirror she could see Anselm lighting a cigarette outside the Tu-Rest Home. He was still looking toward the east and toward the flashes of lightning in the cloud that Camellia was starting to drive under.

Yes, she was thinking, she'd been through storms before, but this upcoming marriage with Anselm—would it not be the biggest storm of all?

The next thing she knew—and it happened all at once—the car inside and outside was ablaze with light, there was an electrical snap or click sound rather than the usual crash of thunder, there was a tremendous impact of something on the windshield, and a blinding downpour of rain.

Camellia felt herself braking the car to a halt, and then there was sudden darkness, blackness...silence...absolutely nothing....

Chapter Six

Was this dying? she asked herself as the mist and the darkness pulled her deeper and deeper into black silence.

Slowly, faintly, through the black silence there came music. She was floating inside the music, and there was a bursting of music inside her. Was this drowning?

Suddenly she felt vibrations under her feet. She was on a road going somewhere. She saw a blinding light ahead, and then no more.

After how many eternities...? A roaring amidst the blackness, the sound of wind, motion, speed, and an overpowering sense of music....

Again no more....

She was coming awake in the dark matrix of something. Lights were all around outside, and there was noise. Inside the matrix someone was saying, "We're at the city bus terminal, lady. We can't take you no further."

A door opened to let her out. A cold air rushed over her.

"Why is it so cold?" she asked.

"It's always colder up here than down on the shore, lady."

"The shore? Seashore?"

Laughter came from inside the car. Then the door closed, and the car drove away.

She stood on the sidewalk in front of the bus terminal, shivering. She walked through the terminal door. It wasn't much warmer inside. She asked for a ticket to New York City. The agent said, "No more buses to New York until morning."

She was cold and put her hands in the pockets of her dress. She had no wrap and no purse. Her hand closed on something inside her pocket. She drew out a twenty dollar bill.

"Where is the nearest and cheapest hotel?"

The ticket agent wrote an address on a piece of paper and handed it to her. "Just down the street to the right from here and about a block."

She walked out into the cold wind and shivered along in her sleeveless dress until she reached a dark and gloomy-looking hotel.

She approached the desk clerk, asked for the cheapest room, and offered the twenty dollar bill. The clerk took it and handed her five dollars change.

"Sign the register, please," said the clerk.

She picked up the pen, then stopped. *She had no name*! She looked to one side and on a wall saw a crumbling poster announcing a Charity Ball. She looked back at the register and to one side saw a faded blue card with the name Professor Croswell, Lecturer on Prehistoric Mammals.

She grasped the pen and quickly wrote "Charity Croswell" in the hotel register. The clerk pushed a key towards her.

She took the key and went down the first floor corridor to a room toward the back, unlocked the door, and once inside with the door bolted, she collapsed in a chair, shaking and shivering until sleep or black out overpowered her.

When she woke up again she was still in the chair in the cold, dimly lit room. She tried to trace backward as far as she could remember anything. She had come down a dark corridor to this room. She had signed a hotel register with the name Charity Croswell. She had been out in a cold city street walking from a bus station. And before the bus station she had been in someone's car. But where had the car come from, and why was she in it? And where was she going? She remembered saying something about New York. But this wasn't New York. It was a city, but which city?

Before she could answer any of these questions she drifted off again....

Later, coming once more out of her stupor, she shifted around uncomfortably in her chair. She was cold, but she rejected the temptation to go lie on the bed and roll up in the spread. If she went sound asleep, she feared she might not wake up again.

She tried again to reconstruct what she could remember, and again got it back to when she was in somebody's car, and again she blanked out.

This time in her unconsciousness she was aware of being somewhere on a dark wet road, and there was music all around her in the blackness. She could hear herself saying I'm going away...away... away...New York City.

Coming to once again, she no longer heard that music, but she was still hunched in her chair, shivering, dozing, half-dreaming. It was no longer as dark in the room. She looked up to the top of a long narrow window and saw shafts of sunlight coming from somewhere. She went to the window and looked out on a court with the outside walls of the hotel going way up all around. At the top she could see the sun. She judged it must be nearly midday.

She remembered again about saying New York City and having some vague plan about going there. She looked at the five dollar bill in her pocket and concluded that was hardly enough to do anything with except maybe get something to eat.

She glanced into the bathroom mirror and saw herself for the first time—a tall, dark-haired, dark-eyed woman with tawny skin, and a handsome, but dazed, look. "Charity Croswell?" She said out loud. The accent was British. Was this London?

Or maybe she had left London and was heading for New York. But why?

She left the room, went to the desk, turned in the key, and checked out of the hotel. She wandered out on the busy traffic-congested street, wondering which city this was. Though the sunshine was bright, the air was cold, and she was cold. She was also hungry.

She saw what appeared to be a restaurant on a corner and walked toward it. As she came in front of it—a dingy-looking, very uninviting place—there stepped out into her path a huge, roly-poly, middle-aged fellow with a white but not very clean apron on. He had a wide smile all over his face, and in spite of the cold air, there was sweat rolling down his face all the way from his back curly hair to the black stubble of his beard. He was carrying a huge, hand-lettered sign even bigger than he was, and it said:

Singing Waitress Wanted
Apply Within
(Must be able to sing in Italian)

"I can sing in Italian," Charity Croswell heard herself say.

The roly-poly, sweaty-faced fellow looked at her with curiosity and exclaimed, "Can-a you, really? Can-a you sling-a da pizza, too?"

He was laughing and calling to someone inside the restaurant: "Hey, Louisa! Come out-a here to your husband, hey? Come and-a see. Maybe we got our singing waitress already, I t'ink. An' I not-a even put-a down-a da sign yet!"

A big moon-faced woman, not very tall and with a whole face full of big smiles and lots of lipstick and mascara, came waddling out the door. She was laughing and humming at the same time. She looked at Charity Croswell and said, "Can-a you sing-a in Italian, dearie? Yes? No?"

She was chuckling enormously, and then she whispered to her husband, "You t'ink-a she can-a sing, Sylvester?"

How dare the woman express a doubt! Charity Croswell thought with indignation. *She* would show them whether she could sing...and in Italian, too. She burst into an aria from Ponchielli's *La Gioconda* right there on the busy street corner and was easily heard above the traffic.

She saw Sylvester and Louisa dancing all around her, clapping their hands and hurrahing and all but sweeping her off her feet and taking her into their little restaurant.

"Wait!" Charity said. "I didn't say I'd *work for you*! I only said I could sing in Italian...and in French and German, too!"

"What are you?" asked Sylvester. "Some sort of opera singer?"

"Well," Charity said, haughtily. "What do *you* think? You just heard me."

Sylvester said, "Then maybe you no wanna work-a for *us*. Maybe you t'ink-a you're too good-a to work-a for us....Aw, come on an' work-a for us. We pay good."

"I'll let you know tomorrow," Charity said in an offhand manner. She started to walk away, but hunger made her turn back. She looked again at Sylvester and Louisa, at their big sign, and the big smiles on their faces.

Something inside her was saying, *You fool, what is wrong with you?* You *are Charity Croswell from England.* You *are an opera singer. You just as good as said so and you sang from* La Gioconda *and proved it. So why would you consider being a singing waitress in a crummy little pizza joint that doesn't look like it's had a customer in it since Christopher Columbus? What is the matter with you?* She again turned to walk away. She saw Louisa waddle back inside the restaurant.

But Sylvester was speaking again. "Aw, come on. Sing-a for us, huh? You sing-a Italian like a pro. And you 'easy on the eyes', too." He looked her up and down with approval. "Come on. Work-a for me an' Louisa. We pay good."

Charity didn't answer him. Yet something was telling her that these two people seemed kind and good. Why not stay here with them for awhile? But she wasn't sure. Then she found herself *listening* intently to something, but it wasn't to Sylvester, who was still yammering.

She glanced at him and said, "Do you have a radio playing inside your restaurant?"

"It's only Louisa," said Sylvester. "She sings, too, but not-a good as you!"

Charity said, "But it didn't seem like anyone *singing*...." Then she recognized it—*that music again*! The same as she had heard in the wet blackness the night before when she had been walking somewhere on the dark road.

She broke into a smile as big as Sylvester's and Louisa's and, going entirely on intuition, she said, "Why...why, yes! I'll sing *and work* for you!"

Sylvester jumped right straight up in the air, and as he came down he grabbed Charity in a big hug and called for Louisa. "Hey, Louisa, come back out-a here. She says she'll work-a for us! Now, what-a did you say-a your name-a was?"

"Charity Croswell! I'm from England," she said loud and clear.

Then, as though hearing the words from a stage prompter, she continued, "Yes, I'm from England. I have sung opera there, yes. But now I am in America, and I am somewhat upset and confused. At the airport a mugger took my coat, suitcase, and purse, and I barely had enough money in my dress pocket for a hotel room last night. So, if I could stay with you for awhile until I get myself together a bit, I would be happy to work for you...singing, serving pizza, whatever I can do to help you."

Louisa had come waddling out to the front of the restaurant again. "Charity Croswell," she said, putting her arm around her, "you help-a us. We take-a care of you. I t'ink God must-a send you down out-a silvery cloud. You see, we had a fire here at-a da restaurant an' we close all up for a year an' we need-a way to get-a da new customers. Sylvester, he t'ink up dis idea—get somebody sing-a in Italian to be our waitress. I could-a do it, but we need-a somebody pretty like-a you are. So, you work-a for us and sing-a for us and we take-a good care of you, Charity dearie. Den maybe real quick-a like, you be singing opera in America, too, just like-a you sing-a in-a da England."

"And we pay good!" Sylvester said for the tenth time or more.

Charity was thinking they didn't look like they could pay at all. But she felt serene and secure inside herself now. She still didn't understand what had happened to her or who she really was, but *she knew she could sing*, and she was certain that with Sylvester and Louisa she had fallen among friends!

Charity sensed that Sylvester and Louisa (whose last name was Valiano, they said) didn't quite believe her story, but they were going along with it because they felt something was more wrong here than her merely being mugged and robbed at the airport, and they sincerely wanted to help her, whatever her problem might be.

They gave her the third floor apartment of their residence at the corner of the block which had been damaged by fire like the rest of the building. These row houses, Sylvester said, were near the Little Italy section of Baltimore. The name Baltimore and the familiar pattern of all the houses joined together and all looking alike on their fronts seemed to rouse some faint recognition in Charity, but she still was unable to connect it to anything.

She spoke without hesitation, however, about her home in the English countryside; about her relatives, Bishop and Mrs. Lowell; about her dear Chloe, her accompanist in concert.

Sylvester and Louisa always listened earnestly to what she was saying, but they asked but very few questions. If Charity spoke of her concert tours in Europe and her operatic roles at Covent Garden in England, they listened raptly, but made no comments. Sometimes she sang excerpt from those roles, accompanying herself on Louisa's piano, and Sylvester and Louisa always applauded her roundly and rightly so, for even though Charity herself knew instinctively something was "not quite right" about her professed identity, when it came to her music, of *that* she had no doubt.

Sylvester and Louisa never questioned her as to why she was not getting in touch yet with anyone in England about her misfortune upon arriving in the United States, nor did they ask her about applying for new identification papers to replace the ones she said had been lost when she had been mugged at the airport.

During Charity's first few weeks of working for the Valianos, Sylvester paid her in cash. Then rather quickly, it seemed, and without his even asking her any information, he had secured an American social security card for her. Charity thought he might be a little on the hinterside of the law, but since "there's honor among thieves," and since she felt herself not quite "on the level," either, she felt even more safe now in the care of these two good-hearted people.

In between times of helping Sylvester and Louisa get their restaurant ready for re-opening, Charity learned the numerous Italian ballads she would be performing as their singing waitress. Sylvester said that since Baltimore was a world port, there might be foreign sailors coming in who would even appreciate songs of some of the more bawdy operatic roles such as Carmen, the gypsy prostitute.

Louisa remarked, "An' our Charity here, she's-a English, but she'sa got good strong gypsy features to go wiz her mezzo-soprano voice."

Charity started to say something herself about gypsies, and then as quickly forgot what it was. But it was little catches every now and then like that, little tugs at some invisible past, that made her somewhat on edge.

And nighttime, too, often brought troubling dreams. She heard strange music and saw wraith-like images that were anything but like the English countryside she spoke of so glibly during the day. In her restless sleep she would sometimes see black people singing and swaying rhythmically together as they worked in a large dark place at long wet tables. She couldn't see what they were working at, but their singing and chanting stirred something within her. Sometimes she would dream of being on the water with green and white waves rising and falling on the horizons all around her. Occasionally she would see huge geared wheels and hulls of boats and hear thumps and whistles, shrieks and bumps. One incomprehensible dream had to do with seeing and hearing a marching band that seemed to march right up into the air, go over the edge of the world, and tumble right down into a fish truck full of seaweed!

For part of the restaurant's grand re-opening, Charity was costumed as the gypsy prostitute, Carmen, from Bizet's opera. She sang—and this time in French—and whirled around the floor as she served. Louisa was at the piano, and together they brought down the house. The word must have gotten around among the sailors and maritime workers because in the weeks to come, as Charity continued to sing Italian ballads and enact the various operatic scenes that she and Louisa adapted from the original arias, the restaurant's business soared. The Valianos couldn't praise her enough.

Things continued to go well for quite a while. Then when Charity was once again in her Carmen role, a disastrous situation arose. Charity had finished serving the food and singing her *Habanera* to one table of appreciative seamen. She then had taken the next table's order and gone to the kitchen for it. She came back through the swinging door of the kitchen with the food just as two additional customers came in. They were a rough-looking pair of loud-talking men wearing hip boots and reeking of fish, and they were very drunk. They were muttering "Where's the wimmin? We need tail. We kin pay for it. Goddamit, we kin pay!"

Where they thought they were Charity didn't know, for in spite of her Carmen character the Valianos's restaurant was not a front for a bawdy house.

The men took one look at Charity, started for her, then stopped short. The bigger of the two, a tall, gorilla-like man, squawked, "My God! It's *Moonlight*!" And the other fellow, who had a knife scar across his face, exclaimed, "Christ, no! It's her *ghost*!" And the two men trod all over each other in their hasty scramble to get out of the restaurant.

Charity was so shaken she could barely set the tray down for her table, much less burst into her next song as she was accustomed to doing. She didn't know why she was so shaken. She managed somehow to serve the food to that one table, and then she hurried back to the kitchen without further singing.

Louisa, who had been playing the piano accompaniment and expecting Charity any moment to go into her usual routine, stopped playing and waddled back to the kitchen to see what was wrong.

Louisa found Charity trembling all over and trying to pour herself a cup of coffee. Louisa said, "Charity, dearie, now what-a is it? Why you no sing-a for our guests? Dose horrible creatures dat come-a in here-a by-a mistake, did-a dey scare-a you? But dey gone-a now. So, come on-a back an' sing-a for our guests, yes?"

Sylvester had come to the kitchen, too, and Charity heard Louisa whisper to him, "Our Charity—she-sa prob'ly lead very sheltered life-a in England before-a come to America. She-sa not used to roughnecks like-a dat. Scoundrels—dey prob'ly come from Eastern Shore-a!"

Charity knew she was a good trouper and that nothing could stop her from singing for long, so she got herself together and went out into the dining area and sang and twirled around as though nothing had happened. But inside her there was a terror and the worst of it was she still couldn't figure out why.

Charity stuck ever close by Sylvester and Louisa, and they seemed to be keeping a mother-hen wing over her. Charity went with them to church, to market, and to meet all their relatives in Little Italy. Thanksgiving and Christmas of that year brought some hilarious moments as all the grandchildren, nieces, nephews, and cousins came to the restaurant for holiday festivities, and they were all delighted with Charity's operatic characterizations as she sang and served the evening meal.

Into the new year, however, another incident, perplexing to Charity and certainly to the Valianos, occurred.

Sylvester had brought into the kitchen of the restaurant a couple barrels of oysters still in their shells. He said he'd bought them "in the rough" because the price for shucked oysters had gone too high for him. But when he started to shuck them himself, Charity watched in shocked amazement.

Sylvester picked up an oyster, looked at it, muttered to himself, laid the oyster down on the wooden table, then picked up a hammer and started banging away at the oyster.

"DON'T!" Charity burst out. "That's not the way to....Don't you have an oyster knife?"

"Oyster *knife*?" asked Sylvester. "We have-a plenty da oyster forks, dose little t'ings you pick up-a da raw oyster to eat-a him with, but oyster knifes, I don't t'ink-a....Hey, Louisa? Did dat salesman what sell us da oyster forks, did he sell us any da oyster knifes?"

Charity said, "No! No! That's not what I mean. Oh, just give me a plain old table knife and I'll show you how to open an oyster."

Sylvester handed her a table knife. Charity picked up an oyster, inserted the blunt end of the knife into the one and only "right place" between top and bottom shell, and flipped open the bivalve for Sylvester slick as a whistle.

Louisa and Sylvester danced all around Charity, cheering. Sylvester said, "England, she wonderful place! You learn-a da opera dere, Charity, and how to shuck-a da oysters!"

But there were tears in Charity's eyes, and she couldn't tell why.

"Whassa matter—you cry?" asked Sylvester.

"It's....It's....It's the salt," Charity said. "Yes, that's it....It's the salt in them. The salt in them always bothers me."

"Thassa funny," said Louisa. "I've heard-a da salt in-a da wound, she hurt-a you, but you not got-a scratch on-a your hands, have-a you, Charity dearie? Maybe you cut-a yourself on-a da shell, yes?"

Charity knew she had not cut herself, and she knew she'd opened that oyster correctly just like she knew she could sing, but she couldn't say why or how or why she had cried.

Charity noticed that Sylvester still had that hammer in his hand and was trying to scoop up the heap of crushed shell and goo from the oyster he had bashed to bits a few moments before. He was so comical with it that Charity burst out laughing. Once again her anxieties fled, and she knew that, whatever was wrong with her, she would still be safe with these two adorably goofy people—Sylvester and Louisa—until she could unravel her unknown past.

Charity often wondered, had she been a criminal in her past? Had she escaped from some mental institution? She felt if she didn't soon work out of her dilemma, she was going to *be* in one or be back in one. Sometimes when practicing on the piano her roles for the restaurant, her fingers would stray on the keyboard, and she'd hear herself playing *strange music* similar to what she continued to hear in her dreams at night.

Sometimes the Valianos remarked about this. Sylvester said, "You compose-a da music, too, huh? But is no sound-a like-a da opera music."

No, it didn't "sound-a like-a da opera music," not the Puccini kind, certainly, that Sylvester was familiar with. It was more a mixture of syncopated jazz and hybrids of soul and folk rhythms oddly superimposed on a classical line. Charity didn't know what to make of it or why she was playing it.

Whenever they could take off from the restaurant, Sylvester, Louisa, and Charity would go to concerts and opera performances in Baltimore. Charity was learning that the Valianos were at home and at ease in just about any social setting. They were colorful and personable and had enough bull and brass as well as enough money to move in and out of both the good and not so good circles. They knew people on both side of society's fence.

Sylvester often gambled at the nearby Laurel and Pimlico race tracks, and sometimes he placed bets for Charity. She won so frequently that Sylvester jokingly accused her of having "connections."

By the time Charity had been with the Valianos for a year or more, she had built up quite a little bank account, a far cry, she was thinking, from the meager twenty dollars she had with her when she first found herself in Baltimore City. She was able now to buy the latest in fashions, have her hair done in the newest of styles, and give nice presents to Sylvester and Louisa. She was frequently wined and dined by various ones of the Valianos's unattached male kin. Life with the Valianos was indeed pleasant. Life as Charity Croswell was indeed pleasant. But like a color print in a magazine that is slightly out of its frame, Charity's life in Baltimore was still not quite right. She knew it and she fretted about it; nevertheless she carried on.

Sylvester said one evening, after an unusually rousing show put on by his singing waitress, "Charity, you have-a too powerful voice an' you too good-a actress to be stuck forever with-a us, much as we love-a you. You once say you come-a to America to sing-a da opera. Why you no find-a good voice teacher and get-a yourself ready to audition for city opera?"

And Louisa said, "We know-a Madame Dupree who could-a train-a you up in-a no time."

Charity went along with the Valianos's suggestion and was taken into training by Madame Dupree. Once she got used to the peppy little French lady's periodic rages about "zeez breezing muzz bee bettaire or weel nevaire get to zee ohperah," Charity made good progress. Madame Dupree got the range of her voice—both top and bottom—improved as well as her "breezing" (breathing) and timing. Madame drilled her in histrionics and even gave her some "lezzons" in acrobatics. "For," said Madame Dupree, "ev-ree ohperah zinger zooner or lataire haz to zing ze final aria upzide down with zee daggaire in zee boo-zome!"

Charity studied under Madame Dupree for nearly a year while continuing with her singing waitress duties at Sylvester and Louisa's. Before Charity made any move of her own to audition for the Baltimore Opera Theater, a scout from there was dining one evening at the Valianos's restaurant, and he asked to see Charity afterwards. With Sylvester's ability at contacts, Charity was wondering if the scout had not been planted there.

At any rate, the scout must have liked what he had seen and heard of Charity's performance that evening, for he told her an Erda for

Wagner's *Das Rheingold* was needed to replace theirs who had quit. Erda, a rather small supporting role, but nonetheless quite dramatic—and spooky—represented the mysterious goddess of primeval wisdom. The character, Erda, figured in two of the four operas in Wagner's *Ring of the Nibelung,* a saga of Norse mythology revolving around the theme of love and lust for women and gold, a rather universal theme, to say the least. Charity had always admired the Erda role when she and the Valianos had attended either *Das Rheingold* or *Siegfried,* the other opera of the Ring cycle that Erda featured in. The scout asked Charity if she would consider auditioning for Erda. Needless to say, Charity was delighted at the opportunity.

After a quick consultation by phone with Madame Dupree, who gave Charity the go-ahead, a time for the audition was set for the next day.

The next morning Charity was trying to hold down her nervousness about the audition by helping Louisa rearrange a cupboard in the restaurant's kitchen. Louisa had gone to the basement of the building to look for some cleaning equipment. As Charity was moving a stack of old newspapers, one fell out at her feet and part of a headline caught her eye: "Body of Missing Bell's Island Waterman Found."

"Papa?" screamed Charity. She grabbed the newspaper and frantically continued reading:

Second Tragedy in Two Weeks Shakes Bell's Island
(Special to The Baltimore Sun)

It was the second tragedy in little more than two weeks for the Thomas Stephens family of Bell's Island on Maryland's Eastern Shore. The body of seventeen-year-old Roger Stephens, son of Mary and Thomas Stephens, missing in a boating accident since last Friday, was found yesterday by marine police dragging operations in the area near White's Point on the edge of the Wintergreen County mainland just opposite Bell's Island.

Stephens's overturned skiff had been located Saturday morning by family members after he failed to return home on Friday. Stephens was believed to have been searching for his sister, Camellia Stephens, age thirty-four, Royal Hall High School Music Director, who had been missing since October 1, after her disabled and abandoned auto was found on a lonely stretch of marshland road between Bell's Island and Royal Hall after a violent thunderstorm.

Police theorize that in the case of Miss Stephens a freak accident must have occurred. A section of concrete road was found torn apart in front of her auto, and the windshield smashed by a chunk of concrete that might have been thrown against it when lightning struck the road.

It is not known whether Miss Stephens, in a stunned condition, may have wondered away from her auto and drowned in the marsh, or whether a late summer tourist in the area may have picked her up and, not knowing who she was or what her condition was, may have taken her somewhere. The investigation into that case is continuing.

Funeral services for Roger Stephens will be held Sunday in the Bell's Island Methodist Church. Roger is survived by his parents, Thomas and Mary Stephens; his wife, the former Doris Thornton of Bell's Island; and a month-old daughter, Virginia, all of Bell's Island.

It was like a rock had hit Charity Croswell.

"ROGER!" she screamed. It was *Roger* who had drowned. A horrid chill came over her. What was the date on that newspaper? *Over two years ago*!

As Charity read and re-read that article, all the blank pages of her memory as Camellia Stephens started tumbling back to her in great shock waves. Also everything out of kilter, currently, made sense now—those odd things that kept troubling her: where that dark, wet road was that she had been on when she'd lost contact with her identity; what the meaning was of all that strange music and her strange dreams; who the two drunken watermen were who came into the restaurant and whom she recognized now as Charlie Stephens, who had once tried to rape her, and Simon Cartwright, whom she didn't trust any too far, either; why she was crying when she opened that oyster, blaming it on the salt, when it was really homesickness for Bell's Island; and how her subconscious mind had drawn on what she knew of Claudie's English background to build her own Charity Croswell identity.

"Mama! Papa!" she screamed again. It had been *two years* since it happened. Could they even be dead, too, by now? And Roger's widow, Doris, and her little baby girl? What had happened to them?

Then tugging at Charity was yet another question: There was somebody else. But who? She re-read the article, but no other names were given. But there was *somebody else* in her life at that time. Anselm! ANSELM! Her "teddy bear"! And they were to have been married....

When Louisa returned from the basement, she found Charity/Camellia sobbing uncontrollably and chattering frantically to herself: "I must phone Bell's Island—the Stephens Tu-Rest Home—right away. But no, maybe I shouldn't. Maybe the shock of hearing from me might be too much for Mama and Papa. And after two years, suppose they aren't even...? I know! I could phone Aunt Lizbeth first. She's right here in Baltimore."

Charity/Camellia began digging in the phone book for the number. Then with one thought after another piling on top of each other, the realization about Roger hit her again and she cried out, "He was looking for *me* when he drowned. *I am responsible for Roger's death*! Oh, Louisa, Louisa! *Help me*!"

It took several hours for Charity/Camellia to even begin to explain to Louisa that the article in the old newspaper had broken her amnesia and revealed her real identity as Camellia Stephens. Even then she wasn't sure Louisa was completely believing her any more than Louisa had when she had first told her she was Charity Croswell from England.

But Louisa did say, "How can-a you be responsible for-a your brother's death, when-a you didn't even know who you were or where-a you were?"

Charity/Camellia said, "I guess you are right, Louisa. Oh, Louisa, what would I do without you."

In the confusion they'd both lost track of how late it was. "What about-a your audition?" Louisa asked suddenly.

Camellia said, "God! I'd forgotten all about that!"

A long hesitation followed. How long had she waited for this chance at an opera audition? How many times in the past had she been about to go forward with her musical career and something at Bell's Island turned her back?

Two years had passed now since she was even on Bell's Island or aware that she was ever a part of it. Roger was now gone. Who knows how many of the others were gone, too? And Anselm? Would he have waited for her? Did she really want to know? Should she get re-entangled again with any of them?

Well, she concluded, she had waited two years through no fault of her own to contact anyone. She could certainly wait two more hours.

To Louisa she said, "I'm going to my audition now. I'll phone my Aunt Lizbeth when I get back."

Louisa beamed a big smile. "Thassa good, Charity dearie. Or should-a I say 'Camellia dearie'?"

"Say 'Charity'," said Charity. "Charity Croswell will be my stage name. And still my official name for awhile longer, too. It's what they know me as at the opera company."

When Charity left the restaurant, all traces of shock and dismay were gone. She was Charity Croswell once again. For the time being, at least, Camellia Stephens had been forcibly put back out of consciousness and could no longer rattle her.

Charity's audition for Erda went perfectly and she was hired on the spot.

She returned triumphant to Sylvester and Louisa's. There was much dancing around and rejoicing. That evening Sylvester went through his restaurant telling all his customers that their singing waitress would be leaving them shortly because she had made it to the big leagues of classical music—the opera!

There was one thing that Charity/Camellia did not do that evening. She did *not* phone her Aunt Lizbeth.

Charity said to Louisa, "I certainly can't get entangled *now* with Bell's Island. Not when I have Erda to perform. But just as soon as this current opera season is finished...."

Did the phrasing sound familiar? *I'll break away from Bell's Island as soon as I have enough money...as soon as I have enough education...as soon as the family is settled down...as soon as this, that, or the other problem is solved....*

Louisa and Sylvester both said, "Whatever you t'ink-a is best, Charity dearie. We still-a be your friends forever, no matter which-a-way you decide."

Sylvester even offered to get a private eye that he knew to check things out on Bell's Island for Charity. That way she could have information on which to base any decisions without having to reveal her current whereabouts or situation to anyone who had known her before her disappearance.

But fear of being entrapped again in Wintergreen County tended to prevent her from even wanting to know. She reasoned as long as she didn't know what was going on back on the shore, she wouldn't have to do anything about it. She explained to Sylvester and Louisa how her family had always been off-again on-again in financial troubles and dependent on her for handouts, and how her mother had always been ailing or else *used* her ailing to get Camellia to do things for her.

Yet it was hard for Charity/Camellia not to think of Roger and the tragic end of his tragic life. And what of her little niece, Virginia, whom she had never seen? And Anselm? She turned quickly from that thought, fearing her "teddy bear" may well have gone to another by now.

On the opening night of Charity's debut as Erda in Wagner's *Das Rheingold*, Sylvester, Louisa, and all the regular customers from the restaurant (tickets complimentary from the Valianos) were there to cheer her on. Louisa was in her best befurred and bejeweled elegance, most of it fake and over-much as usual, but she was endearing as always. Sylvester preened and pranced in his rented white tie and tails.

Erda does not appear until near the end of *Das Rheingold.* The stage becomes dark, and from a rocky cliff at the side there shines out a bluish glow in which Erda rises from below to half her height. She is of noble presence and enveloped in a mass of black hair. (Not unlike the appearance of Charity/Camellia in real life, Charity was thinking.)

Erda warns Wotan to give up the ring he has taken from the Nibelung because it is cursed. And then Erda disappears. Wotan reluctantly gives up the ring, but then the two giants, Fafner and Fasolt, fight over it. Fafner kills Fasolt and gets the ring, Wotan bewails the curse; the gods return to the castle, Valhalla; and *Das Rheingold* ends.

After Charity's successful debut as Erda, after receiving with tearful joy all the congratulations and mounds of flowers in her dressing room from Sylvester and Louisa and their patrons from the restaurant, the next afternoon before the second evening performance, Charity had a special mission:

She went alone to Baltimore's big Greenmount Cemetery and located the grave of her earliest friend, teacher, and mentor. *The dead tell no tales,* Charity reasoned. In the purple shadows of the city twilight she communed with Claudie. She thanked her for her early lessons, her encouragement and help—and yes, even the red mittens!—and she thanked her for the privilege of using her identity the past two years which gave Charity/Camellia the doorway, finally, into the world of opera.

Then Charity/Camellia asked of Claudie's spirit yet another favor—the privilege of *continuing* to use that identity.

Feeling her request had been granted, Charity left Greenmount Cemetery and went on to another successful performance as Erda in *Das Rheingold.*

So it was that Camellia Stephens became and remained reincarnated as Charity Croswell and without ever having died!

When it came time for the Baltimore Opera Theater to put on *Siegfried* later that season, Charity was again their Erda. It was a longer part this time, but essentially the same ingredients. Again it is Erda who is counseling Wotan. Again she rises from beneath in that bluish halo. It is almost like she is covered with hoarfrost. Her hair and garments gleam with iridescent light....

Erda was a good witch, but Charity wasn't adverse to playing a bad witch every now and then. Or any number of other "comprimario" roles such as priestesses, peasants, angels, or gypsies. And she was very good at those gypsies, having "come by it rightly," with her own one-eighth gypsy blood.

Whenever the Baltimore Opera Theater needed a chesty mezzo with a flamboyant style or a contralto who could do a "trousered role" and the same time be someone who was a willing and cooperatative worker, they knew on whom to call. Charity was well liked by both the company and the public. She became quite a pleasant fixture in Baltimore musical circles. Since mezzos rarely got top billing or many principal roles, she had to be content as the less visible, but still important, second fiddle. She was no longer in a leadership position as she had been on the shore. She was now the "little fish in the big pond," but that didn't matter—she was at last singing opera!

Charity/Camellia maintained that Charity Croswell identity on the outside of her self and largely on the inside, too, so she avoided being detected as Camellia Stephens even by some of the instructors at the conservatory under whom she had studied both for her masters and her doctorate. She would occasionally see one or two of them at some of the after-performance gatherings of the cast, and sometimes they seemed to recognize her and seemed about to speak to her as Camellia, but then they apparently changed their minds. Maybe a little "gypsy magic," lightly applied, helped here, too.

For awhile after her entrance into opera, Charity continued to stay at her third floor apartment at the Valianos. But as her income increased from her opera work, her own private voice students, and her ever-lucrative "wise investments," she moved to progressively larger and more expensive residences throughout the city. But she always went back to Sylvester's and Louisa's to be their singing waitress on special occasions and to bask in their ever-loving warmth and approval.

But she never went back to Bell's Island, nor did she contact anyone there nor even phone her Aunt Lizbeth right there in Baltimore. There were plenty of times, though, when loneliness for her kinfolk and for her "teddy bear" and second thoughts about what she was doing—or *not* doing—threatened to overwhelm her. It was impossible at times for her not to wonder what was going on at Bell's Island.

There were times when she even mourned for Roger, though he'd always been the bane of her (and everybody's) existence. And she felt plenty of guilt for not even contacting her parents, Thomas and Mary. Worst of all were those times when she longed for the warmth and comfort of Anselm Jurgensen's body. She longed for it to the point of pain.

But she felt she had her foot in the door of "the big time" now and she still had her eye on The Met, so she wasn't about to let any slips of judgement—like getting involved again with family—jeopardize her progress. She suspected her attitude was pure selfishness, but that's the way she felt, just the same.

Charity dated every now and then the few that remained of Sylvester and Louisa's kin who were still bachelors. Occasionally there would be somebody from the opera orchestra or one of the cast. She did a lot of flirting at the after-performance parties, but it was only a surface pastime. She still had her sensuous charm that ranged all the way from playing hard-to-get to a sultry come-hitherness that could make even the stodgiest old bassoon player sweat. But her heart was not in her coquetry, and she kept all her relationships on a *non-boudoir* basis. One time, however, she did say (jokingly) to her manager, Merv Roth, "If you get me a spot at The Met, I'll go to bed with you." And Merv was the kind of person who would hold her to that, too. But she liked the dapper Jewish fellow with the wiry black hair and cocky smile, and the thought of going to bed with him wasn't all that bad.

Louisa, who was one of those matchmaking individuals who got nervous when one of their proteges stayed unattached too long, often said, "Charity dearie, you been gone-a da Eastern Shore long-a time now, but I do believe your heart, she stay over dere. Sometimes you seem-a so down in-a dumps, I worry about you. Dearie, you can not-a go on-a like dis. You either got-a go back dere to da shore and try to find-a your man Anselm or else forget-a him forever and get-a yourself new lover."

It was at these low times that Charity often turned again to improvising and writing down music. Performing was one thing and a very important thing with her. It satisfied the showoff nature in her and her yen to interpret. But writing music was a way of working out her deepest feelings. Much of it, she knew, was caused by her desire for Anselm, so her scraps—those ever accumulating and unpublished bits of strange melody and rhythm—were her means of accomplishing the supreme sublimation: that of converting sensualism into art.

Charity often thought about Roger's daughter, Virginia, the niece whom she'd never seen. As the years went along, she found herself calculating, *Now how old would she be now? Starting to school, maybe?* And a few years later, *Virginia's at that tomboy age now, I'll bet.* And still later, *Virginia's probably thinking about her first date.*

Charity decided that Virginia was pretty. Doris, her mother, had not been a bad-looking girl—plain, yes, but personable. And there was Mary as the paternal grandmother, and Mary was always pretty. Virginia probably had light hair, Charity reasoned. She could not inherit the dark features of the gypsies because Roger himself had not even been a blood Stephens. Virginia, in personality, Charity reasoned, would take after the ingenuous AND ingenious Doris and not the irascible Roger.

While imagining off and on about Virginia's probable growing-up years, Charity herself passed into middle age without hardly realizing it or showing it. Bits of gray flecked her black hair, but her features remained youthful and, since she was a large person to start with, a little middle-age spread didn't make that much difference in her appearance.

One day in the spring of 1970, Charity's door chime sounded. She walked through the best yet of her apartments with its plush, ivy-covered exterior in one Baltimore's most venerable residential sections. She glanced around quickly to see if everything inside was in order, from the polished-to-a-mirror-finish grand piano to the ivory-colored archways to the Chippendale furniture. All looked well. She glanced at herself in the mirror and was pleased with what she saw—the still "easy to look at" countenance, the black hair attractively flecked with gray, the healthy, matronly physique.

Charity opened the door and there stood a delightfully smiling, willowy-slim young girl of about twenty years—one of the prettiest creatures Charity had ever seen. She was decked out in a white linen mini-skirt with a blue-and-white striped blouse. She had long, wavy, auburn hair and crystal blue eyes that shone with the innocence and idealism of youth.

Charity felt a sudden electrified feeling go through her.

The young girl asked politely, "Excuse me, but is this the home of Miss Charity Croswell?"

Charity said, "Yes." The two were regarding each other intently.

The girl said, "You may not know me exactly. But I think I may know you. I hope you don't mind me checking this out. I'm Virginia Stephens and—"

Charity nearly melted. "Virginia! *Virginia*! My dead brother Roger's grown-up daughter!"

"Aunt Camellia! I have found you!"

They clung together in a huge, joyous embrace that went on and on, and it was hard to say which one of them cried the most.

When they both stopped gasping and Camellia invited and escorted Virginia inside, Camellia said, "The moment I saw you, Virginia, I felt almost sure it was you before you said a word. You remind me so much of Mama as I remember her....Uh, is Mama...?"

Virginia hesitated as though trying to find an easy way to say something hard. She said, as gently as she could, "Your mother, Mary Stephens of Bell's Island, passed away a couple of years ago."

"And Papa?"

"Thomas Stephens, too, shortly after Mary," Virginia said, quietly.

Camellia lowered her head and swallowed hard. "Yes, I should have figured. I've been gone a long time...." Then, remembering she was a good actress and that she must carry on, she brightened and said, "Tell me, Virginia, how on earth did you find me?"

Camellia could not, right then, risk a second blow, so she did not ask about Anselm Jurgensen.

Virginia said, "First, let me say, I did not grow up on Bell's Island, and I will explain about that in a bit. It's only recently I've been anywhere near Bell's island. I am going to college at Halburg State and have been trying to both locate you, Aunt Camellia, and get at my family roots. I went first to the conservatory, your alma mater, but they had no information on your whereabouts since your disappearance from Wintergreen County back in 1950. My mother had told me of your yen for singing opera, so I went to the Baltimore Opera Theatre and asked about you. They had no information but on a hunch I asked to look at photos of their roster. When I saw the photo of Charity Croswell and compared it with a photo I had of you, I felt sure you two were the same person even though the opera company insisted their Charity Croswell was an English lady! But they gave me this address and I took the chance and came here."

Camellia said, sotto voce, "Amazing that nobody else in the family ever thought of that!"

Virginia said, "I can't speak for your family, Aunt Camellia, because I never got to know any of them. My mother, Doris Stephens, and I left Bell's Island when I was still an infant and it's only been in the last few months that I've been back to Maryland or had any contact at all with anyone on Bell's Island. By the way, how did you know my father, Roger, was dead? That's been twenty years ago."

Camellia briefly told Virginia about being struck senseless in a freak storm outside Bell's Island, being picked up by some unknown motorists and taken as far as Baltimore, and then not until two years later being startled out of her amnesia by seeing the old newspaper article about Roger's drowning. "By then," said Camellia, "I was established in my Charity Croswell identity and was on my way to an opera career, and I didn't want to endanger it. That's why I never contacted my family in all these years. Pure selfishness, I guess, but that's the way it's been."

Virginia said, "Most everybody thought you had drowned, and that may be why nobody pursued the lesser theory that you might still be alive somewhere....

"Anyhow, at Christmas of that year that you disappeared and my father drowned, my mother and I—and I was only a couple months old—had a chance to leave Bell's Island and go live with a very well-to-do family that had visited the island as tourists *just one time* back in the mid 1940s. My mother had been just a young teenager at that time, but these people—the Mearses—happened to see her walking along the shell road, and they asked her for directions and general information about the island. They were so impressed with her 'charm in the raw' and she with their friendliness that they all took an instant liking to each other, and they started sending Christmas cards each year thereafter and writing little messages.

"Now, shortly before Christmas of that terrible year—1950—Moonlight Corrigan—you remember her, I'm sure—" (Camellia nodded) "went to see my mother. My mother, a number of years later, when I was grown up enough to understand, told me about all this. My mother had been startled out of her wits at seeing Moonlight at her door. Moonlight looked a lot like you, Aunt Camellia, and for a moment there my mother thought she was seeing your ghost.

"When my mother got over being scared at seeing Moonlight, she went ahead and let her come in the house. Moonlight told my mother a rather confused and weepy story, saying that she—Moonlight—was responsible for my father's drowning. That she had let my father, Roger, talk her into playing some sort of trick on you, Aunt Camellia, to try to make you think Moonlight was messing around with your fiancé of that time, Anselm Jurgensen."

Camellia gave a little start at hearing Anselm's name, but she did not interrupt Virginia's story.

Virginia went on, "Evidently my father assumed that trick had backfired, because when you disappeared shortly after that, he thought that instead of your just breaking up with Jurgensen in a fit of jealousy, you had decided to drown yourself by going off into that marsh during that thunderstorm. He then blamed Moonlight for the whole business.

"In the meantime my father continued to search for you in that marsh and in so doing, he, himself, drowned. Moonlight told my mother that she felt indirectly responsible for his drowning, and she had come to try to make amends.

"Moonlight said she had received an insurance check for ten thousand dollars from being beneficiary of some man she was living with at the time, and he had died. I think she had cashed the check but had not used any of the money. She tried to give that money to my mother. Moonlight said Doc Feldman had told her she had inoperable cancer and only a few months to live, and since she had no relatives to leave the money to, she wanted my mother to have it, because she said she had always thought a lot of my father, mean though he was, and it was all she could do now—just to try to help his widow and baby.

"Moonlight said something to the effect 'Miz Doris, you got a li'l baby girl an' you're a widow now, and you're not much more'n seventeen years old, an' you don't have no money to look out for her an' you. An' if you stay on Bell's Island, your li'l girl is goin' to grow up with people talkin' behint her back, jes' like they've always talked behint Mary Stephens's back an' behint Roger's back, sayin' about him bein' a "bastid" an' all. If you stay on Bell's Island, your li'l girl is goin' to grow up hearin' bad things about her dead daddy an' about her dead aunt an' about how both of 'em drowned an' about how her aunt's lover was mixed up with a common whore'.

"My mother kept protesting that she just couldn't take a large sum of money like that, but Moonlight kept insisting, still believing she was responsible for all the trouble and saying, 'It's all I can do now, Miz Doris. I dint want to do that trick what Roger ast me to do. But I done it for him becuz I always felt sorry for him. He was mean, but I think it was becuz his mother, Mary Stephens, hated him, being he was a "bastid". Please take the money, Miz Doris. It won't help Roger none, but maybe it will help you an' your li'l girl'.

"So, my mother took the money from Moonlight....How about that, Aunt Camellia? My mother and I being subsidized by a dying prostitute!"

"Amazing!" said Camellia, marveling at Virginia's story and her candor in telling it.

Virginia continued. "My mother then got in touch with the Mears family in Louisiana, told them of my father's drowning, and asked if we could come live with them temporarily until she could get a job and a house of her own. She didn't tell them about Moonlight's gift, but made out like the 'insurance money' had come from my father.

"The Mearses welcomed us with open arms that Christmas and became our foster family permanently. There was Papa Gary Mears and Mama Anna—Grand-Anna, I grew up calling her—and their two daughters Sharon and Susan, who were about eighteen and nineteen when we first moved to Louisiana. They just wouldn't let us leave even after my mother got a job and we were financially independent."

There came sort of a wistful look in Virginia's eyes and now it was her turn to swallow hard. She went on, "My mother was very attractive after the Mearses transformed her into a young sophisticate, and she had an assortment of men friends from the Mears's circle, but she never re-married. Rightly or wrongly, she never told anybody on Bell's Island where we were going nor did she contact anyone there in all the years we were gone. She wanted us to have an entirely new life and we did—a good one. We had nearly twenty years together before she passed on last fall."

Camellia murmured, "I'm sorry, Virginia. I always thought the world of your mother. She was 'one fine person'."

Virginia continued, "Though my mother never again contacted Bell's Island after we left, she always *talked* about the Stephenses, and early on she got my curiosity up, especially about you, Aunt Camellia. Shortly before she died, she gave me her blessing to come to Maryland for my college work and to research the Stephenses family, if that's what I wanted. She warned me about all the bad things I was likely to hear about my father, but she said, 'Remember, Virginia, the best of him went into the making of you'. She saw the potential good in my father, if nobody else did. Too bad he couldn't have lived; she might have brought out more of the good in him....Now, for some reason, I had always believed you were still alive, Aunt Camellia, and that one day I would find you. And that is mainly why I came back to Maryland."

After rejoicing some more at having discovered each other, Charity/Camellia and Virginia put together a meal in the kitchen, all the while continuing their excited talk about their lives.

Camellia could wait no longer and asked Virginia, "Do you know if Anselm Jurgensen is still on Bell's Island?"

Virginia said, "Yes. That is, he's always lived there, but for the last six weeks or so he's been in the Veteran's Hospital at Centerbridge, on the shore. I don't know just what's wrong with him, but he's in a coma, and they don't hold out much hope for him."

Camellia drew very silent.

Virginia studied her carefully, then said, "He's never married, Aunt Camellia."

"Nor have I," Charity/Camellia said.

Later in the evening when they were still filling each other in on the details of their past twenty years, the phone rang, and it was Merv Roth, Charity's manager.

"Yes, Merv. Yes! Yes! Azucena? The gypsy mother in Verdi's *Il Trovatore*? THE MET? Are you sure? That's quite a part! Merv, don't be joking with me now....Yes, I know you have 'contacts' in high places....Yes, of course, I'm familiar with the role. I've done it for Baltimore Opera Theater. Madame Dupree can get me in shape for it in no time. How soon do you have to have an answer?...You want me to go to New York with you in the morning? What? You want to come here *tonight?*...Yes, I remember our bargain, but I have a guest here. My niece...from...from England! She arrived unexpectedly this afternoon...No, I'm not just making it up. You want to speak with her? She's right here....Well, okay I'll call you back after I've called Madame Dupree....Yes, love you, too, Merv. G'bye!"

When Charity/Camellia set the phone down, she was ecstatic. "Virginia, can you believe it? *The Met*! *Finally*!"

Virginia was squealing with joy, too. "Wonderful, Aunt Camellia, wonderful! You've got it in your hands now—your lifetime dream! Oh, I'm so happy to be here with you!"

Virginia giggled some more and said, "And I'm so glad you didn't make me talk with your Merv. You say I'm your niece 'from England,' but I don't believe I can do that *educated* British accent as good as you. My Bell's Island blood mixed with growing up amidst Louisiana dialects does not make for *educated* British!"

After much laughing, several glasses of celebration wine, and much rejoicing with Virginia, Charity/Camellia phoned Madame Dupree and got the go-ahead from her for singing Azucena. Then she phoned Merv, saying she would be ready in the morning to go with him to New York City.

Merv again said he wanted to come to the apartment that night, but Charity/Camellia again reminded him that her niece, Virginia, "from England," was visiting and it was just not convenient!

After Charity/Camellia said good night to Merv, Virginia burst out laughing. "You're using me to get out of going to bed with Merv, huh?"

"No, I'm not. If I were to go to bed with anybody on the opera scene, it would be Merv. He's a real doll. But....But...."

"But what, Aunt Camellia?"

Camellia could not say any more except, "Let's try to get some sleep, if that's at all possible."

In the morning Camellia woke with a strange feeling of calm, accompanied by a strong sense of resolve and rightness. It was the feeling you have when you've made a hard decision in which something precious has been sacrificed in order to have something even more precious.

At breakfast Camellia said to Virginia, "I dreamed last night of being back on Bell's Island. I was looking for my old home, the Stephens Tu-Rest Home, where so much trouble took place in the past, but now there was only the impersonal town parking lot there that you told me about.

"I began walking near the docks. A few oyster boats were coming in and going out, and sea gulls circled and screamed overhead. The smell of creosote in the pilings and planks of the wharf mingled with the saltiness of the air above the water.

"I looked about expecting to see Papa at any minute come out of the warehouses with a barrel of oysters on his shoulder. Or to see Amos and Charlie Stephens tying up a work boat at the dock, or Simon Cartwright across the way working on the keel of a new skipjack. Or to see Mama come tripping across the shell road with a plateful of Maryland Beat Biscuits in her hand. Or to see Roger come barrelling across the Bell's Island bridge in that stinky old fish truck. Or to see Grandpaw Azariah walking back onto the island from having been to Moonlight's.

"When I saw none of them I went to the Bell's Island cemetery and stood there in silence and stared at the graves of those I'd last seen alive over two decades ago: Thomas Stephens 1891-1968; Mary Stephens 1891-1968; Roger Stephens 1933-1950; Azariah Stephens 1870-1966; on and on.

"A breeze, salty and moist, came across the island and I heard a whole host of voices—voices of those gone on before—singing softly from the old Irish ballad, '*Come Back to Erin*'....

Come back to Erin,
Mavourneen
Mavourneen
Come back again
To the land of thy birth.
Come with the shamrock,
The Springtime, Mavourneen....

"I cried out in anguish, "Oh, *why* did I wait so long? Why did I wait till all of them were dead?

"Suddenly there was another voice and it said, 'Anselm lives. *Go to him! Quickly!*'"

"Virginia, could you go with me to the shore to that Veteran's Hospital? Today?"

Virginia said, "Sure, Aunt Camellia, but aren't you supposed to go the New York City with your manager, Merv Roth, to see about your role at The Met?"

Camellia said, "I can't do it. I can't go to New York."

Virginia protested, "You mean you can't—or won't—do what you've been dreaming all your life of doing?"

"Virginia, there are some things in this world more important than personal achievement—even than the achievement of a lifelong goal. True love is one of them."

Again Virginia protested, "But Aunt Camellia, you'd risk the accomplishment of your lifelong goal to sing at The Met on just this hunch, this dream you had? We don't even know but that Anselm

Jurgensen may already be dead. And even if he is still alive, what good could he be to you like he is?"

Camellia said flatly, "I don't believe he's dead. I believe he's waiting for me."

Camellia would not be put off by any of Virginia's arguments, so they set out together in Virginia's car for the shore and without even phoning Merv Roth or Madame Dupree.

After crossing the Chesapeake Bay Bridge and several hours of driving, they arrived at the Veteran's Hospital in Centerbridge. They asked at the desk for Anselm Jurgensen and were given passes to his ward. So he *was* still alive, as Camellia had felt certain he would be.

But he was just barely alive, and a couple of nurses accompanied them to Anselm's bedside. Virginia had already told Camellia how much her old lover had aged. But Camellia was largely unaware of the inert, gray-white form lying there, eyes open, but not seeing. Instead she was in touch with his eternal essence, that intangible, invisible identity that she had always known and always loved.

With the nurses standing by, Camellia drew close to Anselm's side. She felt no shock or consternation at his ghastly appearance—his once rusty-red hair having turned a scruffy white, his once ruddy complexion now deathly pale. She felt only the most tender communion with him.

Camellia bent over her old sweetheart of years gone by and said, "Anselm...? Anselm? *Anselm...*? Her voice rose just a bit with each repetition.

Anselm stirred ever so faintly. Camellia laid her hand on his and called to him again, "Anselm. Anselm!" She began caressing his hand. Then suddenly she started to sing—very softly—the old Methodist hymn:

Who at my door is standing,
Patiently drawing near,
Entrance within demanding,
Whose is the voice I hear?
Sweetly the tones are falling,
Open the door for me.
If thou wilt heed my calling,
I will abide with thee.

Anselm stirred again, and this time his eyes blinked. He closed, then reopened them. He turned his head and focused with curiosity on Camellia, and in the clearest of voices he said, "Barnacle Bill?!" and burst into a strangling laugh.

The nurses rushed to him to see that he didn't choke. But he was all right.

Anselm wiggled his fingers and tried to grasp Camellia's hand. She was laughing and kissing his lips. Virginia and the nurses were all smiles and nods. "It's a miracle" one of the nurses whispered. "Praise God!" the other one said.

Anselm didn't speak any more right then, but he kept on trying to chuckle, and he had tight hold onto Camellia's hand. As she bent over to again kiss his lips, he got one arm partly around her and almost succeeded in pulling her down to him.

"Whoa, there, big boy!" she said teasingly. "There'll be time for that when we get back to Bell's Island!"

Explain it how you may, call it spontaneous remission or whatever you like, but to Camellia, Virginia, and those nurses, a resurrection was taking place!

Anselm's condition improved rapidly and steadily over the next couple of days, and by the end of that week he was sitting up in bed, talking, eating, and continuing to marvel at what had happened, as was everybody.

Camellia and Virginia had taken a room in a nearby motel and Camellia went every day to the Veteran's Hospital to see Anselm. They would sit talking for as long as the nurses would let them, gazing into each other's eyes, kissing, and holding hands. The years and the dramatically divergent paths their lives had taken since they'd last been together had not changed either's feeling for the other.

Anselm, in re-telling of the events immediately following Camellia's fateful departure from Bell's Island twenty years before, said:

"Just after you got over the bridge and out of sight, Camellia, there came that lightning and simultaneous thunder crash, and it seemed so close that I had fallen to my knees in the road.

"Your parents came running out of the Tu-Rest Home to see if I was hurt.

"Your mother screamed, 'Did that hit you, Anselm?'

"I said, 'I don't know. Did my cigarette explode?' I couldn't even find the cigarette I'd been smoking, and I was shaking all over.

"Your father said, 'Come on in the house, Anselm. These storms are bad when they come out of the east like this'.

"'That's what I was telling Camellia', I said.

"All of us went in the Tu-Rest Home, into your parents' front room and stood there waiting, as one is likely to do after such a crack, waiting for the next one. But there was no further lightning or thunder. Just a torrential downpour of rain. I kept looking out the window and saying, 'I hope Camellia gets to Royal Hall in time to put her windows down'.

"Your father said, 'I doubt if they had any of this storm at Royal Hall'.

"Your mother said, 'I'll phone Camellia in a bit and check on her'.

"Your mother phoned four times at fifteen to twenty minute intervals and got no answer either time. After the last call—and by now it was very dark—I jumped up and said, 'Well, I'm going to Royal Hall. Maybe her phone is just out for some reason, but I'd feel better to know for sure that she got home okay'.

"There was a cool, wet blackness to the night as I left Bell's Island for Royal Hall. Summer was surely over now, that weird thunderstorm having been its last gasp.

"When I shortly came up on your car pulled over to the side of the road, I couldn't believe what I saw. The windshield was shattered in a million pieces, and a huge chunk of the concrete lay on the hood. I pulled open the door expecting to find—I don't know what. But there was nothing in the car—not even any glass—only your purse laying on the front seat.

"Puzzled, I walked all around the car, shining my flashlight around in every direction and finding nothing unusual except a large section of roadway torn up. I recalled hearing someone once say that lightning can once in a blue moon strike down in a roadway and burst it apart. That must have been what happened—and what the police later thought, too,—and your windshield must have caught one of those flying chunks of concrete. It must have happened right when I had dropped to the road at Bell's Island at the time of that lightning and thunder crash. *But where were you*?

"I was shining my flashlight all around the marsh on either side of the roadway and even walked a ways down the old road toward the abandoned wharf where we'd spent that day cavorting in the fish truck. Then I turned back from there. It was ridiculous to think you would have walked down there in a thunderstorm.

"Finally I decided you must have gotten a ride back to Royal Hall. I called out your name several times, feeling sort of foolish for doing so and hearing nothing in response from the marsh and the wet, quiet blackness of the night. I picked up your purse, returned to my own car, and hurried on to Royal Hall, while keeping an eye out for you in case you were walking along the roadway somewhere. But I saw nothing of you.

"It had not rained in Royal Hall. The streets were dry and there was a coolish, almost chill breeze running through the town. I shivered as I got out of my car in front of your apartment there on Prince Edward Street. No lights were on inside and all your windows were open. I thought maybe you had gone to bed already, before it started to get cooler and just had not put them down.

"I pushed your door buzzer several times, but got no answer. I wondered why you wouldn't let me in. You hadn't seemed mad at me when you left Bell's Island. That business Roger trumped up about my being with Moonlight had not seemed to bother you too much after your first explosion to me about it.

"I buzzed your door a couple more times, then started knocking and calling your name. I didn't want to raise too much of a noise because there were close neighbors. Mrs. Elderkin, however, wasn't home—as usual.

"I felt silly standing there so long trying to get in. And from out of the past there came your voice, singing that solo *Who At My Door Is Standing*? as you had done that morning in the Bell's Island Methodist Church. I laughed out loud, remembering how embarrassingly ridiculous that had been for both of us.

"Then I felt a catch in my chest—something akin to foreboding. I shook off the feeling and reached in my pocket for the key you'd given me. I was still calling your name as I unlocked the door, went in, and flicked on the light in your vestibule. I started walking cautiously through your apartment, turning on the lights as I went and calling your name. I search the place over and found nothing.

"As I came back out into the hallway dividing the bedroom and kitchen from the front of the apartment, I felt something pass by me. It was not a breeze from the open windows, though your filmy white curtains were moving softly here and there. *It was you*! I froze to the floor....

"Then I shook myself and said out loud, 'Oh, crap! What's the matter with you, Jurgensen? You're no psychic. You've never had any experiences like that'.

"I told myself to go call your mother to see if you might have gotten a ride *back* to the island. But I recalled no car passing me in either direction as I'd driven from the island to Royal Hall.

"I phoned anyway only to learn that you were not at the Tu-Rest Home. I told your mother briefly about finding your car, but not about the condition it was in. I didn't want to alarm her.

"Then I quickly made two other calls—one to the Gainsbiddle hospital and one to the hospital in Centerbridge, thinking maybe you had been shaken up by the broken windshield and had gone for aid to one of the houses in that little black village of Satin not too far from where your car was, and maybe someone from Satin had taken you to the hospital. But those two calls turned up nothing.

"I picked up the phone again and this time I notified the state police and the Royal Hall town police.

"Two voices in my head were fighting for attention. The one was saying, 'Oh, she's around somewhere, you'll find her, she's okay, these strange things are always explainable once you get the facts'.

"And the other voice was whispering, 'Camellia's gone, Anselm. You'll never see her again and you'll never know what happened. She's gone, but don't fret; she's okay wherever she is...and she still loves you...'.

"And somewhere from afar off, I could hear music, like nothing I'd ever heard before on this earth....Was I finally hearing—but too late—what you had been hearing for so long and trying to convey to me...?

"And down through the years, since you've been gone, every once in awhile I have heard it again. Like you used to say about your attempts to capture it, I've never been able to hold onto it long enough to write it down, either, or if I did think I had it, it never came out the same as I'd heard it....But now that you're back...?"

Yes! thought Camellia. To be putting opera and public performance behind her would open the way for that other yen—composing—that had never really died. Had she not always heard "that music" most profoundly when with Anselm and in the area of Bell's Island, both to which she was now returning?

"Yes, Anselm" Camellia said, nestling in his arms. "Now that I'm back, we'll find 'that music' again—this time together—we will capture it and it will never get away from us again."

It was not possible for them to even begin to recap to each other all the things that had happened to them in their twenty years of separation, but they got enough of the main events explained to each other to be able to judge where they stood with each other and what their plans should now be.

Anselm said, "You used to say you'd never marry a Bell's Island waterman, Camellia, but you realize, don't you, that that's what I am? I quit—or rather got fired from that bandmaster job at the Royal Hall High the very year you disappeared. I still live in my cabin on Little Bell's and I still tinker with my animal feed experiments."

"Great!" said Camellia, with a big smile. "When all my Baltimore friends and associates come for the wedding, we can tell them you are engaged in high level government research in the field of nutrition!"

Oh, yes—Camellia Stephens—soon to be Camellia Jurgensen—had not forgotten about her image!

Camellia had phoned Sylvester and Louisa two days after Anselm's sudden turn toward recovery and told them where she was and why and how happy she was, and they rejoiced with her and promised not to say anything to anybody for the time being.

It wasn't until the end of that week that Camellia finally phoned Madame Dupree and told her she had been called to England due to a severe illness of a close relative; the relative was better now, thank you, but she would be staying in England during the relative's convalescence, and she would also be officially retiring now from public performance in the music world.

Camellia never did contact Merv Roth, but she knew he'd get the word eventually from Madame Dupree. Camellia suspected both of them would think she'd gotten cold feet about the prospect of singing, finally, at The Met and had made up the sick relative excuse, but no matter what they thought. She was reunited with her "teddy bear" and that was more important to her now than a hundred roles at The Met.

Camellia did not tell Anselm about The Met bid that she'd passed up to return to him. She knew she would tell him eventually but she couldn't do it right then, lest it make him feel like a heel.

Camellia's sorrow in learning of the death of both her parents had been mitigated somewhat by the presence of Virginia, who reminded her so much of Mary with that "you can't tell a book by its cover" personality. Virginia admitted she had been "living with" Nick Carrambarro, a fellow student at Halburg State and "one handsome Italian!" They had not even been considering marriage, but now it seemed advisable to "do something," because Virginia hadn't been feeling well of late and she was fairly sure she "had a slight touch of pregnancy!"

Camellia said, "Well, don't let sad history repeat. Marry, if at all feasible, and love what you two have created. And why not get Nick to come here and we'll have *a double ceremony* at the parsonage of whatever preacher we can find who'll do it for us on the day Anselm is discharged from the Veteran's Hospital. And I'll forget the frills of a big wedding. It's not something Anselm would want anyway."

Somewhat reluctantly Virginia contacted Nick. And to everybody's surprise, that "one handsome Italian!" went along with Camellia's suggestion.

Sylvester and Louisa Valiano, in all their gaudiest togs, came down from Baltimore to stand up with Anselm and Camellia and Nick and Virginia. After the ceremony, there was a lot of back-slapping, wisecracking, and carrying on as the two newlywed couples took off for their respective honeymoons.

Nick and Virginia drove back to the little apartment they had near the Halburg State campus to bring to fruition the seed sown by the mutual lust...AND by Virginia's giddy-headedness (shades of Mary!) in forgetting to take "the pill" regularly.

Anselm and Camellia headed for Little Bell's Island and his cabin to pick up where they'd left off two decades before. They had so many things to do, some new, some old: develop a feed that would grow chickens with all drumsticks and white meat...turn all of "that music" into operas and symphonies...and love, love, love...love...and then love some more!

Part Three

Chapter Seven

The two cars of newlyweds had left the parsonage near the Veteran's Hospital and had followed each other down the shore nearly to Royal Hall. Then Nick and Virginia branched off the main highway and headed toward Halburg State and their apartment near the campus.

As the two cars parted, there was much waving and blowing of kisses, and Camellia and Anselm continued on into Royal Hall.

Suddenly Camellia said, "Tell me everything, Anselm. I can take it. What's it *really* been like with you and everybody since I've been gone?"

"Oh, so-so," said Anselm. "A little bit of good and a little bit of bad. Like with everything."

That was no kind of answer, Camellia was thinking, but she didn't press the matter. She eased her Mercedes into Royal Hall. Yes, her Mercedes. She'd come back to Wintergreen County well-heeled, just as she'd left. But it was not from singing opera all those years. It was from her old standby—"wise investments."

Royal Hall, Wintergreen County's colonial-graced county seat was still as Camellia remembered it—resplendent with beautiful historic homes, brick sidewalks, cobblestone streets, and huge umbrella trees that arched from one side to the other, making Wintergreen Avenue an emerald thoroughfare in the center of town.

At the main intersection of Wintergreen Avenue, Camellia turned west onto Prince Edward Street. Catty-corner across from Royal Hall High School, where she had been music director and Anselm the bandmaster, there was the white colonial mansion where she'd had her apartment. It was where she and Anselm had their first sex—on a Sunday morning just before she was to solo in the Episcopal Church which she had switched to, finding the Episcopal trappings more "royal" than the Methodist. It was where they'd argued about where they would live when they got married—Royal Hall or Bell's Island. Bell's Island—Little Bell's to be exact—had won out. Anselm had a way of bending Camellia's mind that no other person on this wide earth ever had.

Camellia circled the Mercedes around the block one more time, then they headed west for Bell's and Little Bell's.

Before too long they were driving through the miles and miles of marshland between Royal Hall and Bell's Island. There were endless brown and green mud flats on either side of the road, stretching out as far as the eye could see to the south, the west, and the north clear to the milky-blue horizons. The mud flats were crisscrossed in every direction with "guts"—intestinal-like salt water ponds and canals running and twisting around and around every which-a-way.

Camellia wanted to fill in her "disappearance" from the local point of view, so she asked Anselm to show her where he'd found her disabled Lincoln Continental that fateful night. All she could remember was a wet blackness around everywhere and the sound of strange music until a car filled with black people and children picked her up. Then the next thing she knew she was wandering aimlessly around the streets of Baltimore.

Anselm had Camellia slow down when they got past the black village of Satin. "It was along about here, as I recall," he said.

Camellia pulled the Mercedes over and they got out and looked around.

Anselm said, "The morning after your 'disappearance,' cars were parked along here in both directions, and everybody was out here walking along the roadside. I joined the rest and found this spot cordoned off and your Lincoln sitting here with its windshield smashed in. Nobody seemed to notice me. Everybody's thoughts were on you.

"There was a cold northwest wind blowing across the marsh from the Anderson Sound over there and it was no time to be 'drownded' in that marsh, which was what most people seemed to think happened to you.

"Coast Guard helicopters, marine police, and K-9 dogs were all searching the marsh and water on both sides of the road here, and everybody was speculating as to what caused you to disappear.

"The talk I heard the most went something like: 'Well, Camellia and her boyfriend were supposed to be getting married at Christmas, but everybody knows he's been going with that Moonlight Corrigan on the sly, and I think Camellia must of found it out...and...well, I think it was more than she could take, beings she's had a crush on that Jurgensen, the Royal Hall High bandmaster, her 'teddy bear', as she called him, for so long now. I think it was just too much for her, seeing that Moonlight Corrigan is Wintergreen County's favorite prostitute, and so Camellia prob'ly just went out there in that marsh, stepped into one of them guts, and drownded herself. If they keep probing around out there, they'll prob'ly find her body in a bit, just wait and see...'.

"And somebody right away added: 'She could of got swallowed up by that quicksand out there, and they'll never find her. Somebody years ago—a city guy doing some hunting down here—lost a hunting dog in that quicksand. He saw the dog go down, down, down, but by the time he got to him, the dog was gone, buried alive right before his eyes, and he couldn't dig the dog out, either, lessen he get sucked down himself....And I'll bet that's just what happened to Camellia'.

"Then somebody else piped up and said: 'They're wasting time and the taxpayers' money fooling around in that marsh looking for her. I'll bet she never got in that marsh. I'll bet she and Jurgensen staged that accident to her car, made it look like a bolt of lightning struck down in the roadway and threw a concrete chunk against her windshield. Then I bet they had somebody come along and carry her out of the state so she could get an abortion...'.

'Abortion?' somebody asked. 'Was Camellia pregnant?'

"'I don't know, but I'll bet she had every opportunity to be!'"

At that juncture Camellia and Anselm both laughed so hard they nearly fell into the marsh themselves.

Anselm said, "Another theory about your disappearance was that if your car had become disabled by the storm, you may have been stunned by the lightning and wandered along the roadway until you were given a ride to Lord knows where by some late tourist who didn't know who you were, and if you had been stunned by the lightning, you might not have given a correct identification of yourself."

Camellia interposed. "And that's exactly what did happen. I figured it out some two years later when seeing Roger's obituary in an old Baltimore newspaper—the Eastern Shore section. That obituary shocked me out of my amnesia and back into my right mind."

"But you still didn't come home or tell anybody where you were," Anselm said abruptly.

"I'm not proud of that," Camellia admitted. She could tell Anselm was angry at the thought of her deliberately staying away and she knew she had a lot of "making up for" to do.

Still she tried to justify herself and said, "It had taken me so long to break away from here I was afraid of getting tangled up again with the Stephenses and all their problems—financial and every-otherwise."

Anselm said no more on that and resumed talking about her "disappearance." "Suddenly, as I recall, the crowd around me moved like it was one single unit when somebody yelled, 'Hey! What's that going on over there? Have they found her?'

"The crowd turned into a near mob. I felt myself stomped on, kicked, and jabbed in the ribs and in the head as the knots and clots of thrill seekers strained and pressed to see what was going on. Somebody yelled out again, 'They've found her car keys. I'll bet they step right on her body any minute now!'

"The state police had found your car keys hanging out there on one of those white-blossoming water bushes that pop out in the marshes every fall. The bush was near that walkway along the drainage canal, but with all the clumping and stomping of state police feet and police dog paws, any trace of your footprints, if there had been any out there, were promptly wiped out. I was too tired and heartsick to stay there any longer. I knew they weren't going to find you, so I went on back to my room at your parents' Tu-Rest Home and tried to sort my thoughts out."

When Camellia and Anselm got back in the Mercedes, Anselm said, "There was less confusion and concern over your brother Roger's drowning a couple weeks later than there had been over your disappearance. Everybody knew Roger was a 'Peck's bad boy', and maybe people were thinking 'good riddance to bad rubbish'. But the police were again swarming about, questioning your parents and Bell's Island residents."

Remorse bit into Camellia. No, she hadn't wanted to get re-tangled up with her family after finally breaking away, but now in retrospect she knew she should have been willing to risk it in order to save her parents some of their anguish. But too late to do anything about that now....

Anselm was talking on....

"In the wake of Roger's drowning, legends about you began to spring up...."

Camellia laughed. "Yes, Virginia got such a kick out of telling me some of them that Doris had told her. I guess you heard some of the same ones."

"Well," said Anselm, "the weather had turned icy cold and that's when people started seeing and hearing things at night out here in the marsh.

"I saw what appeared to be utility poles burning at their bases in that marsh, in that deep black darkness that only a Wintergreen County moonless, starless night in late fall can have. I believe this was what other people were seeing too, when they reported seeing something like your ghost running through the marsh with your clothes on fire and then suddenly sinking down and disappearing as though the marsh had swallowed you up. Some said it was nothing but St. Elmo's fire or marsh gas.

"As for those voices people said they heard out there in the marsh....Some said they heard Roger's voice just as plain, crying out, 'Sister! Sister! Where are you?' But loons, you know....They sound just like the human voice in distress.

"And there was 'the big bird theory'. Some said your body was never found because a big bird came down the night you disappeared and carried you away."

Camellia laughed. "Loons don't carry people away."

"No, not loons," said Anselm. "Something bigger. But you know how people talk. And some said they heard weird gypsy-like music coming off that marsh—probably your Corrigan-gypsy-Stephens forebears mourning for you—but again there was a reasonable explanation. Probably a radio on somebody's boat out in the river. Sound carries farther on the water and especially at night. Everybody knows if a Gainsbiddler down river takes a pee in a tin bucket at twelve o'clock midnight, we'll hear it tinkling up here at Bell's Island at 11:56!"

They both chuckled, remembering the old Bell's Island put-down of rival port Gainsbiddle, the reverse version of which was used in Gainsbiddle.

They weren't too far from Bell's Island now. Ahead on the horizon lay a shoreline panorama Camellia had not seen for nearly twenty years:

The old drawbridge over the Anderson Sound inlet, the masts of work boats in the harbor, the little community of Bell's Island nestled beneath summer-green trees, the single church spire, and the clusters of white houses.

To their right just before the drawbridge was what was left of the old Moonlight Corrigan gypsy tavern. It was where Camellia's maternal grandfather, James LeCates, had gambled and eventually lost all his money. It was where her paternal grandfather, Grandpaw Azariah Stephens, had found his half-gypsy wife, setting the scene for Camellia's one-eighth gypsy blood. It was where Roger had gone for solace and sex.

Camellia slowed her Mercedes. She knew how bumpy the drawbridge could be even with a slick-driving vehicle. The last time she'd crossed that bridge it had been in that Lincoln Continental....in the fall of 1950, nearly twenty years ago from this sizzling summer of 1970....

On the map, Bell's Island, Maryland, had always reminded Camellia of a huge wrinkled string bean, three miles long and a half-mile wide, being chucked ickily away from the Wintergreen County mainland and consigned to some bottomless tidal garbage bucket.

She had never liked her hometown. It was an Eastern Shore seafood port all too crude, and full of people too crude, especially her father's relatives, who were derivatives of the Bell's Island gypsies and Irish pirates (as was Camellia herself, for that matter).

In her younger years she had always felt herself too big, too musically talented to be confined there. Yet, back then, aside from her stint at the conservatory across the bay in Baltimore, the farthest she had gotten away from Bell's Island had been the slightly more elegant Royal Hall, the Wintergreen county seat where she had been appointed the head of the high school music department way back in 1942. How long ago that seemed now....

Once over the bumpy Bell's Island drawbridge they rolled into that ordinary-looking waterfront community of seven hundred and fifty people, a population predominately lower and lower-middle class that had remained constant down through the generations. The central roadway, once only hardened layers of crushed oyster shells, was now macadamized. Yet the small white clapboard houses with their little flower-dotted yards, the seafood processing places with their slime and untidiness, the wharves and boat yards with their barrels and massive machinery, all looked much the same as when Camellia had last seen them nearly twenty years before. Except that the name Stephens was no longer on any of the seafood businesses or shipyards.

Then Camellia noticed something else missing....Her childhood home, the Stephens rooming house, was gone and in its place there was a parking lot. She didn't feel much regret in seeing it gone. There, so many years before, she had caught her mother in sexual congress with one of the roomers, which resulted in her half-brother Roger, who had tormented her life (and everybody else's).

On the opposite side of the road and down aways there was still the tiny white box-like house where Roger, his young wife Doris, and their little baby Virginia had been living at the time of Roger's drowning, which had been so very soon after Camellia had "disappeared" in that freak storm.

After all that turmoil, Doris and little Virginia had left the island. Virginia had grown up "down South," but she had returned to Maryland only this year, determined to find her "lost Aunt Camellia," whom she'd heard so many legends about.

It had been the spunky Virginia who had reunited Camellia and Anselm. That had been the joyous part, but there had been a trade off. Only don't think of that now.

"Tell me everything, Anselm. I can take it," Camellia said again, as they continued driving along. "Tell me everything about the twenty years I missed."

"Virginia's told you a lot already, hasn't she?"

"Oh, I suppose so." Camellia realized she sounded peevish. But Virginia didn't know everything. Virginia and her mother, Doris, hadn't been in contact all those years with Bell's Island any more than Camellia had.

Camellia wanted to know things, yet she didn't want to know. She would have to set aside her own past twenty years, forget what she left of the other side of the bay, and pick up Bell's Island's past twenty years. It wouldn't be easy....

They came alongside the Bell's Island Methodist cemetery and Camellia parked her Mercedes. She was wearing dark glasses, a head scarf, and insignificant clothes. She didn't want anybody to know—yet—that she was alive and back on the island. She and Anselm got out and walked until they came to the Stephens's family lot. They looked silently, mournfully, at the graves of her mother and father, relatively new graves.

As they paused at the much older grave of Roger Stephens, Anselm said, "I remember so well your brother's funeral. They put Roger in the ground on a cold, drizzly November day some twenty years ago. Your mother Mary was leaning on your father, as usual. That once was the 'proper' thing for women to do, you remember—'lean' on their husbands, both literally and figuratively, in public at least, and no matter what disruptions may have occurred on the inside of their marriages. Mary and Thomas huddled together in this cemetery on that dismal afternoon. Only a handful of Stephens kin and a few friends were here. I remember how a cold wind sprang up and flapped the canvas of the cemetery tent set up around the grave.

"As you well know, your kid brother's short life—only eighteen, he was—had been a tragic one. Different ones told me nobody had ever really loved him—except maybe his wife Doris—and he got back at the world by his meanness. Everybody thought he was too mean to die. But he did. And fittingly for a waterman—he just drowned when his skiff overturned while he was searching in the marshes for you, Camellia, after you 'disappeared' in that terrible storm."

They glanced at the graves of several other Stephenses nearby... some of Camellia's first cousins who had been killed in World War II. "As you may recall," Anselm said, "these kin of yours had military funerals. For Roger there was neither blue nor gold star in your parents' front window at the Tu-Rest Home. There were no army officers to fold and hand your mother an American flag from off the casket. There were no bugles blowing 'Taps'. There was no singing of *Nearer,*

My God, to Thee. There was only the cold wind flapping the canvas of the tent and a dreadful sob coming up from your mother's throat as if her soul was crying out, 'Eighteen terrible years and it's finally over. Why, oh, why, Lord, did it ever have to start?' Not only had she lost you, she had now lost Roger, though he had been a mistake to start with, but still and all...."

Why, oh why, Camellia was thinking, did Anselm have to say all that? But it was she who had wanted to stop at the cemetery, and she who had been saying all along, *Anselm, tell me everything. I can take it.*

It was bravado talking. And the nagging curiosity about the past mixed with an overload of guilt. What had she done to everybody, Anselm in particular, by staying away so long? She could have come back or at least contacted someone. After the first two years in Baltimore her amnesia had lifted. But no, she was having too good a time, to much success singing opera....But not to think of that now.

She glanced at Anselm and perhaps for the first time realized how bad and old he looked for only forty-five years old. Yet he'd always looked older than he was. Still, in her initial joy at his sudden emergence form his coma when she and Virginia had arrived a the Veteran's hospital, she had overlooked much. Anselm had always been a heavy-set man, but now his clothes bagged on him. His once bronze-red hair had turned a scruffy pinkish-white. He no longer had his own teeth and refused to wear his false ones because he said they hurt.

By contrast, Camellia's thick dark hair had attractive highlights of silver, and there remained a voluptuousness to her body that middle age had not yet marred. Yes, she knew she carried her fifty-four years well. But so do many women, especially women performers and singers. Only she would perform and sing no more....But not to think of that now.

They left the cemetery and drove on to the end of Bell's Island's central roadway where, off to the right and close to the water's edge, was a large weather-beaten building with its doors and windows boarded up.

"Something else that's still the same," remarked Camellia, "my mother's parents' inn still standing...and still closed. Way, way back I had some mighty good times there as a child, singing and performing for all the Baltimore tourists of that day. Claudie, my first music teacher, lived there, and she and Mama used to write little musical skits based on operas and I was always the star!"

Camellia had told Anselm all that years ago, but try though she might, she couldn't stop thinking about singing and performing.

They left the main Bell's Island roadway and drove into the narrow bush-lined causeway onto that strange appendage—*Little* Bell's Island.

Back in there Anselm still had his cabin, the old hunting lodge he had bought after getting out of the army and starting work as bandmaster at Royal Hall High and as handyman at the Stephens shipyard. It was the place Camellia and Anselm had been fixing up for their honeymoon suite some twenty years before, the honeymoon that never came about because Camellia had "disappeared."

What they found at the cabin now was the most gruesome and grisly mess Camellia had ever encountered. Anselm took one look and said in despair, "I thought Jim Stephens, my pal and your sole surviving cousin and relative on the island, whom I left in charge here, was going to clean this up, but I see he hasn't. Too busy with his game warden duties, I guess."

Anselm had already explained to Camellia what he was doing with his animal feed experiments—his hobby of years before that had become a near obsession in Camellia's absence. He collected garbage form the county dump on Little Bell's, sorted, sterilized, and recooked it, then fed it selectively to his menagerie of stray dogs and cats, waterfowl, and wildlife that had taken refuge at his cabin. Before he'd gotten sick and gone to the Veteran's hospital, he had built a dehydrating apparatus and was scientifically distilling the garbage for the vitamins and proteins.

The old hunter's cabin was both his *laboratory* and his residence, but it had gotten in a horrible shape. The roof was falling in on one side, and there was something like old rotten scaffolding around part of the cabin. On the scaffolding were rows and rows of sea gulls and other flying waterfowl.

As Camellia and Anselm got out of the Mercedes, the birds all flew up in the air at once—or tried to—as some had broken wings and couldn't, and they set up a squalling, screeching noise that set off a howling, whining, yelping tirade from inside all kinds of pens and cages sitting around in the yard, piled on top of one another and filled with beagles, ducks, racoons, geese, and God only knows what all.

Everywhere they looked there were piles of trash, junk, old boat motors, rotting hulls of abandoned skiffs, old tires, overgrown brush and brambles, and swirls of tangled-up wire. There were woodpiles and crude drainage ditches, bent gutters and downspouts fashioned into some sort of distilling apparatus, washboards and melting red soap, continuously wet places where wash water had been dumped out, piles of cinders and ashes from a crude outdoor furnace, broken bricks and concrete blocks, and rusty, scorched incinerator drums covered with ragged screen wire and smoldering continuously.

And all around everywhere there were piles of animal excrement and carcasses. Flies—the green-headed, fiercely biting kind—were swarming over everything. The stench was unbelievable, what with the sultry heat trapped in beneath the pines where practically no air was circulating.

There was such a cacophony of noise outside with all the birds shrieking and dogs barking that Anselm said, "Maybe we'd best go inside. Quieter there."

They worked their way up to the door of the cabin and Anselm pushed it open with his foot.

Inside the cabin it may have been quieter, but it certainly wasn't any more appetizing. Every level surface was covered either with a hulking animal or bird of some sort or else the excrement they'd left behind. The floor was heaped up with stained and broken crates, and cartons and rusty cages with piles of rags and newspapers lay everywhere. There were broken dishes and tin plates on the floor with decaying dog meal, soured milk, and dreggy water scummed over with bits of Lord know what—hair and flesh or pus or something or other—floating in them. The whole place was exuding a smell guaranteed to make a roach retch.

And roaches were in there, too—strands and strands of them, hanging like brown-beaded festoons, like ghoulish Christmas tree garlands, hanging all around the room, from the ceiling, around the window frames, across all the crates and cages. They were enmeshed in cobwebs, but at first glance Camellia thought they had somehow all joined hands—or feet—to form those chains.

In a dirty little alcove were stacks of guano-stained college textbooks and governmental reports on everything from animal husbandry and chemistry to physics, mechanics...and music!

Camellia sadly sensed this was the way Anselm had been normally living because it couldn't have gotten all that bad no longer than he'd been in the Veteran's hospital. She didn't know how much longer she could stay in that cabin without becoming ingloriously sick, when finally Anselm said, "Let's get away from here and go find a motel. I'm sorry you had to see the place like this."

Just before they left, Anselm went back into the cabin to get some books and papers. Jim Stephens drove up through the pine trees in his game warden's truck. He and Camellia, seeing each other for the first time in twenty years, embraced and wept. She'd never liked her "low class" Stephens cousins, but this one was all she had left of a past too easily gone.

Jim was as goofy as ever. He was telling Camellia about the weather being so hot that morning that his revolver had gone off all by itself! Camellia recalled his mother and father—her Uncle Amos and Aunt Lois—and how goofy they had been, always going everywhere together—even to the outhouse together—because neither could find the way back home without the other's help. But it was said of them, "They never did nobody no harm." And Jim was just like them. He'd been about the only friend Roger had, Camellia recalled. And he had been befriending Anselm, too.

As for Anselm's menagerie, Jim said, "I've been takin' care of 'em. Couldn't find nobody what wanted any of 'em. I've been 'tendin' to shoot 'em. Most of 'ems half-dead, anyway. A lot of 'ems been injured, as you can see, an' Jurgensen had been tryin' to nurse 'em back to health. Feedin' 'em special vitamin food he was experimentin' with.

"Some of 'em he'd made pets out of. One of 'em died jes' when we was about to leave for the Veteran's Hospital. Nothin' but an old fuzzy mutt dog, but it was one of his favorites. I think it was the last straw for him. We'd done come out of the cabin there with his little bag of clothes, an' that dog was lyin' right out front there like he always done. Jurgensen reached down to pet him goodbye, an' he never moved.

"That dog had been okay before we'd gone into the cabin to get Jurgensen's stuff, an' he'd looked up at us an' wagged his tail, but when we come back out an' Jurgensen reached down to pet him, he never moved. Jurgensen got down on his knees to him an' talked to him an' lifted his head up in his arms, but it warn't no use. The dog was dead, an' I think Jurgensen was as good as dead right then, too.

"I thought it would break his heart because we didn't have no time to even bury the dog. I come back here after I got back from the hospital an' buried it. I felt like I was buryin' Jurgensen instead.

"I often wondered what did he have all of them animals an' birds for anyhow? I thought he was crazy to have 'em. But after he lost you, Camellia, I guess he turned to them animals an' birds for somethin' to love."

Camellia was relieved when she and Anselm got away from both Little Bell's and big Bell's and settled down at an air-conditioned motel outside Royal Hall.

Yet neither the Bell's Island far past nor the Baltimore just-past would let her alone. That lost Met opportunity....But not to think of that now.

At the same time, Camellia dreaded living on Bell's Island again. Dreaded facing up to all those things she could have done—should have done—yet didn't do. When Virginia had told her about her parents having both died only a few years ago, all the accumulating years' guilt over never having contacted them had rushed in on her. And that guilt was continuing to bug her.

And Anselm looked so poorly. But at least he was alive....

As Anselm turned out the light over their bed, Camellia recalled, "When Virginia told me where you were, I was so scared we wouldn't get to the Eastern Shore and the Veteran's Hospital in time to see you before you died, I canceled my Met appointment." *Camellia could have bitten off her tongue. She hadn't meant to say that.*

"*You canceled what*?" Anselm said with a strange squawk.

"My dental appointment," Camellia said with a quick lie.

"That's not what you said!" Anselm sat bolt upright. *You had a Met audition scheduled—something you'd waited a lifetime for—and you canceled it just to come to the Eastern Shore to see me when you didn't even know if I'd still be alive when you got here*?"

"Uh huh," said Camellia, swallowing back the tears.

"Can it be rescheduled?"

"I doubt it. I didn't formally *cancel* it. I just didn't show up for it. I later told my teacher, Madame Dupree, I was retiring and going back to England. I left it up to her to pass the word along. Everybody in Baltimore and around abouts, except Sylvester and Louisa, knew me as 'Charity Croswell, the English lady'."

Anselm fell back on his pillow. "I feel like a louse. What role were you to audition for?"

"Azucena."

"Azucena," repeated Anselm. "The gypsy mother in Verdi's *Il Travatore*. A real plum of a role. Why didn't you tell me about this in the hospital?"

"I didn't want to make you feel bad."

Camellia couldn't decide whether she was telling him *now* to make him feel bad. *She* was feeling bad. He might as well, too.

Had she acted too hastily, too recklessly, in ending her entire performing career just to come back to Bell's Island because she knew that's where Anselm wanted her to be?

In the morning it seemed a tad cooler, so they decided to go back to Little Bell's Island for another look. Anselm wanted to check on his birds and beasts and start cleaning up the place. It was where his heart was and Camellia intended to humor him, to live wherever and do whatever he wanted. She was determined to make amends for her past neglect.

Whether or not Anselm was thinking of making anything up to her for her sacrificing her Met opportunity to come back to him, she did not know.

After a quick look again at Anselm's cabin on Little Bell's, they knew it was useless to try to do anything with it by themselves, so once again they left and returned to their motel.

Later, with Jim Stephens' help and several weeks of intense shoveling, scraping, scrubbing, and finally disinfecting everything from floor to ceiling, they made the cabin and its immediate surroundings passably liveable once again. They removed the caged animals and birds from the inside the cabin and put them in a new shelter under the pines. Some of the more hopeless ones, both from inside the cabin and on the outside, they euthanized.

The cabin was still dark inside from sooted-up walls and lack of paint, but otherwise it was remarkably clean compared with how Camellia had first seen it. She was starting to feel almost at home there and some of the bite of her sacrificed singing career was beginning to fade. Some, but not all....

Chapter Eight

The first night they stayed over at the cabin, they fell asleep to the soft sighing of the pine trees, their tops pushed about in the ever-restless wind moving over the island.

Camellia was up early the next morning and starting breakfast when Anselm came straggling into the kitchen with his pants half falling off. He had lost so much weight while at the Veteran's Hospital, there weren't enough eyelets left in his belt to take up the slack.

He was a sight, but Camellia looked at him adoringly. As she was fixing his breakfast, she reached over every now and then and rumpled up his once bronze-red hair, now polar bear color—*dirty* polar bear.

Camellia's eyes kept meeting Anselm's, which were roaming over her body, still lush and curvy under her filmy, thin nightie, as if to say "All that is mine again!"

Camellia gave a little giggle. She was good in the bed (and she knew it), but she was not so great in the kitchen. She had fixed a soft-boiled egg and some toast for Anselm (about the only thing he could eat in the morning), but unfortunately she was one of those people who never learn how to properly open a soft-boiled egg. She had left bits of shell in it.

On the first bite, Anselm got a piece of shell hung up in the roof of his mouth and he went into a gagging, spluttering, cursing spasm, using some sort of three-language variety of oaths that he confessed to using when he was out on the water, trying to handle his crab boat, which he never quite learned how to do. Camellia started laughing at him, that glorious laughter that only she was capable of.

When Anselm recovered from the choking, he said in a deliberately exaggerated foreign accent (a little something he'd picked up from his German-born mother and which he sometimes used when agitated), "Iss it not enough that you leaf schell in der ekk, Camellia?

Do you haf to laf your head off at me, too?" But he was not angry at her, really.

At that point Jim Stephens came in the cabin and, having witnessed Anselm's plight with the egg, he offered some helpful (?) advice:

"Jurgensen, when you've got a wiggly digestive system in the mornin', what you oughta do for 'schell in der ekk' is try the 'Gainsbiddle Sure Cure for Seasickness:'

"Take a piece of fat-back an' tie a long piece of string around it. Then put the fat-back in your mouth an' swaller it slowly, leavin' the free end of the string hangin' outa your mouth. Then take a-holt of the string an' pull the piece of fat-back slow...ly up outa your gullet 'til it's back in your mouth again, then sl..ow..ly re-swaller the piece of fat-back, still leavin' the string hangin' outa your mouth. Then take a-holt of the string and sl..ooow..ly pull the fat-back up into your mouth again, then...."

"FOR CHRISSAKE, JIM STEPHENS, GET OUTA HERE!" Camellia and Anselm yelled at him both at the same time.

Jim laughed and headed outside, saying he'd brought some fish for their supper and would start cleaning them. Camellia went out to help with the fish, leaving Anselm to contemplate the "Gainsbiddle Sure Cure for Seasickness" and further choke on "der schell in der ekk."

While Camellia and Jim worked on the fish, Jim got into some sad talking about how all the Stephenses had either died or moved away from the island:

Camellia's Uncle Charlie—who had once tried to rape her and she'd thrown him a double whammy with her "gypsy magic," leaving him with a recurrent unbearable pain in the top of his head that haunted him the rest of his life—had died many years before with a heart attack.

Jim's parents—Camellia's Uncle Amos and his wife Lois—had moved away from the island, as had her Aunt Amanda and Amanda's husband, Simon Cartwright.

Jim said with Amos and Lois gone, none of the other Stephenses, including Jim's wife, would give a home to Grandpaw Azariah, who had taught Camellia her "gypsy magic" and had lived with Amos and Lois yet wouldn't go with them to the mainland. He ended up freezing to death in an abandoned Stephens warehouse after even the old gypsy place had thrown him out because he'd gotten so nasty in his habits.

Snipsey Cartwright Jones, Camellia's first cousin and her sidekick when they were kids, had died in a house fire on the island many years back and two of her children perished with her.

Jim paused in his doleful list to say, "You've never forgot how to clean fish, have you, Camellia?"

"Unk uh," said Camellia, filleting the critters with a deftness that only an island breeding and the agility of a pianist's hands could afford.

Jim said, "I guess it's like sex an' riding a bicycle, If you ever done 'em once, you never forget how."

Camellia barely heard his wisecrack, for she was thinking about that time in Baltimore before she had come out of her amnesia, when she was shucking some oysters for Sylvester Valiano, her mentor and restaurateur boss, who had been trying to open the shells with a hammer! She had been crying at the time and couldn't understand why. Later she realized it had been subconscious homesickness and anguish for deserting her people.

Trying to keep from being overwhelmed again with grief, Camellia pitched the ball back to Jim and said, "All the Stephenses are gone from the island except you, Jim. You say even your wife and kids left! How come you stayed?"

Jim got that goofy look on his face and his ping-pong ball eyes bugged out a little further in preparation for telling a whopper: "How come I stayed? Well, you remember them warehouses the Stephenses had, an' they was built part over the water an' part over the shore?"

"Um hmm," said Camellia.

Jim said, "An' remember them toilets in some of 'em—jes' an inside outhouse, and ever'thing would drop down through a big hole cut in the floorin' under the seat an' would end up on the rocks an' oyster shells underneath the warehouse? But it wouldn't stay there long because the tide would get it."

"Um hmm," said Camellia.

Jim went on, "An' you know that television commercial: 'Tides In, Dirts Out'? Only, remember how the Stephenses said it: 'Tides In, Turds Out'?"

"Um hmm," said Camellia, wearily, wishing she hadn't asked. "Get to the point, Jim."

Jim burst out laughing. "You ask how come I stayed on Bell's Island? Can't you see? *I've been the only Stephens turd what the tide couldn't wash out*!"

Camellia laughed in spite of herself. She wanted to hug Jim because he represented the only "scrimption" left of a past long gone.

The next guests at Anselm's cabin later that week were Virginia and her bridegroom of one month, Nick Carrambarro. Virginia came striding up the long path, through the pines, her auburn hair swirling about her shoulders. Nick was striding alongside her.

Watching them at a distance, Anselm noted, "There's a wholesomeness to Virginia, like she's not been out of the Girl Scouts long."

Camellia whooped. "Well, they must be learning new things in the Girl Scouts these days. Virginia got illegitimately pregnant four months ago."

"Ummm. Like grandmother, like granddaughter," Anselm noted, undoubtedly thinking of Mary's encounter with the roomer.

"At least Virginia knows the *name* of the father," snapped Camellia.

Anselm frowned. "You won't ever forgive your mother, will you?"

"Not for Roger, no."

"Hard to realize Virginia is Roger's daughter," said Anselm. "She's so pretty. Roger was a mess. He had that glary red hair and those long, stringy arms and legs and the biggest feet and hands. And he turned the cuffs of his shirts and pants way up and that made him look all the more like a scarecrow. Doris wasn't much to look at, either—a real plain Jane. But Virginia...."

"Virginia looks like Mama when Mama was real young. Creamy, pink complexion, thin facial features, clear blue eyes....Hush now, they're within earshot."

Nick gave Camellia a big hug and called her Aunt Camellia. He was one of the most handsome specimens of Italian descent Camellia had ever seen. With his black hair and eyes, bronzed skin, and the taut, trim physique of an athlete, it was easy to see why Virginia fell for him. And he had a coiled-spring inner tension underneath the surface of his laid-back personality that even stirred up Camellia at times.

Nick, the budding lawyer, gave Camellia some information on her tangled-up finances resulting from her twenty-year absence from the local scene and her many unclaimed securities and bank accounts. And there was the big problem of re-establishing her Camellia Stephens legal identity since she had been officially going under the name "Charity Croswell" for so many years now, and she continued to use it locally wherever an identity was required.

Then Camellia asked Virginia if she'd located any of her mother's people, the Thorntons, on Bell's Island.

Virginia said, "Jim Stephens said my grandmother Thornton was dead, but" (and here Virginia gave a short laugh and a half-vexed, half-sad shake of her head) "I found my grandfather 'Hambone' Thornton. My mother hardly ever spoke of her father. He's a big, beefy, ignorant sort of man. He came to the door in a dirty T-shirt and I didn't even get to finish my first sentence. I tried to say, 'I'm Virginia Stephens, Doris's daughter, your granddaugh—' and he slammed the door in my face. I wanted to say about my mother having passed on, but I didn't get the chance."

Camellia chuckled sympathetically. "Yes, the Thorntons never did forgive your mother for marrying Roger. But don't worry about the Thorntons. They're not much."

Virginia said, "I think that's partly why my mother wanted to cut all ties with Maryland when we had the chance to leave here. Her Thornton family was pretty rough. She never contacted anyone again after we were gone. She had no real quarrel with the Stephenses and she hated to break my grandmother Mary's heart by never writing. But she felt she was doing the best thing."

Virginia paused for a moment, reflecting. "I often wonder about my other grandfather...."

Camellia said, "You mean Roger's father, I assume?"

Virginia nodded.

Camellia said, "I only caught a quick glimpse of him after he got unjoined from Mama. I couldn't tell you what he looked like. Nor could Mama. These one-time-only things....And I'd unintentionally scared both of them by yelling 'The house is on fire!' Mama had left her stew pot untended, and it caught on fire while she was seducing that roomer."

"Camellia, your mother wasn't a bad woman," Anselm hastened to interject.

"That's what *my* mother always said," Virginia added. "She said it was well known around Bell's Island about Mary's husband, Thomas 'Pumpkin' Stephens, that he'd 'got religion and forsaken sex'. Little wonder my grandmother did what she did. But that 'unknown sire' in my genealogy, well it troubles me. Some day I hope to find him."

Anselm laughed. "You did okay in finding your Aunt Camellia."

Camellia thought briefly about a cryptic entry in one of Doc Feldman's old logbooks which Anselm had found on the Little Bell's Island dump and showed to Camellia. The entry had mentioned that Doc had not given Mary the abortion she requested, but the entry sounded ambiguous as to who Doc thought might be the father. Even though Mary, Doc, and Roger all were dead now, Camellia decided to say nothing for the time being to Virginia about the logbook.

It was when Camellia and Anselm settled down at night that Camellia began asking him questions about her parents and their failed business and all that had happened to them in her absence. She had been unable to get much of anything out of Jim Stephens or Virginia.

Anselm also was reluctant to talk about her parents' misfortunes. Thomas and Mary Stephens had been like adoptive parents to him and they had "taken onto" him like the son they wished they'd had instead of the terrible Roger. Watching the Stephenses and their business gradually collapse had hurt Anselm as much as losing Camellia.

"If you don't tell me," Camellia threatened, "I'll go look in your diaries and find out for myself." One whole shelf in the cabin was taken up with Anselm's handwritten record of the past twenty years.

"Well," said Anselm, "in the year after you had disappeared and I had been fired from my bandmaster position at Royal Hall High, I went to work full time for the Stephens firm, in their shipyard and on their oyster boats. I did this for a couple of years and then as the firm began to founder and your Stephens uncles pulled out, I did, too, and went oystering and crabbing on my own and came here to the cabin to live.

"The Stephens Enterprises were sliding further and further into debt while the dilemma over your finances remained unsolved. Nobody, including your parents' lawyer, seemed to know whether the statute of limitations had run out, whether or not you could be declared legally dead, whether or not your funds—which were considerable, in the way of unclaimed bank accounts and securities—could be tapped into by your next of kin.

"Those funds could possibly have bailed out the Stephens Enterprises once again like you had done so many times for them when you were around.

"The Stephenses didn't have either the proper counsel or sufficient wit and wisdom of their own to make any constructive moves. Your father, though he remained titular president of the firm, was ineffective, and your mother, though intelligent enough, always deferred to him. She didn't have that guile that most women have that enables them to get their advice across while making it seem like it is the man who has thought of it first. So mostly she just kept silent.

"Your mother was like a willow tree—frail and thin, but, for all the tossing the winds could give her, she seemed only to bend, not to break. She stayed outwardly as cheerful as she had always been even after you and Roger were both gone, and somebody said to her, almost sarcastic-like, 'Well, Mary, you certainly have gotten over your troubles quickly, haven't you?' But to me, she said, 'Oh, Anselm, if people *only knew* what I feel inside.'

"She felt nobody loved her. That God had punished her for Roger's illegitimacy by taking away from her not only Roger, but you, too.

"As the years went on, her physical condition continued to deteriorate and the Stephens firm continued to go further and further downhill. In 1966 it closed down completely, except for the Tu-Rest Home.

"I used to clean the Tu-Rest Home for your parents; do repair work to the tourist side, though there were practically no roomers there any more; and take care of what were left of the beagle hunting dogs that your mother had once raised. And I gave your parents my pocket cash when they seemed to have a special need for something.

"If your father stepped up his little kindnesses to your mother, such as giving her that little platonic kiss of his more often or offering to do the supper dishes for her, it seemed only to irritate her that much more. If he just let her be, thinking she wished to be alone with her thoughts, she claimed he ignored her.

"She was getting to be a holy terror to live with, even for your mild-mannered, religiously devout father. Your mother talked his ear off by day and you could hear her high, thin voice yammering at him almost down here to Little Bell's. And then she would weep half the night with pains stabbing her insides 'til your father called old Doc Feldman, who by then was aging and ailing himself and barely able to keep up. Doc would go to the Tu-Rest Home, give your mother a *needle,* and all was quiet for awhile.

"Sometimes in the daytime I would see her sitting at the front window of the Tu-Rest Home, with her snow-white head bent over almost on her chest. She was bowed together so terribly by then that I found it hard to look directly at her."

By now Camellia was softly weeping and Anselm said no more.

Though Anselm had stopped talking about Camellia's parents when she started crying that night, Camellia still wanted to know more. The next time she asked him it was in the middle of the day:

"When Mama died, did she go hard, Anselm?"

Anselm evaded her question and instead got off on another facet of the Stephens's last years that was just as painful for Camellia to hear....

"You mean Mama and Papa were actually *on welfare* toward the end?"

Anselm nodded.

Camellia hung her head. "And to think I could have helped them... and didn't. But at least you did."

Anselm laughed bitterly. "What I gave them was next to nothing, as I had next to nothing. I've always loved the water, but I've been no good as a waterman. I'd get to daydreaming about you—thinking I was hearing you singing—and then, not paying attention to what I was doing, I'd swamp my boat and have to call for Coast Guard help. Jim kept a lookout for me, too.

"Anyway, the county welfare department was after me a few years ago because of what little money I did give your parents. A case worker named Connie Cerajik came back here to see me. Later your mother happened to mention Connie was a distant LeCates relative of hers. Connie did somewhat resemble your mother's features when

Miss Mary was much younger—the ash-blond hair, the aristocratic face. But there the resemblance ended.

"I took an immediate dislike to Connie Cerajik. For one thing, she had a bohunk married name and no doubt had married into that same filthy, hateful east Wintergreen County clan of Slavs and Poles that my brothers and sisters all married into. Not that my Scandinavian/Kraut family was any better, but still and all....

"For another thing, I didn't like people coming here to my cabin, stirring up my critters. And I was not about to disclose to this Connie Cerajik any amounts of money I was giving to your parents and that's what she was trying to find out.

"She also was after me for another reason. She said she was clearing welfare eligibility for a Karl and Maude Jurgensen in east Wintergreen County, and they had told her they thought their youngest son, Olaf, was living on Bell's Island, but he had run away from home when only a teenager.

"Connie Cerajik asked me, 'Would you happen to be related to the Karl Jurgensen family who lives over there in back of old Camp Conover near that Mennonite settlement?'

"'Never heard of 'em,' I said. 'And my name's *Anselm* Jurgensen. I'm from South Dakota originally'.

"I don't think I convinced her one little bit because she kept on talking and said that the income of all adult children of an aged couple applying for welfare had to be determined in order for the couple's eligibility to be established. She said she had gotten income statements from all the other Jurgensen adult children.

"'Well, I'm sorry I can't help you,' I said and motioned her toward the door. She left mad as a hornet and I felt unnerved. But I don't think she ever mentioned my local family to your parents. Your mother never brought the subject up to me. And Connie Cerajik never came back here again, either.

"For all those years that nobody but you, Camellia, ever knew that I was really 'from around here', and I wasn't about to have your parents find out then. If my people had been any kind of decent people, it would have been different. My 'ole man' was nothing but a bit of Danish-Norwegian crap that filtered out from the Delaware Swedes. But oh, my! He thought he was all-American and, true, he was second generation or so and he had no accent. My mother, however, was a German immigrant girl in New York City, trying to make a living prostituting and nightclub singing. The 'ole man' claimed he 'saved her from a life of sin by marrying her'. Hmph! Some life she had with him. Drunk all the time on his moonshine whiskey so she wouldn't feel the pain when he beat her up. But I've told you all this before, years ago."

Then Anselm added: "The only good thing I ever got out of growing up in that family was learning the principle of the distilling apparatus the 'ole man' used to make his moonshine whiskey.

"The 'ole man' made whiskey out of everything he grew on the farm—even tomatoes. Sold that moonshine to the Mennonites at cut-rate prices so they'd let his kids attend their parochial school. Everybody thought we were Mennonites, but we weren't anything. The 'ole man' was a dropped-out Lutheran; our mother a kicked-out Catholic. But I've told you all this before."

Camellia murmured, "Umm, umm." She didn't want to hear about Anselm's family. Her heart was still aching for her own.

A week or so later Camellia again asked Anselm about her mother's death. When he again changed the subject, Camellia knew she was going to have to get into his diaries if she was ever to have an answer.

The next day she waited until he took his boat out in the river to check its repaired engine. Then she started her search. Anselm had not hidden the diaries and it wasn't too hard for Camellia to locate the entries for which she was looking of a couple of years back:

> *All night long I tried to locate a doctor to come to the Tu-Rest Home. A neighbor lady was caring for Miss Mary as best she could. After Doc Feldman died last winter, it was as good as the end of Miss Mary, too. For all her church going and church serving, she still had doubts about God's goodness and forgiveness, but she did not have any doubts about Doc Feldman's needles!*
>
> *A doctor from Royal Hall came at 2:30 A.M. He walked past me and into the downstairs bedroom where Miss Mary was dying. I could feel the hot night air still hanging heavy over the island, and that sense of ominous foreboding, that kind of bad night so often filled with sickness, sadness, and death.*
>
> *Mr. Stephens and I waited in the hallway next to Miss Mary's downstairs bedroom. Mr. Stephens was sitting silently, his forearms across his knees, his hands clasped, his head down. I winced at the sounds of anguish I heard coming from the bedroom.*
>
> *In my mind I heard bits of music*—Nearer, My God to Thee:
>
> Though like a wanderer,
> The sun gone down.
> Darkness be over me;
> My rest a stone.
> Yet in my dreams I'll be
> Nearer, my God, to thee....

The sounds in the bedroom ceased. Miss Mary's struggles were over. The doctor and the neighbor lady came into the hallway. She took Mr. Stephens's hand and said quietly, "Mary's gone, Thomas." He gave a short sigh and a nod of his head, and somehow I felt—in spite of all the past, Miss Mary's one misstep and all that resulted from it—that he was now seeing her safe in Heaven.

Or if on joyful wing
Cleaving the sky,
Sun, moon, and stars forgot
Upward I fly.
Still all my song shall be
Nearer, my God, to thee,
Nearer, my God, to thee,
Nearer, my God, to thee.

Whether it was "on joyful wing" for Miss Mary or not, I do not know. But for those of us left behind, the long hard wait was over.

Some other neighbors, aroused by the arrival of the doctor, came to the Tu-Rest Home to "see to" Mr. Stephens. I slipped quietly from the house.

I walked out into the roadway and headed back toward Little Bell's. There was a cooling in the air, that cooling that often comes after an oppressively hot and humid summer night, that cooling that comes just before the first light in the eastern sky signals the new day.

In this new dawn, everything seemed to be breathing a sigh of relief and whispering that the heat, the fever, the anguish, and the dying of the previous night were over now and peace had come to the one who had struggled so long. Peace and a brand new day.

It was 4 A.M. now and I could hear the first waterman in their boats preparing to leave the harbor. That slow, rhythmic, repetitive "tok—tok—tok—tok" of the work boat engines sounded to me like a requiem for Miss Mary. I knew I wouldn't be going out to fish my trot lines today. Bell's Island and working on the water *would never be the same again.*

It's not so much that Miss Mary died in physical torment—many of us are destined to do that—but that she died (as she had lived), feeling she was a sinner. How strange that although Mr. Stephens forgave her, she could not see God *as forgiving her.*

The tears were pouring down Camellia's face and she didn't notice Anselm come in the cabin until she heard him say, "Damn motor still won't run right."

Seeing her with his diaries and crying as she was, he said, "If you haven't already done so, might as well go on a few months ahead and read about your father's death."

Camellia did....

> *It was a quick and easy death from a stroke and a few moments before the end, his speech came back a little and he said, "...just...want to be...with...Mary...." Then he smiled vaguely and slipped away. It was like he was really seeing Miss Mary...and seeing her in Heaven...beckoning to him.*

Camellia pushed the diaries aside and said irritably, "Papa always did see Mama from the surface. Just because a woman *looks like* an angel doesn't mean she is one."

"True," said Anselm. "*You* look like a *whore* (and I mean that as a compliment), but you aren't. And your mother wasn't a bad woman, either. Troubled, maybe, but not bad."

Camellia could tell Anselm was still downhearted over losing his surrogate mother.

He said, "I bet half the married women in the world and most of the single ones have dreamed of, if no more, of doing what your mother did with that roomer at the Tu-Rest Home. Just one-time-only physical sex and nothing more. And I'll bet plenty of married women have actually done it, too—with the delivery man, with the preacher when he visited when hubby wasn't home, or with a brother-in-law. Whoever was available and not waiting for your mother's type of rationalization: that their husbands had quit sex for religion. Most of 'em don't get pregnant. Your mother did."

As Anselm jabbered on, two ideas kept revolving around each other in Camellia's mind. Maybe it was because of her recent conversation with Anselm about Virginia's mother, Doris, and past tourists on Bell's Island. Maybe it was the realization that Virginia Stephens Carrambarro was all Camellia had left of her Mama. And though she couldn't do anything for Mama now, she could for Virginia. And though the island's past glory with tourists was gone, the old Bell's Island Inn was still standing. How odd that our buildings outlive their owners!

"Anselm, what if I were to buy the old Bell's Island Inn and reopen it as a grand hotel? Even after I pay Uncle Sam all the back taxes and penalties accumulated on those old accounts of mine, there'll still be enough, Nick says, to do pretty much anything I want. I'd also like to set up a trust fund for Virginia's twins—the doctor says it's going to be twins, you know."

Anselm didn't say anything. Did Camellia detect jealousy? Did he want *all* her affection and attention...and...money?

Maybe she'd better lay low for awhile on the Bell's Island Inn suggestion, but she did intend to see that Virginia's kids had something special.

Whenever Camellia and Anselm or Camellia by herself went out from the cabin and onto Bell's Island or into Royal Hall to buy groceries and supplies, Camellia wrapped a scarf around her head and put on dark glasses. She still didn't want to be recognized. And she was egotistical enough to think people would still recognize and remember her after twenty years absence.

She wanted to remain incognito, yet in a sense she didn't want to. The singer/actress in her couldn't stand to be ignored indefinitely. Anselm said she looked like a tourist; only there weren't any tourists on Bell's Island any more. The thought of the old inn of her grandparents kept recurring to Camellia. She wished she could turn the clock back to those glorious days when tourists *were* on the island.

Chapter Nine

Camellia and Anselm couldn't say, "The honeymoon is over," because they didn't have one. They were snipping at each other almost from the start of their residence on Little Bell's. Maybe it was the summer heat that wore on and on clear into the autumn.

Or maybe it was because, although they had been lovers in the sex sense a long time back, they had never actually lived together in the day-to-day grind of cooking, cleaning up, doing the laundry, etc., within elbow reach of each other.

Now, though they had a compulsive need to be near each other all the time, they were getting on each other's nerves.

Camellia had vowed to humor Anselm, but she was often out of patience with his endless explanations about what he was now calling his "chicken experimental station." And Camellia knew he was equally bored with all her talk about her scraps—those half-done musical compositions she was going to complete just as soon as her piano was shipped down from her former Baltimore apartment. She felt she had to at least talk out loud about composing because she dared not say anything more about performing—that part of her musical career now gone.

Camellia still wasn't cooking to suit Anselm. And he hadn't entirely given up the sloppy ways he'd gotten into as a hermit—like not taking a bath very often. Camellia one day gave him the classic Bell's Island insult: "Anselm! You smell like a Gainsbiddler!"

Though they had done a superb job of cleaning up the cabin and the area immediately around it, they had missed some spots. The little island every now and then resounded with Camellia's shrieks as she opened a cupboard or closet door and was confronted with a skeleton or two of some of Anselm's long-deceased wildlife critters. More than once, Virginia, when coming to visit was greeted at the cabin door by Camellia holding up what was left of some by-now-barely-recognizable species.

Virginia fussed with her Aunt Camellia for humoring Anselm so much. "Why does he expect you to wait on him all the time? Why doesn't he undo his own soft-boiled 'ekk', and why isn't he the one—not you—to take outside these old animal carcasses you keep finding? He's not that sick now. And his sickness probably wasn't anything but depression anyhow."

Camellia said, "He's trading on my guilt for having deserted him and my family those twenty years. You know, I could have at least contacted someone when I came out of my amnesia after the first two years in Baltimore, but I was enjoying a good career with Baltimore Opera Theater, and I was afraid of getting caught up with the Stephenses all over again. They did sponge a lot off me—emotionally as well as financially. And the longer I waited to contact anyone, the more I feared Anselm would have found himself another woman. If he had, I didn't want to know about it."

Virginia said, "Jim never mentioned anything about Anselm having any other woman, and I think Jim would have told me because he's a talker, you know. Frankly, Jim thought Anselm was going to die. And so did the Veteran's Hospital, and I think he would have if you hadn't gotten there when you did....Have you told him about The Met yet?"

"Um hmm. I didn't intend to ever tell him, but it sort of slipped out."

"It's been on your mind, surely."

"Yes, but I wanted Anselm more than The Met. Without him no success would mean much. With him success is no longer necessary."

"Do you really mean that, Aunt Camellia?"

"Virginia, don't get me confused," snapped Camellia. "I'm having enough trouble keeping my eggs in the basket these days."

They heard a whoop from inside the cabin and Anselm exclaiming, "There's another one! There's another one!"

"Another corpse, carcass?" yelped Virginia.

Camellia laughed. "No, I think he means another 'Camellia-rism.' I should have said 'keeping my wits about me' or 'getting my ducks in a row' or something. Anselm's been collecting those malapropisms of mine for years. He's got a whole notebook full. Just between you and me, I don't think I ever said half of them. I think he made most of them up to pass the time away when he was out in his crab boat fishing his trot lines all those years I was gone."

Anselm's book of "Camellia-risms" got them all in a jolly mood, and when Virginia said she was good at sketching, they let her have a go at illustrating some of the "Camellia-risms," which were accompanied by Anselm's translations. There was quite a list from which to choose:

Anselm, have you ever read that dirty book—Lady Chitterling's Lawyer (Lady Chatterley's Lover)?

That'll put salt in your pepper (lead in your pencil).

Your advice fell on stony ears (stony ground/deaf ears).

It's clear as a bell pepper out tonight (clear as a bell).

That's a slap-ass way of doing anything (slap-dash/half-ass).

Don't rock the apple boat (rock the boat/upset the apple cart).

She was wearing a broomtail skirt (broomstick skirt).

Is the band ever going to learn to play Entrance of the Gladiolas (Entrance of the Gladiators)?

Let sleeping dogs bury their own dead bones. (Let sleeping dogs lie./Let the dead bury their dead.)

Anselm, you do things in such a half-hazard way (hap-hazard/half-assed).

I heard it through the grapeyard (the grapevine).

My investment counselor says I should purchase some more blue chopsticks (blue-chip stocks).

It's a kettleful of different fish (horse of a different color/fine kettle of fish).

I think blacks could get in the D.A.R. if they could prove they were related to Custis LaCrisp (Crispus Attucks).

Well, you certainly have thrown a fishhook into my plans (a monkey wrench).

Don't just rest on your paddles (your laurels/your oars).

Happy as a cow at high tide (clam).

Do you think we should try sixty-one (sixty-nine)?

That's nothing but an old cock-and-cunt story (cock-and-bull).

Don't put all your pennies in one pocket (eggs in one basket).

That's terrible. That's nothing more than the cat calling the pottle back (pot calling the kettle black).

We're having hail balls as big as gallstones (hail stones as big as golf balls).

I can't get my eggs in the bucket today (ducks in a row).

It's time to separate the sheep from the chaff (sheep from the goats/chaff from the wheat).

It will drive you bazookas (bananas).

You're nothing but an old night hog (night owl).

Don't put all your chickens in one pot (eggs in one basket).

Are you all screwed away (squared away)?

Anselm, if you really believe in what you are doing, wild monkeys won't be able to stop you (wild horses).

Anselm, we argue too much. We are always nitsplitting (nitpicking/hairsplitting).

A bird in the hand is worth a fish in the bush (two in the bush).

I hear the writing on the wall (see the writing).

You're getting your kettle of fish (pound of flesh).

You have to do it, so you might as well button down to it (buckle down).

You can't put all your potatoes in one basket (eggs).

She dropped him like a hot tomato (potato).

Don't let anybody pull the fur over your eyes (the wool).

If I stay cooped up in this cabin much longer, I'll get hydrophobia (claustrophobia).

That's a slip-ass way of doing anything (half-assed/ slipshod).

You didn't come within a tinker's damn of it (a country mile).

They are feathering their own pockets when they do that (feathering their nests/lining their pockets).

You can dish it up, but you can't take it out with you. (You can dish it out, but you can't take it.)

There's a mosquito in here as big as a tomahawk (as big as a hawk).

You're nothing but an old jerk-off (old goof-off).

You've got to grab the bull by the balls and go ahead with it (by the horns).

It came by mail. What did you think it came by—pony pigeon (pony express/carrier pigeon)?

This pump has lost its hard (its prime).

We've all been bull-dozzled (bamboozled).

Just sitting there waiting for the anvil to fall (the gavel).

Like six in one, three ounces in the other (six in one, half-dozen in the other).

Don't put all your shoes in one box (eggs in one basket).

You're really burning your bushes behind you. (Your bridges, though sometimes she said britches!)

He's nothing but a clothesline homosexual (closet).

Nervous as a fishhook (as a fish).

When it starts to freeze, wrap it. (An old Gainsbiddle expression—"When it starts to rot, freeze it.")

*They got on each other's hair (each other's nerves/*in *each other's hair).*

Anselm, will you never learn to keep your drawers closed (the cupboards in the kitchen)?

Anselm, we fit together just like tongue-and-cheek molding (tongue-and-groove molding).

You're quiet as a tombstone tonight (as a tomb).

If your power mower won't start, maybe it needs a new fireplug (spark plug).

He's nothing but a tin-pot journalist (tinhorn).

You said a handful there (a mouthful).

The sky is as yellow as saccharin (as saffron).

It's like eating your dessert before you put your socks on (like washing your feet with your socks on).

We hadn't done it for so long; that's why you went off like Old Friendly (like Old Faithful).

They've left you in libido (in limbo).

*Everything has two sides—even a bottom. (A board, although a bottom—a butt—*does *have two sides)*

Quiet as a church mouse (as a mouse).

You've got more problems than Job's got liver pills (than Job/than Carter has liver pills).

You've got the ass before the cart (the cart before the horse/ got things ass-backwards).

Deep in Davy Jones' bosom (locker/Abraham's bosom).

You're getting your quart of blood (pound of flesh).

Blind as a goose (as a bat).

I've got other fish in the fire (fish to fry/irons in the fire).

That's one way to kill the bull with two stones (kill two birds with one stone).

When things get really bad, you can always throw in the dishcloth (the towel).

It's just somebody's screw-pot theory (crackpot).

Anselm, you're way off in center field (left field).

As honest as an open-end sandwich (an open-face sandwich).

What is the tune of that Australian national anthem— Marching Matilda (Waltzing Matilda)?

As hard as trying to find a nigger in a haystack (a needle).

I think it's a white herring (red).

A caged bird dies hard (?).

You better do it before the boomerang falls (the gavel/ the guillotine/before the boom is lowered.).

Maybe we could build a little placebo down by the water (gazebo).

You first have to get your balls in a row (ducks).

You don't want to bite the hand that laid the golden egg, do you (bite the hand that feeds you/kill the hen that lays the golden egg)?

He's still green behind the ears (wet).

You have to hammer first before you can nail. (You have to crawl first before you walk.)

People who live in glass houses should wear umbrellas (?).

Seems to me they're beating up a dead tree (beating a dead horse/barking up the wrong tree).

Anselm, you look like the goose that swallowed the golden egg (cat that swallowed the canary).

A dog could do the same thing if he had a tail (if he had a hand).

Happy as a clam at half-tide (high tide).

Anselm, you are more of a physic than you think (a psychic).

You don't have to read music to be a musician any more than you have to read Chinese to be a Chinaman(?).

Anselm, you need somebody on which to try your ideas out. You need a pissing post (a sounding board).

People who live in glass houses should have two sets of keys (?).

They just want to get a finger in the pudding (in the pie).

He's a sort of jackass of all trades (Jack-of-all-trades).

Do you want me to put saltpepper in your peter (Saltpetre in your pepper—or in your food)?

It's like having a kink in your intestinals (what? where?).

I like wash 'n roll clothing (wash 'n wear).

I don't want to grassle with that right now (grapple/ wrassle).

You have to take this with a bar of soap (a grain of salt).

It's different kettle of figs (kettle of fish).

Where is your octoruna (ocarina)?

He's going from petal to post (from pillar to post).

Sometimes I think you are a pig in a china closet (a bull— said of my clumsiness).

It's a case where you're no longer going ahead, but just spinning your oars (spinning your wheels/resting on your oars).

He's got so much hot air in him, if you threw him overboard, he'd float like a bobbin (a bobber—how could a waterman's daughter miss that one?).

Well, I guess they are just beating their own horn (their own drum/blowing their own horn).

Anselm, I've got a crow to pick with you (a bone).

I heard it out of the corner of my ear (saw it out of the corner of my eye).

It goes over like a wet balloon (lead balloon).

It'll get you climbing up a tree (up a wall).

You might take a petal from their rose (a page from their book).

Another turner has been crossed (corner has been turned).

Anselm, you must burn your britches behind you (your bridges).

They were so unreceptive, Anselm didn't even get to second base with them (first base).

He seems to have soft palate of the brain (softening of the brain, maybe?).

The trouble with us in those days, we never had our wheels on the ground (our feet).

Do you see any moondogs, Anselm (sundogs—rainbow coloured patches in the high thin clouds over the sun)?

You cling to a cobweb as though it were a rope. (Another way of saying "grasping at straws.")

He's not used to getting a square shake from anybody (a square deal/ a fair shake).

Don't sit there like a toad on a log (a bump on a log).

It's like bumping your head against a dead wall (a stone wall/coming to a dead end).

You wouldn't want to be swallowing any live raisins, would you, Anselm? (whole raisins; she was chiding me for trying to eat raisin bran without my teeth.)

Are you trying to say I hootchy-kootchy'd you into getting appointed bandmaster at the school? (Probably "hocus-pocus'd," because everybody said she used her "gypsy magic" to get me that job.)

You wouldn't want to buy a pig in a bottle, would you (a pig in a poke)?

Virginia was stumped at the very beginning as to how to illustrate *Lady Chitterling's Lawyer*.

Camellia said, "Haven't you ever eaten chitterlings, Virginia, you being raised down South?"

"Well, ah—ah really doan know," Virginia drawled.

"Or maybe you called them 'chitlins'."

Anselm butted in. "Which is polite talk for '*shit*-lins'. They're fried hog guts—poor people's food. Colored folks love 'em, so I've been told."

Virginia never admitted whether she was on talking—or eating—terms with chitterlings, but she sketched a chic, curlicue'd intestinal-like creature regaled in laces and jewels and labelled "Lady C." and had her entering the law office of D.H. Lawrence, Esq. with a mysterious brown-bagged package under her arm, looking suspiciously like a book.

Yes, Virginia was familiar all right with *Lady Chatterley's Lover*, but as for the chitterlings...?

Virginia had the most fun with this one, drawing a very unhappy bull and a very courageous Anselm:

"Anselm, you've got to grab the bull by the balls and go ahead with it."

Camellia liked this one the best: A devilishly smiling, slanty-eyed Oriental stockbroker holding up a pair of blue chopsticks with dollar signs on their ends. "My investment counselor says I should purchase some more blue chopsticks."

They played "Draw Us Some Camellia-risms" almost every time Virginia came for a visit. And in the meantime Camellia continued to humor Anselm and grant him his whims.

His most absurd request was when he asked Camellia to take a gang of his animals and birds to the Royal Hall vet. He claimed they needed all sorts of shots and checkups, and though he had managed to get his old truck in running condition and had loaded it with crates and cages full of wildlife, at the last minute he said he just didn't feel like going himself.

He tried to get Jim Stephens to do it, but Jim flatly refused, saying, "I ain't gonna take no screamin', howlin' load of shitty livestock to no goddam vet!"

Jim was one of those kind who'd go a long way with anybody, but when he decided to stop, that was it.

Anselm looked at Camellia....

At first she said, "I cawnt drive no truck!" She was fracturing the King's English and doing it with her British accent.

Anselm again looked at her...pleadingly....

"All right, I'll do it, but only if Nick or Virginia will drive."

Nick had some of his pre-law classes at Halburg State, but Virginia was free, so she and Camellia went off to Royal Hall in Anselm's rusty old pickup with all those rickety, rusty, manured-up crates and cages full of screaming, screeching, yowling critters jammed into the back.

Camellia was putting on her best front ever, theatrical-wise. More appropriately she should have put on a pair of coveralls, but for some unfathomable reason, since she always dressed down when going out, she was decked out like a prima donna at a reception following some gala opening night.

She was adorned in high heels, sheer black hose, and lots of black lace. She was carrying on her wrist a sheer black lace hanky that she was swishing around in the air. Her thick dark hair with attractive highlights of silver was elaborately done in masses on top of her head, ringlets about her face, and tight curls around her shoulders.

She was ultra slick and chic, poised and posing, and somehow she managed to stay that way without getting a spot or wrinkle on her attire or even uttering a single Bell's Island cuss word the whole trip to Royal Hall, even though she and Virginia had stop the truck several times to adjust and rearrange those crates and cages full of squealing critters as they kept falling over and causing their wire doors to fly open, threatening to set loose the whole menagerie on the roadside.

When they got to Royal Hall and the vet's office, Camellia was still all smiles, and there was that delightful twinkle in her dark eyes that nothing could obliterate. But she did seem somewhat out of breath as she and Virginia went in the vet's waiting room.

This particular vet did not make appointments and took patients on a first-come, first-served basis, so Camellia approached the attendant behind the desk and began to say who she was and why she was there.

She was about to launch into one of those stilted sentences, the kind she often fell into when she was overwrought about something and overacting to compensate for it, sounding almost as though she were translating literally from some foreign language into English. Still and all, she was cheerfully loud and self-assured and brimming all over with smiles. With the deep resonance of her mezzo-soprano voice, she announced, "Good ahfternoon. I ahm Mrs. Jurgensen. I hahve come for the sterilization of Mr. Jurgensen...ulp!...."

She had run out of breath! That was as far as she could get on first crack. The vet's attendant and the whole waiting room full of people and pets had been watching and listening to her, for she had that commanding presence and beautiful visage which, when she was in the right mood, could draw immediate and admiring attention wherever she went.

So, everybody fell into dead silence and waited eagerly for further revealing words on the "sterilization of Mr. Jurgensen." But they didn't come. Had Camellia forgotten her lines? Perish the thought!! And what was this about sterilizing *Mr. Jurgensen*?!

Someone in the waiting room said, *sotto voce*: "She's Mrs. Jurgensen and she's come for the 'sterilization of *Mr. Jurgensen*?'" And another voice said, also *sotto voce*, "What she wants is a urologist, not a veterinarian!" And yet another voice said, and this one a little louder, "Maybe 'Mr. Jurgensen' is a cat!"

Camellia, though she'd heard every word that had been said, was not the least bit abashed, but turned and smiled graciously at everyone, then turned back to the vet's attendant and started all over again. This time she got through the whole sentence: "I've come for the sterilization of Mr. Jurgensen's ducks!"

The attendant, who must have been new on the job, was all the more confused now and stated incredulously, "You've come for the sterilization of Mr. Jurgensen's ducts: d—u—c—t—s?" A ripple of laughter went all around the room.

The veterinarian himself, hearing all this from one of his examining rooms, stepped out, all smiles in his white coat, and ventured to say, "Ah yes. Yes! The *immunization* of Mr. Jurgensen's ducks: d—u—c—k—s and his geese and shore birds and all. Ah yes! And you're *Mrs.* Jurgensen. How nice! How nice!" He was looking Camellia up and down and probably marveling that Jurgensen, whom he'd known for a number of years, had finally gotten himself a wife...and such a wife! "Yes, *Mrs. Jurgensen*!" the vet kept repeating.

"Yes, that's what I said," Camellia returned, with an air of pique, but she tempered it with that ever-engaging smile of hers and that twinkle in her eye. She added, "It's the chicken shots I think he gets."

Again the waiting room went into a titter. What on earth were chicken shots? But the vet clarified things by saying aloud, "Yes. Yes! We do them periodically for Mr. Jurgensen for his waterfowl and the distemper and rabies shots for his raccoons, rabbits, beagles, and squirrels. Ah yes, *Mrs*. Jurgensen. Yes. Yes!"

Camellia eventually deduced that "chicken shots" and rabies shots for anything but cats and dogs were probably ineffective and little more than sugar and water injections, but if Anselm *thought* they were good for his critters, the vet, like all good doctors, apparently went along with him, believing in keeping one of his best customers happy.

Meanwhile, Camellia's way of handling the vet was beginning to get results. It was hard to say which it was—her innate charm, the vet's curiosity about her, or maybe even a bit of "gypsy magic," but Camellia was taken next in line over that whole gang of others waiting.

The vet did all the administering of shots, etc., right at the truck, and he even repacked the crates and cages more securely so that nothing would fall off or out of place on the way back to Little Bell's Island.

As Virginia pulled away from the parking lot, Camellia was still graciously smiling, and the vet was waving his "bye-byes" to her and chuckling for all he was worth. No doubt he was fixing it all soundly in his head so as to be able to tell it over and over again to his colleagues about that glorious day when he had performed "the sterilization of Mr. Jurgensen's ducts...!"

Chapter Ten

It was coming on winter 1970 by the time Camellia's piano was shipped down from her former Baltimore apartment and placed in a side room in Anselm's cabin where—in spite of the rough-hewn walls and time-and-tide warped timbers—all was bathed in shafts of early morning sunshine cutting through the wind-swept limbs of the pine trees.

Camellia often started working on her "sunshine scraps" before dawn. Using the full range of her piano, she was simulating the effect of high, thin trilling violins as the first rays of light came into the sky. Then there was the tumbling bump of the drums, signalling, she said, "the quickening heartbeat of early dawn." Finally came the nuance of a tinkling chime bell as the first edge of the sun appeared above the horizon on the far shoreline.

Music like that indicated contentment and, reflecting that contentment, Anselm would often get breakfast for the two of them, undoing his own soft-boiled "ekk" and avoiding "der schell" that Camellia tended to leave in it.

Sometimes, though, Camellia stopped in the middle of a phrase and Anselm called out, "That sounded good. Why did you stop?"

"I didn't know where to go from there." That's the way Camellia was. She never forced her music—always let it come from her Muse. When her Muse shut up, she did, too.

Sometimes her improvisations revealed a white-hot vexation. Hearing some of it, Anselm said, "Did that music come out of *you?*"

Camellia replied, "Who knows if it's out of *me* or if it's just life in general with all its wretchedness that I am mentally picking up and tossing back?" She still could not get it out of her head that to gain one thing, you so often must give up another: Her returning to Anselm had meant letting go of The Met.

Much of what she was improvising had a disquieting air of mystery. She was trying to capture—now as in the past—those strange mental melodies and rhythms she always heard when driving through the Wintergreen County marshland outside Bell's Island. Was she hearing the lingering thoughts and emotions of her Corrigan-gypsy-Stephens forebears? Or was the marsh reflecting the dark midnight of the soul, that primordial something or other that is deep and hidden in everybody, but of which nobody cares to be reminded?

All too often there was a disturbing sadness in her music as her past neglect of her family continued to haunt her.

Some of her music was downright prurient. Nick got teed off about it one evening when he and Virginia came to visit, and Camellia was improvising concoctions of rock, spirituals, rhythm and blues, and honky-tonk all mixed together.

Her structure had thrown to the wind all the so-called "good" musical influences of the European classical school in which she had been trained in her early years, when she had been learning both voice and piano AND composition. In place of the melodic line Camellia was now using suggestions of irregular and weirdly traumatic shrills and moans and underlying rhythms that were pulsing and driving—in short, a boiling, wailing, low-class sensuality that offended Nick.

"Did *you* compose *that stuff*?" Nick chided.

"I most certainly did," said Camellia, huffing up as only she could do.

"I'd call that 'porn in music'," said Nick, shaking his head.

"Call it what you will," said Camellia, unconcerned.

Virginia started chuckling. "Aunt Camellia, I understand Wagner worked out his sexual hang-ups through his music. Is that what you're trying to do, too?"

Camellia really got angry now. "What's the matter with you two? Anything that doesn't sound like a Strauss waltz, a Sousa march, or a Methodist hymn, you don't think is music."

They all, including Camellia, laughed good-naturedly and a potential tiff was avoided.

With Camellia still working on her scraps, the holiday season was fast approaching. Christmas festoons all around the cabin replaced the horrible strings of roaches of the previous summer. There was even a light snow falling, and all seemed perfect for the holidays.

As the Carrambarros' main present, Camellia revealed she had set up a huge irrevocable trust fund for their twins-to-be, the interest on which would come monthly. However, instead of being joyously received, the gift was spurned, and the nasty scene that followed ruined everybody's Christmas and nearly fractured Camellia's relationship with Nick and Virginia.

"I don't need handouts for my kids," Nick said furiously. "Yeah, I'm still in college, but I'll be a lawyer soon and earning my own way."

Nick's parents were subsidizing him at the moment and he was embarrassed enough over that. And Virginia was the kind who reacted adversely to whatever Nick reacted adversely to. Camellia was doubly hurt because she felt Nick and Virginia were both spurning her help and preventing her from working out through Virginia some of her guilt about her mother.

The rift didn't last long, however, for come the end of January, Nick and Virginia—proud as peacocks to display their girl and boy twins, Flossie and Jesse, to "Auntie Cammie" and "Unky Andy"—were visiting again at Anselm's cabin, and the trust fund was reaffirmed in all its original magnitude.

Often when the Carrambarros visited, they found Camellia and Anselm in a hilarious mood over their renewed sexual capers. Those capers, Camellia admitted, could get interrupted if she got a musical inspiration or if Anselm heard in his head a new formula for his "chicken experimental station." Neither would hesitate to hop out of bed (often at a crucial moment) and go write something down.

Camellia said, "I lost my diaphragm one night doing that. I thought I'd left it on the piano, but I couldn't find it anywhere."

Virginia whooped. "What do you need a diaphragm for, Aunt Camellia? You're well past the change of life, aren't you?"

"Yes," said Camellia, "but you never know about Anselm!"

That kind of reasoning was challenging, to say the least. But Anselm did look great. He was fleshing out and looking like her "teddy bear" once again after six months of rejuvenated sex, "schell in der ekk," a new set of dentures, and Camellia's humoring his every whim.

"Auntie Cammie" and "Unky Andy" turned out to be top-notch baby sitters for little Flossie and Jesse. Sometimes Camellia and Anselm went to the Carrambarros's apartment near the Halburg State campus if both Nick and Virginia had to attend classes at the same time and their regular baby-sitter wasn't available, or else they brought Flossie and Jesse down to Little Bell's Island.

Camellia and Anselm took turns with each twin—feeding, diapering, and bathing—so that they wouldn't develop any partiality to one or the other.

Though Camellia was no stranger to baby-ing, having practically raised Virginia's father, Roger Stephens, those many years ago, this was an all new experience to Anselm. He had *been* the baby in his family, and even as he had gotten older and been around younger nieces and nephews, he had no shine for them and stayed away from them as much as he could.

But with Nick and Virginia's twins, he seemed to get a kick out of caring for them, although he wouldn't admit it and often complained, "If I have to change one more shitty diaper, I'm going back to being a hermit!"

But Camellia always shushed him, saying, "Now, Anselm, it's the closest we'll ever get to being parents ourselves, so let's be grateful for the opportunity to help Nick and Virginia."

In her continuing willingness to help the Carrambarros, Camellia knew she was trying to make up for having deserted the Stephens family for those many years she was careering in opera in Baltimore. Virginia was now the only one left of her immediate family, so she was heaping her attention—and her money—on this niece and her nestlings.

But she was not neglecting Anselm. Unlike many couples who find sex to be enough and so don't talk much, this pair was jabbering continuously, and there seemed to be nothing they wouldn't joke about.

Camellia told Anselm that at one time in her early life when everything was going wrong at home, especially after the birth of Roger, she'd even considered becoming a nun. "But I wasn't sure they'd take non-virgins."

(Camellia had, a long time back, told Anselm about her early and only sex encounter prior to him, and that had been with a young fellow, long since deceased, on the island.)

"Not take virgins?" snorted Anselm. "Hah! If there were any such rule, there'd be a lot of empty convents, doncha think?"

One evening they were lazing around in the cabin with the door open, listening to the peepers. The long nights and short days of earlier in the new year of 1971 were giving way to more light and milder temperatures. Camellia had been writing music all winter. She was running out of ideas. And Anselm was running out of conversation. Camellia asked him:

"Didn't you do *anything* around here during the '60s when all that racial and political unrest was going on?"

Anselm said, "I do remember one incident—the riot in Royal Hall. I had grown a big flowing red beard. I'd bought a guitar and had it strapped on me, and I was up on a platform in front of the court house, leading a choir of black singers from Halburg State in a bit off-key but nevertheless soul-tugging rendition of *We Shall Overcome*.

"Suddenly the police came with their fire hoses and billy clubs and German Shepherd dogs. They were followed by a mob of up-county rednecks and Gainsbiddle watermen armed with baseball bats and rotten eggs. The platform was shoved down and there was a grand *melee*.

"Someone in the mob saw me and yelled 'Hey, looky there! Ain't that the "Big-Bellied Dutchman" what used to be our bandmaster at Royal Hall High?'

"And the fellow beside him said, 'Yeah! And will ya lookit that red beard! Wonder what happened to the woman of his'n?'

"'What woman?'

"'Oh, you know....That fancy lady music teacher we had at Royal Hall High. What was her name? Miss Camellia something or other. She warn't from around here, I don't think. Didn't talk like she was.'

"'Oh, yeah. I remember her. She drownded in the marsh off Bell's Island.'

"'Naw, that warn't it. She went away somewhere to have his baby and never come back.'

"'No, no, that warn't it. She got out there in that marsh to drown herself because he'd done got *another woman* pregnant, but a big bird come down and et up Miss Camellia's body, and that's why they never found her.'

"'Naw, you've got it all wrong. It warn't that way at all. It was....'

"'Hey! Willya stop hollering your rotten beery breath in my face...!'

"'I will if you quit shovin' me...!'

"And the two of them got to hitting on each other and soon dragged others from the mob and the police into it. The Wintergreen County farmers and Gainsbiddler watermen were more interested in cursing and beating on each other and on the police with their baseball bats and rotten eggs than they were in using them on me or the blacks or the choir...or on...."

Anselm stopped abruptly in mid-sentence.

"Or on what?" asked Camellia.

Anselm shrugged off her question with "Amazing, isn't it? The local rabble's nit-sized mentality."

Anselm would say no more. He seemed troubled about something. Then Camellia realized one day that Anselm's diaries were not where he usually kept them. She couldn't find them anywhere in the cabin. Was there something in them he was trying to hide?

It was not until Camellia was nosing around in Anselm's boat, after he'd pulled it up on the shore, taken off the motor, and carried it to Gainsbiddle in his truck for more repairs, that she spied the diaries. And it was just too much temptation not to look for entries around about the time of "that Royal Hall Freedom March" back in the '60s.

She found only one entry written almost a year later. Anselm was philosophizing on a variety of subjects like injustice, fate, etc., and inevitably the entry got around to women. Anselm had never had much use for women in general, Camellia recalled....

Women....They're not worth taking our pants off for....

Like that Myra I found during that Royal Hall Freedom March. When I fell down on her to keep her from being mauled by the police dogs, something happened. I wanted to stay down on her.

When the riot was over, she was still around. I asked did she want us to go someplace. I had my truck.

I didn't want to take her to Little Bell's Island. She said to drive over toward old Camp Conover way.

She was a day student at Halburg State. But she was also a bohunk. Enough to make me stop right there. But the animal in me wouldn't let me stop....

There was an old trailer in back of the old cannery—once one of those fat silvery things—now more like a flat rusty thing. She said we could go in there. It was her uncle's trailer, but he had died and the trailer was unused...and unlocked....

Camellia was getting madder by the moment. Not so much mad that Anselm had a woman back then, but mad that she had not seized a similar opportunity and had a man—such as Merv Roth, her manager, when she was singing for Baltimore Opera Theater. Merv had wanted that sort of thing, but Camellia had resisted.

Resisted up until the time Merv had her booked for The Met audition, and then she had promised him "Yes!" But she never got to pay off that promise, nor get to The Met. Virginia had come on the scene and it had dramatically changed.

Camellia read on....

The trailer was at the end of a bad lane and we had to walk up. There was one other shack-like house back there with a crippled man living in it.

That night the pine trees were dark against the rising moon. The cannery was still stinking, though it probably hadn't been in operation for fifteen years. The crippled man passed by us, limping out to the end of the lane to check his mailbox, and his dog was limping along beside him. Myra said he wouldn't come out in the daytime. He never got any mail except his social security check once a month, but he limped out to the end of the lane every night anyhow to look in the mail box.

No cars could get up that lane. Myra said a fire engine once tried it. Somebody had seen a blaze back there and turned in the alarm, thinking it might be the crippled man's home, and they had pity on him.

The pine branches arching over the lane were hitting the firemen as their truck moved along, and they were chopping them off with their axes. The blaze turned out to be only the crippled man burning trash.

Well, Myra was willing and able, and that's about all that could be said of her.

She was a bohunk. Myra Wrokje. She might have been a cousin of mine for all I knew. The Jurgensens had a habit of cohabiting with the bohunks. Looks like I wasn't exempt, either.

She was a little chickadee-like woman—cute for the time being—but the kind who when she gets older, will turn into that typical, fat, dumpy, bohunk woman with the blank look on the face.

Most of the mornings when we'd wake up together, the first thing I'd see was that dirty white ribbon she tied around her hair at night, and one loop of it was always undone.

She had a soft, little girl, whiny-type talk, and that made me angry. She asked if I was the Jurgensen who ran away from home. And that made me angry, too. I must have become a legend out there. A legend like Camellia. Dammit! I was being reminded of Camellia. Even by this temporary little tart. After three months of Myra, I'd had enough.

To have a woman that you don't love...it's only a tad better than masturbation.

Camellia laughed out loud at that last observation. Anselm was a hopeless romantic!

Like the animal in Anselm that had needed its day, Camellia's need for public performance and public adoration was working on her. She had been hibernating with Anselm on Little Bell's for going on a year. And though she loved the soughing of the pine trees and even found a certain resonance in the shrieking of Anselm's experimental birds, which she incorporated into some of her music, she was yearning like crazy for public exposure.

Finding out about Anselm's woman and being sharply reminded of her own never-consummated affair with Merv Roth and her aborted Met bid made Camellia think again about buying and re-opening the old Bell's Island Inn. She could be hostess there like her Grandmother LeCates had so nobly been.

She could be a "*singing* hostess" like she'd been a "singing waitress" in Valiano's restaurant in Baltimore before getting her start in opera.

She still resisted saying anything to Anselm about all this, knowing he wouldn't want her to get involved with something that might cause her to neglect him. He hadn't responded too negatively to her trust fund for Virginia and Nick's twins or to babysitting for them because he liked the Carrambarros, and he knew Virginia had been the one who had reunited him with Camellia.

Buying and reopening the inn was a different matter. Then it occurred to Camellia if she financed and applauded a bona fide "chicken experimental station" on Little Bell's for Anselm, maybe he wouldn't mind her indulging a hobby, too, one that was a little more "out front" than the isolation of composing music. Also, maybe they could move out of that cramped cabin and into a grand suite in the inn. Camellia was made for luxury and she couldn't stay away from it for long.

So, as spring 1971 blossomed on Little Bell's, it was time to officially come out of the wraps. No doubt Jim Stephens had already whispered it around that Camellia was alive and back on the island. Yet nobody she passed on the street or in the stores, either on Bell's Island or in Royal Hall, gave any indication they recognized her, even when she stopped using her "tourist" disguise.

In a few places, like the Royal Hall bank where she had opened an account in the name of Charity Croswell, she remained just that, as it was the name on her driver's license, marriage certificate, credit cards, and even her social security card. Charity Croswell had been her official identity in Baltimore and was what she had brought with her to Wintergreen County, and she'd been slow to change it.

Anselm often pointed out people to her on the street and said who they were. Camellia wouldn't have otherwise recognized them because they had changed so. She was egotistical enough to believe *she* hadn't changed, and she hadn't, not all that much.

As for Anselm, beyond a mere nod of recognition or a grudging "Hello," nobody was paying much attention to him when they went out together. Hermits are not all that popular, though Anselm had been well liked years before when he had been working for the Stephenses.

Jim Stephens had intimated that the legends of Camellia's disappearance that had been so entertaining at the time had now all but been forgotten.

The younger ones growing up who had never known Camellia couldn't have cared less. The older ones just forgot, had died themselves, or moved away.

Since no "Camellia Stephens Day" had ever been instituted on Bell's Island or in the county, there was no way she could have been immortalized.

Anselm was not one for publicity, and since he had no money back then, he could not have, even if he had wanted to, made some large donation to something or other in memory of Camellia and thus have gotten at least a bronze plaque with her name on it installed somewhere.

Realizing all this, Camellia was beginning to think nobody really gave a hoot about her then—or even now that she was alive and back. Well, she'd show 'em. She bet they wouldn't forget her again....

Her first step, with Nick's help, was to get her Camellia Stephens name back with its new appendage Jurgensen. This necessitated much consultation and verifications from the Valianos in Baltimore, her friends and mentors who had gotten her Charity Croswell identity established for her early on in her stay there. Proving that Charity Croswell and Camellia Stephens were the same person was a little tricky. But the Valianos were savvy people and had remained as good friends even after Camellia left Baltimore.

Once the name adjusting was done, the way was cleared for Camellia to retrieve her unclaimed accounts and securities and settle her tax debts with Uncle Sam and the State of Maryland. Still having plenty of wealth left, she put up the securities for a construction loan and encouraged a delighted Anselm to start building his "chicken experimental station" on Little Bell's.

Then she bought the inn....

Chapter Eleven

When people saw work starting at the inn, Camellia, with her old flamboyance renewed, said, yes! she had bought the inn; yes! she was "the" Camellia Stephens; yes! she was alive and well, thank you; and yes! the "new" Bell's Island Inn was going to be a colossal thing.

The initial work of renovating had given her some additional ideas. She had pondered her early youth there when her first music teacher and mentor, Claudie, and her mother, Mary Stephens, had put on those little amateur musical productions for the out-of-town guests. If amateur productions then, why not real opera now? Camellia's brain was working overtime.

Yes, she told everybody, the inn was to have a grand ballroom with a mammoth stage at one end, and some of the guest rooms were to be designated as quarters for aspiring young opera singers. Her opera school workshop, Camellia said, would be in the old gypsy tavern across the inlet on the Wintergreen County mainland.

Camellia was also telling everybody she saw on the island and in Royal Hall that she was going to have the inn painted white with red and black trim on the outside—red around the window woodwork, black shutters, red railings on the upper porch deck, and red chimneys. The columns on the front and the remainder of the facade would be white.

When some of the island people seemed amused and said to Camellia, "Sounds like you're turning it into a steamboat!" she only smiled her magnificent smile and said, "Oh, you'll like it when you see it!"

But Anselm said he'd heard some people say, "Steamboat, hell! Sounds more like a damn whorehouse and she aims to fill it with a bunch of hippie musicians from out of town."

And others were saying, "Maybe we'd better look into the county zoning laws and see if we can get a case against her before this goes too far."

Camellia said to Anselm, "Looks like the people of Bell's Island feel their provincial way of life is being threatened."

One thing for sure, they wouldn't forget her this time!

Camellia said an additional feature of the "new" Bell's Island Inn would be a tour boat to take the inn's guests and other persons visiting the island all around the river and sound and out into the bay on excursions. "I have designated Anselm to be the captain of the tour boat," she announced proudly.

But Anselm protested and said, "Camellia, If I run a tour boat, when will I have time to work with my chickens?"

Camellia replied playfully, "I was hoping you'd let me turn those damn chickens into tetrazzini for the inn's cuisine!"

Anselm raised his hands in mock horror. "Ca-mel-lia, have you no respect for my potential as an inventor and scientific investigator?!"

Throughout the summer and into the fall of 1971, while Anselm was getting things "screwed away" (i.e., squared away) at his "chicken experimental station," clearing out all previous shore birds and wildlife and getting his "herd" (i.e., his flock) of experimental chicks placed in his new broiler house, Camellia was supervising the remodeling of a gorgeous suite of rooms for her and Anselm at the inn.

The rooms had originally been Grandmother and Grandfather LeCates's suite. Camellia, when growing up, had fancied herself looking like the elegant Lucille LeCates. She had resembled Grandmother Lucille in her size and bearing, but Camellia's thick, lustrous, black hair, tawny skin, and dark eyes could have come from nowhere but the Corrigan-gypsy-Stephenses.

Camellia had the old LeCates suite modernized, making a music studio out of the original parlor and putting a modern kitchenette and bathroom between the studio and hers and Anselm's bedroom.

Camellia's studio windows looked out, one northwestward toward the Anderson Sound, and the other southwestward toward the pines of Little Bell's. Her piano, brought from Anselm's cabin, flanked the southeast wall which was painted an oyster white. French doors opened from the studio onto the upper porch deck where she could walk out and contemplate the Anderson Sound or the stars.

From their southwest bedroom windows, she and Anselm could peer through the middle branches of a big maple alongside the inn and see the pines of Little Bell's and, also, on extra clear nights the lights of Gainsbiddle down river.

Camellia was "happy as a clam at half-tide" with their new home. Anselm was a little less enthusiastic. "Sex," he said, "was better back at the cabin."

Camellia, ever willing to please her "teddy bear," said, "So, we'll go back there for sex." Which they did, quite often, until their inn suite became less formidable to Anselm.

But it was not for sex that Camellia had gone back to Little Bell's one day when Anselm was in Gainsbiddle getting supplies....

Camellia had been having some of her shorter musical compositions recorded by a folk rock group from Halburg State. These were certainly not *classical works*, but the local *better musical circles* had gotten wind of Camellia's return to Wintergreen County and assumed they were, just because she was remembered as a performer and teacher of *better music* from two decades before.

Mrs. Dunston-Ayres, Royal Hall's current *patroness of the arts*, was trying to find Camellia to see whether she might like to perform some of her compositions at an upcoming Community Concert. Mrs. Dunston-Ayres had not been able to locate Camellia at the "new" Bell's Island Inn, but a workman there said "try Little Bell's."

Camellia was there at Little Bell's all right, but not "with bells on." She had on coveralls and knee boots, and she was adorned with flies and chicken crap from ear lobe to tippy toe. There were fluffs of white chicken feathers in her hair, and her face was flushed and glistening with perspiration. She was cleaning out the holding pens for Anselm's experimental chickens!

Usually Anselm or sometimes Jim Stephens did that, but on occasion Camellia would, too. It was being said around Bell's Island, "Camellia will do anything for her 'teddy bear', even nigger-work!"

When Camellia saw Mrs. Dunston-Ayres, instead of folding up in mortification, the actress in her suddenly rose to the occasion. She greeted her guest with a sweepingly flamboyant *presence* just as though she were a prima donna attired in her finest and taking curtain calls at the Baltimore Opera Theater.

"Mrs. Dunston-Ayres!" Camellia beamed. "Such a pleasure to *see* you! On this bee-you-tee-ful summer day!"

Actually it was a cold, raw, *fall* day, but Camellia was feeling no chill, considering what she was doing to those chicken pens and considering that Mrs. Dunston-Ayres had suddenly turned aghast at the sight of someone like Camellia shoveling shit like a pro! And it wasn't exactly smelling like a perfume factory around the premises, either.

Now, Mrs. Dunston-Ayres had some stage presence, too, and once she recovered her bearings, she oozed with oiliness at Camellia as she said, "Ah, yes, Mrs. Jurgensen—or should I say 'Miss Croswell?' Uh, that was your stage name at one time, my dear, wasn't it? Uh, we are so hap-pee to have you back with us in Wintergreen Coun-tee a-gain and so hap-pee to hear you are composing now in your retirement.

Tell me, my dear, have you had any oratorios or concerti recorded lately? We would be so hap-pee to feature you performing some of them on our upcoming Community Concerts program."

Camellia could never decide even for herself whether she intended to say what she said to Mrs. Dunston-Ayres so as to deliberately get the snooty patroness's goat or whether she actually made one of her more famous "Camellia-risms."

Anyhow, Camellia turned a huge smile on Mrs. Dunston-Ayres and with all the graciousness and bowing and scraping of a born actress, she announced, "Why, my dear Mrs. Dunston-Ayres! Why, yes! Of course, yes, and by all means! I would be sooooo privileged to perform for your Community Concerts program one of my *latest recordings for piano and voice—'Chicken-Shit Blues'*!"

The ensuing silence was deafening. Even the chickens were embarrassed and stopped squawking. Actually, Camellia had recorded something she called "Chicken *House* Blues," but that was *not* what she had just said.

Mrs. Dunston-Ayres was so startled that her countenance distorted wildly. She spun around on her high heels and flounced away toward her car—flounced as far as she could get, that is, for she suddenly encountered a gob of Camellia's "latest recording" on the ground, and but for Camellia catching her by the arm, she may well have slid all the way back to Royal Hall!

What Mrs. Dunston-Ayres may have thought of the whole episode, Camellia didn't give a hoot. She heard nothing further from the incensed patroness of the arts, nor did Camellia contact her. But Camellia did hear later that Mrs. Dunston-Ayres was saying around the county that she had been highly insulted and wanted no further dealings with "that gypsy!"

Which was okay with Camellia, because to her way of thinking, performing for the Community Concerts was rank amateurism. She had bigger and better things to prime herself for....

She had bought the old gypsy tavern over on the Wintergreen County mainland and was mapping out plans for its renovation and the opera training program she aimed to set up there. The Bell's Island School of Opera would be in tribute to Claudie, her first music teacher. She had thought also of Madame Dupree in Baltimore, but quickly decided against that as she did not want to open a can of worms and be reminded again of her own terminated performing career.

Almost from the start there had been a terrible odor problem with Anselm's "chicken experimental station" and it wasn't just from "good ole chicken shit."

As for the fine points of what Anselm was doing, chicken-wise, that created such a compound problem, it would take a bio-chemist to explain adequately. It was enough for Camellia to know that his dehydrating apparatus, in which he "boiled down for the nutrients" the garbage, crab scrap, etc., that he added to his poultry feed, sent billows of fetid white smoke into the air. One whiff of that choking, burning smell and one would think some of Camellia's Corrigan-gypsy-Stephens ancestors had been kicked out of Hell and dropped, still smoldering, back onto Bell's Island.

Anselm's ground drainage system was at fault, too. Everything went into it, from discarded oils and chemicals to decaying chicken carcasses, innards, and blood. Since many of his young chickens succumbed to the often too-potent doses of chemicals he used for inducing growth, for disease and vermin control, and whatnot, he was forever dissecting the corpses and peering through his microscope to try to find out why, and then afterwards dumping the remains into his homemade septic system.

Whenever it rained or the tide washed back onto Little Bell's Island, there arose into the air a stench "strong enough to gag a maggot," to use a good ole Bell's Island expression.

The Gainsbiddle *News-Dispatch* even printed a bit of doggerel about it:

Little Bell's Island
Is "wasting" away.
But the culprit is not
The Chesapeake Bay.
A wacky inventor
There has his tent.
A "crud plant" he's built
With gallant intent.
From crab scrap and garbage
Nutrition is pressed.
He hopes to breed chickens
All drumsticks and breasts.
But from the smell of the place
(If you dare to sail past),
The breed he's got now
Is already all ass!

Nobody needed a poem in the newspaper to deduce that.

"It's got to stop!" Camellia screamed at Anselm. "Your 'crud plant' will drive away the inn's tourists before they even get here!"

Whether Martin Cerajik, boss of the county health department, would have come anyway because of that poem, it's hard to say. But he got to Little Bell's Island for a more urgent—and dangerous—mission one sunny but extremely windy Sunday afternoon in late November.

Camellia and Virginia were coming back from Royal Hall where Camellia had been visiting with the Carrambarros. As they drove along the Wintergreen County marshland, they saw off on the horizon to the west a tremendous amount of smoke.

"Aunt Camellia!" said Virginia. "That smoke off there! Isn't that in the direction of *Little Bell's*?"

"My God! It is! Anselm uses so many chemicals in his formulas and cleaning agents for his machinery, I've always feared one day there'd be an *explosion*!"

As they got closer and closer to Bell's Island, the conflagration kept getting bigger and the smoke higher and higher.

Fire trucks from Royal Hall were running right along with them on the road and the closer they got to the Bell's island bridge, the more cars filled with sightseers jammed the roads. Camellia knew the county people's innate love of a good fire out of control. They would drive for miles to see one in progress. The only other thing they liked better was to witness a bang-up crash on the highway with plenty of human gore all intermingled with the broken glass and twisted metal.

Camellia couldn't even begin to get her car onto the Little Bell's Island causeway, so choked it was with fire engines and equipment. And the marsh edges were lined with sightseers on foot. Virginia and Camellia also ran on foot the rest of the way. They spied Anselm, none the worse for wear, but he was in a fierce argument with the fire marshall and with Martin Cerajik (who was also Connie Cerajik's husband—Connie had been the welfare worker several years back who had gotten after Anselm for possibly giving money to Camellia's parents before they died).

"At least Anselm's okay," gasped Camellia. Then her relief turned to annoyance at him. "I *told* him sooner or later he was going to catch if from Martin Cerajik and the health department, but he never *listens* to me."

Virginia questioned a fireman who was hustling by, and he said Anselm had been burning trash in back of his "chicken experimental station" (against Maryland law in itself as it was before 4 P.M.), and the high wind had blown sparks into the dry brush. The fire had creepy-creeped along until it got to the marsh where it erupted into a massive blaze. So far nothing had been burned *but* the marsh, but if the wind, high as it was, changed, the fire would get into the Little Bell's woods and then "kitty bar the door."

Camellia couldn't get to Anselm for the tangle of equipment that was in the way, but she latched onto the next fireman going by and begged of him, "Please, would you tell yonder idiot Viking I want to talk to him?"

The fireman looked at Camellia with a puzzled expression on his face and said, "'Yonder Idiot Viking'?!"

"Yes," said Camellia. "That fat guy over there talking with the health department man and the fire marshall."

The fireman said "Oh, yes!" and he yelled as loud as he could over the noise of the crowd and the roaring fire, "Hey! 'Yonder Idiot Viking'! Lady over here wants to talk to you!"

Immediately Anselm turned around and, seeing Camellia frantically gesturing at him, he left off arguing with Martin Cerajik and came toward her.

Virginia giggled and said, "He knows his name, doesn't he, Aunt Camellia?!" And from then on, Anselm had a new moniker—"Yonder Idiot Viking"—to go along with "Camellia's teddy bear," as he had been known years before in Royal Hall, and "Miss Camellia's Danish Ham," as he was more recently known by the kitchen staff at the "new" Bell's Island Inn.

Anselm came up to Camellia and Virginia in a rage and for all sorts of reasons. He was mad at himself for having started the fire, for which he would now have to pay a fine for burning trash at the wrong hours, and he was mad at Martin Cerajik for being a Royal Hall fireman. Martin had unintentionally found out about Anselm's makeshift septic system.

"That goddamn bohunk!" Anselm fumed. "I'm not the only one dumping contaminants into this marsh. What about all the germs in that Little Bell's Island dump? Oil, garbage, junk metal, God knows what all, have leached into the ground and seeped into the marsh, the river, the sound, and the bay for hundreds of years, and nobody's done anything about it. But now Martin blames *me* for all the pollution in the bay, and he's going to close my 'chicken experimental station' down in thirty days if I don't fix it!"

Later, after the marsh fire was under control and the thrill seekers gone home, Anselm, Camellia, and Virginia were back at the inn, commiserating.

"What I need is an e-gret," said Anselm. "Christ! I need an e-gret."

"You need a what?" asked Virginia.

"An e-gret to run the overflow off somewhere."

Camellia stepped in and translated. "He means an 'egress.' I'll swear, Anselm, for an educated and intelligent man, you talk like a bohunk." (Which was almost as bad as calling him a Gainsbiddler.)

Anyway, Anselm said the "e-gret" business so often that Virginia, who was forever making dolls and little animals for her twins, Flossie and Jesse, took some of the dry goods, made a pattern, sewed together a skinny, little, silly-looking white bird, stuffed it with little shreds of foam rubber, and gave it to Anselm.

"And what in hell is this!?" Anselm wanted to know, when Virginia handed him the stuffed bird with Camellia looking on.

"It's an 'e-gret'," Virginia said. You keep saying you need an 'e-gret'. You need an 'e-gret'. So now you've got one!"

Anselm took Virginia's nonsense—and her "e-gret"—good-naturedly, and he hung the stuffed bird onto the rearview mirror of his truck. The "e-gret" became quite a conversation piece at Bell's Island.

But an "e-gret" or "egress" was not the best way to handle the drainage problem and certainly would do nothing to sanitize the smoke. Camellia worried about both. She said to Virginia, "Anselm could fix things out there if he wanted to. He's got the brains to do it. Tomato canneries in the county have learned how to control odors and processing wastes over the years. Anselm could do the same, but he's so pigheaded about things sometimes."

The inn opened around Christmas time 1971 on a limited basis to a few commercial customers. Camellia was using them a guinea pigs to bring to the surface any dissatisfactions with the inn—its rooms or cuisine. She had suggestion boxes in the rooms, at the front desk, and in the restaurant/cafeteria (the dining room had not yet been completed).

One of the "suggestions" crassly put it: "*Do something* about your septic tank smelling!"

Well, it wasn't the septic tank at the *inn*. It was Anselm's "crud plant." For all his "brains," he still could not get his "chicken experimental station" to stop smelling like what it was.

And he wasn't getting any sales or patents for his feed formulae, either. He had tried to interest the seafood biological lab in Gainsbiddle in his chemical recommendations for chicken feed made from crab scrap and garbage, but they thought he was nuts. They said, "We do fish, not fowl," and they slammed the door in his face. He tried the Agronomy Department of Halburg State but couldn't even get a conference with them. But he remained undaunted.

Camellia said to Virginia, "About the only thing Anselm is successful at is sex!"

"*Well, that's not to be sneezed at, certainly*!" Virginia exclaimed.

Was Virginia finding her husband Nick somewhat wanting in that department? Camellia wondered.

Camellia said, "Don't tell me you're sex-starved like your Grandmother Mary was."

Virginia said, "It's not that I'm sex-*starved* exactly. It's more like sex-*bored*. Or perhaps *Nick*-bored says it best....

"Some would say Nick is the perfect husband and father. But I'm afraid he is turning out to be one of those perfect and perfectly boring mortals who does everything right—even sex. Nick rarely gets angry or in trouble. He's doing well with his studies at Halburg State and he'll probably end up working well and uncomplainingly eight hours a day, forty hours a week, on the same job, perhaps in the same law firm, for fifty years, then receive a gold watch upon his retirement, immediately give the watch to his oldest grandchild, and then fold his hands across his chest and die, totally happy that he'd had a good life.

"Don't get me wrong, Aunt Camellia, Nick is a good man—just like I understand my Grandmother Mary's husband, Thomas Stephens, had been a good man. And I should be grateful to have a husband like Nick. BUT MAYBE I DON'T WANT 'A GOOD MAN'. There are times when I even envy you your off-center Anselm. A lot of people say Anselm is a lazy leech, aiming to live off your investment wealth, and capitalize on your guilt for having deserted him those years before. But 'the Luther Burbank of the poultry set' is not afraid to 'follow that other drummer' and you can't help admiring him."

"Oh, I suppose so," Camellia granted. Anselm's individuality did have a certain pull, but Camellia had always found her "teddy bear" *sensually* attractive because he came across to her with just the right proportion of animal lust and angel innocence to stir her up no matter where her mind happened to be at the moment, even if it was on MUSIC.

One evening at the inn a man named Akaido Li registered as a guest. Anselm recognized him as the Japanese investor and entrepreneur who had recently blown onto the local scene and was snapping up flagging businesses in the Wintergreen County area and reorganizing them.

Anselm had gotten so conservative over the years he was scared of anything and everything that was not 100 percent WASP, and it amazed Camellia that he would even talk with Akaido Li.

But talk they did, almost the whole evening. Camellia figured Anselm must surely have been desperate about the future of his "chicken experimental station," for the next thing she knew a big sign went up at the entrance to Little Bell's Island, announcing to the whole wide world that the "crud plant" was now the Kami-Yaki Super Chick Corporation!

Although Anselm was a painstaking and innovative researcher and inventor, he was no good as a manager, organizer, or public relations man, and Akaido Li was. What's more, Li claimed to be a chemist and said that correcting the smell at the plant would be no problem. Still, Anselm didn't take the *partnership* very happily. "Give the country over to the Japs! Didn't we fight a war to prevent that?" he fumed daily.

The two partners had yet to prove each other out on a personal level. Anselm claimed Akaido Li gave him the willies. Anselm couldn't even get an argument going with this epitome of Oriental unflappability, this ever-cool cat who came gliding out of the inn in the morning wearing his perpetually and inscrutably pleasant visage. This was not a "bohunk" Anselm was dealing with.

Anselm thought he remembered some things from the karate days of his early manhood spent in Wilmington, Delaware, with Johann and Wilma, two older cousins from a different—and slightly better—branch of his Jurgensen family. So one day Anselm suddenly tried to put a karate hold on Akaido Li and immediately found himself flipped gently but decisively onto his back in front of the Kami-Yaki Super Chick Corporation's big new sign. Anselm developed a rather instant respect for Akaido Li after that, and the two came to at least tolerate each other.

At the Kami-Yaki Super Chick Corporation things were soon going great guns. Akaido Li advised Anselm not to try to market the feed locally ("a prophet is not without honor save in his own country" sort of reasoning) but to go for the out-of-state-trade. In a big promotion scheme during the early months of 1972, they printed up clever brochures, all complete with samples of their best, most promising formulae, and sent the new products to target areas all over the country. Orders for the feed stated pouring in! They had to hire a bona-fide work force to process, package, and ship the orders out.

People began taking Anselm more seriously. Camellia noted one evening, "Anselm, your Kama-Sutra chicken place has been written up in the newspaper again—a little more complimentary this time. What are you cooking in that feed these days?" (The smell was practically all gone! At Li's suggestion, Anselm had begun experimenting with synthetic vitamins and minerals instead of cooking so much garbage and crab scrap.)

"'Ka-mi-*Yaki*'. 'Ka-mi-*Yaki*'!" hollered Anselm, correcting Camellia's identification of the plant.

"'Kami-Yaki'? You're cooking 'Kami-Yaki' in the feed? What's 'Kami-Yaki', anyhow?"

"It's only a brand name, Camellia. Kami-Yaki—Kama-Sutra? Goooood Lord! Shades of Lady Chitterling's Lawyer!" And he reached for his notebook to rack up another "Camellia-rism."

"But what does 'Kami-Yaki' mean?" Camellia persisted.

"Oh, I don't know. Broiled God, maybe."

"Broiled cod?"

"Broiled *God*. God, God, God, as in God, the Father."

Anselm's religion—or the lack of it (although he had attended the Lutheran Church when he'd lived with his cousins Johann and Wilma in Delaware)—needed to be broiled or cleansed or something, Camellia was thinking. She was planning on returning to the Episcopal Church in Royal Hall to keep her connections open to the local *better* music scene as she was still intent on starting an opera school at Bell's Island. Her run-in with Mrs. Dunston-Ayres was still getting her some bad publicity around the county. Fortunately, Mrs. Dunston-Ayres was a Presbyterian, so there would be no face-to-face combat at the Episcopal Church.

Camellia talked Anselm into going to church with her, but after the first couple of Sundays, she wasn't so sure it was a good idea. Anselm's version of the Lord's Prayer—à la his every-now-and-then German accent mixed in with the poor white trash brogue he'd picked up from the Gainsbiddle docks—sounded like this:

Air fodder,
Witch-art in heffen,
Hollow be thy name.
Thy kinkdom come,
Thy wool be done,
In eart'
Ass-it iss
In heffen.
Giffus this day,
Air daily brett,
An' forgiffus
Air ditts,
Ass-we forgiff
Air ditters.
An' lead a snot
Into timptation,
But deliffer us
From a-vil.
For thine
Iss-da kinkdom,
An' the pair,
An' the glurry,
Foreffer.
Hay-min!

Anybody sitting close by might wonder what sort of goon Camellia had married. But Anselm was still "good in the bed," and that covered a multitude of sins and made up for a lot of disappointments, even that lost Met bid which still jabbed at Camellia's memory every now and then.

Chapter Twelve

Camellia spent most of the early months of 1972 getting ready for the grand opening of the "new" Bell's Island Inn, slated for Memorial Day, and to be dedicated to her mother, Mary LeCates Stephens, and her grandparents, James and Lucille LeCates.

Restoration work was just about complete and Camellia had purchased a huge yacht to be used as the weekend tour boat. She still wanted Anselm to be the captain, but Jim Stephens said it was doubtful whether Anselm could even qualify for the pilot's license.

Jim said the local Coast Guard at Gainsbiddle regarded Anselm as "a navigational hazard" because he had always been so clumsy with his work boat. During his hermithood days on Little Bell's Island he had swamped the boat and radioed the Coast Guard for help so many times that the Gainsbiddle station had begun saying they wished he would just go ahead and sink the work boat once and for all so they could get on with more important matters like repairing buoys and making channel surveys. So perish the thought that he should ever become the captain of a tour boat!

So Camellia found somebody else for that post, but she did get Anselm to be the tour guide. He was to give the passengers a running commentary about wherever they might be sailing past at any given moment. Camellia tried to talk him into accompanying his commentaries with sea chanties like The Wreck of the John B. But Anselm said the only sea chanties he knew were the kind the Gainsbiddle watermen sang, and if all the blue lines were censored out, in deference to the ladies and little kiddies who might be on the tour boat, there wouldn't by any lyrics left to sing. Camellia said well, scrub the sea chanties, then. Thus a passel of trouble was stopped before it had a chance to start.

Camellia knew Anselm would far rather spend the entire summer with his chickens on Little Bell's. His lack of motivation toward normal red-blooded American male pursuits such as money and status didn't bother her as much as it had twenty-some years before when they had been lovers in Royal Hall and she had been social climbing. Now—and even though she fussed about it—she was both fascinated by and proud of Anselm's ability to work his ass on some invention or notion such as his chicken feed experiments, and, thanks to Akaido Li's continuing help and partnership, the Kami-Yaki Super Chick outfit was purring (or cackling) along nicely.

Memorial Day came with weather in its early summer glory, and amazingly large crowds of both local people and out-of-towners pushed onto Bell's Island for the event. Politicians and public officials swarmed everywhere. Chambers of commerce, tourism bureaus, and historical society representatives from all over the state had a heyday.

Camellia had advertised extensively in the Baltimore and Washington news media as well as locally, and she had also sent out myriads of invitations to all important people and institutions.

The flyers spoke glowingly of the "huge three-story white hotel with black and red trim, remodeled to resemble a majestic steamboat... completely modernized inside, with every convenience imaginable... the luxurious ballroom...the exquisite cuisine with food unsurpassed anywhere in taste and quality...the mighty tour boat...."

Ah yes, that "mighty tour boat!" It glided down the Anderson Sound on its maiden voyage the weekend of the grand opening with Anselm as tour guide. Camellia had made him dress up in a commodore's outfit. Anselm quipped, "I feel like the organ grinder's monkey!"

Anselm didn't like the straight spiel Camellia made him give about the local islands, the tributaries, the shoreline, and the history of the area. He would have preferred to ham it up like he'd done years and years before during World War II, when Camellia first knew him as a young soldier-entertainer with the USO in Royal Hall, where he'd sung dirty little ditties like Barnacle Bill the Sailor to homesick GIs, eager to hear anything funny to take their mind off their lonesomeness, and the more vulgar the humor, the better.

But this was a different time, a different occasion, and a very different audience. Camellia said their new business would do best by confining all "Danish ham" to the restaurant part of the inn. So she insisted that Anselm "act respectful" to tourist and countian alike, to both history past and history present.

So, as Anselm jabbered away and jumped around like the "organ grinder's monkey," he had to "tell it nice" about Wintergreen County and Bell's Island's "wonderful heritage." He did not—not even once yield to the temptation to use that famous little dialogue:

Tourist: What do you natives do here for kicks? Don't you get bored?

Bell's Islander: Oh, we have variety. In winter we fish, oyster, and fuck. In summer, we fish, crab, and fuck.

After the aquatic tour, with the safe return of the boat to its dock beside the inn, there was the official grand opening banquet at the inn that evening.

The Eastern Shore Choral Society and a joint high school band ensemble performed some of Camellia's latest compositions—modern classical music, she called them. They were full of jumpy cadence and broken rhythm, part calypso, part gypsy czardas, part Gilbert and Sullivan mishmash, and part God only knows what. Camellia told everybody she was influenced by the modernists Philip Glass and John Cage. Whatever the influence, the music was sending Virginia (and probably others, too) rustling through her handbag in search of aspirin and antacids.

After that part of the entertainment, the banquet hall and stage were turned into the grand ballroom for the formal dance that evening. The orchestra then settled in to a more traditional dance band style, but not without a scattering of rock tempos which Camellia adored.

Camellia and Anselm shared a table with Virginia and Nick Carrambarro and Sylvester and Louisa Valiano, who had come down from Baltimore for the grand opening. The Valianos, at home in any arena from Baltimore's Little Italy to political and cultural bailiwicks anywhere in the state, were a big hit with everyone. Big, fat, jovial Sylvester had shed his none-too-clean restauranteur's apron for a rented tux (also none-too-clean), and big, fat, mothery Louisa had redoubled her usual double dose of mascara and lipstick and tripled the length of her dangly earrings. Both of the Valianos were as goofy and endearing as ever.

Lighthearted talk somehow got around to Camellia and Anselm's choice of a tombstone for their cubbyhole in the Stephens lot in the Bell's Island Methodist Church Cemetery.

The tombstone was one of those big deals, a massive obelisk-type monument, a more or less archaic critter, the kind you rarely saw anymore and they had to have it custom-made. It had the name Jurgensen cut into the marble in German script, but in its ostentatiousness it was very un-Anselm, and everybody knew Camellia had been the one who dreamed it up.

Nick had been drinking all afternoon and he was "feeling no pain" by the time of the dance. He and Virginia had seen the tombstone for the first time that day, and he kept bantering Anselm about it and all but hollering, "It looks like a phallus! It looks like a phallus!"

Embarrassed, Virginia whispered, "For heaven's sake, Nick, be quiet!"

Camellia said to Virginia, "Oh, shoot! Let Nick talk. Nobody here knows what a phallus is, anyway."

And Nick kept on blabbing, "It looks like a phallus!"

By now Camellia was getting a little miffed, and she huffed all up with that brand of withering hauteur that only she was capable of. She said to Nick, "Why, of course, it looks like a phallus! That's exactly why we chose it!"

Sylvester, not to be left out of the fun, asked, "Camellia, does-a your tomba-stone look-a like why-a George-a Washington is call-a da father of-a his country?"

A joking reference such as that, only a Baltimorean or an alert tourist familiar with a side view of Papa George's monument at Mt. Vernon Place could appreciate. For there in the heart of the city stood the father of his country, with his arm extended diagonally, giving the distinct impression of something else extended when seen from a distance.

Camellia knew what Sylvester was talking about and she said, "Uh, huh, only bigger."

Anselm, beer'd up and feeling no pain, either, must have known, too, for he guffawed and said, "Yeah, I'm bigger than George Washington by about ten inches. And that's because I'm one-third German, one-third Danish, one-third Norwegian and 100 percent atheist. Camellia is one-eighth gypsy and one half-assed Episcopalian. We're going to be buried together under a phallic tombstone bigger'n George Washington's cock and in a Methodist cemetery. And you know what? We can screw for all eternity and neither the Devil nor the Lord will think of looking for either of us there!"

Nick, three sheets to the wind though he was, had not lost his analytical sense and he said to Anselm, "One third, one third, one third—what kind of genealogy is that?" [Correctly stated, Anselm was one-half German and one-quarter each of the other two nationalities.]

But for the rest of the evening, Nick joshed Anselm, no longer about his phallic tombstone, but about the mathematical and physiological impossibility of his proclaimed pedigree.

The successful grand opening led into a successful first season. The kitchen staff of the inn were mostly local cooks and bus boys, and some were still finding it hard to get used to the rapid-fire pace expected of them in catering to out-of-town tourists. Especially vexing all that first summer were those moments just preceding the arrival back to the inn of the Saturday and Sunday tour boat with its load of hungry passengers.

Whenever the boat was first sighted on the horizon of Anderson Sound, the call would ring out "Kee-ryst! Here comes the boat!" All hell would break loose at the inn's restaurant.

Bus boys and waitresses who had been lounging around just waiting began frantically snuffing out cigarettes, tossing away half-empty beer cans, and bumping wildly into one another in haste to get to their posts.

In the kitchen, the cooks, in order to get things warmed up or iced down in time, were creating general havoc, dropping pots, pans, and utensils and letting fly choice curse words, Bell's Island-style.

An older employee within earshot (probably deliberately) of Camellia lamented that the years were long gone on the island when "all anybody had to do for a living—and for fun—was oyster and crab, fish, and fuck." Now those carefree days were gone forever and all because Camellia Stephens had come back to the shore and "let in all them Baltimore and Washington city slicker tourists."

Anselm, too, was still not quite up to city ways. Being a daytime person after so many previous years of working—or making out like he was working—on the water, he often still got up before dawn. He would go down to the restaurant part of the inn and fix himself a snack before he and Camellia had their regular breakfast upstairs in their suite. Sometimes after his snack he'd curl up in one of the booths and go back to sleep. Usually he'd wake up before the kitchen staff came in to work and he'd go back upstairs, unnoticed.

But sometimes he'd oversleep, and the staff would find him still clad in his shorts and T-shirt, snoring away in one of the booths.

Camellia found him like that one morning, with the cook, the clean-up girl, and several of the waitresses standing over him, giggling.

Camellia was about to clobber him, but the clean-up girl suggested, "Take a straw and tickle him awake on the bottoms of his bare feet."

Which Camellia did, even though she remained furious over Anselm's carelessness. She had lost a lot of her particular brand of stuffiness since being back on the shore, but in the presence of "the help" she got re-stuffy all over again.

She heard one of the waitresses whispering to Jim Stephens, who'd come in with a basket of fish, "'Miss' Camellia don't even cough like she's 'from around here'. J'ever notice? It's that cute little 'hoo hoo hoo' kind of cough."

"Yeah," said Jim. "Any native Bell's Islander ought to be able to cough a genuine old 'oyster cough'. You know—that harsh 'AAAARRRGH RACK-RACK-RACK-RACK' that is always followed by a big 'KER-EEESSSH-SPLOOT' of phlegm that usual lands right inside the bucket of shucked raw oysters that the waterman is bringing in to the restaurant here."

Well! Camellia and the now wide-awake Anselm were about to stretch Jim's neck. "JIM STEPHENS, FOR CHRISSAKE, GET YOUR ASS OUTA HERE!" they blared at him in unison.

True to her intentions, Camellia "dressed to the nines" as hostess of the inn, from the dangly earrings, jingly bracelets, and hair piled high on her head to the sweeping nearly floor length gowns, up just high enough to show her four-inch heels and lacy black hose.

And she sang, too, usually light ballads good for the diners' digestion and usually with Anselm accompanying her on the piano, or if he were out with his Kami-Yaki chickens, she became her own accompanist.

But one day in early fall as the first successful season of the inn was winding down, wisdom, "gypsy magic," or whatever told Camellia to not be so flamboyantly decked out this time....

She was wearing just a plain mauve gown as she and Anselm chatted at the front desk with the newest visitor to register at the inn:

"Just call me 'Izzie'," Rabbi Israel Epstein offered cheerily.

The good Baltimore rabbi was staying at the inn for his vacation, and he mentioned to Anselm and Camellia that he had known of the late Doc Feldman, Bell's Island's favorite and only doctor, Bell's Island's favorite and only Jew of "long time back." And Izzie said he'd known in person Doc's nephew, Asa Yittelman of Baltimore.

Anselm commented that he had spent many a pleasant hour in front of the drugstore or on the Bell's Island docks joking and philosophizing with Doc Feldman. Anselm said there were only two people on the island back then who could carry on a decent conversation—Camellia's mother Mary Stephens and Doc Feldman.

Anselm may have liked Doc Feldman, but Camellia hadn't had much use for him. She'd even called him—to his face—a no-good Baltimore Jew who came to the island to practice medicine because the islanders couldn't afford anything better. Camellia never forgave Doc for not giving her mother the abortion Mary had asked for, which would have saved everybody the burden of Roger.

Izzie's mention of Doc's nephew, Asa Yittelman, reminded Camellia of that page in Doc Feldman's old logbook, the logbook which Anselm had found on the Little Bell's Island dump which mentioned Mary's request for an abortion. That logbook entry had also mentioned somebody named Asa, whom Doc said was his nephew.

Camellia wondered whether Izzie might provide a lead as to the identity of Roger's father, that "other grandfather" that Virginia often still spoke of as wanting to find. So Camellia decided to "take the bull by the balls" and try to find out whether the Asa Yittelman that Izzie had just spoken of was the same Asa mentioned in Doc's logbook.

After Anselm went off to check on his chickens, Camellia phoned Virginia to come to the Inn. Izzie had agreed to talk with them in private.

Now, Izzie was a craggy-faced, squeaky-voiced old Jew with a bit of wiry gray hair left on top of his head and a scraggly set of whiskers running around his face. In personality, though, he didn't seem at all rabbinical. There was something vaguely humorous about him, and one felt like one could tell or ask him anything without embarrassment. This was a good thing because the subject matter Camellia and Virginia were about to discuss with him was a little delicate.

They all went into Camellia's office at the inn where Camellia showed Izzie and Virginia the crucial page from Doc Feldman's logbook:

> 15 November 1933—Patient: Mary Stephens. Diagnosis: three months pregnant. Wants abortion. Said baby not her husband Thomas'. No sex with him for years. She admitted she had sex one time with one of the roomers at the Tu-Rest Home. Said she didn't know which one it was. Said she'd been in a daze.
>
> Comments: My nephew, Asa, was down from Baltimore and staying at the Tu-Rest Home at that time. He was investigating the island's hurricane damage for the State Relief Administration.
>
> Prescription: Mild sedative. I told Mary, No abortion.
>
> Comments: I could not risk killing what might be my own kin.

After reading the logbook entry, Izzie said, "Yes, Asa Yittelman did indeed work for the State Relief Administration during the Depression, but whether he ever came to the shore to do hurricane damage evaluation, that I could not say definitely, but I think you can take Doc Feldman's word for it."

Izzie also recalled that one time he and a bunch of his pals, including Asa Yittelman, had gotten together over beers and were swapping stories about their sexual adventures. (This was before Izzie had thought about becoming a rabbi.)

The young men were talking about whether a man should accept "favors" from a housewife if the man's trade, such as, carpentry or meter reading, took him inside a house when a husband was not at home.

Izzie said one of the men, who was a plumber, said he'd gone into a fashionable lady's home to do some work while her husband was out of town. While the plumber was dismantling the kitchen sink, the lady came and squatted down beside him with her kimono open and no undies on, and asked him, "Would you like to play tiddlywinks?"

Izzie laughed and said the plumber, who was a timid soul, confessed that he had been so startled that he picked up his pipes and wrenches and ran out of the house so fast that the lady not only didn't get to "play tiddlywinks," she didn't get her kitchen sink fixed, either!

"Then," said Izzie, "somebody asked Asa Yittelman what would he have done in a similar situation and Asa said, 'Well, one time I was staying a couple of days at a rooming house and the woman who was running it came to my bedroom door one morning—and she didn't have much on, either—and she asked me if I would like to have 'something extra special' in the way of 'room service'."

Izzie said, "We all asked Asa, 'Did you?' And Asa grinned and winked and said, 'What do you think? But I almost got the hide burned off me because right in the middle of it, the damn rooming house caught on fire and I had to run for my life!'"

Virginia yelped and said, "That's him That's my GRANDFATHER!"

And Camellia said, "Yes! Those words about 'room service' were the very words my mother said she said when she was explaining to me how she had gotten with that man. And there was a fire in the Tu-Rest Home right at that time! It hadn't been much of a fire, but it filled the house with smoke, and it had scared me as I had come back home from the drugstore with a prescription for Mama—and Oh! What a cold morning it was—all the heat was in the Tu-Rest Home and not from just from the smoking stew pot on the stove, either! I caught my mother with that roomer when I ran upstairs yelling, "The house is on fire!" It scared that man so bad he ran like the dickens out of the house. He didn't even get his pants buttoned up!"

Izzie said Asa Yittelman had not said where the rooming house was that he had been involved with the woman, but it could well have been on the shore and it could well have been the Stephens Tu-Rest Home.

Virginia asked Izzie what Asa Yittelman had looked like. Izzie said he had been a blond sort of Jew and not very good-looking. As for genetics, Izzie thought it was possible that Asa could have produced a red-headed son like Roger Stephens.

Virginia asked Izzie if he knew whatever became of Asa Yittelman. Izzie said he himself had left Baltimore after that time and had gone to Washington to begin his rabbinical studies, but he had heard that Asa Yittelman had quit state employ, had enlisted in the army air force, and had become a fighter pilot, but he had been killed during the Japanese attack on Pearl Harbor.

Virginia and Camellia both bowed their heads for a moment in memory of someone they had never known and whom they couldn't even be sure was the right person, but Virginia seemed satisfied enough that it was the right person.

Virginia said, "My father Roger might well have been proud of his unknown sire, dying in the defense of his country."

Camellia said, "Roger had always wanted to be either an airplane pilot or drive a tank, and he was always disappointed that he'd been too young to enlist in World War II. And he had had a strange and sudden rally from pneumonia right at the time of the radio's announcement of the Pearl Harbor attack. He had come out of his coma making like an anti-aircraft gun and yelling, 'Att-att-att-att-att! Get 'em goddamn fuckin' Japs! Att-att-att!'"

Izzie said he was neither a psychic nor a psychiatrist, and he couldn't begin to say whether such a phenomenon meant that Asa and possibly his unknown son, Roger, were somehow communicating telepathically at the moment of Asa's death and at the moment of Roger's near-death, or just what it all might have meant.

But they all agreed it had been a strange phenomenon. Camellia and Virginia thanked Izzie profusely for his willingness to discuss all this with them, and Virginia said she felt she had come as near as she ever would to uncovering the identity of her unknown grandfather. She seemed quite proud of her possible new heritage. And Izzie seemed quite happy that he'd helped somebody.

That evening Virginia asked Camellia, "Do I look 'Jewish'? Even one-quarter 'Jewish'? Anyways at all 'Jewish'? Auburn hair, fair skin, pale blue eyes, and what you might call 'chiseled features'. Anything 'Jewish' here? Medium-tall, slim physique, though still a bit misshapen from the twins. 'Jewish' at all?"

Camellia could tell Virginia was pleased at the possibility of being part Jewish. Anything to counterbalance the heritage of "Hambone" Thornton, her no-so-glorious legitimate grandfather.

Chapter Thirteen

As long as Camellia kept her Bell's Island Inn a top-notch tourist accommodation that also had a good restaurant that even local countians flocked to, all was "beauty on Bell's Island." The local citizenry and business people tolerated the tourists as well as profited from their dollars. During that first season and into the next, curio, gift, and sportswear shops proliferated like ants on a sugar bun.

But Camellia still had it in her head to make Bell's Island a retreat for aspiring young opera students. In spite of local grumblings, she had been working on this during both the summer of 1972 and the winter of '72-'73, and into the summer of 1973. She had the old gypsy tavern rebuilt but had it done in such a way as to retain its original aura.

Then to soften the terrible past reputation of the old place, Camellia named the workshop "The Bell's Island School of Opera" and used a ship's bell as the logo. "Everybody loves the idea of a bell," she said. "Bells connote 'nice things'. There is the dinner bell, the church bell, the door bell, the Liberty Bell, wedding bells, and Christmas bells. And the bell that most certainly 'says' Bell's Island is the ship's bell."

Camellia was as good a businesswoman as she was a musician, and she formed a legal organization called "The Bell's Island School of Opera." She screened her applicants as carefully as possible and not just for their musical and acting potential but for their character. She made it a rule at the very start both for the students and the instructors—NO DRUGS!

Her applicants came from all over the mid-Atlantic region as she had catchily advertised in musical journals, newspapers, and on TV. Some came from local high schools and colleges, others from stints with amateur groups and summer stock, and still others were those who had not quite made it at the regular conservatories or opera companies.

When the first group of accepted students and instructors arrived on Bell's Island in September 1973, in spite of all the screening, they still *looked like* "a bunch of drug-crazed hippies" with their long hair, sloppy clothes, and careless mien. Bell's Islanders rose up as one and were about to have Camellia's scalp. Everybody feared their beloved island homeland was going to be turned into "another damned Woodstock."

But Camellia managed to calm down some of the initial outcry by assuring everyone that this was "*culture*" and not "*cult*" being brought to the island.

Camellia had sufficient leadership qualities and organizational ability left over from her early teaching days in the county to manage a small ensemble. She could "get things done." She still had her boundless energy and her ever-flamboyant personality—composed of "bull, brass, and brawn," as someone put it.

Camellia knew how to "pour on the molasses"—how and when to flatter and cajole. She had accurate enough intuition to know who to say what to—who to deflate and who to expand—in order to get the best and most out of her students and instructors.

That fall, however, one of the young black students—yes, Camellia's opera school was "an equal opportunity institution"—got Virginia (who was helping to do sets) all stirred up and without really doing anything. His name was "Ace" Cunningham, which made him sound more like a race car driver than a potential Othello. He was "so black he was almost purple" and on his chest was a mat of black, velvet-like hair, unusually thick for a Negro. When Virginia saw him for the first time, walking shirtless around the old Corrigan-gypsy workshop getting stage props set up, she told Camellia she was just aching to wiggle her bare toes around in the thick, black, velvet-like mat of hair!

Camellia said to her, "Whoa, Virginia! You've got Nick or doesn't he have the right mat?"

Virginia threw her hands it the air in a "no hopes" gesture. Clearly she was still bored with the too-perfect Nick, yet Camellia could tell Virginia knew a good thing when she found it and was not about to ditch her husband or even run around on him. But Virginia could dream, couldn't she?

Virginia brought the twins with her while she was helping with the art work. Flossie and Jesse—toddlers now and amazingly good toddlers—quickly became the mascots of the Bell's Island School of Opera!

So far so good. Then just as Camellia was getting ready for the opera students' first season in early 1974, new trouble came on the horizon of Little Bell's Island.

The business that the inn was bringing to Bell's Island made the state and county think the tourist trade could be exploited a bit further, and a proposal was afloat to turn Little Bell's into a state park.

Anselm first knew of it when he and the couple of other property owners on Little Bell's got letters from the authorities offering to buy their land.

Anselm admitted to Camellia a state park would be good for the inn's business, but the thought of giving up his little cubbyhole in the brush was not so joyful. The Kami-Yaki Super Chick Corporation was still thriving under the guidance of Akaido Li and Anselm's continuing experimentation.

Or it *seemed* to be thriving. Some checks had bounced from out-of-state feed dealers who had bought the Kami-Yaki Special Mix, but Akaido Li, with his usual Oriental graciousness, had made them good.

Camellia began to feel uneasy about Li, but Anselm's main concern lay elsewhere:

"If I have to leave Little Bell's, where will I put the Kami-Yaki?" he wailed.

Well, Camellia didn't *know* where he'd put it, though at times she felt like telling him where and in no uncertain terms. But she was not about to be mean to Anselm. He was giving her what she needed—plenty of sex—which continued to fire her ambitions....

Camellia's Bell's Island School of Opera undoubtedly aided the 1974 tourist business in Wintergreen County. With Anselm as assistant director (a complimentary post to which Camellia appointed him even though he didn't do much, spending most of his day at the Kami-Yaki) and Camellia continuing as "head one," the students put on productions for the entertainment of the inn's guests, for boaters docking at the Bell's Island wharf, and for tourists visiting the island by auto.

In addition to learning to perform abridged versions of regular opera and operettas—abridged to accommodate to the old Corrigan-gypsy workshop's limited amount of space, props, and personnel—the Bell's Island School of Opera concocted musical plays and skits of their own with operatic overtones.

Camellia strutted around at the workshop in tight pants, head scarf, and dark glasses—her old tourist incognito outfit—very different from her hostess attire at the inn.

"How wonderful," she said (to anyone who cared to listen), "for my students to be learning to perform *Grandpaw and the Gypsies*" (her own composition) "in the very spot where it all occurred so many years ago!"

Lest something *current* occur, Camellia had to watch out for some of the women opera students who tried to "get into Anselm's pants," finding him *teddy bear* cute, even as Camellia had found him a quarter of a century before. The key topic of conversation among the female students was "Who gets to play with the 'teddy bear' today?"

When the troupe did *The Mule and I* (composed by one of the students) for the first time in public, there was such an impressive representation of the mule given by two local stuntmen in costume that a talent scout from New York City offered the two men the opportunity to audition as the understudy for Brunnhilde's horse Grane in Wagner's *Die Walkure* at The Met. How ironic, thought Camellia, if *that* should get to The Met and I didn't!

But the stuntmen, who were two Bell's Island watermen with histrionic proclivities, said "Naw! We don't want to go to no New York City. We want to stay right here on Bell's Island." Greater loyalty hath no man than that, as the saying goes.

The only time Camellia's opera school got into trouble was when they put on the black-and-blue musical comedy (written by Virginia and Camellia) called, *All of That—AND FISH, TOO*? The local D.A.R. chapter, the NAACP, the Wintergreen County Historical Society, and the Lower Shore Ministerial Association all picketed the Bell's Island-Royal Hall road and the Bell's Island bridge one whole month, warning incoming tourists of the X-rated fare that awaited them—"shameful and degrading to all races, governments, and religions, past, present, and future." Actually the tourist count jumped by 150 percent during the picketing. Nothing like having free advertising!

So the name of the Bell's Island School of Opera was getting voiced around. Before too long Camellia was getting invitations to bring her troupe to festivals, events, and "do's" all over the state. And they did do a lot of traveling around, sandwiching engagements here and there between regular performances at Bell's Island.

Needless to say, Camellia was immensely enjoying her *second career.*

But what had happened to her guilt? Camellia wondered. She rarely thought of her deceased parents anymore, so busy she was with her Bell's Island Opera School and its successes. The Bell's Island Inn, which she had dedicated to her mother and grandparents, was doing well and providing her and Anselm a luxurious home.

Camellia still humored Anselm, but he in turn still "had a good cock," and it was his way of saying "thank you" to Camellia for all her indulgences.

If all this was the result of absolving guilt, then *Viva la guilt, oiu*? But Camellia was uneasy. Now she was feeling guilty about no longer feeling guilty! She seemed to think more of a sacrifice should have been involved. True, she lost out on her Met bid by returning to Anselm, but her Bell's Island School of Opera was filling that void.

Still she thought there must be something more she could do, especially to square things with her departed parents.

Anselm fussed with her sometimes because of her uneasiness: "Your folks—and I, too—brought most of our troubles on ourselves. It was not altogether because of your disappearance and failure to come back.

"For one thing, I didn't *have* to become a recluse and nearly starve to death because I was such a poor waterman.

"The Stephenses didn't *have* to depend on your money to bail them out. They could have used the opportunity to prove they could make it on their own...and permanently.

"Your mother didn't *have* to pine away for you and Roger and suffer continuously for all sorts of IMAGINED sins; she could have found redemption or some sort of rationalization.

"The rest of the Stephenses didn't *have* to stay in the firm as long as they did—some did pull out early—but most of them seemed to want to go down all hanging onto each other.

"So what happened on Bell's Island in your absence, Camellia, was not entirely your fault at all."

Camellia agreed, but she still felt there must be something more she should do to square the past....

Then one evening Anselm was reminiscing about his earliest visit to Bell's Island. It was when he was a GI stationed at Camp Conover and, like the native New Yorker who's never visited the Statue of Liberty, he was a native Wintergreen Countian who'd never been on Bell's Island until World War II.

"I was on leave and decided to go down to Bell's Island. When I got there, I was drawn right to your mother's little lending library."

"Yes," said Camellia. "Mama always wanted to do something for Bell's Island. Give it culture."

Anselm said, "She kept her library going as long as she could, even after you were gone. But the Stephens money was running out. It was a sad day for me and her, too, when she had to close down the library because she could no longer pay the rent or the electric."

Right then Camellia knew what she was going to do....

With the island and, correspondingly, the county, flourishing from tourism, thanks to Camellia and her Bell's Island projects, she knew now was a good time to press the county library system for a branch of Bell's Island.

She told the "head ones," "I'll donate whatever it takes to get it started and all along the way until its completion." She had a tendency, like her parents before her, to spend lavishly when things were going good, rarely thinking of anything but the present moment.

And money does talk, as the saying goes, so before 1974 was over, the Mary LeCates Stephens Memorial Library on Bell's Island was a reality.

The state and county dickered around all that summer of 1974 and into the fall about whether or not there should be a state park on Little Bell's. Anselm felt it was a certainty, but he still couldn't decide what to do about the Kami-Yaki. He doubted the state would pay him enough for his land to buy or rent elsewhere, so he remained in the proverbial quandary.

It was along about this time that Anselm's estranged family out in east Wintergreen County realized his marriage to Camellia had put him "in the chips." No one could look at that elegant display—the "new" Bell's Island Inn—and think otherwise.

Anselm's older brothers, Harald and Kurt, came to the Bell's Island Inn to see him one evening while it was still hot that summer of 1974. Harald, nearly twenty years older than Anselm, was a stockman by trade and he looked like he smelled like the cattle he tended. He was burly and unkempt and wore his shirt open to his navel, exposing a big, gray-haired chest and belly that hadn't seen soap and water lately.

Kurt was several years younger than Harald and a far neater, cleaner-looking man. He was an up-county farmer, tall and sunburned with mahogany-colored hair, a muscular build, and a certain quiet dignity to his bearing.

The two brothers argued with Anselm for nearly an hour, asking for money to get their parents into a nursing home. Anselm refused to contribute anything.

Camellia could hear part of their conversation. Anselm was saying, "The 'ole man' whipped me as a kid every chance he got and so did our mother. I've never forgot any of that. I'll never give a cent for them."

"So what if they did whip you?" Harald jeered. "They whipped all of us. You were the only one who couldn't take it and you ran away."

Anselm retorted, "No decent creature could or would stay in a home like that, if there was any way possible to get away. Our mother was sodden drunk all the time from the 'ole man's' rotten whiskey and he was the filthiest beast God ever created, beating on our mother like she was an old horse, and then messing sexually with our sisters when he couldn't get any more out of our mother. And she wasn't much better, yelling and cussing at him in German and broken English even when he dared her to say a word and knocked her around like a soccer ball."

Not too many days after Anselm's brothers had been at the inn, his sister Margarethe came. Camellia heard a knock on the suite door. Anselm wasn't there, and Camellia was glad he wasn't.

Camellia had never seen Margarethe Dietz before and at first didn't realize this was one of Anselm's sisters, although he'd told Camellia a little about Margarethe.

Margarethe was the only one of the Jurgensen household who had not married a "bohunk." Instead she had married Will Dietz of the neighboring Mennonite clan and had been absorbed into their religion and culture.

Margarethe was a stocky woman of middle years with still-blond hair braided in a circlet around her head. Her skin was fair and she had a serene and pleasant face. She was neatly and simply dressed and had on a little white net cap, indicative of her Mennonite affiliation.

"Mrs. Jurgensen," she said to Camellia, "I'm Margarethe Dietz, Olaf's sister. I'd like to talk with him, please, if he's home."

Margarethe's smile, her milky blue eyes, and slightly protruding little white teeth reminded Camellia of Anselm's look of mock innocence when he was about to launch into some racy and mischievous banter. But there was no outpouring of off-color humor from Margarethe.

Margarethe continued, "I know that Olaf has chosen not to be a part of the Jurgensen family for many years now. But I've always prayed he would one day forgive the things of the past, and maybe that would make everybody, including Olaf, feel better."

Camellia gave a twisted little smile. One sure way *not* to make Anselm Olaf feel better was to call him "Olaf," the middle name Anselm hated because it was what his family had called him. My! She was glad Anselm wasn't home.

Margarethe said, "I hope Olaf will find it in his heart to help us with some money so we can get our parents into a nursing home—a *good* one, not just a state-run thing. They need the attention so bad."

That evening when Camellia relayed Margarethe's message to Anselm and said she had found his sister engagingly polite, Anselm made a distasteful face and said, "Margarethe gives me the willies. She always did, even when we were growing up. She strikes that pious Mennonite pose all the time. She was the only one with which the 'ole man' didn't mess when we were growing up. Her halo must have got in the way."

"Where was she wearing her halo?" Camellia asked, with a sly wink.

Anselm dismissed the witticism and yammered on. "Margarethe acts like she's an agent of God, worrying about my soul. I understand she keeps saying to everybody, 'Oh, I wish Olaf would turn to the Lord before it's too late'. 'Olaf'. '*Olaf*'! Oh, for Chrissake! I go to church with you sometimes; doesn't she realize that? But you don't like the way I say 'Air Fodder, Witch-art in heffen' and I suppose Margarethe wouldn't, either."

Camellia said, "I thought Margarethe was very nice. She seems to want to do the best by your parents."

Anselm looked disgusted. "Camellia, are you so stupid you can't see through all that 'nice' business? A 'good' nursing home instead of 'a state-run thing'? You know what they plan to do?—put the 'ole man' and my mother *in* a 'state-run thing,' for which Social Security will pay and then keep for themselves any money *I* would give for a 'good' nursing home for them."

Camellia knew when to lay off, but Anselm's kin didn't. The next to come to see him was his sister Ilse Bronck.

Anselm and Ilse hadn't seen each other for almost as long as Camellia and Anselm hadn't seen each other. Ilse was back in the county now, but for a long time she had been living out of state and had picked up a nurse's education and a measure of sophistication. Anselm's reaction to her was far different than his reaction to his brothers and to his sister Margarethe. Camellia could see that he liked Ilse. Also, Ilse called him Anselm and not Olaf, and that helped a heap, too.

Ilse was short and plump like all the Jurgensen girls. A one-time strawberry blond, she now had steel-gray hair, clipped short, and there was an impish gleam in her clear blue eyes.

Ilse wasn't saying anything about money to get the parents into a "good" nursing home. Instead she and Anselm began reminiscing intimately about the family's earlier days. It was as though one moment Ilse was talking just to Anselm and the next moment talking to both Anselm and Camellia, who was sitting there all ears.

Ilse said the Jurgensen children had been—with the exception of Anselm—a rowdy, quarrelsome, hyperactive bunch, though all of them, including Anselm, were reasonably healthy. "Even sex with the 'ole man' didn't hurt physically," Ilse said. "We girls were too stupid to be embarrassed by it or troubled that it was immoral."

Where ignorance is bliss, etc., etc., Camellia was thinking.

Yet there was one story that was downright chilling. Ilse said she couldn't remember which older sister had told her, but seems after Anselm's birth, each time the "ole man" flopped down on their mother and got up dripping, he would thunder at his wife, "Remember, Maude, NO MORE BABIES!"

Maude knew what her husband meant: He wasn't about to feed any more kids, so if she got pregnant, she was supposed to kill it or else he'd throw her out of the home. Maude feared it would be worse (if that were possible) *away* from Karl and being out in the world again, so when she found herself pregnant again a year or so later, she swallowed an extra large dose of Karl's moonshine and rammed herself with an extra large knitting needle to cause the necessary abortion. She also got blood poisoning and nearly died, but she never got pregnant again even though Karl continued to use her until he found his daughters and granddaughters served the purpose just as well.

As to Karl's beating on the family, Ilse said, "As long as we and our mother behaved, none of us got hurt. It was either do what the 'ole man' said or suffer the consequences....But we, including our mother, were like the children of Israel—a stiff-necked people—and we did misbehave a lot, and we got licked severely for it."

Ilse reflected a moment, then said, "Intimidation? Cruelty? Good? Bad? Who can say? The 'ole man' always said that's the way God worked, and you could find plenty examples in the Bible of God's severe punishment for disobedience.

"He saw no wrong in anything he did because God was his role model. Annnd...he was respected among the Mennonites as a good father. They, too, believed women and children should be kept in their place. Annnd...the 'ole man' was a role model for the young bohunk boys down at the cannery. My husband Laszlo worshipped the 'ole man'. Uh...that's why I left Laszlo after two kids and went to Wilmington to live with cousin Johann and Wilma just like Anselm had done earlier."

Camellia asked, "How did you girls keep from getting pregnant by your father?"

Ilse winked. "Let's put it this way—he didn't always have sex with us the conventional way. And some may gave gotten pregnant. Not me, but Raghnild (we called her 'Ranny') or Gerta may have. And they may have done the same thing our mother did—abort it. Or they may have passed the 'ole man's' babies off as their husbands' children.

"It was often said at the cannery that Anselm wasn't our mother's kid, but Gerta's by the 'ole man'. But I don't think that was so....

"Gerta told me—after I was grown up a little—that I was in my crib in the bedroom that morning our mother birthed her last one—Anselm. Gerta said there was the stink of blood and fluids on the bed quilt and a wicked gleam of hot sunlight coming in through the cracked green window shade.

"Ranny and Gerta were there with our mother. Margarethe, I guess, was off somewhere downstairs—polishing her halo, maybe." (Both Anselm and Ilse laughed fit to kill themselves.) "The boys, who by then were married to bohunk girls and starting to have kids of their own—Anselm's despised cousin, 'Peachie,' for one—those boys were out with the 'ole man' working in the tomato fields.

"Ranny went and told our father he had another son, which should have pleased him because he'd lost two boys along the way: Gunter died of pneumonia when he was ten and Hjalmar was thirteen when one of the bohunk boys dared him to climb way up high on our windmill and jump off. Hjalmar did and he landed wrong and broke his neck and died. A girl, Dagmar, had died, too, before her first birthday.

"Well, anyhow, Ranny went and told the 'ole man' he had a new son. Gerta said he came upstairs, took one look at the baby and said, 'Chrissakes! Is that the boy?'

"Gerta said, 'Yes'.

"The 'ole man' said, 'Aaaarrrgghhh! Looks more like a rotten cantaloupe'. He never liked Anselm from the very start."

After a pause in which Camellia served some iced tea and cookies, Ilse continued. "Although the 'ole man' was an uneducated and uncouth person, he still believed his family should have fun."

"So long as it didn't require much thought," Anselm said with a wry laugh.

Ilse said, "There were plenty of hayrides and picnics, barn dances and song fests—mostly with the bohunks. And the barn dances were held in the house rather than in the barn!"

"Which helped to tear up the house, as if we kids hadn't already torn it up enough," Anselm added.

Although Anselm had been the only one in the family with any real musical talent, they all could and did sing after a fashion, and the bohunks always brought their fiddles and accordions, sometimes getting so drunk they left a fiddle or an accordion behind which Anselm appropriated for himself and taught himself to play, and soon he became their prime accompanist. And their mother, when they could catch her sober, would play the old piano that was in the house.

Anselm said, "Our mother tried to each me the piano as I showed some interest in it, but she was so wrought-up all the time she had no patience with my mistakes and spent most of her time cussing me in German and broken English. But she was a broken woman and I suppose she couldn't help being like she was."

Camellia shuddered, thinking on what Anselm had only recently told her about his mother—that Maude Vogel had been trained as a classical musician in Germany before coming to the U.S.; that when she did get here, she did *not* make it as a classical musician and ended up as a night club singer; and then, failing that, too, she became a prostitute, which was what she was doing when Karl Jurgensen found her and "saved her from a life of sin" or so Karl bragged to everybody, especially the Mennonites.

Anselm, a long time back, had merely told Camellia his father had found his mother nightclub singing and selling sex on the New York streets. Maybe he'd said nothing back then about his mother's *classical* musical background because he hadn't wanted to upset Camellia.

But now Camellia shuddered again, thinking of Maude Vogel Jurgensen: *There, but for the grace of God and the Valianos of Baltimore, go I. Groping around, as I had been, on the streets of Baltimore, not knowing who I was or what was going to happen next.* And Camellia was grateful all over again to Sylvester and Louisa for truly "saving" *her* when she had been down and out in Baltimore.

Ilse recalled that the Jurgensen family never actually went hungry, although the home-grown food was of poor quality and poorly prepared. Anselm laughed bitterly and said, "Like the boiled pig ear—with the hair still on it—that showed up in my school lunch bag one day. And the Mennonite kids all laughed at me for having a pig ear sandwich for lunch."

"I had a pig ear sandwich once in a while, too," said Ilse. "Anselm, do you remember how Ranny used to take you, when you were two or three years old, to her shack by the cannery after she was married, pull you along for a mile or so in the little wagon? And she'd always steal a watermelon from the Mennonite patch on the way back to our parents' home and set you on top of it so the Mennonites wouldn't see it, and then she'd give the watermelon to our mother. And then the next time she took you to her shack, she'd steal the watermelon on the way there and set you on top of it, so her husband and kids could get a free watermelon, too."

Anselm laughed a little and said, "Yes, that's the only reason she took me to her shack, so I could be the cover-up for stolen watermelons!"

Ilse recalled that when growing up they usually had enough clothing to keep them covered, but it was shreddy, cheap stuff they never bothered much about repairing or even laundering. Their mother was too drunk all the time to sew any homemade clothes, so they bought most of what they wore from city fire sales and second-hand shops whenever they went to Wilmington, Delaware, on the train to pick up wholesale sugar from their cousin Johann Jurgensen's grocery for the "ole man's" moonshine operation.

Anselm said, "The 'ole man' had once been a laborer in a Wilmington railroad freight yard and somehow he got a train pass which he used for forty years to get his family free train rides back and forth from Wintergreen county to Wilmington. No conductor dared challenged the validity of the pass because he was so persuasive in his bullshit about how he and the president of the Pennsylvania Railroad were life long friends."

Anselm and Ilse both remembered how the family had driven the train conductors and other passengers nuts when all the Jurgensens, including the grandchildren, piled onto the day coach with hilarious horseplay and baskets of picnic food—most of it half-spoiled. And before they got to Wilmington, four or five of them always managed to get wondrously train-sick.

Ilse and Anselm talked for hours and yet Ilse made no request that Anselm contribute anything toward getting their parents into a "good" nursing home.

Then just before she left, she did ask for money, but not for their parents. "Anselm, my son Sten and I have a chance to go in business. Right how, Sten drives a truck for his Uncle Harald, carrying cattle to market, and he hates it, just like I hate the thought of ever having to go back into nursing. The restaurant in Gainsbiddle where I'm working now as a cashier is for sale. Sten and I can get the money, but we need somebody to guarantee our note. Do you think you... maybe? Could you come down to Gainsbiddle sometime and look the place over?"

Anselm gave a non-committal grunt and Ilse didn't press the matter.

After Ilse was gone, Camellia couldn't decide whether she liked her or not. There was something sly about her that was both intriguing and cautioning. Camellia's "gypsy magic," that intuition which of old had guided her around and out of scrapes and bad deals, didn't seem as operative as before.

Anselm said, "I wonder what will happen to the old farm if the parents do go into some kind of nursing home."

"What's it to you?" Camellia said, "You never liked it."

"I was thinking about the Kami-Yaki if I have to leave Little Bell's. If I keep on the good side of Ilse, maybe she could talk the others into letting me rent a piece of land at the old place and I could put the Kami-Yaki out there. As I once told you, the farm was originally Mennonite property on which the Jurgensens started out as caretakers, and when the owners never came back, my parents became squatters there and eventually owners. When the county started sending them tax bills, they never would pay until the county advertised the property for tax sale and *then* they'd pay and plus the interest, too. They never cared about the place, but they never wanted anybody else to have it, either. Funny people."

Camellia asked, "If your parents go in a nursing home, even a state one, won't the nursing home get the farm?"

"Not if the 'ole man' can help it. Before they go in any nursing home, he'll probably put the property in his children's name—all but me, that is. He may be an uneducated louse, but he's shrewd. Always has been. He used to wield a silent power over everybody in east Wintergreen County from the Mennonites to the sheriff because he was supplying whiskey—a needed product that didn't used to be easy to get. And even after Prohibition was repealed, he still earned most of the family livelihood from bootleg liquor. Sold it cheap, though illegally, because he neither charged nor paid the federal tax on it."

Camellia felt exhausted after hearing again The Jurgensen Story with all its new additions. She had thought her own family bad enough, but Anselm, when growing up, had not had an easy row to hoe, either. So she felt it was stupid of him to get involved again in any way with any of them. But Camellia was somewhat like her mother, Mary Stephens. She decided to keep her thoughts to herself and let the *boss* of the family make his own decisions, for better or for worse.

Chapter Fourteen

Before investigating Ilse's restaurant in Gainsbiddle and getting into something that might be unwise, Anselm did decide to first look at the old Jurgensen farm out in east Wintergreen County to see whether it had any potential as a place for the Kami-Yaki.

He hadn't been on the farm since he'd left it as a kid and gone on his own, and he hadn't seen either of his parents since then, except at a distance, and even that had been a number of years ago.

He'd "heard through the grape-yard," as Camellia put it, that his sister Margarethe was staying most of the daytime with his parents and Ranny and Gerta filled in at night.

Anselm said this was good as he now could prove to Margarethe that he was interested enough in their parents to come to see them. Maybe she would think he was going to give some money after all to get the parents in a "good" nursing home. Maybe Margarethe wouldn't stand in the way of Anselm's renting some of the Jurgensen land.

Camellia and Anselm drove out there in Anselm's truck. The farm was big, with most of the tillable acreage on the front and the woods, house, and outbuildings to the rear.

The corn was brown and awaiting harvest, but it didn't look like much. Anselm's older brother Kurt and Kurt's sons and Margarethe's husband, Will Dietz, the Mennonite, had been tilling the farm for a number of years since the "ole man" had been out of commission.

As they drove up the long lane, Anselm said, "You can never really see the condition of the house from the main road and that's probably why the Mennonites tolerated the family in the past."

Then he exclaimed, "The oak tree's gone! It used to hide the whole house."

Camellia saw where a large tree had been sawed off level with the ground.

"Makes the house look different," said Anselm. "Better, I think. The place could use a little sunlight to purify things."

They turned from the lane where Margarethe's car was sitting and drove onto the yard where the oak tree had been. They stopped at the side of the house, a house that rose high up, having an above-the-ground cellar. Near where the wider front joined the narrower back section there was a door at the beginning of the back section. The door had a long narrow oval glass and a flight of concrete steps with a curved pipe railing that had come undone at the top.

Anselm and Camellia got out of the truck, walked up the steps, and peeped through the dirty oval glass in the locked door. They could vaguely see into the living room where Anselm said the Jurgensen children and grandchildren tore up the hardwood floors with homemade scooters concocted of rusty roller skate wheels and wooden tomato crates.

"And sometimes," Anselm continued, "when Ranny or Gerta came up here with their kids from the cannery shacks where they were living with their bohunk mates, when they came up here to clean—yes, clean...joke! joke! Anyway, when they came here, they'd always find a little pile or two of dried-up something or other on the stairway, and they'd get into an argument over whether it was from one of our dogs or cats or left from one of their own kids on a previous visit!"

Margarethe must have heard Camellia and Anselm arrive, for she called cheerily from an upstairs window, "Just a second, Olaf, and I'll be down and let you in."

Anselm cringed at that "Olaf" designation. While waiting for Margarethe, he and Camellia went around to the back of the house. There was the same old bloodied tree stump Anselm remembered from his childhood where chickens got their heads chopped off in preparation for Sunday dinner. But the fact of chicken blood had not left anywhere near the impression on him that the ungodly, endless screaming of a pig whose throat had just been sliced in preparation for the winter's pork chops had. "I can still hear those pigs," Anselm noted with a shudder that went clear down to his toes.

The backyard was in a state of chaos with rickety clothesline poles and broken wire, graying sheets besmirched with bird droppings, trash blowing around in the wind, and a lazily smoldering grease drum loaded with burnable scraps mixed in with nonburnable tin cans, bottles, light bulbs, and anything else you could think of. Anselm said food garbage probably got dumped into the smoldering drum, too, as the farm no longer had pigs or dogs and not many cats.

Camellia and Anselm went up on the back porch with its falling-in floor. The back door was locked, too, so they peeped in the kitchen window.

Anselm said, "There's that same bilious green paint in there, still peeling off the walls and ceiling. They used to have a hand pump on the sink, but I don't see that now. It use to regurgitate rusty water from the shallow well that they used when the windmill well wasn't working. Even the 'ole man's' rot-gut liquor tasted better than the water from either well. He used spring water, as I recall, for his moonshine."

They left the porch and glanced toward a cellar door which was padlocked. Anselm said, "I'll bet there're still rotting vegetables and fruits under there from years back, from when our mother never got around to all the canning from one season to the next because she was too hungover to ever finish anything she started."

They walked around to the front of the house and found the front porch overgrown with weeds and vines. Anselm said, "Looks just like it did when I was a kid. I guess they never did—in seventy-some years of living here—ever get around to using that front entrance."

They walked around to the back yard again. Camellia motioned toward the crumbling barns and outbuildings and said, "That long red shed over there....Was that once a chicken house?"

"It had chickens in it when I was a kid. The 'ole man' made me candle and sort eggs until I thought my head would explode."

Anselm gave a short laugh. "It was back there that Peachie—my brother Harald's oldest daughter—when we were both about fifteen, and her bohunk girl pal tripped me with a rope one evening, made me fall backwards, and the two of them jumped on me and tickled me unmercifully and not on the bottoms of my feet or in the ribs either."

Camellia remembered Anselm's having told her that tale years before.

"...And then they had the gall to run up to the house and tell the 'ole man' that I—'Uncle Olaf' they called me—that I was trying to do something nasty to them. *I* to *them*, yet!"

Margarethe had come downstairs now and was at the back door, motioning Anselm and Camellia into the kitchen. Inside, everything stank of dark oldness, old dirtiness, old rugs, old upholstery, old curtains, old mouse mess, old sick people.

In a back room downstairs, they found Maude Jurgensen, now in her nineties, lying propped up and motionless in her bed, all shrunken and dark like a mummy. That she was even alive at all after a lifetime of drinking "the ole man's" whiskey was remarkable, Camellia was thinking. Remarkable even though Anselm had said his mother had been a hefty, healthy, broad-hipped German woman to start with. Now she was totally unrecognizable to Anselm, and as expected, she did not recognize him, either. She stared at him uncomprehendingly through wide, brown, unseeing eyes.

Things were no better in the next room, there they found Karl, "the ole man," also in his nineties and his legs almost totally useless, but he was alert and restless. His skinny frame, which had once been hulking and formidable, was strapped in a wheelchair beside his bed, but he was giving the wheelchair a rocking fight because the wheels were purposely locked and wouldn't roll.

Margarethe explained to Anselm that if she didn't restrain him AND the wheel chair like that, he would be rolling up and down the house, trying to get into their mother's room and into her bed or else trying to roll the wheelchair down the back porch steps.

When the "ole man" looked around and saw Anselm he was at first surprised, then scornful. "Olaf! Hah! 'The corn on the outside row.' Hah!" Then he turned back to fiddling with the wheelchair.

"The old shit-fart!" Anselm muttered. "C'mon, Camellia, let's get out of here."

Without even saying "Good-bye" to Margarethe, Anselm pulled Camellia along with him, and they left the house and the Jurgensen farm in a proverbial snit. All the way back to Bell's Island, Anselm kept muttering, "God, that was awful! God, that was awful! That was the awfulest trip I ever made to anywhere."

Camellia, just as puzzled now as when Anselm a long time back had mentioned about his father calling him "the corn on the outside row," asked, "What did your father mean by calling you 'the corn on the outside row'?"

Anselm said, "It's a derogatory expression. Haven't you ever noticed how corn on the outside row is always shorter and of poorer quality than the rest of the field?"

"Yes, I suppose so," said Camellia.

"Then never plant corn on the outside row."

"But what's that got to do with you?" Camellia asked.

Anselm said, "The 'ole man' always referred to me—to my face and to others—as 'the corn on the outside row' because I was his last child and he didn't like me because he couldn't—even with whippings—get the obedience and work out of me that he could out of Harald and Kurt. And he hated me because I wanted an education—something more than third grade when he took his kids out of the Mennonite school and put 'em to work on the farm, only he let me stay the full seven grades because he couldn't get any good farm work out of me anyhow. Every moment I could steal away, I went to the attic of the old farmhouse and tried to read books I'd smuggled home from Cousin Johann and Wilma's in Wilmington.

"I can see the 'ole man' now, hulking up the attic stairs with an old slouch hat on his head, looking for me. He told everybody he wished I'd never been born because I was like the corn on the outside row—it never amounts to anything. So you shouldn't plant it in the first place. You are wasting your seed."

Camellia turned that over in her head a couple of times, then said, "But, Anselm, if you don't plant corn on the outside row, the next row becomes the outside row and if you don't plant corn on that row, either, and if you keep that up, then by and by...no corn at all planted!"

"Exactly," said Anselm with a mirthless laugh. "For a waterman's daughter, Camellia, you show a remarkable understanding of agriculture."

Camellia, still grappling with the aphorism, said, "...And if you don't have the last and youngest child, the next youngest becomes the last one and then....Why both statements are ridiculous to start with."

"Of course they are," said Anselm. "Beautiful *reductio ad absurdams*. But the 'ole man' didn't say them for the paradoxical humor in them. All he meant was that I was his last child—the corn on the outside row—that never amounts to anything and should never be planted in the first place."

Camellia, quickly rising to the occasion, said, "Anselm, *I* don't think of you as 'the corn on the outside row'. To me, you've always been and always will be top quality, prize-winning 'Silver Queen' at its very best!"

Camellia knew she'd not always thought that way. In the past she'd had questions about whether or not to marry Anselm because of his indolence and lack of ambition toward attaining the "proper" things of life—money, status, etc.—things at that time she was pursuing so rapidly herself. And sadly enough, things which she seemed to be pursuing all over again today.

Another winter was coming on. Frost was on everything, and skims of ice formed on puddles after every rain.

The Bell's Island School of Opera was into its second year of instruction. The Bell's Island Inn and the mighty tour boat had wound up another successful season.

Anselm still had not been to see the restaurant Ilse wanted to buy. But the state and county had notified him they would be compensating him for his land on Little Bell's, though they hadn't reached a figure yet. So the state park was indeed coming and the Kami-Yaki would definitely have to be moved now.

Anselm said to Camellia, "Well, we could go down to Gainsbiddle and at least look at the restaurant where Ilse works. Doesn't mean I have to commit myself to anything."

But Camellia could tell Anselm had already made up his mind to guarantee Ilse and Sten's note in exchange for Ilse's putting in a good word for him at the Jurgensen farm.

Camellia had little desire to go to Gainsbiddle or be involved there in any way. She still had plenty of ground-in Bell's Island enmity against that rival port, which was larger and generally conceded better than Bell's Island.

Her memories of Gainsbiddle were mainly those connected with her earliest music teaching years when she had been the itinerant singing teacher for the county elementary grades. That had been during the Depression years when the physical condition of the Gainsbiddle school building and its pupils had been only a little less than horrible.

The only bright spot of her once-a-week "Gainsbiddle Day" was the lunch hour she spent with Bessie Travis, longtime friend of the Stephenses. But Bessie and her husband Norman were both dead now, so no redeeming feature of Gainsbiddle was left.

Anselm phoned Ilse at her home and found she was on her day off, and she said that Sten, who also lived in Gainsbiddle, had the day off, too, so it was arranged that Camellia and Anselm pick up both Ilse and Sten, and they all would go down and look at the restaurant.

They stopped first on Chester Street to pick up Ilse. Earlier in the week there had been a "nor'easter" which had left tide and rain water trapped in low areas of town, and now that water had frozen on the edges and sidewalks of Chester Street.

Ilse's house was one of those turn of the century working-class homes that had no front porch and only one short wooden step to the narrow front door. The house sat almost on the street with no yard, only the sidewalk, in front. Ilse could almost step out her front door and into her curbside parked car with one step. When there was ice, however, that was a little tricky.

Ilse had to leave home in the morning around 4 A.M. in the dark of Chester Street since the downtown restaurant served breakfast to watermen preparing to start their pre-dawn haul out into the river. But Gainsbiddle—dark or light, Chester Street or the waterfront—held no terror for Ilse. Before settling in Gainsbiddle, she had been a nurse—one of those tough kind, the kind that had to be tough—a nurse in a Veteran's Hospital in Pennsylvania. Anselm smiled every time he thought about it, having been a patient in a Veterans' Hospital himself and knowing just how much disabled men can do—or think they can do!

Ilse slid—literally—into Camellia's car, and then it was on to pick up Sten. Tidewater had mostly drained out of the part of downtown where Sten and his family lived. The apartment house was a long narrow structure on a jib lot between lower Main Street and the railroad tracks. It was a frame building covered with deteriorating brick-like siding. The bottom floor of the building housed an auto parts store, and the second floor was chopped up into apartments.

Camellia, Anselm, and Ilse started their climb up what seemed like a forever flight of frigid-cold, inside-the-dark-wall stairs to the second floor. Way up in the ceiling at the top of the stairs they could see a single bare light bulb nearly burned out and casting a weird glow on the top landing. A curtainless window in the back wall looked out on toward the marsh, a marsh frozen stiff with leftover tide. This window was the access to the fire escape down the backside of the building.

Once at the top of the stairs they were treated to the choking smell of rancid fried meat and boiled cabbage seeping out from the apartments and filling the narrow hallway. In the ceiling down about midway the hall there was another bare bulb nearly burned out. Numerous doors flanked either side of the hall.

Sten's apartment marked 2A was the first on the left.

"Thotcha'd never get here," Sten said, meeting them at the door of the first of two rooms—the kitchen.

Sten had a bohunk head—the short forehead and small fat face. Of only medium height, lean of body, and small-boned, he was still just as full of bullcrap as his Uncle Harald's stockyard.

Sten ushered them into the kitchen where there was a single window in the outside back wall with a thin cafe curtain over the bottom sash and nothing, not even a pull-down shade, at the top. On the wall to the right a cracked mirror hung over a sink which doubled as a wash bowl. The one and only bathroom for the entire floor of six apartments was at the opposite end of the hallway.

Sten's kitchen had a greasy gas range, an old-model refrigerator, a kerosene stove that was doing next to nothing to warm the room, and a beat-up washing machine against the wall opposite where the sink was. The rest of the room was taken up with a couple of storage cabinets, a baby's play pen, a table with several chairs, and a baby's high chair. The floor, what little was visible of it, was covered with broken and stained linoleum. The ceiling with its one bare light bulb was so low anyone ever six feet would have to duck passing under that bulb.

Camellia and Anselm caught a glimpse of the family's sleeping quarters through a curtained doorway next to the sink which led into an adjoining room where there were a number of beds and cots jammed together and a couple of chests of drawers stacked up against the wall. There appeared to be no heating appliance at all in that room. There was, however, the single bare light bulb in the middle of the ceiling.

Sten's wife, Sue, was not a bohunk. No telling where he got her. She was a sinewy-looking, long-haired girl with a small face and brown eyes, and she had one hand with a sponge scrubbing the sink and the other hand with a wash cloth wiping the baby's face. Considering what she had in that crowded apartment, she did about as well as could be expected in keeping the place liveable.

She appeared to have a storehouse of nervous energy which she surely needed to keep their six kids in line...three of which were preschoolers...to keep them from falling out the apartment windows which had no screens or from falling down the stairway or from getting out on the fire escape (where they liked to play) and falling off it.

Camellia saw no crucifixes sitting around, but she got the feeling the family was Catholic or Eastern Orthodox (like the bohunks from which Sten's father had sprung). Whatever they were, they must not have believed in birth control!

The restaurant where Ilse worked and which she and Sten wanted to buy had originally been an old concrete block oyster packing house. Camellia remembered it from her "come to Gainsbiddle on the boat" days of her early youth. Now it had been remodeled—no, that's too charitable—*remade* into a restaurant. It sat right on the edge of the downtown mud which was straining against the bulkhead lining the harbor. Tide from the recent "nor'easter" had poured over the bulkhead and run into the building.

Everything was dark and cluttered inside and still damp even after much mopping and sopping. The furniture and fittings were obviously second-hand. Ilse ducked behind the cashier's counter to pick up some figures and information to show Anselm. Short as she was, she was almost hidden by the piled up, cracked and bent cookie and candy dispensers, the razor blade displays, the flashlight batteries, and the posters advertising beer and wine.

Anselm, Camellia, and Sten sat down in a booth and ordered some sandwiches. Sten, who must have been trying to impress Camellia about whom he'd undoubtedly heard stories of grandeur, said, "Did you know my mother and I..." [not bothering to include "Uncle Olaf" in this] "...have *a genuine American Indian princess in our ancestry*?"

They could hear Ilse behind the cash register trying to suppress a laugh.

When Ilse joined them in the booth, she apologized for Sten. "He tells everybody that."

Anselm snorted and spoke as though Sten wasn't even present: "I guess he heard the 'ole man' say that. The 'ole man' tried to tell that same bullshit to everybody, too, especially the Mennonites, whom he was always trying to impress."

Ilse, sticking up for her son and maybe "the ole man," too, said, "Yes, but, you know, there may be some truth to that 'genuine American Indian princess'. When I was staying with Cousin Johann and Wilma after I left Laszlo, Wilma said the first Jurgensen, Hjalmar Jurgensen, didn't come directly to the United States the first time. He went to Canada to do some fur trapping. He lived with a Canadian-Indian girl, and they had some children. Then the Canadian-Indian girl died, and all the children but one died. Then Hjalmar Jurgensen took his one surviving child, a son, with him back to Denmark.

"Hjalmar then married a Norwegian girl and later the son married a Norwegian girl, also, and all four of them came to the United States. These were the stowaways with that boat load of Swedes that the family always talked about that ended up in Delaware. Hjalmar and his Norwegian wife had children in the United States, and from that branch came Cousin Johann and Wilma. Hjalmar's son whose mother had been the Canadian-Indian and his Norwegian wife had children and our father came out from that branch. So our father was right in one sense to say there was a genuine American Indian in his ancestry, although she was a *Canadian*-American Indian, not an *American*-American Indian, and probably no princess!"

Anselm turned that over in his thoughts and said, "Come to think of it, the 'ole man' looked as much Indian as Scandinavian. I always though he was dark-skinned form being sunburned and weather beaten. He had tough-looking skin and sinewy arms and that graying black hair—real straight black—Indian hair, maybe. I guess we kids got our red hair from our henna-headed mother."

Sten snorted this time. "The 'ole man' *looked* as much Indian as Scandinavian? *Had* Indian hair? Doesn't he still? Uncle Olaf talks like Grandpa was dead a'ready, yet." Sten apparently liked "the ole man."

Anselm came close to swatting Sten for that "Uncle Olaf," but a concerned look from Camellia stopped him.

Sten got up from the booth and went toward the juke box and put in some money. It must have been a whole fistful of quarters.

The juke box had its revolving colors no longer revolving, but its turntable played over and over and over again an out-of-date novelty tune containing the lines: "Bouncy-bouncy...bouncy-bouncy...bouncy-bouncy/Just-like-a-rubber-ball/I come boun-cing back to you."

Camellia felt like her head was a rubber ball, endlessly bouncy-bouncing against the dark walls and ceiling of that restaurant, as Ilse explained to Anselm a bunch of figures and stipulations regarding the loan that the bank would give if there were a guarantor. Anselm promised Ilse nothing. Ilse still did not press the matter. Sten had a shitty, sneery look on his face, but he, too, kept quiet.

Before Camellia and Anselm got ready to take Ilse and Sten back to their homes, Anselm went to the rest room. It just said REST ROOM, no specific men or women designation.

After Anselm and Camellia had dumped off their two passengers and returned to Bell's Island, Anselm said he'd been surprised to find the REST ROOM at the restaurant was merely an "inside outhouse" (where everything dropped down to the tide-soaked ground beneath), as Jim Stephens had referred to the "facilities" in the Stephens' warehouses in the old days.

"But these are not 'the old days'," Anselm protested. "Why hasn't the county board of health been onto this? They raised enough hell over my 'chicken experimental station' on Little Bell's."

"Anselm, don't you know?" said Camellia resignedly. "The restaurant is in Gainsbiddle and that fact covers a multitude of sins."

Anselm agreed and said he was all for giving up on Ilse and Sten, the restaurant, AND the Jurgensen farm as a place to put the Kami-Yaki.

Then in early 1975 when the state and county informed Anselm of the amount he was going to get for his land on Little Bell's and it turned out to be—pardon the expression—*chicken feed,* Anselm gave in, signed Ilse and Sten's note, and got Ilse's promise that she would try to get him some of the Jurgensen farm front acreage for his Kami-Yaki and get it "at a reasonable price."

In the meantime, as Anselm had figured, when his brothers and sisters saw they weren't going to get any money out of him to help put their parents in a "good" nursing home, they went ahead and put them in a state-run nursing home. But not before old Karl, who was still sharp mentally, had the chance to sign the Jurgensen property over jointly to all his children—all except Anselm, that is.

Then stubbornly, and in spite of Ilse's entreating, the others balked on renting or selling Anselm any of the front acreage for his Kami-Yaki.

"I wish I had the money to buy the whole farm!" Anselm said to Camellia. "I bet they'd sell then."

Camellia frowned. "Why would you want to buy something that has so many bad memories for you when there are surely other places in the county that you could rent or buy to put the Kami-Yaki on?"

"I want to joy of burning it down!" said Anselm gleefully of the old homeplace.

Camellia, who still had more money than brains, said, "Well, if the only way you can get any of it is to buy all of it and if you can get them to sell, then I'll consider helping you out on it."

After Anselm sent the word out by Ilse that he wanted to buy the whole farm, he said to Camellia, "I can just hear them saying now, 'Let's soak him on the price. He's got the money'."

And soak him they did. But even though he agreed, and apparently they agreed, a couple of weeks before the closing, the brothers—notably Harald—and Margarethe reneged.

Ranny and Gerta couldn't have cared less who got the farm as they were already licking their chops at the thought of "a little pin money" as their share.

Margarethe, though, thought "Olaf" should become a *born-again* Christian as a condition for *her* signing any deed.

Anselm again enlisted Ilse's help, reminding her he'd guaranteed hers and Sten's note for their restaurant.

So Ilse tried again and suddenly both brothers and Margarethe capitulated and the old Jurgensen farm became solely Anselm's.

"What do you suppose Ilse did to make them change their minds, especially Harald?" asked Camellia. "He seems to dislike you the most."

Anselm snickered. "Don't know what Ilse did about Margarethe, but she probably slept with Harald!"

"But he's her brother!"

"No problem. I understand she's done it before."

"Whatta family!" Camellia muttered.

Anselm shot an incredible glance at Camellia.

She came back at him with, "Yes, I know what you are thinking, Anselm. The cat shouldn't call the pottle back...." [The pot shouldn't call the kettle black.]"...But the incestuous-minded Roger was only my half-brother, and no matter how he carried on, I didn't do it. You know that."

"Of course I know that," Anselm said with a chuckle, "but when it comes to virtue, if a Jurgensen and a Stephens went up to the Pearly Gates and St. Peter said, 'Only one vacancy left', which one do you think would get in?"

"The one who had the most money," said Camellia, wearily.

"I can't argue with you there," Anselm replied.

Chapter Fifteen

Akaido Li was out of town on some of his other entrepreneurial ventures when Anselm signed over his Little Bell's Island land to the state and county and received his *chicken feed* payment.

Some of the Kami-Yaki, mainly the shell of the concrete block experimental building, would be used by the state park. The boiler and dehydrating apparatus Anselm dismantled and stored temporarily in back of the opera school workshop to be taken eventually to its new location out in east Wintergreen County on the now *former* Karl Jurgensen farm. But Anselm's cabin was not usable by the park nor sound enough to stand the trip to east Wintergreen, so it was to be torn down.

The roar of the crane and its bucket drowned out the early spring soughing of the pine trees as the demolition began.

Seeing that bucket with its mammoth jaws chomping into his old home—his shelter for so long both from the elements and the world—almost brought tears to Anselm's eyes. Camellia, too, was sobered. It had been there, two decades and a half before, in the dusk of many a summer's evening, they'd had their first playful chases around and around inside and outside that cabin before flopping down on an old cot inside and finding heaven in each other's arms.

It had been there Anselm had wiled away the hours and days and weeks and years after Camellia was gone, finding in his pet wildlife and feed experiments some measure of solace and meaning.

It had been there, in their second stay, only a handful of short years ago, that Camellia and Anselm had renewed their lives and soothed each other's past hurts.

An old relic that had no more utilitarian value, it still held a nostalgic and sentimental charm and both of them hated to see it go. In spite of the new park and recreational facilities that would come in its place and spell out many tourist dollars for them and the inn,

Little Bell's Island without that cabin would never be the same to them again.

Along about the middle of that summer of 1975, there was a subtle change in Camellia's usual robust health. She realized she often gave the impression to her opera students of being "indisposed"—a delightful Victorian term and also used by musicologists to explain why an understudy is replacing the leading lady for the evening performance. It could mean anything from having a bad menstrual spell to a final heart attack.

For Camellia to suspect anything was wrong with her—the physically invincible Camellia Stephens—was a terrifying experience.

She realized that Anselm also noticed something disquieting about her. Sometimes the two of them would be alone in their suite at the inn, talking at random about "this 'n' that" or just sitting around, reading a newspaper or a musical score or whatever, and Camellia would suddenly get tense and unusually silent. It was almost as though she were listening for or to something that she knew was beyond Anselm's range of perception.

That music again? Hadn't she pursued that elusive music enough?

A sudden fear went through her the first time she thought about what would happen to Anselm if she died. She had always believed—*hoped* maybe is the better word—that Virginia would look out for him if she were no longer around. Virginia surely would do so in gratitude for all Camellia had done for her and her family. Wouldn't she?

But Virginia and Nick were talking about leaving Wintergreen County. Nick felt he could better his law career by moving back to Brooklyn instead of staying with the Royal Hall firm that had given him a position.

Camellia knew Anselm would never go to Brooklyn with them, even if they asked him, anymore that Grandpaw Azariah had been willing to leave Bell's Island and go to the mainland with Amos and Lois. And Azariah, abandoned and neglected, eventually froze to death one winter on Bell's Island. Camellia shuddered.

After a while Camellia decided she wasn't sick but merely in some sort of letdown period following so many radical changes in her life in the past five years since she had rediscovered Anselm; returned to Bell's Island; and been involved in so many *projects*—the "new" Bell's Island Inn, the Bell's Island School of Opera, her musical works, Anselm's harebrained schemes for his "chicken experimental station," and her own recurrent longings to capture *that music* and fashion it into a symphony.

Since she had been successful with all these things except for her symphony, she was beginning to wonder if she was becoming a bit like Napoleon who was said to have sat down and cried because there were no more worlds to conquer.

Or was her indefinable uneasiness something that portended trouble—maybe even big trouble?

Nick and Virginia and the twins did leave Wintergreen County in August. That wasn't exactly trouble, although it was heartbreaking to see them go, especially Flossie and Jesse, who cried and cried when it was time to say "good-bye" to "Auntie Cammie" and "Unky Andy." But Nick had a better job awaiting him in Brooklyn and he wanted to get settled before the twins entered kindergarten.

Although the state park on Little Bell's was complete enough to be in action before the summer of 1975 was out, Anselm was slow on starting the relocation of the Kami-Yaki at the old Jurgensen farm. He wanted Akaido Li's help, but Li was making himself very scarce around Wintergreen County these days.

Then—

"That goddamn chink!"

"What's the matter, Anselm?"

"That goddamn chink! His Baltimore phone has been disconnected and a whole handful of my letters to his Baltimore address have come back 'Unclaimed. Left No Forwarding Address'."

"Hmmm," murmured Camellia, thumbing through a card file at the inn's front desk. "He's been gone from here for a month without paying his last month's bill or turning in his room key."

Camellia, though not Anselm, had become very suspicious of Akaido Li several months earlier when there was an increase in the number of checks bouncing from feed dealers across the county who had bought the Kami-Yaki product. Li had made some of the checks good and made excuses and promises for the rest. Still and all....

"Anselm, I'm afraid you've been dealing all along with phony businesses and a phony entrepreneur," said Camellia. "Remember how intent he was that you not market the feed locally, but 'across the country'? How much have you paid Li in the past three years as 'partner' and 'adviser'?"

"Too much," sighed Anselm, realizing the probable truth of what Camellia was saying.

Though not a very good bookkeeper, Anselm nevertheless quickly figured he'd spent more for supplies—baby chicks, feed corn, chemicals, synthetic vitamins, etc.—and paid his workers more in salaries and Li far more in commissions than he'd ever gotten back from the "good check" buyers of his feeds.

Needless to say, none of the rest of the accounts receivable paid—with either good checks or bad—after Li's departure.

As for what Li may have done to other businesses in the area, Anselm didn't know for sure except for one building supply outlet whose owner was cussing Akaido Li for all get out. Said the dealer, "Li had his truck—not mine—deliver all these out-of-town shipments and he made out phony invoices, and God only knows who got the stuff. One thing for sure, I never got the money."

Anselm said to Camellia, "And if my feed didn't actually sell, either—except to phony businesses, there's no point in taking the boiler and all to east Wintergreen and rebuilding the Kami-Yaki, is there?"

"Not unless you plan to start all over again and call it something else," said Camellia.

"I'm not eager to. Not out there in Jurgensen land. I thought I had a sure thing in that Akaido Li. I guess if he'd been any good he'd never have done business with me and a worthless product to start with, right?"

Camellia didn't answer that.

Every time Anselm glanced toward the dismantled Kami-Yaki boiler and dehydrating apparatus sticking up through the weeds in back of the opera school workshop, he muttered, "Monument to a failure."

Camellia was thinking, Anselm's main assets today are a defunct project and a useless piece of land—the old Jurgensen farm.

After letting go the Kami-Yaki and his chicken feed experiments, Anselm had more time to help Camellia with her opera school.

Camellia still had feelings of both physical and mental uneasiness now and then, but she and Anselm and her opera students launched into plans for the coming year's big event—the Our Nation's 200th Birthday Celebration on Bell's Island.

All the publicity, including photos of herself, that Camellia had stirred up in the past couple years on both sides of the bay for her Bell's Island School of Opera had apparently led Baltimore Opera Theater to deduce that their former "Charity Croswell" and Camellia Stephens was the same person. Sylvester and Louisa had told Camellia that Madame Dupree surmised it and probably Merv Roth, too. But neither Dupree nor Roth had come across and acknowledged anything to Camellia, so she wavered as to whether to invite them to the Bell's Island Fourth of July fete.

In truth she didn't want to see either Madame Dupree or Merv Roth and be reminded again of her lost Met opportunity. There was always that little twinge of regret, a feeling she knew Anselm must have experienced, too, whenever he looked at the junked Kami-Yaki boiler and dehydrating apparatus and was reminded of the demise of his chicken dreams.

So Camellia skipped the invitations to Madame Dupree and Merv Roth and, with Anselm's help, plunged herself even more vigorously into the major preparations for the summer of 1976. And as she did, her feelings of uneasiness vanished and once again she was on top of the world.

The town of Bell's Island, the state park on Little Bell's, the Bell's Island Inn, the docks, wharves, work boats, and visiting yachts, including the mighty tour boat, even the old gypsy tavern/opera school workshop, were all decked out in American flags and red, white, and blue bunting.

The Fourth of July weather was perfect and the midday parade through the island's main street went off beautifully.

Camellia's Bell's Island School of Opera put on their new opera buffo, "Yankee Doodle Diddle Doo!" at the band shell in the state park and received a rousing ovation.

There was a crab feast in the park and a big banquet at the inn in the early evening, a quick spin around the harbor and mouth of the river by the mighty tour boat, and then a mammoth fireworks display.

Everybody who was anybody was present, from the governor and assorted state and county legislators to Jim Stephens, President of the Game Warden's Association, from Sylvester and Louisa Valiano of Baltimore and Nick and Virginia and the twins from Brooklyn, New York, to Mrs. Dunst—? Could it be? Really? Yes! *Mrs. Dunston-Ayres of Royal Hall*!

Mrs. Dunston-Ayres even personally congratulated Camellia (a.k.a. "that gypsy") on her opera school's composition and performance. And Camellia accepted the congratulations with warm graciousness. The old hatchet had been buried!

As usual, when Camellia didn't have music on the mind, she had money on the mind. Hardly was the successful Fourth of July celebration on Bell's Island completed than she was thinking about putting on something for Labor Day.

The receipts at the inn and state park and all the other businesses on Bell's Island over the Fourth had been overwhelming. Like with playing the slot machines, the more you win, the more you want to play. And Camellia also thought it was time to remodel the inn, especially hers and Anselm's suite, so they could use the extra money an additional bust over Labor Day might bring in.

Come the last Sunday in July, Camellia had planned to sit down that evening and talk it over with Anselm about "something for Labor Day."

Then, around eleven o'clock in the morning, an hour before the tour boat was to leave the dock, someone phoned to say the captain had been rushed to the hospital with appendicitis, and the backup pilot couldn't be located.

Camellia knew rain checks or refunds could be given to those who'd already bought tickets for the tour, but Anselm said, "I can pilot that boat. I've taken the wheel many a time when my organ grinder's monkey duties were in intermission. I've sat beside the pilot at other times and watched and absorbed everything he did and said."

Camellia hesitated. "I don't know, Anselm. What if the Coast Guard stopped the boat for some reason and found *you* at the wheel as an unlicensed pilot? They know you, remember?"

"I'll take Jim Stephens with me." Anselm said quickly, "and give *him* the wheel if the Coast Guard gets nosey."

Camellia still didn't think it was a good idea, but as usual Anselm won out.

By midafternoon Camellia, who had stayed ashore for the trip, noticed the sky over Bell's Island had turned a strange gray-yellow. A single cloud covered the whole sky, which was like a quilt with rippled ridges. The air was dead still and smothering, something unusual for a place where the wind was almost always blowing.

Camellia knew something was wrong and she searched the horizon for any sign of the tour boat, but all she could see was a long gray mist where sky and water came together.

She instinctively jumped at the one and only flash of lightning and the heavy roar of thunder which seemed to start right overhead and then go down to the four corners of the earth and sea, reverberating, echoing, and re-echoing.

An hour or so later Coast Guardsmen were landing on Bell's Island in ambulance helicopters. Other helicopters were in the air hovering over the stricken tour boat as it crunched to a halt at the inn's dock. (Jim Stephens, who had been aboard, had radioed for help.)

The typhoon-like storm in the Anderson Sound had, for close to an hour, thrown the passengers around the cabin like toothpicks, and it nearly took the tour boat and all with it to a watery grave.

Camellia watched aghast as the Coast Guardsmen began removing the numerous injured tourists, those with broken bones, shock traumas, and heart attacks. There were no fatalities, but one woman, five months pregnant, did have a miscarriage.

Anselm, with Jim at his side, stumbled off the boat, looking like death in a bucket.

"We brought her in," he gasped. "Jim and me, we brought her in. Nobody washed overboard, I don't think."

When Camellia got Anselm to their suite in the inn, he collapsed completely. It was the first time she'd ever known him to be seasick from a boat trip.

The storm that had caught Camellia and Anselm's tour boat by surprise (there had been no unusual weather warnings nor any tip-off from "gypsy magic') resulted in numerous lawsuits against them. Though Anselm had been the unlicensed captain of the tour boat that day, Jim Stephens said—and later testified in court, as did the regular captain—that Anselm had done all any navigator, including the regular pilot, could have done.

Still there were massive charges of negligence—the boat operated by an unlicensed pilot, not enough life preservers aboard, etc. The boat itself came through the storm relatively undamaged, but many tourist passengers, in addition to receiving numerous physical injuries from being tossed about the cabin, had *mental* problems as a result of the experience and they had to spend much money on "psy-ack-a-trists" (to use a good ole Gainsbiddle term) to get their heads straightened out.

The Coast Guard testified to Anselm's incompetence as a pilot, citing the many times he had negligently swamped his own smaller craft and required their help to save him.

The judge and juries (and even Nick who had come down from Brooklyn to help legally) concluded the tour boat trip should have been cancelled for the day if no qualified backup pilot was available. Better to refund a few tickets and disappoint a few tourists than to risk everybody's life.

It was conceded by the prosecution that if only the licensed back-up pilot had been in charge there would have been less justification for so many lawsuits even if there had been just as many passenger injuries.

Camellia's insurance company wouldn't pay anything, either, saying the policy on the tour boat had been invalidated because of an unlicensed pilot and other failures to live up to the agreement.

With lawsuits that went on for an excruciating eighteen months and damages figuring in the millions, Camellia and Anselm were cleaned out of everything—the inn, the Bell's Island Opera School, the tour boat, and practically all of Camellia's "wise investments"—everything gone except the old Jurgensen farm, which was in Anselm's name and which nobody knew they had or surely the lawyers and the claimants would have gotten that, too.

"This makes three times now something similar has occurred in my family," Camellia said as they sat huddled at Jim Stephens's house where Jim was giving them lodging for as long as they needed it. "The first time was with Grandfather LeCates. His gambling debts led to his bankruptcy and the loss of the inn back in the 1920s. Then Mama and Papa were always on the verge of bankruptcy because they had no sense to put anything away in reserve when times were good. And now me."

Though Anselm continued to wail about "what I've put you through," Camellia knew it had ultimately been her fault for letting him pilot the tour boat that day.

Yet she felt no anger or resentment toward Anselm or herself. She felt only relief that Anselm had not perished in that storm. And there was a certain amount of relief, too, that now their business ventures were all gone from them, she could finally write music and do nothing but write music...*that music* and turn it into a symphony, maybe ten symphonies!

They knew they were not going to stay forever with Jim Stephens, yet with not even the cabin on Little Bell's to run to, the only thing left was to go to the old Jurgensen farm. That purchase which at the time had seemed ridiculous to Camellia and just another incident of her humoring Anselm now seemed a godsend, although Anselm didn't quite agree....

Though he remained racked with guilt over "what I've put you through," he still was his own man and said he would *not* live in the old farmhouse—"I'd have us live in a Boy Scout tent in the field there before I'll live in that house," he swore.

And since the Kami-Yaki never got rebuilt on the front acreage, they didn't even have that to resort to as a shelter.

Sten and Ilse, before the tour boat lawsuits were over, and as a surprise to no one, had defaulted on their note. To save their hides and their restaurant, Anselm had paid off their note with the money he'd set aside for the Kami-Yaki. Although he'd decided not to rebuild the Kami-Yaki anyhow, that money would have come in great now to build some sort of home for him and Camellia. But he no longer had the money.

Then Virginia, along with Nick, who was still disheartened at not being able to help Camellia and Anselm more in defending themselves in their lawsuits, took from the money they had been saving for a home of their own in Brooklyn and financed a log cabin home for Camellia and Anselm.

Camellia and Anselm had the little log cabin built in the woods in the rear of the Jurgensen farm, where they saw neither the Jurgensen house nor the front fields, and it was to their liking. It even had a log outhouse!

The Carrambarros—Nick and Virginia and the twins—returned to Wintergreen County briefly in the spring of 1978 to help Camellia and Anselm move in.

The twins were the one bright spot in an otherwise sobering time. Flossie and Jesse were growing up nicely. Both had black hair like Nick. Jesse had Nick's mild personality, whereas Flossie was so very pretty she was "set on herself," somewhat like Camellia had been in her early years.

At seven years, the twins were old enough to understand a little why Camellia and Anselm couldn't lavish gifts on them as before. Virginia had explained to them now it was *their* turn to help "Auntie Cammie" and "Unky Andy."

And help they did, carrying music books and music paper into the log cabin from Anselm's truck, and at one point they emptied their piggy banks and presented the coins to Camellia and Anselm, saying, "For some ice cream, if you get hungry."

It was a gesture that made Camellia turn away momentarily to keep from weeping. She remembered a time when only a child herself and her parents were hurting from poor judgement and lack of money and food in the home, a time when her cousin Snipsey used to give her things from her school lunch box. Snipsey and her folks didn't have much to spare back then, either, and Camellia knew this was true now of Virginia and Nick, in spite of the income they were continuing to receive for the twins from Camellia's irrevocable trust for them, one item, at least, that did not get touched by the tour boat lawsuits.

Weep though she wanted to over Flossie and Jesse's presentation, Camellia's innate graciousness came to the fore and she smiled broadly and said to the twins, "Oh, how wonderful! *Thank you*! 'Unky Andy' and I *are* hungry *right now*, so let's *all* go get some ice cream!"

Before they started off in Nick's car, Camellia rustled through her handbag, and finding neither bills nor change, she whispered to Anselm to give Nick a fiver so he could replace the twin's coins. Then emotion overwhelmed Camellia again and she clung to Anselm, murmuring, "I have *nothing* anymore to give to anybody."

Anselm soundly rebuked her and said, "*Oh, yes, you do*! Give to the world your music—your *written* music!"

Anselm couldn't have said anything more fitting. A warm glow encircled Camellia as they headed off for their ice cream.

Later that night, Anselm, Nick, and Jim Stephens *removed*—read that, *stole*—the upright piano from the closed-down Bell's Island School of Opera and brought it in Anselm's truck to the log cabin. They didn't dare try to get the baby grand from the inn. But at least Camellia again had something on which to compose.

Here, with no longer the distractions of either her guilt-absolving projects on Bell's Island or Anselm's "chicken experimental station" or her desire to compose "people pleasers," Camellia was able to write music, do nothing but write music and write it in a way her heart, not her vanity or her pocketbook, dictated.

There was an exit through the woods to another county road so they could get out to anywhere without having to pass by the old Jurgensen house. They did their grocering in Cocquemac, a border town, way far from Bell's Island or Royal Hall. They seemed away from it all—from Wintergreen County and the Jurgensen farmland, in a world separate from everything and everywhere.

There was even a creek through the woods where, when the summer of 1978 came fully on, they went several times a week to catch fish and crabs. The woods reminded them somewhat of the Little Bell's Island woods, but it was not the kind of reminder that made them either homesick or anguished over their business failures.

Anselm couldn't even begin to find the site of his father's old whiskey still, so there was none of that unsavory past to bedevil him.

What they had here was good in and of itself.

In order for them to have some means of income, Anselm sold the old farmhouse and the tillable front acreage to a Mennonite relative of his sister Margarethe's husband, Will Dietz. After nearly seventy-five years the bulk of the farm was finally and rightfully back in Mennonite hands.

Camellia and Anselm were able to live—meagerly—on the mortgage payments. There was nothing left over at any time for "wise investments." Camellia no longer felt the urge to gamble. She no longer craved luxury. It was enough to still have Anselm and a sylvan setting in which to listen for and finally begin to capture *that music*. Then....

Then...Anselm, who was nature's ultimate in clumsiness, dropped a sofa on Camellia's right hand when they were rearranging the furniture!

She got two lovely mashed fingers. Even though Anselm kept tearfully singing the ballad *You Always Hurt the One You Love,* the injury wasn't all that serious, and it would heal. But the Cocquemac doctor's huge dual bandage did slow down her composing.

Camellia could have laid off the piano for awhile, but fearing her Muse, who'd always been a temperamental creature, would get disgusted and walk out on her, she continued to compose, trying to play both clefs with the left hand at the same time, which was a little challenging.

So Anselm began helping her by letting her play the treble notes with her left hand and he filled in the bass notes as she said or sang them. Soon they discovered he was playing—and writing down for her—the exact notes *before* she said or sang them!

And even when they switched positions and Anselm was poised to play the treble notes as Camellia called them, they found he was again playing the exact notes at the same time or even *before* she said or sang them. They were both responding to the same Muse, *both* of them now were hearing *that music*! *That music*—indescribable in human words, knowable only as divine sound.

Camellia and Anselm—they'd always been "together in body"; now at last they were "together in soul."